UNHOLY SIN

"Dear Heavenly Father," came the warped voice, "again I succumbed to the will of the flesh." The strap cracked through the air again. "This is my penance. I do it lovingly for You." His hand rose, halted, then came down with more force, the strap almost falling from his grip, his legs buckling at the knees.

Rhoades straightened his racked body, his head tilted back, and in the darkness his mind saw a bluish white vapor hover above. "It is You, Father." Letting go of the strap he sank to his knees and cupped his head in his palms. "I gratefully accept the curse as a test of my obedience to You. My penance serves to strengthen me so that I might carry out Your Will . . ." Each tear that fell into his palm brought back the reality of pain. "Sweet Jesus," he pleaded, "help me. Please help me."

MARC BRELLEN

CROSSBEARERS

LEISURE BOOKS ∞ NEW YORK CITY

A LEISURE BOOK

Published by

Dorchester Publishing Co., Inc.
6 East 39th Street
New York, NY 10016

Printed in the United States of America

CROSSBEARERS

1

Jones Street in New York City's Greenwich Village swarmed with people. The cool summer night's breeze succumbed to the smoldering of the food vendors' barbeque pits. Flashing colored lights enticed more crowds into the area. Hung across Jones Street was a large banner announcing the annual start of Our Lady of the Shrine Fair.

In front of the church bearing the same name as the banner stood a life-size statue of Our Lady of the Shrine, a long swath of purple cloth draped about her shoulders. One, five, and ten-dollar bills were pinned to it. By the Fair's end money would be pinned upon money. Two plainclothes policemen stood guard over the growing tribute. A tourist with a camera posed his wife and child meticulously in front of the monied statue.

The pungent aroma of sizzling sausage, green peppers, and onions lured Frank Miller through the crowded street. Despite his average looks, his deliberate strut conveyed a measure of importance and power.

"Buongiorno, Mr. Miller," called a vendor.

He nodded in response.

Another vendor sought recognition. "Hi ya, Mr. Miller."

Mr. Miller nodded, stopped, inspected the sausage, and moved on. More hellos. More nods.

A faint voice summoning, "Mr. Miller, Mr. Miller," was barely audible above the clamor of the crowd.

Mr. Miller turned and extended both arms to greet his friend. "Father D'Angelo."

Father D'Angelo's sixty-eight years of age and thirty extra pounds of weight had curved his back and slowed his pace. "Glad you could make it, Mr. Miller," he half shouted so as to be heard. His flesh turkey neck, concealing the white square of his clerical collar, jiggled as he spoke. "I prayed you were not ill. Not showing up for the feast's opening night, that was your first miss in many years. I've even forgotten how long. You know the Fair doesn't feel truly underway until you're here."

"Thank you, Father. . . ." A tantalizing hunk of sausage caught Mr. Miller's gaze. Indicating the specific piece, he ordered "lotsa peppers and onions."

"Yes sir, Mr. Miller," replied the vendor, rapidly obeying.

"Unfortunately, Father, yesterday there was an emergency at work that only I could clear up. That's the only thing that could keep me away from this Fair."

He's a hard working man, Father D'Angelo reflected. A devoted family man and religious. I'm thankful he belongs to my parish. "Nothing troubling, I hope."

"No," Mr. Miller replied as he inspected his oniony sandwich. "Where's my garlic?"

A young blond man standing nearby quickly handed over the jar he was using.

Mr. Miller shook it until it looked as though it had snowed over his sandwich. He took an enormous bite. "Very tasty," he complimented the vendor. "Can I buy you one, Father?"

"No thank you, Mr. Miller. God has granted me a serene life but imposed an ulcer just to remind me of my mortality, I suspect. My joy of food is relegated to watching others consume it."

Picking their way through the throngs, they proceeded toward the church. The people who accidentally bumped into Mr. Miller were strangers; those who recognized him were more careful.

Frank Miller's cheeks bulged. His yellow-stained teeth furiously chomped away and his neck strained as he forced the half-chewed pieces down his gullet. Wiping his mouth with an embroidered white silk handkerchief, he remarked, "That was good, but they seem to make 'em smaller nowadays." He licked the saliva from his lips. "How 'bout some calamari, Father? That won't upset your stomach." He let out a belch, and pressed his hand against his chest. "Too much garlic. My doctor told me to be careful." He belched again.

"Perhaps a drink would settle your stomach."

Miller pressed both his hands against his abdomen. His breathing intensified. "I'll walk it off." But his legs faltered, and he clutched at the elderly priest for support. "My legs won't move." He clutched his sides for a moment, and suddenly his torso pitched forward. As he sank, a wheezing sound came from deep in his throat.

"Oh my God, Mr. Miller, can I help you?" implored the priest as Mr. Miller collapsed in his arms. "Help! Please God, somebody help!"

Mr. Miller's face shaded into blue and black as Father D'Angelo lowered him carefully to the ground. The crowd huddled around the two men as police shoved their way through.

One of the officers knelt and administered mouth-to-mouth resuscitation. Father D'Angelo clasped his crucifix, looked toward the church, and saw Father Rhoades standing at the top of the stairs shaking his head in warning. "It is not for us to decide," whispered Father D'Angelo as he administered the Last Rites. Other patrolmen encircled the trio. One felt for a pulse, then listened for a heartbeat.

"Too late," reported the officer. "He's dead. Call the M.E. and Homicide," he directed a colleague.

Within minutes, sirens shrieked from all directions. Detective Barry Martin pushed his way through the crowd. Only his badge clamped to his brown sports jacket distinguished him from the onlookers. He always wore a variation of brown in the belief that it made him appear thinner. Maybe even younger. His five-foot ten-inch height was increased by his curly dark brown hair.

Many faces in the crowd were familiar to Barry. He knew practically everyone in the precinct. It always amazed him that death drew such crowds. During his seventeen years on the police force, the last nine as detective assigned to the homicide division, he had never found death fascinating or tantalizing.

A patrolman and Barry, side by side, made their way toward Father D'Angelo, the patrolman filling Barry in on the particulars before returning to his normal routine. Seven years of friendship lay behind the supporting arm Barry provided as he led Father D'Angelo up the Church's marble stairs and away from the pandemonium.

Barry allowed the priest to regain his composure before inquiring, "Is there anything you can recall, Father? Something incidental? Did somebody bump into Miller or was there a particular person near him when he collapsed?"

"As I told the other officer, aside from the people on the street there was only," replied Father D'Angelo, his left hand still clenching his crucifix. "It must have been a heart attack. He should not have eaten that sandwich so fast."

Barry withheld any response, although he suspected there was something missing in the priest's diagnosis. "You said Miller ate the sandwich too fast. In a crowd this size, there must have been other customers around the booth when he ordered it. Does any particular person come to mind?"

"God forgive me for not having thought of it before. Yes, there was a young blond man who handed Mr. Miller a jar of garlic powder."

Barry urgently summoned a uniformed policeman and ordered him to confiscate all available jars of garlic powder and have them sent to the lab for testing. "Father, can you describe the blond man? Age, height, weight, clothes, anything at all?" He reached into his breast pocket and took out a small notebook and pen anticipating a lengthy description.

Father D'Angelo shook his head before answering. "All I can remember is that there was a rather large white cross hanging around his neck. I'm sorry, Barry."

"It's okay, Father," Barry said, returning the notebook and pen to his pocket. "Have you ever seen this blond man before?"

"No. I know all of my parishioners and neighbors. I'm quite sure he does not live around here." Father D'Angelo sighed and mumbled. "May God have mercy on his soul."

"Martin! Martin!" came the all too familiar and unwelcome voice of Captain Adams, the precinct commander, chewing on his ever present cheap cigar, and sporting his constant glistening mustache of perspiration. His men referred to it as Adam's 'Pinocchio

Nose': the more he lied, the wetter it became, and it was rarely dry. Politics was his platform and his forte was ass-kissing; he was skillful at both. But regarding police work, he had forgotten the little he ever knew. Promotion was the only thing he craved. Lately his ambition was to become Chief of Detectives, and he was constantly politicking for it. His men had little respect for him. Barry had even less.

After filling the captain in on what had happened, Barry said, "I need a partner again. My caseload is up to nineteen, not counting this one. Captain, assign someone to me for a few months, just so I can catch up?"

The captain spat a glob of brown saliva onto the church stairs. "Obviously you jest, Martin," he responded. "New York City's in the midst of a budget crisis and the Mayor has ordered all departments to tighten their belts. Mine will be the tightest. You're handling this case by yourself."

"Captain, you have Dave and two other detectives investigating that murder on Bank Street. I need only one. Give Dave back to me for a while. We were a good team."

"Can't do it, Martin. That's an important murder. Oh, it's almost nine o'clock, gotta run. Can't be late for the Mayor's party. The press will be there." He slapped Barry on the back. "Carry on, Martin."

"Schmuck!" responded Barry, but not loud enough for Adams to hear. Money talks, even after death. The other murder victim was the sole son of a bank president, and naturally that got top priority all the way around. Nobody cared about Frank Miller, and with good reason.

The Medical Examiner, unimaginatively nicknamed Doc, tapped Barry on the shoulder. "It was some type of fast-acting poison that attacks the nervous system. He didn't have a chance."

"Murder!" Father D'Angelo exclaimed. "Dear God, it makes no sense. Mr. Miller was a community leader, a good Catholic."

Barry ordered a full autopsy report along with the results from the jars of garlic powder.

"Everything's rush, rush, rush," Doc sneered. "I should have entered private practice. I could be at my private country club sloshing down martinis and cheating on my wife."

Barry turned his attention back to the priest. "I'm afraid your opinion of Miller is inaccurate, Father. Between selling plants and flowers he operated a major numbers racket for the syndicate."

"A criminal? I've known him and his family for over twenty years. I christened his two daughters."

"Sorry, Father, but that's the truth."

Father Paul Tobin, one of the young priests, and a friend of Barry Martin, bounded up the stairs two at a time. He wore sneakers, jeans, and a sweatshirt, and was badly in need of a haircut. Paul was one of the causes of Father D'Angelo's ulcer, yet he still couldn't help liking the young priest. During the eighteen months since Paul had been transferred back to New York, Father D'Angelo had developed a fatherly feeling for Paul.

"A priest should look like a priest," Father D'Angelo never tired of preaching to Paul. "You also missed Mass again. Where were you?"

Paul gawked at the ambulance and police commotion as he answered. "There was a rally at City Hall to legalize abortion . . ."

"Oh, sweet Jesus, close thine ears from his young tongue," Father D'Angelo implored as he crossed himself three times, then retreated to the sanctity of the church.

"You're gonna drive him crazy," Barry told his young friend who was still watching the goings on. "One of your parishioners, Miller, was killed tonight."

Paul shifted his gaze to Barry. "Miller? Was he mugged?"

"No, murdered." Barry held up his hand as if he were stopping traffic. "Don't tell me, Miller was a community leader and a pious Catholic."

Paul nodded in agreement. "Wrong. He was employed by the syndicate. I'm disappointed in you, Paul. A priest of the people who dresses like the people, you should have known."

"I had no idea," Paul said, also disappointed in himself. He went out of his way to be the modern, community-minded, non-preaching priest, by way of being involved in the people's daily lives, not just on holidays or special occasions. And now this. "Do you know why he was killed?"

"It's either a syndicate feud or it was time for him to retire. I have to go back to work. We're playing racquet-ball together this week, or are you gonna chicken out again?"

"For someone who constantly loses, you're very eager to play. I'll give you a call unless my dear sister gets into another argument with my folks. Oh, by the way, happy birthday. You should get my card tomorrow. It's the big forty, isn't it?"

"Thirty-nine!" Barry carefully articulated.

"Thirty-nine? Well," said Paul mischievously, "you ought to know; you've been it long enough."

Barry gave a curt smile before walking back to his car. He thought of Jenny, Paul's sister. Beautiful. A damn shame though.

Loitering near Barry's car was a young man clutching a small brown paper bag. He stared at Barry's badge number and silently repeated it for memorization. As he stepped back, a boy bumped into him and the bag fell open, exposing a blond wig. Quickly he stuffed the wig back into the bag and headed for his car and waiting companions.

Paul opened the over-sized wooden church doors, automatically dipped his fingers into the bowl of Holy Water, genuflected, then entered the priest's study behind the pulpit area. Father D'Angelo and Father Rhoades were arguing again. It was almost a daily event, usually instigated by Father Rhoades. Rhoades was in his early forties, had a Roman profile, and believed he possessed Roman wisdom, although his abrasive manner often belied this. Paul had been at this Church since his sister's accident eighteen months ago, and from the first day he disliked Rhoades, and vice versa. Paul chalked it up to a personality clash, especially since Rhoades' cryptic personality clashed with everybody. If there was ever a politically motivated clergyman it was Rhoades. And he was so dogmatic, obsessively so. Yet no one could deny the certainty of Rhoade's faith, even if it was charged with more fire and brimstone than most could tolerate.

Certainty. That was the key. And Paul's key had, over the past two years, tarnished. But how does one polish faith? Paul was still searching himself for the answer.

"Did you find out why Miller was killed?" Rhoades asked Paul.

"Barry said it's either a syndicate feud or they wanted him to retire." Paul took a seat. "What are you two arguing about now?"

Rhoades aimed a finger at Father D'Angelo. "He administered the Last Rites to Miller. I saw him. Cardinal Alden specifically decreed that there were to be no Last Rites for criminals; they're infections that fester and corrupt Mankind. Such diseases do not deserve prayer, that's why the ruling was made. He deliberately defied the Cardinal's word."

"He didn't know Miller was a criminal," Paul offered in Father D'Angelo's defense. "I didn't even know about

Miller, so how can you condemn Father D'Angelo?"

Father Rhoades inhaled deeply before unleashing his denouncement of their naivete. "It's time both of you learned the truth about some of our parishioners. Going to Church does not make one religious; I'm surprised you haven't learned that by now, Father Tobin."

At that, Paul drew himself up in indignation, but realizing that only a useless argument would ensue, bit his lip in restraint.

"There are people out there who prefer sin," Rhoades continued, "and we cannot talk people out of something they enjoy. It's that simple."

"Then what," Father D'Angelo bellowed, "is the role of the priest, Father Rhoades?"

"To make sure that the Catholic religion survives, no matter what!"

"And what do we do with people like Miller?" Paul asked. "Forget about them?"

"Precisely. The wicked are no longer entitled to receive God's grace. It's the new order."

"Says who?"

"Me!" Father Rhoades proclaimed. "Even Cardinal Alden agrees with me; that's why criminals aren't allowed the Last Rites. They have forfeited them. It was their choice."

"Did not our Lord Jesus take two criminals to Heaven with him as he lay dying on the cross?" asked Father D'Angelo.

"I know the story, Father," Rhoades answered sarcastically. "The old ways are gone. People have changed, the Church must change. You, Father D'Angelo, still conduct Mass in Latin for some of our parishioners even though they don't understand what the words mean. It's priests like you who impede the Church's progress."

Father D'Angelo's throat quivered. "And what do you propose to do with us older priests who believe in tradition?"

"We take over the parishes and give them a well-deserved retirement."

"Your words are finally in tune with your actions, Father Rhoades. I regret my eagerness to show you how this parish operates, but I am still the elder priest and this is my Church!"

"*Was* your Church. I have petitioned Cardinal Alden to make this *my* parish. He will undoubtedly agree."

The unexpected revelation drained the life from Father D'Angelo's face. His lips parted slightly, but he said nothing. After a moment of silence, he left the study.

Until now, Paul had excused Rhoades' "fostering of the new order of things" as a mindless aspect of his renegade personality. But the attack on Father D'Angelo was deliberately hurtful. Paul turned on Rhoades. "There was no reason for you to talk to him that way. He's devoted his entire life to the Church and he deserves—he's earned—our respect."

"He hasn't earned mine. Now, if you'll excuse me . . ."

Outraged, Paul blocked Rhoades' path. His mind sifted through a surge of derogatory remarks he wanted to utter, but the years of religious indoctrination toned down his statement to "There are times when I find you disgusting, Rhoades. This is one of them."

Rhoades, displaying a holier-than-thou grin, simply side-stepped Paul and left.

Paul found Father D'Angelo kneeling in front of the pulpit and knelt beside him. "You're a good priest, Father D'Angelo, and our parishioners need you. The Church needs you."

The aged priest kept his head bowed as he spoke.

"Can you smell it, Paul? The burning candles used to give this church a scent all its own. They often would flicker, but I can't recall one ever going out before the wax had melted away. No more. Now, for a quarter, we have slot machines with electric bulbs shaped like candles. No more flickering, no more scent." He raised his head. "You're a good architect, Paul. The new pulpit you built is beautiful. The old one had to be replaced; the old ones always have to be replaced."

Father D'Angelo grasped the railing for support as he stood up. His gait was lifeless, limp. He was walking like an old man. Slapping the railing, Paul muttered, "Damn that Rhoades!"

The exterior of the new Sixth Police Precinct Headquarters was modern and contrasted sharply with its Greenwich Village neighborhood. But inside, the concentration of people had already worn away the newness. The detective unit was housed on the third floor, which resembled a station for recycling paper. No desk top was visible. Papers were piled on top of the file cabinets that lined the walls. The smells of stale coffee, cigarettes, and cigars polluted the air. The noise of telephones ringing, people talking or yelling, and typewriters clacking was endless.

Barry assumed his thinking position, feet up on the desk, body slouched into his chair, head back, a cup of luke warm coffee in one hand, and today, the Medical Examiner's report on Miller in the other. Cause of death: A massive dose of thallium, used in rat poison, orally ingested in a mix of garlic powder. The jar of garlic powder containing the poison had not been found. That was no surprise. Miller was definitely the target, and the killer, the blond man, knew he'd be at the feast and that he'd use garlic powder. Probably followed Miller from booth to booth waiting to switch the jar of garlic. A set up, and by someone who knew Miller's routine and eating habits. The syndicate? It wasn't their style, but then again styles change. If it was a syndicate hit, the case would never be solved, and nobody would care. Barry didn't. Miller deserved it.

Detective Dave Smith, seated in front of Barry, busily handled two telephone conversations at once. They had been partners for four years, until the city's budget was slashed. It was unfortunate. They had finally reached that point where each could anticipate what the other would do in any given situation. Neither one had ever let the other down during an emergency. Once, Dave had even crawled out of a sick bed to back up Barry on a drug bust. Barry trusted Dave implicitly.

Dave swung around and pointed at Barry's phone. His face was bloated but thinner than it had been. He had lost twenty-five pounds, yet he was still fat. "It's her again, the one with the sexy voice. But then all your women have sexy voices. I'm not going to answer your phone any more. It's not fair to my excitable imagination."

"Go home and see your wife."

"I'd rather take a cold shower," Dave joshed, not meaning what he said. He was one of the rare policemen who had a successful marriage. He knew it and he was thankful for it.

Barry gritted his teeth before picking up the phone. Ann. He'd forgotten all about their date last night. On purpose? It was happening again—boredom had invaded the relationship. This time it had taken a mere two months. His relationships were getting shorter.

Ann skipped over his apology and in her sexiest voice cooed, "I was eating a banana and thought of you. Are we on for tonight?"

"I'm working late," he offered as an excuse. "I'll give you a call." Hell, he didn't even want to talk to her any more. Why couldn't he meet the right woman? But Barry knew all too well the staggering divorce statistics of policemen. It seemed absurd to try something when the odds were stacked against you. If only the loneliness didn't bother him so much. And sex, rather than curing it, only made it worse.

Dave held up a glossy magazine picture of a seven-layer chocolate cake and crooned, "Now that's better than all your girlfriends." His eyeslids closed halfway as he tried to recapture the taste. "I hate diets. And I hate people who tell you to go on diets. I've read six diet books over the last few weeks, and you wanna know something? All the authors are thin. Thin people shouldn't be allowed to write about diets, they can't understand what it's like to be fat. Besides, it's common knowledge that all thin people have tape worms; that's why they're so thin. Fat worms, thin bodies."

Barry felt queasy. "That's disgusting."

"The truth usually is." He leaned across the desk and snatched the coroner's report out of Barry's hands. "You got the Miller case. You'll never solve it. The killer's probably in Vegas living it up, all expenses paid." His voice lowered. "Help me with the banker's son's murder. I'm really getting the squeeze from all sides."

"Who else besides the Captain?"

"The Chief and the deceased's father. He calls me up twice a day, once in the morning, once at night. I feel like a stock broker quoting him what's going on with the case."

"And?"

'It's a depressed market. Nobody saw anything, nobody knows anything. Right now I'm running down a lead on somebody who saw a witness leaving the scene."

"The Captain and the Chief are really on your back.

If I get some free time I'll help. On the Q.T."

"Thanks, partner. I'd much rather have you than those rookies. They need a manual just to pick their nose."

"I'll never understand how Jane has stayed married to you all these years."

"She doesn't listen to me," he retorted as he swiveled back to his desk.

Barry's phone rang. If it's Ann I'll see her tonight. "Detective Martin."

"Is this Badge 5746?" came the muffled voice.

"Who is this?" Barry flung a pencil at Dave's back and motioned him to have a tracer put on the call.

"Badge 5746, you haven't picked up your morning mail yet." Click.

Dave pointed thumbs down; there wasn't enough time for a tracer. Barry contacted the bomb squad, then hurried down to the mail room. Two men from the bomb squad were already sifting through his mail with a hand-held detector. They were outfitted in protective flak-jackets and enclosed by special moveable reinforced plastic partitions which they had erected around the mail room. To everyone's relief the results of their search were negative. One letter, printed in red ink, was hustled down to the Forensic Department and was returned thirty minutes later. Attached to the letter was a memo: "Smudges of white powder, as sometimes on disposable surgical gloves, were found on the letter and envelope. No fingerprints. Detailed report ASAP."

Barry took the letter into the Captain's office and read the four lines aloud:

He that is not with me is against me.
Miller was against me.

The wages of sin is death.
Miller has been paid in full.

The Crossbearers

Captain Adams took the cigar out of his mouth and spat a hunk of saliva into the wastepaper basket. Barry gagged at the sight. "Goddamn religious fanatics, they're a pain in the butt. You ever dealt with religious fanatics before, Martin?"

"No sir."

"I did. Once. Cardinal Beck's assassination. Solving that case got me my promotion. The Chief's too. I enjoyed that case."

As the captain babbled on about the old case, Barry reflected on this one. For the moment, Miller's death could not be assumed to be a syndicate feud. Or it could be then again, and the telephone call and letter were merely distractions. He'd have to investigate it both ways, he concluded. He tuned back to the Captain's jabbering.

"We'd better keep the lid on this case, especially from the goddamn media; no sense starting a panic when none exists yet. And listen, let's not spend too much energy on this case, it's not worth it."

Barry had expected the last statement.

The police chaplain knocked on the door, ending the meeting. Holding an armful of books, he exchanged hellos with Barry commenting on the relief everyone felt when no bomb was found in his mail. He rested the books on the Captain's desk and shook his arms, explaining, "I'm in the final phase of getting my pilot's license and I can't stop reading. It's become an obsession. I'll be happy when it's over, although it is exciting. Do you like to fly, Barry?"

"Only if the plane's headed toward the Caribbean."

The captain cleared his throat signalling Barry to return to his work. He hated idle chatter, unless, of course, he was involved in it or the subject of it.

Barry returned to his desk. The captain is right, he grudgingly admitted, a case such as this could easily be blown out of proportion by the media. He reread the letter. How did the caller know he hadn't picked up his mail? Barry scanned the people in the office. Detectives, uniformed officers, some lawyers with their clients, suspects, handymen. Barry bet his money on one of the mail clerks, although it seemed too obvious. It's the place to start. He'd investigate all of them.

His telephone rang. "I see you got my letter, Badge 5746. I took great pains preparing that letter; nothing is traceable."

Barry glanced about the room to see if anyone was talking softly into the phone. Half the staff was. This is crazy, suspecting other cops.

"Are you there, Badge 5746?"

"Yeah, I'm here. I was just going over the Forensic report concerning your letter." That was the lead-in. Here came the bait. "According to this, you have blond hair, about 5'10", 170 pounds. We have two definite prints from the stamp plus a sample of your saliva which can tell us your blood type. Pretty soon we'll know your name and where you live. Why not save us the trouble?"

"My ass. That description ain't worth nothin', and the rest is bullshit. You ain't very smart, Badge 5746."

Not even a nibble. But admitting to the bluff could be interrupted as a sign of weakness on Barry's part, and Barry wouldn't allow that. "We've already distributed a composite picture of you on the street. You can't hide forever. Why don't we talk, you and me, face to face?" Barry listened carefully for any recognizable noise.

23

"No way, Badge 5746. We ain't never gonna meet, at least not with you knowing it." A sadistic laugh accompanied his words. "I'll speak to you again. Have a good day, Badge 5746." Click.

"Just what I need," he said to Dave who had been listening in on the phone conversation, "a friendly psychopathic killer."

"And on your birthday too." He handed Barry a small white box. After all these years, Barry knew that the present was a dozen of Jane's home-made double fudge double nut brownies. "You're going to have your hands full with this case. You'll never have time to help me. But I'd rather have my case than yours."

"I know what you mean," Barry said. "My first year as a detective I was involved with a psychopath. There were four detectives assigned to the case, yet he still managed to kill seven people before we nailed him."

"Psychos can really drive you crazy. They can also make you feel so damn stupid. Everything they do is so unpredictable . . . you feel like a dog chasing its own tail—you get nowhere fast. But you'll crack the case, you're one of the best detectives we have." Dave held his head erect. "Of course you did have the best teacher."

"You're damn right I did." Barry placed two brownies in Dave's hand. Dave's testimony to his professionalism was true, and Barry was proud of it. Sure, some cases took a long time to crack, and sure, some were still unsolved, but nobody could solve them. I *am* a good detective, and I hate being made to look like a fool. Have no fear, blond man, I'll get you. All by myself, if necessary.

Barry leaned across his desk and shook Dave's hand. "Thanks for the present, and give my love to Jane. By the way, how come you haven't asked me how old I am?"

"Why should I. You'd only lie. I know I do." Before turning back to his work, Dave teased, "Have a good day Badge 5746."

"Cute," Barry replied as he got ready to leave. He had to start the investigation somewhere. First, Miller's family; second, Miller's successor. He did not anticipate any cooperation from either source. But what made matters more difficult was that somebody close was spying on him. In a room full of fellow officers he suddenly felt conspicuous and uncomfortable. Who the hell was watching him?

Father Tobin shuffled aside the blueprints of houses he'd designed until he found the diagrams of the rocking chair he was planning to build for Father D'Angelo's approaching birthday. The good Father needed a boost to cheer him up now.

Paul's architectural ability was well known and highly in demand in the neighborhood. He could have been successful as a professional architect had the lure of the priesthood ever left him, but it never did. College and graduate school were his ways of combatting his urge to join the priesthood. Young men shunned the priesthood, but he didn't. His parents didn't understand. His sister didn't understand. Especially his sister. That Sunday dinner . . . He had waited for the family Sunday dinner to make his announcement about entering the priesthood. Mother gasped, Father eyed him queerly, and Jenny alleged 'You're too good-looking to be a priest.' But her joke turned sour when she realized he meant it. No big brother to protect her, to talk to, to have fun with and learn from. It was outright desertion. An older brother who was different from her girl friends' brothers. An oddity by choice.

That was six long years ago, and people do change. His parents were proud of him now and so was Jenny, although occasionally she hinted to Paul that if he wanted to he could still be a husband and father. "Thirty-four isn't that old" Jenny had said a few months back, shortly after she herself turned thirty.

Paul had changed too: There are some goals in life you desire, but when you achieve them, it's not the way you imagined it would be. That was the priesthood. Paul wasn't expecting to convert the world, not even a part of it. He loved God and wanted to have others believe as he did. Some did, the majority didn't, but that was okay. New Mexico was not. It was his first assignment as head of a parish, small and out-of-the-way as it was. But that only magnified his enthusiasm. Then came an aspect of religion he had never before encountered: converting American Indians into Catholics by barter. You become a Catholic, we'll give you education and medicine. Catholicism was their castor oil. The tribal elders treated Paul like a leper, keeping their children at a safe distance from what they considered his contaminated ideas. Then came news of Jenny's automobile accident and her permanent blindness. God's anger struck the wrong member of the family. Regardless of how much Paul rationalized, he could not escape the guilt of his sister's tragedy. New Mexico, like an expert criminal, had unlocked the door to his safe-guarded belief. And once open, he found it harder to close. There were even times when, by itself, the door opened wider as if some unknown force was manuevering him out of control. Yet he was most fearful that his struggle to close the door, to restore order and faith, was not as strong as it could be. Resignation? Desire? Allowance? One of these was the reason the door had remained open. But Paul remained detached from the search of his inner self; he wasn't prepared for the truth, not yet anyway.

Paul came upstairs and spotted Rhoades in the

hallway sorting through the incoming mail. He was always the first one to pick up the mail. Sometimes he even waited on the steps for the mailman and became upset when delivery was late. Paul and Father D'Angelo knew Rhoades had family, but from his lack of reference to them the two assumed they were not close. Judging from Rhoades' intensity as he checked the mail, Paul had theorized that he was waiting for a letter from his family that would end whatever problems existed. Father D'Angelo's theory was less cerebral: Rhoades was in charge of the Church accounts so he wanted to collect the bills before they had a chance of getting mislaid.

Father D'Angelo is probably right, Paul thought, as he approached Rhoades, although Rhoades' attitude of urgency made Paul feel as though there was more to it than just safeguarding bills. Before Paul could speak, Rhoades said abruptly, "There's no mail for you, Paul." His right hand lowered the mail to his side.

"I wasn't expecting anything. I'm on my way to the lumber store and I want to know if I can write a check for about a hundred dollars?"

"What do you need lumber for? The Church account is to be used strictly for Church business."

"It is Church business. May I write the check?"

"I must know precisely what the money is to be used for." With hands on hips and an expression of authority as if it had been struck in stone, he waited for the answer.

Paul calculated that the truth might not be approved by Rhoades so he avoided it and offered instead, "I'm trying to get a head start on the Christmas pageant this year. The wood is for the manger and platform."

Rhoades consented.

As he was about to leave, Paul spied the corner of a manila envelope sandwiched between a stack of magazines on the round lobby table. He withdrew the envelope from the stack. "This is my article on 'The Church and Politics.' You said you'd deliver it to the League of Independent Voters."

"I forgot. I must have been busy."

"They were going to print my article . . . but it's too late now. You should have told me you couldn't deliver it. I would have mailed it. I wasn't that sick. Why didn't you deliver it?"

"I said I was busy!" Rhoades' manner, as often occurred, unpredictably changed. This time it was toned down. "Mrs. Weaver thought she was dying again, so I had to rush over to administer the Last Rites. Another false alarm and a waste of my valuable time."

She'd done that to all of them. But why would she ask for Rhoades? Father D'Angelo must have been too busy. Paul reluctantly accepted the answer and left.

A handful of teenagers greeted· Paul on the church stairs, their usual after-school hangout. Paul sniffed the air. "Where's Bobby?" he asked no one in particular. "I want an answer." The movement of their eyes secretly gave him the information. Around the far corner of the church a group of kids huddled close to the church wall. One look-out clapped his hands signalling Paul's approach. They scattered. Bobby, a thirteen-year-old, wore a silk monogrammed shirt, blue designer jeans, and genuine leather cowboy boots. He jammed his hands into his pockets.

Paul's face reddened with anger; his voice was un-controlled. "I told you I don't want you selling drugs around here. As a matter of fact, I don't want *you* around here any more."

The boy belligerently replied, "Hey man, you don't own this corner. And I don't sell drugs neither."

Paul grabbed Bobby's arm and pulled it out of his pocket. Two plastic bags containing grass and pills dropped to the ground. Tearing the bags open, he dumped out the contents and mashed them with his foot. "If I see you around here one more time, I'm going to call your parents and the police."

"Who cares?" Bobby snickered. "They can't touch me, I'm under age."

Paul raised his hand warning, "They won't touch me either. Now get out of here!"

Bobby retreated a few steps, then gave Paul the finger before running away.

The other kids were watching from across the street. "My warning applies to everybody," Paul shouted. "If there's a next time I'll call the police. Now go home." With expressions of guilt and apology, the youngsters quietly dispersed. But Paul knew it was only temporary; they'd be back, buying and taking drugs again. Drug abuse was one problem Paul had no success with. No matter what he said, they wouldn't listen. Another of my failures, he accused himself. Too many failures. Way too many.

He crossed the street to the fruit stand, bought an apple, and continued on his way to the lumber store. The bill for the lumber was only eighty-eight dollars. That should please Rhoades, Paul thought.

Miller's family lived in a townhouse on Washington Place. Barry estimated the price at three to four hundred thousand dollars. Miller had to sell a lot of plants and flowers for that kind of money. Mrs. Miller answered the doorbell and seemed less than pleased at seeing Barry's badge. He followed her into the livingroom. Protective plastic coverings were on everything, including the lampshades. The furnishings were old bulky styles in offensively vibrant colors. They weren't worth protecting.

Miller's two daughters joined Barry and their

mother. The family resemblance was evident but not flattering. The oldest daughter, speaking and acting in a masculine manner, began the discussion with a defense of her deceased father. "For years, you cops have harrassed my father for no valid reason and now you come here looking for help. We know you won't investigate the case properly, so why do you bother us?"

Those were the kindest words spoken during the short meeting. Barry wisely remained silent while each family member reviled the police for disgracing their father by innuendo and false gossip.

A complete waste of time, Barry thought, yet wondered if those women really believed Miller to be a law-abiding citizen. Maybe they just refused to accept the truth. If so, that was their problem.

Next stop was Miller's terrarium shop on busy Seventh Avenue, two blocks away from his house. King-size glass windows displayed an exotic assortment of plants and flowers. It was a successful business and Miller could have made a decent living without hooking up with the mob. Inside, a bulldog of a man waited on customers. As he bent over to water a plant Barry observed the outline of a pistol sticking out against his smock. It wasn't for protecting the plants.

Barry showed the man his badge. "Is Avery in?"

"He's expecting you, Detective Martin," the man said gesturing to a door in the rear of the store. "You can go right in."

Barry guessed who tipped them off. He walked into the rear office. Robert ("Buddy") Avery was sitting behind an old wooden desk. Not one piece of paper was visible anywhere. They really were expecting me, he joked to himself. The rest of the office was bare, with no plants or flowers anywhere.

"What can I do for you?" Buddy stated in a surly

voice, disregarding all formalities. He was not a very big man and his voice was anything but authoritative. An unlikely candidate to be Miller's successor, but he had the appropriate connections and got the job done, and that's what counted.

"You're going to tell me who killed your predecessor," Barry stated as he roamed about the office browsing for something they might have over-looked during their cleanup.

"How am I supposed to know who killed him? You're the cop, not me. You tell *me* who killed him."

"Maybe you did. There's a lot of money in plants today." Barry sat on the edge of the desk. Buddy's lips grew taut but he said nothing. "How many plants do you have to sell in a year to buy a four hundred thousand dollar townhouse?"

"I'm a legitimate business man, Martin, and I don't care for your insinuations. Ask your questions, then get out."

Barry got off the desk, wandered over to the window sill, picked up a small pair of shears, snapped them open and shut a number of times, and returned to the edge of the desk. "I don't like to be rushed when I'm working on a case," Barry said snapping the shears in Buddy's direction. "Who killed Miller?"

"I don't know." Buddy's eyes followed the snapping shears. "I had nothing to do with it. I was bowling that night with three other men. They can verify it."

'No doubt they can. The only problem, though, is that you have a motive for wanting Miller dead that nobody else does."

"You're not even in the ballgame, Martin."

"You ever hear of a group called the Crossbearers?"

"No." Then, in a solemn voice he added, "None of my acquaintances wanted Miller dead. That's all I can say."

Barry tossed the shears at Buddy who fumbled the catch. "Don't plan any vacations for a while," Barry offered as he left. Buddy's final statement that none of his acquaintances wanted Miller dead confirmed Barry's suspicions: Miller's death was not a syndicate hit, which led him back to the sole alternative, the Crossbearers. It would have been a lot easier if it was a syndicate feud. With all the other cases pending, Barry didn't want to spend too much time on this one. Maybe it's a one-shot deal, but he had a premonition Miller was not the first or the last.

Barry got off duty at six-thirty and went directly to the address on East 56th Street that Paul had given him. Paul would already be there with his sister, Jenny. Her last argument with her folks was the culmination of a build-up that eventually would have to end in her leaving home. Jenny was a marvelous girl, woman, he corrected himself. At thirty she had strikingly beautiful features accentuated by long straight black hair. Her skin was soft, and Barry enjoyed watching her smile, although she didn't do that too often any more.

Barry knocked on the door and Paul let him in. The luxury apartment was in accord with its upper East Side status: Modern furniture, art and sculpture everywhere, and oversized rooms with high ceilings. Obviously who-ever lived here had money.

Jenny, pacing off the steps to the door, gave Barry a hug. "Thanks for coming, Barry. I need all the moral support I can get."

"Paul's message sounded urgent so I rushed over." She looked lovelier every time I see her, Barry reflected. Black velvet slacks, a purple silk blouse, one simple silver necklace, and boots. Just right. Except for the ever-present dark sunglasses which hid the tiny scars around her eyes. Barry had never seen Jenny without those glasses.

He planted a brotherly kiss on her forehead. "Whose apartment is this?"

"Mine," came a pleasant female voice from across the room. Firmly, the lady shook Barry's hand. "I'm Mary Evans, Jenny's friend. Excuse the jogging suit, I wasn't expecting company."

"That's quite all right," Barry seduced her with his eyes. Short matronly styled auburn hair, a proportionate figure enhanced by the designer jogging suit, some gold chains about her neck, and, if they were genuine, a set of expensive diamond stud earrings. Flagrantly ostentatious for jogging but that's the Upper East Side, Barry concluded. He checked her fingers. No wedding band or discoloration on the finger. She was available.

Barry sat next to Mary while Paul and Jenny sat the other end of the livingroom discussing the family quarrel. Barry concentrated hard to keep his eyes from Mary's legs. "How do you know Jenny?"

"I'm a psychologist at the Institute for the Blind. Jenny has been my patient since she began attending the Institute. Now she's also one of my assistants. A paying job is a positive incentive to a handicapped person. She'll do fine."

"I wasn't aware psychologists made this kind of money," pointing to the art. Barry examined a wooden horse on the coffee table. "Oak. I made one like this in workshop at high school."

"That's an original sculpture by Brellen. It costs twenty-four hundred dollars," Mary said, retrieving it from Barry's hands and cautiously replacing it on the table.

"Twenty-four hundred dollars?" Barry repeated in amazement. "It doesn't even contain any gold or silver. That's a lot of money for a piece of wood. You must have wealthy parents."

"I do," Mary answered, then quickly stressed, "But everything in this apartment was purchased with my money. Women *can* be successful at a career, you know. We can be successful at anything."

"I never said otherwise." He glanced at Jenny and Paul still conferring over the family problem.

"You're one of Jenny's favorite topics," said Mary, noting the direction of Barry's gaze. "She's extremely fond of you."

"We've become close friends over the past year. She has such an endearing personality. I remember her first day at the Institute. Paul and I drove her there. It was like escorting a prisoner to the gallows."

"My encounter was worse. I was the first person she met at the Institute. And her reactions were typical: scared, defensive, self-pitying, and wanting to believe her blindness was only temporary. She's matured a great deal in the past seven months. Of course Jenny should have been attending the Institute for the past year and a half. If only parents didn't shut the handicapped in closets as though they were freaks, it would make my job much easier."

"Parents or no parents, sudden blindness is one helluva shock. And the saddest part is it never goes away. Jimmy, the boy who was driving that night, was killed in the crash. Jenny considers him the lucky one."

"It's heartbreaking, but in time, and with the proper support, Jenny will rebuild her self-confidence. She's already enrolled in sculpture class again, working with clay. She was a gifted artist before the accident and now she can be a good sculptor. All it takes is hard work, determination, and many failures." Mary ended the sentence with a smile. "She can do it if she wants to."

Paul and Jenny's conversation grew louder and more intense. Paul apologized. "She refuses to go home," he said, raising his hands in surrender.

"She can stay with me," offered Mary. "My father has been blind his entire life, so I know the procedures. Besides, we women have to stick together."

Paul sighed. "My parents are going to oppose this all they can." He looked at Jenny. "I suppose you want me to break the news to them."

"Priests are good at breaking unpleasant news. Tell them I'll be fine."

Paul went into the kitchen to make the call and Mary readied the second bedroom for her guest.

"Barry, where are you?" Jenny's voice was fearful that she was alone.

Barry joined her on the couch and held her hand. "I hate those dark glasses." He wanted to take them off, but she pushed his hands away. "They detract from your beauty." Her hands held her glasses in place. He changed to another subject. "Mary's extremely competent; she'll take good care of you, Jenny. Things will get back to normal."

"Normal is no longer in my vocabulary," she said. "Don't you know that blind people frighten other people? It's true. They either help too much or not at all, and it's usually not at all. When Mary and I walk down the street I can hear people's footsteps change direction to avoid my tapping cane. And crossing a street, I can feel their eyes glaring at me as they ponder whether or not to help me. That's my normalcy."

"You can't blame people, Jenny. They just haven't been educated properly. One day, it'll change."

"I'm thirty years old. I can't wait until I'm eighty to have a normal life."

"Jenny, I've seen other blind people live a full life but the first step is up here," he tapped gently on her head. "You smiled. You should wear that smile more often."

Jenny placed her hands on Barry's face, as she did

every time they were together. "I can feel your smile. Five o'clock shadow. Your broken nose from high school football. I like your face, Barry, I wish I could see it."

In a contrived falsetto voice he answered, "Nobody looks upon the face of the Medusa and lives to tell of its beauty."

"You make me laugh, and you also treat me as a normal person. I like that. I like you."

"Jenny, one day you're going to meet some nice young man who can keep that smile on your face."

Jenny held Barry's cheeks in her hands and whispered, "Maybe I already—."

"Jenny," Paul cut in, entering the room. "Mom and Dad were terribly upset but I straightened them out for now. Tomorrow I'll bring some more of your clothes over. Of course you neglected to mention that you left without telling them where you were going. I caught holy hell for that."

"Transference," Mary answered professionally. "They were upset with Jenny but speaking to you, so they took their frustration out on you."

"I'll say. Anyway, I told the folks you'd call them tomorrow, just to tell them you're all right. Are you listening to me, Jenny?"

"They just get me so mad."

"Will you call them tomorrow?"

"Yes. But I'm not going back there."

"I told them that. But call, please."

Mary motioned to Paul to calm down. He sat beside his sister, draped an arm over her shoulder, and said, "You'll be fine, Jenny. Together we will solve your problems. This time, I'll be here when you need me." He hoped that this second chance, this reprieve, would negate some, if not all, of his guilt. *Never again will I leave her. Never.*

Barry moved toward the door. "Since things are somewhat settled, I'll be leaving. Take care of yourself, Jenny." Then to Paul, "And I'll speak to you tomorrow. Miss Evans, it was nice meeting you and I hope we see each other again real soon." First chance, he'd call her up for a date.

When Barry left, Jenny's face clouded. "Mary," she confided, "I'm tired. It's been a hectic day. Big brother, thanks."

"Just remember to call Mom and Dad tomorrow."

"I won't forget." Jenny answered as Mary guided her to the guest room. Sitting on the bed, Jenny admitted meekly, "I'm sorry to be such a burden to you, but there was no other choice. If there had been—"

"Jenny, I invited you to stay. If I didn't want you here, I wouldn't have offered. And you're not a burden. A friend is never a burden." Before leaving, Mary described the layout of the room for Jenny's benefit: the bathroom at seven o'clock, the dresser at two, and the closet at three o'clock.

Rejoining Paul in the livingroom, Mary noticed his pensive expression. "You remind me of Atlas with the weight of the world on his shoulders," she said as she poured two more cups of coffee.

"When I'm with Jenny I feel sorry for her and when I'm with my folks I feel sorry for them. They shouldn't have shut her in as they did, but they did it out of love. And now that she's not coming home they're even feeling responsible for her blindness."

"I expected that reaction. They'll get over it. Meantime, this separation will be beneficial to everyone. Your parents can return to a normal routine, Jenny can start her independence, and all anxiety will be relieved. It's just traumatic at first."

"And you are bearing half the burden," added Paul.

"My father promised himself that if he ever became

successful he would aid other blind people. I'm helping him fulfill that promise. Besides, being a female in today's society is difficult enough, but being a blind female is almost unbearable. And, if I may be so candid, religion often hampers our cause."

"I know the lecture."

"And? . . ."

"And you are correct. But changes in religion happen as fast as evolution." Paul chuckled. "Look at poor Galileo. After all these hundreds of years the Church finally confirmed that he was not an anarchist, just a scientist."

"I don't believe the leaders of the Equal Rights Amendment would be enthralled with your span-of-time example."

Mary refilled the coffee cups and their socio-religious conversation continued until the neighborhood church bells chimed one o'clock.

During the night Jenny's sleep once again plunged her into reliving the car accident. Muffled moans of distress became tense sounds of panic. Her hands clawed at the air above, her body twisted to and fro. Suddenly her eyelids snapped open only to see more darkness. Another nightmare. What was it this time? her half-awake mind asked her subconscience. A lone man standing in the middle of some street, and Jimmy's car almost hitting him. As usual the remembered bits and pieces of the nightmare made no sense.

Her eyes throbbed with headache pain. Reaching over for the bell on the nightstand to signal her mother, she felt only emptiness. A moment of panic—a loss of place—riddled through her mind before clarity returned. "I'm at Mary's," her hand struck the bed in anger. "I'm driving myself crazy," she thought, fearful that her nightmares were becoming as permanent as her blindness.

A refreshing breeze from an open window brushed against her face. Fully awake, Jenny moved off the bed, felt her way to the window and, in a yoga position, sat in front of it. Faint street noises echoing from below went unheard as the results of the fight with her folks consumed her thoughts. "And now I'm on my own," she stated to the darkness, her constant companion and secret confidant. "I'm so tired of fighting for my independence; of having to rebuild my life again. It's like being born twice, only I don't like my second life." She tilted her head down allowing more truth to trickle into her thoughts. I want someone to take care of me . . . to love me. Barry came to mind but she quickly dismissed the fantasy. Nobody falls in love with a blind person.

In one graceful motion, Jenny untangled herself from the yoga position and stood up. She placed her right hand against the warm window pane. It was a beautiful summer night, and she imagined the sky cluttered with stars. She found herself reciting "Star light, star bright, first star I see tonight; wish I may, wish I might, have the wish I wish tonight. I wish . . . I wish never to be alone."

2

Barry gulped down his morning coffee as he rummaged through his mounting case load, but his mind was absorbed in the Miller case and the strange telephone caller. The same disturbing thought continually re-occurred: If it was a fanatical religious group who murdered Miller it could be the first of many. Amateur killers, picking their victims at random, killing them at random, and no patterns to their kill.

Dave sauntered in, opened a brown bag and pulled out a thermos of coffee and an extra thick jelly doughnut which he positioned in the middle of his desk. "Isn't that a beautiful sight? Do you want it?"

"I don't like jelly doughnuts."

"You what?" he said aghast. "I always had an inkling you were a communist." Gingerly he picked up the doughnut and held it in front of Barry. "You have to eat it for me, Barry. If I don't see somebody else enjoying this I might have to, and you don't want me to break my diet, do you?" He moved the doughnut closer to Barry's face. "Please."

"Give it to the Captain."

Dave drew the doughnut closer to his chest as if he were protecting a child. "Only if it was laced with arsenic." He sat down facing Barry. His voice was hushed. "I was here until midnight last night conferring with the Captain and the father of the victim. There are now five detectives assigned to this case, and so far each one has investigated the same leads and the same people. We're bumping into one another. It's crazy."

"What are you doing?"

"Staying away from the others as much as possible. I don't even tell the Captain what I'm doing. I accomplish more that way. The Captain and the Chief really want promotions again and my case could be their ticket. I'd enjoy this job a lot better if both of them were off my back. I'd better get to work. Making any headway with your case?"

"Nothing noticeable. I'll keep you posted."

Dave swung around to his desk while Barry took to the streets to find out what the informants knew. As he cruised about the city, a blue Oldsmobile Cutlass sedan followed from a safe distance, matching his every move. Barry's first stop was the newsstand, then the wandering dirtballs, as the bums were called, then the shoeshiners. Next were the unimportant street corner drug pushers whom he knew only by their first names, and finally the paid informants.

One of them, known on the street as Ripley because you could believe him or not, was the hungriest for money. They met in a corner of Gramercy Park.

Ripley's physical appearance was devastatingly ugly. He had been punched in the face so often by those he had informed on, or thought he had informed on, that no one remembered what any of his features originally looked like. Also, his left hand was missing. Two stories circulated as to how this happened: Ripley's and the truth. Ripley contended that during the late 1960's he was a C.I.A. agent attempting to infiltrate the K.G.B. He would have been successful if a reporter had not accidently published a top secret list of agents stationed in the West German sector. The K.G.B. arrested him, interrogated him, and when that failed, resorted to physical torture; crushing each finger and then his hand with a hammer. As the story evolved, the C.I.A. rescued Ripley because he was so valuable and then they disclaimed any knowledge of him and his actions, abandoning him as a wounded animal to fend for himself.

It was an intriguing story. The truth was different. In a drunken state, Ripley stole a bicycle in Central Park, rode it into heavy traffic, fell, and a passing car ran over his hand. Short but true. Ripley, however, adamantly stuck to his version, and to buy information from him Barry was mindful of which story to refer to.

Wearing mismatched and ill-fitting clothes resurrected from the garbage, Ripley circled closer to Barry. A stench of cheap wine permeated his body. His eyes constantly scanned the area. Using his ventriloquist's trick of speaking without moving his lips, he asked Barry for fifty bucks.

"First the info."

"It's solid. Fifty bucks." Ripley's right shoulder twitched. "You wired?"

"No. And I checked the area for you, no C.I.A. or K.G.B.," Barry offered as a temporary pacifier. "What do you have for me?"

"Miller's death weren't no feud," he informed Barry.

"Avery told me that. How about a private contract?"

"They ain't even sayin' it's murder. They're agreein' with what your Captain said to the papers . . . uhm . . ."

"Miller's death was still pending further investigation."

43

"Yeah, that's it. I even heard some say he might have died from a heart attack."

"Then the syndicate's not searching for the killer."

"Nope. They ain't doin' nothin'."

Barry peeled off the money and handed it to Ripley. "If you hear anything else let me know."

Ripley rapidly disappeared.

Barry relaxed in the car, puzzling over the information. With the syndicate's direct line into the Medical Examiner's office, they had to know that Miller was murdered. Then why agree with the Captain's obvious lie to the newspapers? *They know something I don't know. Now all I have to do is find out what it is.*

Barry drove down Eighth Avenue in the Village and spotted Paul leaving a lumber store. "Hop in, I'll give you a lift back to the church. You look upset."

"I bought some lumber the other day and the check bounced. I don't understand it; Rhoades said there was enough money in the church account."

"It happens to millions of other people."

"Not Rhoades, he's meticulous about everything. What are you doing down here?"

"Visiting the local A.P. members, and—"

"A.P.?" Associated Press?"

"No. Asshole Population, and the membership is growing uncontrollably. You're laughing, but I have to deal with 'em thanks to our beloved Mayor who closed a lot of the psychiatric wards. Do you know what it's like to talk to someone who thinks he's a kangaroo, who attacks a sidewalk vendor because the man thinks they're using his missing tail in the meat? It's scary as hell."

Paul couldn't stop laughing.

Barry handed him a copy of the letter he had received from the Crossbearers. "I also came to see you, if you can stop laughing for a minute. I received that after Miller was killed. Notice the two quotes from the Bible."

"I knew they looked familiar," Paul teased. "Who are the Crossbearers?"

"Damned if I know. What about the quotes or the name Crossbearers? Any special hidden meanings?"

"One of great thing about quoting the Bible is that you can make it support almost any opinion." Paul handed the letter back to Barry. "They sure are stretching the Bible to rationalize Miller's death. Maybe that's why we're losing so many parishioners; we have a hundred answers for one question. Sorry, that's my problem. You think the Crossbearers will kill again?"

"Absolutely, but I don't know who or when."

"Another syndicate man?"

"That's my guess. By the time I find out who these Crossbearers are, everyone in the syndicate might be dead."

"They deserve it. My God, that's terrible, isn't it?"

"You're not alone in your opinion. Whenever there's a syndicate war everyone moves to the sidelines. Nobody cares if they kill each other, and it's cheaper than prosecuting them. Miller's death didn't even make the front pages."

"Then why are you so upset about it?"

"I don't give two shakes about Miller, but if more Millers are marked for death, sooner or later an innocent bystander will get hurt."

"I didn't think of that," admitted Paul.

Barry pulled up in front of the church. "By the way, Mary Evans is a good looking woman. How long have you known her?" His voice strained to be casual.

"Jenny had mentioned her name to me but last night was the first time we met. She is attractive."

"Priests aren't supposed to notice things like that, Paul. You'll go straight to Hell."

Paul forced a smile as Barry drove off. He did find Mary physically attractive, but more so, he was drawn to her dedication toward her work and toward her friends—like Jenny. He pushed the confession out of his mind. Temporarily.

Father Rhoades, in the midst of a phone conversation, hung up immediately when Paul entered and informed him, "Your sister called about an hour ago. She wants you to meet her at the Institute for lunch tomorrow."

Paul acknowledged the message then remarked, "I had to go to the lumber store; the check I wrote them bounced. How come?"

"An oversight. It won't happen again."

"But you said there was enough money in the account."

"I said it was a mistake!" His voice was agitated; it annoyed him that anyone should question him. "Father D'Angelo, our cook, and our maintenance men habitually write out checks without informing me. They're trying to make me look bad, and I know why. Father D'Angelo's their friend and they can't stand to see him replaced. It's no secret. I know. But it won't work." He walked away still babbling.

He's crazy, Paul judged entering the study. Father D'Angelo was gazing at a framed photograph of himself, the Pope, and others. A small glss of cognac was nestled in his hands. Not wanting to disturb his reflections, Paul started to leave when the elder priest begged, "Don't go, Paul. I didn't realize I had aged so much over the last few years," comparing himself to the photograph. "Old age is ruthless, Paul. Before it kills you it makes you depressed and useless, so bad sometimes that death is a relief." Father D'Angelo sipped some of the cognac.

Paul saw through the elder priest's inner thoughts. "You're allowing Rhoades to get to you, Father. Don't.

He'll never be the person you are, no one will."

Father D'Angelo swung his chair around and faced Paul. "You're too young to understand my thoughts, Paul, although I appreciate your words."

"You heard Rhoades from in here, didn't you?"

"His voice carries like a death knell. His spirit is troubled."

"Nothing a good exorcism wouldn't cure," Paul jested in an effort to bring some life back into his friend's worn face. It was hard to imagine that two or three years ago Father D'Angelo was one one of the most influential priests in the United States. He wasn't powerful, though; that aspect had been relegated to the late Cardinal Beck, Father D'Angelo's best friend. Following the Cardinal's assassination the ensuing power struggle simply bypassed Father D'Angelo and he remained as he always was—a simple parish priest.

Paul examined the photograph on the wall and asked the good Father, "Did you ever dream about becoming Pope? Having all that power!"

"You mean responsibility. I never did, although many do." He sipped his cognac.

"Does Cardinal Alden?"

"He promotes himself very well and I've heard he is well liked."

"I never heard he was well liked, just quietly powerful. An American Pope . . . Think it will ever happen?"

"I would venture to say that it is doubtful."

Paul grinned. "You say no so nicely." As Paul spoke more on the subject he flipped through the file cabinet and pulled out the Church's checkbook. "We have only ninety-eight dollars in the account?" He checked the prior month. Over seven hundred dollars. He showed it to Father D'Angelo. "Is this correct?"

"Father Rhoades takes care of the books. He takes

care of everything. I take care of nothing."

Paul sorted through the cancelled checks. The telephone bill exceeded a hundred dollars. Another check made out to cash for four hundred dollars, with Rhoades' signature on it. Being so preoccupied, Paul did not hear the study door open.

Rhoades stared at Paul. "Have you uncovered the mystery?" came his challenging voice.

Paul held up the checks. "Three months of telephone bills exceeding three hundred and fifty dollars. And this check, signed and endorsed by you for cash, for four hundred dollars."

Paul and Father D'Angelo braced themselves for Rhoades' tirade, but instead he calmly sat down and explained "A church policy, which I oppose," looking askance at Father D'Angelo, "allows our parishioners to use the Church phones for their personal calls. And apparently they have relatives all over the country. It is a total and unnecessary waste of our money."

"That is not *our* money," Father D'Angelo bellowed. "Our parishioners donate that money even though some are so poor they cannot afford a telephone of their own. We are a church dedicated to this community, and our parishioners will continue to use our telephones as they wish."

Wanting to pursue the check matter further, Paul interrupted the oncoming argument with "And the four hundred dollar check made out to cash?"

"Mrs. Weaver," Rhoades answered. "She had no money for her heart medicine or her rent because her social security check was late. Another foolish policy of this church."

Father D'Angelo's jowls shook with anger; his face reddened. "This is God's house! Not a bank! It was built by the parishioners for the parishioners and they can use every facility we have here, regardless of cost. A priest should know that in his heart!"

"The heart doesn't make the church run—money does. A priest should be able to understand that!"

Father D'Angelo's aged hands encompassing the glass of cognac grew taut until there was a shatter. Glass and cognac spilled over the desk. Luckily there was no blood. Disregarding what he had done, Father D'Angelo silently left.

Rhoades commented, "He doesn't understand the priesthood any more. He should be forced to retire."

Paul, laying a paper towel over the top of the desk, responded, "I used to believe that priests with outdated convictions were a detriment to the Church, but your radical ideology is also contaminated. So are those who uphold it."

"And your beliefs are correct?"

"I used to think I was right. Now I think all three of us are wrong."

"I'm not. The Church has to change to the New Order or else it will fail . . . and the changes must occur at any price." As Rhoades spoke he rubbed his lower back. Pain was evident on his face. "The New Order is the Church's only salvation. And the Church must survive. It's that simple."

The New Order again. Paul was tired of hearing about this new plan which supposedly would bring Man and God closer together. It was even stranger that Rhoades declined to explain it fully. "This New Order you always speak of, how hallowed can it be if priests such as Father D'Angelo are excluded from it?"

"You speak of a mere individual while I speak of saving the world. You are young and foolish, Father Tobin. That is why you have not received the Word of the New Order."

"And who gives the Word, Father Rhoades? You?"

Rhoades laughed at Paul and his remark. "Your thoughts are as old and clouded as Father D'Angelo's and your fate is also the same."

"What do you mean by that!"

"God has created three types of people in this world: leaders, followers, and those who fall by the wayside. As a fellow brethren I must warn you not to get hurt as you fall. Good day, Paul." Adding a dramatic nod, he left.

Paul remained alone in the study. Rhoades is so damned defiant, he thought. So sure of himself. But Rhoades is wrong. His "new order" is wrong. Paul relaxed in Father D'Angelo's musty chair. Such defiance Paul had encountered only once before, but that person had been absolutely right. That man, almost two years ago in New Mexico, was Chief Robert Strongarm, leader of the Navajo reservation. Before Paul had set foot on the reservation, the Chief's name had become familiar to him. The townspeople who spoke of this arrogant Indian either admired him or hated him, and those who hated him were afraid of him because of his influence over his people. The Indian vote was negligible, but in a close election the politicians needed every vote, even if it was cast by someone they considered a second class citizen.

The first few weeks on the reservation were chaotic for Paul, and he almost forgot about Chief Strongarm. It was eleven o'clock at night, and Paul was rearranging the chairs in the leaky church, trying to find dry floor space following a rain storm, when the doors swung open. Against the backdrop of darkness, a man approached. He was of average appearance, but Paul couldn't guess his age; the Indian population tended to look older than they really were.

Paul recalled his first welcome to the stranger. "May I help you, my son?"

The stranger came face to face with Paul and in an acid voice retorted, "I know who my father is, and he is not you."

Even now Paul's skin prickled at remembering those words.

"The phrase 'my son' is only a figure of speech. I am Father Paul Tobin, the new parish priest."

The stranger's burnt orange face was motionless. "I am Chief Robert Strongarm," he proudly announced. "I have come to ask you to leave this reservation. You and your God have no place here. My people do not want you."

Paul summoned his courage and attacked. "You mean *you* don't want me here. But I have seen the faces of your people; they need the Church."

"It is not the Church they need, it is food."

"And we give them food."

"As a trapper gives to the prey."

Paul would never forget that sentence: As a trapper gives to the prey. That was what the Church had been doing to those people. Chief Strongarm's lack of education was no deterent to his intelligence. Paul remembered defending the Church, its right to be on the reservation, its enlightenment to the people, and its duty to spread the word of God.

Motionless, Chief Strongarm listened, and then asked, "Why must we believe in your God? Why is He better than our Gods? Our Gods belong to us; for an outsider to believe in them would be meaningless, yet this is what you ask of us. Leave us alone. Take your God to another place where there is no God. They will want Him. We do not!"

That was the first and only time Paul ever saw Chief

Robert Strongarm. But those few minutes were powerful enough to place a doubt in Paul's blind acceptance of Church policies. I've never been the same, Paul reflected. Now I challenge policies. But maybe I challenge them too much—almost to the point of hoping to find fault with them. Perhaps it's time to just accept everything, and regain my peace of mind.

3

Barry met Mary for their dinner date at a restaurant around the corner from her apartment. She thought it wise not to tell Jenny she had a date with Barry.

Mary looked marvelous in a soft yellow dress that outlined her figure yet did not put it on display. Barry wore his favorite dark brown sports jacket.

"I'm glad you were free tonight on such short notice," Barry said as he imagined her long slender legs wrapped around his body, her lips rhythmically in tune with his, her breasts pressed against his chest. "How was your day at work?"

"Frustrating. The Institute is attempting to push some legislation through that would require companies to install special equipment for the handicapped, but in this recession no politician wants to speak up. The other day one company reported that they could not afford to build a ramp leading into their building, that the staircase would have to do. It's disgraceful."

"The economy's taking its toll on everyone. Instead

of doing away with patronage jobs and paper pushers they cut back on police and firemen. I'm glad I carry a gun."

"Does the weapon make you feel more masculine?"

"No, safer. You're thinking of cowboys," he joked.

Mary did not laugh. She didn't even smile. Even if she did smile, it couldn't match Jenny's, he assured himself. "Are you always so serious?"

"My responsibilities make me serious. So should yours."

"Six years ago a fourteen-year-old mentally retarded boy was adopted by a group of neighbors where the boy had been living in an abandoned house. Nobody knew him, where he came from, or where his parents were. He still does odd jobs for the people, he's well fed, properly clothed, has a roof over his head, and he's got the greatest belly laugh you've ever heard. I choose to remember things like that."

"That's a typical avoidance syndrome or defense mechanism."

"It works."

"But is it truthful?"

"Who cares, as long as it works," he answered, finding it difficult to talk to her. He felt more like a patient than a date.

"May I ask you a personal question? Have you ever taken a human life? Why are you smiling?"

"It's a popular question to police officers. The answer is yes, prefaced by I learned the hard way. My fourth year on the force I was pursuing an armed robbery suspect on Twenty-third Street. He was in my sight, and I could have killed him on the spot. Instead I shot him in the leg and he fell. I waited. He didn't move, so I approached him. Before I could react, he rolled over and shot me. The back-up units nailed him, but I was in the hospital for three weeks and spent three more weeks at home recuperating. After that episode, I've never given anyone an opportunity to shoot back at me."

"You're proud of that." Her tone was frigid and condemning.

"I've heard lawyers, judges, politicians, and psychiatrists all spout that. But they all have one thing in common—they've never been shot. It's not like the movies where the guy falls dead or makes a long dying speech. Getting shot hurts like hell." He pointed to his stomach where he had been shot. "The bullet explodes into your skin like a burst baloon. Your heart races faster while the blood spurts out of the wound. You're coated in perspiration and you feel numb and cold, ice cold. Then heat consumes you and your muscles go haywire as if you're having an epileptic fit. Nausea chokes your throat. You can taste it. Finally your mind can't sort out all the pain and you just lie there as your body retches against itself. If you're lucky, you slip into unconsciousness." Barry paused and smiled. "It's not something I wish repeated."

Mary's appetite ended with the story, and so did her enthusiasm for the date. Barry realized he should never have answered the question. Conversation like that does not lead to the bedroom, and that was tonight's goal. It was time to switch subjects. "How are you and Jenny getting along as roommates?"

"No problems, but she's so vulnerable. She needs a friend as much as she needs a psychologist."

"And you're both to her. I told her she was in capable hands."

Finally Mary smiled. "Paul mentioned you two met a year ago at the racquetball club. A priest and a detective. An unusual friendship, isn't it?"

"Paul's an unusual priest and an easy guy to like."

"Yes he is. And he's handsome too."

"For a priest."

"No, for a man," Mary corrected him, not hiding her feelings.

One more try. "How about an after dinner nightcap at my place? It will only take us fifteen . . ."

Mary's eyes lit up, but her gaze was directed toward the front door of the restaurant. It was Paul.

Shit, Barry thought, what's he doing here?

Paul joined them at the table. "I went to your apartment, Mary, and Jenny said you were here." He looked apologetically at Barry, clarifying, "Jenny didn't mention you were here too."

"It's okay," Mary answered for Barry. "It's just a friendly dinner. Join us for dessert."

Barry's posed smile began to hurt. There goes the bedroom. "Is there anything wrong, Paul?"

"No, I just wanted to see Jenny and Mary. Are you sure I'm not intruding?"

"Not at all," Mary said. "Why don't we all go back to my place for dessert?"

Barry watched them nod to each other as though he, Barry, were invisible. He paid the check.

"Thank you, sir," the waiter said. "Enjoy the night."

"Not a chance," Barry mumbled, hurrying to catch up to Mary and Paul.

As the three strolled toward Mary's apartment, a tortured wailing scream from around the corner drew everyone like a magnet. A figure engulfed in flames scrambled down the street toward them, the high-pitched squeal still emanating from the figure.

Paul ran toward the human inferno, ripped a jacket from somebody's arm and tried to smother the fire. But it was too hot, too intense. The man fell to the ground, writhing. Barry yanked Paul away as the body became still. The odor of burning flesh filled the air as police sirens neared.

Paul and Barry stepped back as the police sprayed the body with a white fluffy foam. Paul was unable to move, his eyes transfixed on the foam-covered corpse. "I've never seen anyone die before," Paul stammered.

Mary noticed Paul's blistered hands and directed him to the arriving ambulance where a paramedic applied a white petroleum ointment over the sores.

Paul winced.

"The ointment will minimize the pain," the attendant assured him.

Mary held Paul's arm for moral support. She shied away as the police wrapped the charred remains in a black plastic bag and lifted it into the Coroner's car. Barry was conferring with other detectives.

Paul gasped for air. Mary squeezed his arm at each involuntary cringe. "Paul, you should go to the hospital."

"I'll be fine. The ointment's beginning to take effect."

Barry left the police huddle and rejoined his friends. "Somebody threw a Molotov cocktail at him. A young blond male was seen in the area heading toward the subway."

"Who was the victim?" Paul inquired.

"Arnold Frederickson, entrepreneur of prostitution and drugs for the syndicate. He also had a reputation of beating his girls. Three or four years ago one of the girls didn't survive."

"Why wasn't he in jail?" Mary snapped, visibly outraged that such an animal was free.

"The witness contracted amnesia. We see a lot of that disease. Sometimes I wonder how we ever make a conviction."

"The blond guy, didn't Father D'Angelo describe somebody like that at Miller's death?"

"Yeah. It's the Crossbearers again. Another death,

another letter and telephone call to look forward to and still no leads."

Paul's view drifted to the chalked outline on the street. Two detectives were laughing about something while another one was cleaning his nails. The crowd of spectators had increased, hypnotized by the primitive cave-like art outlining the form of a human being. Rotating colored lights from the patrolcars and ambulances cast an illusionary spell over the sordid reality. Distance and shadows obscured his view, but, craning forward, he distinguished a man peering out at the activity. The shadowy figure's movements seemed familiar to him. He had to find out why.

Mary caught hold of his arm. "Paul, where are you going?"

Paul continued forward. Barry and Mary followed. The figure disappeared before they reached the area. Paul searched the alleyway but found nothing.

"What are you looking for, Paul?" Barry asked.

"There was a man here—watching."

"Probably a bum," Barry guessed.

"No, there was something familiar about that man."

"Describe him."

"I couldn't see his face, just his shadow. Boy, that's familiar . . ."

"I think you're in shock, Paul. Let me take you to the hospital."

He shrugged off Mary's suggestion. "I'll go back to the church and rest. Barry will drive me."

Television news cameras surrounded the murder scene, recording every detail. Speaking into a microphone, the reporter indicated the chalked outline. The camera zoomed in for a close-up.

"Mary, make sure you tell Jenny I'm okay. I don't want to upset her."

"I'll do it. Get some rest and when you're feeling

better come to the Institute and I'll give you a personal tour."

Barry and Paul drove off. Barry noted the lack of invitation for him to visit the Institute.

"Sorry I ruined your date, Barry," said Paul, his eyes squinting with pain. "If I had known you were with Mary I would have stayed away. And now this . . ." holding up his hands.

"No harm done," Barry answered, thinking of another night in an empty bed. "You sure you won't go to a hospital—just for observation?"

"It's unnecessary. I'm just so tired. Whew, I've never seen anything like that. Wish I hadn't seen it. Burned . . . agh, what a way to die. And you're not even upset over his death, are you?"

"No."

"He was still a human being, Barry. That in itself calls for remorse."

"You're going religious on me, Paul."

"Can't help it. Burned like that. I can't get it out of my mind."

Barry pulled up in front of the church and accompanied Paul inside. Father D'Angelo, noticing Paul's blistered hands, gasped, "Oh, dear God. What happened?"

"It looks worse than it is, Father." Paul said. "I'm exhausted. Barry will explain everything. If you'll excuse me."

Barry and the elder priest adjourned to the study. Father D'Angelo listened intently, crossing himself at each ominous adjective Barry used in describing the night's event.

"Paul informed me of this group calling themselves the Crossbearers. Are they responsible for tonight's tragedy?"

"I'll know tomorrow. You look tired too, Father.

What's the matter?''

"Nothing, my son.''

"My son! Now I know something's wrong. Your voice has no life to it, you haven't smiled since I've been here and you haven't enjoyed your favorite drink.'' Barry resisted the word "old" but that was what he was thinking. "Is it Rhoades again? Paul keeps me abreast of what goes on between you two.''

"Tonight on television there was a special program on endangered species. The commentator used the expression 'extinction is worse than death.' Not so. Becoming obsolete is worse than both. In God's divine scheme of the universe, the one fact that does not fit is obsolescence. No Heaven, no Hell. When a person becomes obsolete, he lives only to die. In my sixty-eight years of life, that is the only mistake I have found God to have made.''

Barry hesitated before speaking. He wanted to say something intelligent, meaningful, and sympathetic. "In most cases, extinction is beyond the animals' control. Becoming obsolete may also be beyond human control, but a person can choose another path out of the predicament. God didn't make a mistake, Father, the person who forgets that he has an alternative—a choice—makes the mistake.''

"You speak wisely, Barry. You should have become a priest.''

"It never crossed my mind for a minute, Father.'' Barry stood. "I have to get going. I'll call Paul tomorrow to see how he is.''

As Barry drove off, in the rear-view mirror he noticed a car moving up on him. It was a blue Oldsmobile Cutlass Sedan with a missing front license plate. He turned the corner, and the other car did the same.

Are you following me, Mr. Sedan, Barry thought, or

are you simply going my way? I'll find out.

Barry drove onto Sixth Avenue and turned left on Fourteenth Street. The sedan shadowed him. Barry made a left-hand turn onto Seventh Avenue. The mystery car did the same. Street lights allowed Barry to discern two white males in the car. Nothing else. No blond man. Too bad.

I don't know who you are or why you're tailing me, but you're no expert, Barry deduced.

Staying in the right hand lane, Barry purposely slowed down, catching a red light near Christopher Street. His shadow was three cars behind him. Barry turned right on the red light, stepped on the accelerator, took two more right turns, and was now four cars behind the Oldsmobile sedan. Much better position, he observed, although in this traffic congestion if he couldn't catch the strangers within five blocks he could lose them. The traffic light blinked green. The sedan squealed forward, cutting off other cars. The strangers had figured out Barry's moves. Barry took to pursuit. In seconds the speedometer registered 65. The sedan braked, making a sharp right. Barry's car skidded past the street. By the time he backed up and followed, the sedan had disappeared.

A bedlam of near misses reverberated from behind Barry. The suspects had copied his trick. Barry shoved the car into reverse, slammed down the accelerator, and just as he emerged onto Seventh Avenue, collided with another car. The sedan roared down a side street out of sight. Wildly pounding his fists on the trunk of Barry's car was the irate citizen whose car he had smacked.

Barry leaned his aching head back, swearing like a banshee at himself. Damage of city equipment meant three days of writing down each detail of the accident, in triplicate. And on top of that, another flagellating lecture from Captain Adams. "Yeech!"

* * *

Paul propped himself up in bed as Father D'Angelo entered carrying a breakfast tray. With each breath the old man's fleshy turkey neck swung from side to side as if it were a pendulum regulating his heart beat. Paul smiled while Father D'Angelo carefully placed the tray on the bed. He recalled the day he first met the good priest. An uncompromising man swelling with tradition, faith, and an honesty Paul had seldom encountered before. And within the past six months a true friendship had developed. Paul considered Father D'Angelo one of the Church's most prized possessions.

Father D'Angelo rubbed his chin. "You're staring at me. Do I have jelly on my chin?"

Laughingly Paul said, "I was thinking of the first day we met."

"Ah, yes, the Second Coming. You entered my Church with hair over your ears, a sports shirt, jeans, and those horrible looking cowboy boots that smelled like a stable. I said to myself, 'There's a lost soul.' And then you introduced yourself as Father Paul Tobin."

"You checked my credentials four times."

". . . That you know of." His tone of voice dropped. "Lately the past has been consuming my present." Father D'Angelo shook the depressing thought out of his mind. "Jennifer and Barry telephoned this morning to see how you were. I told them you were resting comfortably, but I don't think your sister believed me. Another woman telephoned twice but didn't leave her name."

Mary, Paul hoped. "I can feed myself, Father," Paul said twiddling his fingers for proof. "I'd better visit Jenny today to prove that I'm okay. She always thinks we withhold bad news from her because she's blind."

Father D'Angelo crossed himself at the mere mention of Jennifer's disability. He shuddered. "I haven't seen Jennifer in a year. She had the prettiest long black hair I'd ever seen. An angel. I shall visit her now that I have so much free time. Father Rhoades does all my work." A hurt came through his voice. "Paul, I'm going to retire at the end of the year."

"You mean you're going to let Rhoades defeat you? You can't do that, Father, there are too many parishioners who need you. No one needs Rhoades."

"Paul, please don't speak about a fellow priest in that manner. After all, we are all servants of our Lord Jesus Christ."

"Not all servants are good, Father."

"That is blasphemy, Paul. Father Rhoades simply has his own way of doing things."

"Bullshit! He wants to be head of this parish and beyond."

Father D'Angelo showed no reaction to Paul's choice of words.

Paul wouldn't let up. "Rhoades is power crazy. Everybody's afraid of him, so he's getting away with it. He even has Cardinal Alden agreeing with his stupid ideas. It wouldn't surprise me if Rhoades had something to do with my having been permanently transferred back to New York. A novice priest who wouldn't get in his way."

"Only a Cardinal can determine transfers, Paul."

"With some prodding from others."

"Does being in New York truly make a difference in your life, Paul? You said you didn't care for New Mexico."

"It wasn't New Mexico, it was the way the Church operated out there. There was an Indian Chief I briefly met on the reservation. He was quite intimidating. I would like to see him again now that I understand him better. We'd make a unique team."

"I'm sure Jennifer's accident also influenced your

decision to remain here. If I recall correctly, you didn't protest the transfer that strongly.''

''There were other considerations.''

''So I have gathered. Don't look so surprised; experience and age allow me to notice more. From our conversation concerning the irreverent converting of Indians in New Mexico, I suspect that your faith was tampered with, maybe irrevocably. Then came Jennifer's accident and, well, your guilt is discernible, Paul.''

''That obvious, eh?'' Paul relaxed. ''Thank God she's improving mentally. And so am I.''

''But what of your faith, Paul? Was the damage great?''

''Unknown at this time. Failure isn't devastating if you have some success, but I haven't had any of the latter. One success, that's not much to wish for. And having to cope with a priest like Rhoades doesn't help either. It's too bad Cardinal Beck isn't alive; he'd put Rhoades in his proper place. Oh, I'm sorry, Father, I forgot. . . .''

''Cardinal Beck died a few days before you arrived at this parish. We were almost like brothers—we *were* brothers. At Divinity School our teachers thought we were . . . uhm, odd.''

''Gay?''

''That's the word they used, but it wasn't true. And yet I did love him. A day does not pass that I do not say a prayer for his soul.''

Paul tactfully moved to another subject. ''Father, if you want I'll speak to Cardinal Alden and see if I can't talk some sense into him about your retirement.''

''I have made my decision, Paul. It's best this way. I hope your hands will soon be better.'' He lifted the tray off the bed and left.

''Damn that Rhoades!''

Father D'Angelo backed into the room. ''I heard

that, Paul. And, God forgive me, I agree with you."

They parted laughing.

Paul dressed for his visit to the Institute for the Blind.

Barry re-examined the reports of the two murders. On both occasions the young blond man was seen in the vicinity, but no accurate description was obtained from witnesses. The method of the two killings differed, except that they both occurred at night. And not one clue had been uncovered, not even by Forensics. Killing people was becoming too common and too easy.

Barry's phone rang. The Crossbearers, he was sure of it. He looked around the squad room. Three detectives were on the phone. He knew they were not the ones spying on him, but still he had to be certain.

Dave gave Barry a querulous look. "Aren't you gonna answer it?"

"I know who it is. They'll call back." Barry sauntered over to the first detective on the phone and gesturing for a DD5 form, listened for the voice on the other end. He pulled the same stunt with the other two detectives. All three were cleared. Barry's phone stopped ringing only to ring again a few minutes later.

"Martin speaking."

"Badge 5746. You haven't picked up your mail yet."

"Was that you calling a minute ago?"

"Yup. You must have been late gettin' to work. That ain't good."

"I wasn't late, I was reading my mail," he lied. Silence. "Blond man, are you there?" The phone went dead. Barry scurried down to the mail room. His mail was lying on the counter neatly wrapped.

"Excuse me," Barry summoned the clerk. "Where's the phone down here?"

The clerk pointed to the wall behind Barry.

"No other phone in this room?"

"Only the one on the supervisor's desk, but that's for in-house calls only."

"Where's the supervisor's desk?"

The clerk pointed to a desk that was still in easy view of Barry's bundle of mail.

"Are all the mail clerks at work today?"

"Yes sir."

Barry returned upstairs and opened the letter printed in red ink:

> He that is not with me is against me.
> Frederickson was against me.
> The wages of sin is death.
> Frederickson has been paid in full.
>
> The Crossbearers

His phone rang. "You tried to trick me, Badge 5746. I don't like bein' tricked."

Good, he's pissed. Maybe I can push him. "I don't give a shit what you like. You're nothing but a punk hiding behind God's name." Faintly in the background Barry heard a female voice and took advantage of the situation. "Is that your Mother telling you it's nap time?"

The phone slammed down on the other end. Nothing works with this guy, Barry thought, and he doesn't stay on the phone long enough to have it traced. There's got to be a way to get him to say something revealing.

Five minutes later Barry's phone rang again. "Badge 5746. Getting me mad won't make me say something stupid. But I've decided that one day you and I are gonna meet, and I'm gonna blow your brains out!" Click.

"I sure scared him," Barry mumbled to himself.

"Martin!" Captain Adams commanded. "In my office."

Barry closed the door behind him. "Captain, I just received another—"

The Captain handed Barry a stack of papers: insurance forms for the accident and an estimated repair bill for over three-hundred dollars.

Barry explained, "The accident occurred while I was on duty, Captain. A blue Oldsmobile sedan had been tailing me . . ."

"Chasing him backwards? You were backing down a one-way street, Martin."

"I realize that, sir, but . . ."

"This isn't going to look good on your record, Martin."

He means *his* record, thought Barry.

"We expect accidents to occur, but not so blatantly. Reword your report. Call it a rear-end collision and we'll blame the other guy."

"I hit him!"

"Makes no difference. Since no-fault insurance nobody gives a crap who hit who. Besides, the insurance companies can afford it, they just up everybody's premiums. That's not a request, Martin."

"I'll rewrite the report."

"That's the spirit. Anything on the Frederickson murder?"

"Another note, another phone call."

"And the blond suspect?"

"Nothing."

A momentary pause preceded a flurry of chomps on the cigar. "I wrote a memo to the Chief telling him you were investigating some positive leads, that the case might be broken soon. He carboned the Commissioner. The Chief and I don't like being made to look like liars. Know what I mean, Martin?"

Grudgingly, Barry agreed. He had no choice. *Making promises that stick me in the middle. Adams shouldn't* be Captain of Detectives, he shouldn't even be in charge of a flock of sheep. Same goes for the Chief and the Commissioner. Goddamn politicians screw up everything.

Paul took a cab to the Institute of the Blind. The blue Oldsmobile sedan now trailed him.

Jenny was sitting at her desk in a room full of other occupied desks. Here nameplate was printed in Braille letters on her desk. Jenny tilted her head to the side. "Paul, is that you?"

"That's good. How'd you know?"

"Not too many of our visitors wear sneakers. On this floor they squeak." She stood up and felt his shirt. "As usual you're not wearing your collar." Paul moved his hands away from her touch.

"Are you in pain?" she asked.

"No, they're just sensitive. I'm fine, honest."

"Good. I was speaking to Father Crowley before you came in. Since I've moved in with Mary, we haven't seen each other. I miss his visits."

"One day Father Crowley and I will have to arrange our schedules so we can meet in person. 'Thank you' over the telephone always seems impersonal, and we owe him a great deal. His weekly visits after the accident helped Mom and Dad too."

Jenny interlocked her arm with Paul's and escorted him down the corridor using the metal guard rail along the wall as a guide. Mentally she counted off the steps to Mary's office. "We'll get Mary and give you a V.I.P. tour of the Institute."

Mary stood up to greet her guests. "Paul. I mean, Father—"

"Paul is fine."

"How are your hands?"

Paul held out his hands for inspection. "I can't do

any woodworking, but that's about it. I do thank you for calling to inquire about me."

Jenny tilted her head toward Mary, then toward Paul. "Mary called you, eh? That's nice."

"Jennifer, have you completed the memo on the new Braille signs?" Mary asked in an authoritative voice.

"This morning. I typed them myself." Then to Paul. "The typewriter keys are in Braille but not the letters. This way a blind person can type standard business letters. We'd use more of these typewriters but they're incredibly expensive."

"The money will be raised in time," Mary confirmed. "Shall we begin the tour?"

For the next hour Mary gave a guided tour of each section of the Institute, accompanied by a concise monologue on its function. Her words and tone were suffused with dedication, respect, and hope for everyone at the Institute. She was an extraordinary woman, Paul judged.

Mary ended the tour with "I hope it wasn't boring. Sometimes I get carried away."

"You did, but it worked," responded Paul. "I feel compelled to make a contribution. You're a good saleswoman."

"She raised the most money for the Institute last year," Jenny announced proudly.

"In time you'll be able to do it," Mary said. "Just don't give up; we all make mistakes."

Jenny explained Mary's last statement to Paul. Last week Jenny had given a practice tour for Mary and inadvertently explained the audio/visual room while they were standing in the training room. "I was so embarrassed. What if it had been a real tour?"

"Nobody would have said a thing," Mary assured her. "But we still prefer describing the room we're in," she said with a laugh.

Jenny touched her Braille watch. "12:10. Time for lunch. Paul, you'll join us."

Before Paul could answer, Jenny wrapped her arm around his and led him to the cafeteria. Her perceptive mind noted the apparent attraction between Paul and Mary. They had to be alone. Once there, Jenny snapped her fingers stating, "I forgot to type the letters to the Library of Congress. You two start without me. I shouldn't be long."

Paul had an inkling as to what his sister was up to and secretly approved. Mary busily read the menu as if she had discovered a plot to it. Her gaze shifted from the menu to the people in the cafeteria, back to the menu. The only person she did not make eye contact with was Paul.

"You feel awkward being seen in public with me, don't you, Mary?"

"No," she said, but not convincingly.

"Then it must be my appearance. Why else would you look at everything and everybody but me? I didn't mean to embarrass you, but I'm used to it. It's like meeting one's mistress at a social gathering with your wife and friends; suddenly you're at a loss for words."

"I didn't realize it was that obvious. I apologize."

"As I said, I'm used to it. That's the main reason I so rarely wear my clerical collar. It immediately inhibits people from being themselves and I never get to know the real person."

"You sound bitter."

"Disappointed is a more accurate description. The Church is so different from what I imagined it to be. I fight to change it but nothing happens."

"I used to be fairly religious." Mary's voice turned skeptical. "During college a sorority sister of mine became pregnant and wanted an abortion. Unfortunately as on most campuses news traveled fast. One of the local priests paid her a visit and lectured her on the evils of abortion. He also told her parents on her. A week later she tried a self-abortion. What should have been a simple operation left this nineteen year old girl with permanent damage, including no chance of ever conceiving again. If I have a daughter she *will* have more options available to her than my sorority sister did."

Mary relaxed for a moment. "I didn't mean to sound so harsh toward you."

"I've heard worse. But at least we're both fighting for the same changes; I'm simply doing it from the inside."

"That's not the most objective position to fight from."

"Are you suggesting that my efforts are useless? There are other priests who agree and protest against such things."

"But there aren't enough of you. Besides, you're still a priest which means that the Church still owns you, and you can rebel only so far."

Her words resurrected Chief Strongarm's image into Paul's mind. Little by little his belief was being chipped away by such uncomprising logic. Paul refused to think about it for the moment. He was more interested in Mary. "About last night. I'm sorry I intruded on your date with Barry. He's a great guy."

"It was only a friendly dinner. As a matter of fact we spoke about you and your nonprofessional appearance. I mean a priest should quote the Bible, wear a clerical collar, and be old with a big belly and a cigar sticking out of his mouth. That's what Jenny's priest Crowley looks like, according to her description."

"I've never met him but I've met many priests who do fit that description. Give me a few more years and I'll probably look like that too."

"I'm sure you won't." Her voice trailed off.

"Thank you," Paul said embarrassed. "I'm not used

to compliments like that."

Mary nervously pushed her coffee away and stood. "I just remembered there's a meeting I must attend. Thank you for lunch."

Paul sat there a minute mulling over her abrupt departure. Was it something I said or did she really have a meeting? I must have offended her in some way. Why is this upsetting me? Help me, dear Lord.

The same Oldsmobile sedan followed Paul's taxi back to the Church. Another cab drove off with Father Rhoades inside. He's never around anymore. It's probably Mrs. Weaver again, Paul figured.

Inside the Church, Father D'Angelo was sitting in the last pew, his head bowed, his lips moving in silent prayer as some of the parishioners were doing.

"Are you okay, Father?" Paul asked in a hushed voice.

Father D'Angelo's head remained stationary as he answered. "I spoke to Cardinal Alden and mentioned my intention of retiring soon. He accepted my resignation. He didn't even attempt to talk me out of it. Instead he said: 'It's a wise decision.' Forty-three years in the priesthood ending in a one minute telephone conversation."

"He can't do this to you. I won't let him. Father, you can't retire. We'll talk to Cardinal Alden together. Let me help you, Father."

Father D'Angelo glanced about the church. "This has been my home for many years, Paul. I remember when we received the statues of the Saints; the community turned the day into a festival. We had so many parishioners then. Sometimes people had to stand to hear my sermons. No more. Nothing is the way it used to be." He faced Paul. Tears flooded his eyes. Chokingly he said, "In my heart I wanted you to take over this parish, to continue making it feel like a haven for those

72

who needed it. My church is no longer mine and the haven has become a business." His eyes closed and his head lowered. "I'm very tired, Paul." He crossed himself, struggled to his feet, and walked out of the church.

Paul kicked the wooden pew muttering "Damn them!" Some of the parishioners looked up in amazement.

That night at precisely ten o'clock, at the corner of Sixth Avenue and West Tenth Street, Joe Ricart, minus his blond wig, picked up the public telephone on the first ring. "Are you a believer?" asked the disembodied voice.

Joe gave his usual response. "Yes sir, I am, and I'm ready to do your bidding."

"Have you gathered the Crossbearers together so they can observe you?"

"Yeah. I mean yes sir," Joe replied, watching the waiting three men and one woman across the street. "Each has studied the folder you sent. We're ready to go."

"Then it's time. The sacrifice should be carried out by the end of the week."

"I can do it tonight, sir. I studied the folder and we've been watching him for the last two days. We're rarin' to go."

"As you wish, Joseph. You will not be carrying any wallet or identification on you."

"I don't have to be reminded every time, sir."

"Of course you don't, Joseph; you're an intelligent man. Were the others pleased about the extra thousand dollars I sent you?"

"Yeah, that was really great. Thanks." His voice lowered to a half whisper. "You send me the folders through the mail and then we talk on the phone. When am I gonna meet you? I have a lot of good ideas."

"I'm sure you do, Joseph. We shall meet soon." The line cut off.

Excited over the prospect of meeting the leader of the Crossbearers, Joe approached his group, all of whom wore white enamel crosses. Roger and Doug Mollahan were engaged in their favorite pastime, reading comic books. They always carried at least two on them although it took them weeks to finish just one. Simply by looking at them, one would guess they were brothers. Both wore baggy pants, had long dirty hair and very few teeth. Doug's only true friend besides Roger was his switchblade, which he constantly fondled. Their other joy in life was watching each other masturbate, with Carol Lynch as the imaginary recipient of their lust.

Carol, however, had no desire for such inadequate men. She detested them. At the moment, her preference was Joe unless she could get her hands on another woman, as she was constantly trying to do. Her other enjoyment was teasing Joe as she teased everyone. Usually dressed in a tight tee-shirt with jeans or shorts, she would make Joe jealous by sleeping with Hank Wynn, another member of this sect of religious mercenaries. And Hank received no greater pleasure than to rub their lovemaking into Joe's face. Hank was good-looking, dressed well, and was the only member of the group without a weapon. Money was never a problem for him, although nobody knew where he came by it. And he put his money to good use, buying friends, buying Carol, and if Carol was not available, young prostitutes, the younger the better. But at present his primary goal was to eliminate Joe and take over the group. And Joe knew it.

"The Crossbearer gave us until the end of the week to carry out the sacrifice," Joe informed the others. "I'll do it tonight. Right now."

"It's too soon," Hank argued for the hell of it. "We only received the folder two days ago. I say we observe the target a few more days. Even the Crossbearer said so."

"I don't need more time, and what I say goes. You wanna fight over it?" Joe's hand moved to the knife in his pocket. "C'mon!"

Doug and Roger raised their eyes from their comic books. Carol moved closer to Joe, a gleam of excitement covering her face at the thought of a fight. Goading both of them on, Carol belligerently charged, "Let's find out who the real man is. Take your knife out, Joe. Cut 'im. The winner gets me all to himself. Anything he wants."

Doug and Roger swung their gaze to her out-thrust breasts, her nipples tantalizingly outlined under her flimsy tee-shirt. The same lecherous desire infested both their minds: One day they'd get her. Get her good.

Joe, his hand still toying with the knife in his pocket, spread his feet to a fighting stance.

Past experience taught Hank that Joe would like nothing better than to slice his body apart. And even if Hank had a knife, Joe's skill would overwhelm him. Hank begged off. "No sense in us fighting, Joe; we're not the enemy. Tell yah what, after tonight's sacrifice I'll buy drinks for everyone. Whaddya say, Joe?"

Joe's tense body eased. He had won again. "You're on."

"Can we have ice-cream instead?" nagged Doug while Roger clapped his hands like a child. "Can we? Please!"

"Sure," Hank indulged them as his mind sorted through ways of killing Joe, by surprise of course. Maybe even get Doug or Roger to do it. Carol too, if he gave her enough money. Hank would find a way.

Joe, ordering his group to follow in his car, walked to

the corner of West Eleventh Street and Sixth Avenue. Eleven o'clock. Right on schedule. The street lights glazed the expensive townhouses with an orange hue. Mixed with the dog walkers were tourists admiring the century-old townhouse. 11:06. Any time now. Joe slipped the blond wig out of a bag and put it on.

A prosperous looking man walked out of one of the houses. He was being hauled by a full-grown St. Bernard, who immediately wetted down a car tire. Joe took from his pocket a small object in the shape of a stop watch. The rest of the group observed him from the car as he approached the victim.

"That's a magnificent looking St. Bernard. Does he bite?"

"No, he's real friendly."

"Can I pet him?"

"Sure."

Joe knelt to pat the dog, clipped the object to the dog's collar, and depressed the button starting the device. "They're beautiful dogs but they don't belong in the city." He patted the dog on the head. "Have a nice night." Walking at a fast pace, he counted off the seconds. Twenty-eight, twenty-seven, twenty-six . . . He removed his wig and stuffed it under his shirt.

A thunderous explosion jolted the nearby houses. Dogs barked. Lights flicked on. Front doors opened. Police sirens whirled. Joe hopped into the car and the group took off.

"I wouldn't do that if I were you," Doc warned Barry, his hand grasping a corner of the sheet covering the body. "There's not much left of him."

Barry backed away. "Who is it?"

A uniformed policeman handed Barry the deceased's wallet, then returned to his other duties. Barry stepped under a street light and read the driver's license. "Ralph Tora." Barry, pointing to the corpse, asked Dock for confirmation. "Are you positive it's Tora?"

"The keys we found in the deceased's pocket were Tora's, his wife identified patches of his suit, and his wallet was found near the body. It's Tora. He was walking his St. Bernard. The explosive device must have been attached to the dog; there wasn't enough left for stew meat. This is a major hit, Barry."

"Tell me something I don't know. The syndicate's top attorney. Three syndicate hits in a row. There are a lot of nervous *families* tonight. What type of explosive device was used?"

Doc handed Barry a few small fragments of metal. "Plastic explosive with a simple timing device. Home-made. Probably nothing's traceable." He paused to jot down more notes, then continued. "I overheard some of the neighbors' statements. Your blond man again. The Captain should assign more detectives to the case."

Barry waved that off. "I want your Forensic team to comb every inch of this area. Give me one piece of evidence to prove this murder is linked to Frederickson's and Miller's. One piece."

"We'll try, but whoever's committing these murders knows what he's doing. He's a professional."

"You mean he's an amateur who's as good as a professional. No pro would hit the syndicate like this." Three murders and no leads. They were making him feel stupid. God, he hated amateurs. "Doc, scrounge up a clue for me, will you? Anything."

"I'll try, but don't hold your breath; we're still scraping up parts of Tora and his dog."

What a nauseating thought. Barry felt a tap on his shoulder and hoped it wasn't Captain Adams. "Father Rhoades," Barry exclaimed, relieved. "What are you doing here?"

"I was on my way back to the Church when I heard the commotion. Anyone I know?"

"Ralph Tora, but I'm afraid you're too late for the Last Rites."

"We're not allowed to administer the Last Rites to criminals anymore by order of Cardinal Alden."

"Who said Tora was a criminal?"

"I'm not Father D'Angelo," Rhoades answered with a smug grin. "I am well aware of what my parishioners really do for a living." Rhoades pointed to the victim. "He is, was, a syndicate attorney who kept a number of criminals out of jail by tricks of the trade. He made the newspapers quite often. Well, it's late. I wish you luck with the investigation, Barry."

"Excuse me, Detective Martin," interrupted the reporter. "I'm from the Action News Team. Would you care to issue a statement?"

"Do you know who was killed here tonight?" Barry asked the reporter.

"Why, yes. Ralph Tora, but—"

"Do you know what kind of business he was in?"

The reporter nodded while trying to figure out how he got to be the interviewee. "We did a special report on professionals and organized crime a few months ago. Tora's name came up a number of times. Now about your statement . . ."

Lost in thought, Barry strolled away, not even hearing the reporter's plea for a story. A patrolman relayed a message to Barry that the Captain wanted him back at the precinct immediately. It was after midnight. Maybe the blond man had called.

Barry closed the office door behind him as the Captain replied into the phone, "Yes Sir, I'll take care of it," and hung up.

He must have been talking to the Chief, it's the only one Adams calls Sir, Barry deduced.

Captain Adams took the cigar out of his mouth, and spat into the wastebasket.

"I heard about Tora's murder. These religious fanatics are killing 'em like flies." He held up DD5 forms, Barry's follow-ups on each murder. "I've read your reports. Any leads on this blond male wearing a white enamel cross?"

Barry shook his head. "I've run through a long list of religious groups, but none go by the name of Crossbearers and none wear a white enamel cross. If the computer couldn't find it, that means it's a new group. It's down to leg work."

The Captain switched his cigar to the other side of his mouth. "The syndicate, you think they know who he is?"

"They're not looking for him; at least that's what my informants say."

"They're crazy. Why wouldn't the syndicate want these murderers?"

"It's bad for business when word leaks out that you can't protect your own people."

"Good thought, Martin. It should be in your report. Well, you seem to be up on everything. But what you need is an assistant. The Chief and I have discussed this manpower shortage. We can't transfer detectives off of cases that involves innocent victims, it wouldn't be fair to our citizens, now would it Martin?"

Before Barry could answer, the Captain continued. "The Chief and I have decided that an unusual case such as this requires unusual treatment. You're one of the best detectives we have in the field, Martin, and maybe if we eliminate some of the paper work you could devote your full energy to the investigation."

Barry squinted at the absurd proposal. "Captain, the field is precisely where I need the extra—"

"The Chief and I know what we're doing, Martin.

You're going to have a new partner, a silent partner, so to speak. Me. You'll handle the field work, I'll handle everything else, including statements to the press. From now on this case is confidential. Just you and me."

Barry sat there with a blank expression while his mind was lighting up like a pinball machine. A Captain who wants to become Chief of Police and the Chief of Police who wants to become Commissioner. And what better ammunition for their personal quests than a media type case involving religious fanatics and mob killings? Far better than Dave's case. A nice game plan, only he, Barry, was stuck in the middle again.

"One more thing, Martin. Your habit of selectively suspending the civil rights of some criminals in order to gather more information—don't do it! I don't want any trouble from some drippy-nose public defender accusing us of violating his client's rights. Do you understand me, Martin?"

A long pause passed before Barry regained control of himself. "Captain, so far only syndicate men have been hit. What happens when a bystander gets hurt?"

"You just continue investigating and let me worry about that."

"Captain, I'd like to go on record as being fervently opposed to this arrangement. You're jeopardizing—"

Wham! Captain Adams's fist struck the desk top. "The matter is closed, so's the discussion. You're dismissed." His gaze lowered to his paperwork.

Barry plopped into his chair, furious at himself for giving in so easily, of allowing himself to be used again. I'm no different from all the other lowly detectives; brave enough to walk the streets yet scared enough of what Adams might write in our personnel reports that we kowtow to his insane orders. Pride exchanged for job security. Shit! He felt like talking to somebody, or rather yelling at somebody. But there was nobody waiting for him at home. There never was. He didn't want to talk to Paul. And as for Jenny, it was too late. Dave. God knows he'd understand.

Minutes after Barry left, his phone at the precinct rang six times, then stopped. Joe retrieved his coin from the pay phone and told the others, "Seems like our Badge 5746 didn't go back to the office either."

"I told you it was too late," Hank said.

"Call him at home, Joe," Roger panted. "He's waitin' to hear from us, he expects us to call. Call 'im, Joe. He's waitin'."

"Sssh," Joe ordered. Other night people in Washington Square Park were milling about. "I don't think we should call him at home."

"Can't you decide for yourself?" Hank needled Joe. "Why don't you call up your boss and ask him what to do? He might even let you see his face some day." Hank laughed and rubbed his hand over Carol's back.

"I've seen the Crossbearer," Joe lied, "and I'm the only one who can see the Leader because I'm the only one he trusts."

"You can trust me, Joe," Doug said flipping his knife from one hand to the other. "You can always trust me, Joe."

"Me too, me too," added Roger.

"Nobody trusts a person with an I.Q. of three," Hank retorted.

"You can't tal to me like that. Can he, Joe?" Doug flicked his knife open. "Now you take that back, Hank. Tell him to take that back, Joe."

"I'm sure your knife can persuade him better than I can." Joe grinned.

Carol massaged her hand over Doug's chest. "Put the knife away, Doug, you don't want to hurt anybody."

Doug looked at her but the knife stayed in place.

Carol spoke to Joe. "Tell him to put the knife away.

81

We don't want any cops over here."

"He's his own boss, just as I'm my own boss. You'd better apologize, Hank."

"Okay, okay, I apologize. You're so fuckin' temperamental, all of you." He handed Doug a twenty dollar bill. "Go eat yourself sick on ice cream. Looks like tonight's meeting is over anyway."

"Is it, Joe?" asked Roger, hoping to be treated to some free ice cream by his brother.

"It's over."

Doug and Roger left immediately. Joe seized Carol's arm, forcing her closer to him than to Hank. "We're going back to my room," he informed Carol.

Hank unraveled a thick wad of bills and temptingly counted off a hundred dollars. "Carol, this is for rescuing me from Doug. If it's not enough I have more at my apartment."

Carol caressed the money with more passion than she ever did with a man, and without looking back, walked away from Joe's car in the direction of Hank's apartment.

Hank, displaying a thoroughly enjoyable shit-eating grin, jabbed at Joe, "She loves my cock up her ass." He ran after Carol, put his hand on her shorts and traced a finger along the inside seam.

Joe's mind seethed with blinding anger. Another betrayal of love in his life by a woman. First it had been his mother. Joe had loved her so much and she him. He remembered lying beside his mother asking her never to leave him and she promising never to do so. A year later she was dead, abandoning the young boy to a sadistic drunken father. Now it was Carol deserting him. God how he hated her, yet cursed because he loved her. His body shook, his teeth ground against each other. Pacing and stomping around the park, he stopped and furiously battered his bare fists against a tree, his skin ripping like tissue paper. He was oblivious to the pain. Blood stained the tree. It wasn't enough. His mind wanted more, it compelled him to do more. Too many cops here. He had to do something and fast.

Dave's house in Queens was a small, modest, row house that in the 1980's inflated market would be unaffordable for most policemen, even detectives. The exterior was pleasant, as was the inside, Jane, Dave's wife, being an obsessive cleaner.

12:30. Maybe it's too late to go in, Barry pondered. Ah, what the hell, I'm here. Besides, Dave disturbed me plenty of times. He whimsically recalled the four o'clock intrusion three years ago. A reputable pharmaceutical company was caught selling prescription drugs to the local street peddlers, and at a very handsome profit. Dave cracked the case after three months of intense investigation. Then, that night, one of the company executives offered Dave a bribe—thirty thousand dollars. Throughout the night that's all Dave could say, "Thirty thousand dollars!" But he didn't accept it. The next day both of them went out and got roaring drunk, and still he repeated the figure.

Smiling over the memory, Barry rang the doorbell. Jane opened the door and flung her arms around him. As usual, she was wearing an apron.

"I'm so glad you came, Barry. I've never seen Dave this upset."

"What are you talking about? What's the matter with Dave?"

"You didn't hear?" She stepped back, her eyes red and swollen. "He's in the back yard. Please talk to him. He'll tell you."

Barry marched through the house and stepped out into the small, well lighted, fenced-in yard. Dave was sprawled in a chaise lounge, a cigarette dangling from his fingers. On the ground was a pile of half-smoked cigarettes, a large glass of scotch, and a bottle for refills.

Barry pulled up a chair and faced his colleague. More red swollen eyes. He didn't appear drunk but in a daze. "What happened tonight, Dave? Dave, can you hear me?" Barry jostled him. "Dave, it's Barry. Tell me what happened."

In a voice of anguish tinged with hysterical laughter, Dave blurted out, "You mean I didn't make the headlines or the TV news? It must be too early or too late. I can never tell the difference."

Barry knocked the glass of refilled liquor out of Dave's hand before it reached his mouth. "Goddammit, Dave. What happened?"

"I shot. . . ." He bit his lower lip. "I killed a twelve year old kid tonight. I'm such a good fuckin' shot. I blew his heart out. Can you imagine that . . . a twelve year old kid with no heart?" He shielded his face and wiped the tears away.

Barry's personal problems flew out of his mind as he tried to help his one-time partner. "Did the kid have a gun?" praying the answer was yes.

"A snub nose thirty-eight revolver that fires caps. A toy! Oh, it looks like the real thing all right. Give the kids what they want. Realism. So the toy manufacturers give it to 'em. And you wanna know something? My son had one just like it. His grandfather gave it to him for his birthday. Thought it would be cute."

From the corner of his eye, Barry spotted Jane listening at the glass door, crying her heart out for the ordeal her husband was going through and the hopelessness of it all.

Barry patted Dave's shoulder as a gesture of reassurance before inquiring how it happened.

"I got a lead on a delivery boy who could have witnessed the murder of the banker's son. The boy works at a pizza place on Fifth. I walked in, nobody was waiting on the customers. I went into the kitchen, saw the back door swing shut; the owner started screaming he'd just been robbed so I pursued the suspect on foot a black male. I identified myself and fired a warning shot. He spun around, with the gun in his hand. I crouched and fired. I only needed one shot. Ha, Internal Affairs told me not to worry, that I'd be exonerated.'' Dave clasped his hands and covered his crying face. ''It happened during the commission of a crime, they said. No jury would ever find me guilty. Shit! I feel like I've killed my own son! And they're telling me not to worry. Jesus Christ, how can I live with this? How!''

Barry sat motionless, refusing to let his emotions react to the situation. He had to remain strong and rational, even detached, if he was to help Dave. Fighting not to cradle and comfort his friend in his arms, Barry asked Jane to make some coffee and then, in a harsh voice, ordered Dave to calm down. Before the night's end he wanted to get Dave to admit that the shooting wasn't his fault; that it was done in the line of duty. They sounded like empty words, but Barry had witnessed too many careers and lives destroyed because of an incident like this. He wouldn't allow it to happen to Dave. Barry was ready for a long hard night.

Joe ran to the subway and boarded the first downtown train that came along. The train was empty. His fingers rapidly contracted and expanded as blood from his hands dripped on the seat. His eyes burned, his mind uncontrollably rambled to thoughts of his father and the leather belt striking his naked back. The pain was intense. Joe's body spasmodically moved about. More pain. His fists beat against the plastic seat. Faster. Harder. He remembered the last time his father tried to beat him. Joe had grabbed the belt away and struck out at his father. Revenge. He couldn't stop. His father's pleas made it all the more pleasurable.

"Hold it!" came a yell. A man ran to the train just as the doors closed on his arm. The man struggled to get free, but just as his arm began to slip out from between the doors, Joe grabbed hold. "Let go!" The man screamed. The train began to move. Through the door window Joe mocked the stranger's panic-stricken gaze as he screamed "Stop the train! Please! Let go! Please!" His body bounced up and down as he struggled to keep up with the moving train. His fingernails dug and clawed at Joe's grip, his eyes overflowing with tears, his face contorted in sheer terror. The train neared the tunnel. The stranger's cries of mercy echoed in the empty station. With both hands, Joe yanked the stranger's arm through the slit of the double doors, almost lifting him off the platform, his feet dragging, desperately curling his shoe tips into the concrete in a futile attempt to brake his movement. The car was approaching the tunnel. Joe released the stranger's arm and, with delight, watched his body smash into the platform wall. The train roared into the tunnel.

Cooling perspiration glistened on Joe's face. His breathing was ruthlessly fast, but he felt good. Real good. The crotch of his pants was stained with semen. He was exhausted, but his mind was eased. Now he could get a restful night's sleep.

Barry arrived at work more than two hours late. He'd been up all night consoling Dave and rehashing the unfortunate incident, but nothing was resolved. He was too overloaded with guilt to view anything objectively. And the obligatory phone calls from the Captain and the Chief were useless: "Don't worry, it wasn't your fault," or "Forget about it." Dumb statements from dumb men. And now this; protest marchers circling the front of the precinct with placards aimed at Dave and the rest of the police force. The majority of inscriptions and chants were racial in nature; others were downright vulgar. Thank God Dave was off for a few days.

Inside, detectives and office personnel inquired about Dave as they went about their normal routines. Nothing stops the normal routine. For the first time in his working life, Barry did not want to be at his job. Last night, while sharing Dave's anguish, he even entertained the thought of quitting, but he had no other skills. A transfer to another division wouldn't remedy the situation; the same problems existed everywhere. Why all of a sudden did he feel stymied by it? Age? Perhaps. Or maybe he was at the stage in his career where he couldn't escape the violence and where he had to play the political game. That was it, he decided. No longer was there a choice. It was a matter of survival.

The top brass understood the system, how it worked, how to beat it. Adams and the Chief were using the Crossbearer case, as they were using Dave's case, for their personal advantage. Maybe I should do it too, Barry pondered. A promotion would mean more money, and who can't use more money? Sure, why not? His phone rang.

"Good morning, Badge 5746. I tried calling you last night but you weren't at the office. Tora's murder must have tuckered you out."

"All of your murders have," Barry replied, in an attempt to coax this joker into revealing something. "You're very good at what you do, especially the plastic explosive around the dog's collar. Did you learn that in Viet Nam?" As he spoke, he tried again to distinguish some background noises. There was nothing specific.

"I didn't serve in Viet Nam. Too bad . . . they could have used me over there. Hey, how come you haven't asked me about my poetry concerning Tora?"

Barry sifted through his mail until he found the letter with the red ink. Everything read the same except for the Victim's name. "How'd you get this letter to me so fast? You must have mailed it before you killed Tora."

"Very smart, Badge 5746. But I gotta go now. Be talking to you."

Barry grumbled to himself as he leaned back in the chair glancing at the Captain's empty office. A religious fanatic who gets thrills from bragging about his kills, a political fanatic like my silent partner, Forensic can't turn up any evidence, and poor Dave . . . no wonder I'm in a foul mood.

His gaze fell on the framed photograph of his parents. Mary's comment on how much Jenny cared for him came to mind. No, they were like sister and brother. She was a great-looking woman, though. Nice sense of humor, down to earth person, no heavy artificial make-up, he liked everything about her. Even her being blind didn't matter . . . He stood up. Enough daydreaming, time to go knocking on doors and discover what new religious cults were cropping up. Before leaving, he did a quick check of his calendar. Racquetball tonight with Paul. Good, he could use the diversion.

Side by side, Carol and Hank strolled through the park, but their thoughts were far from the same. Carol fingered the two hundred dollars Hank had given her for last night's activities. She didn't mind going to bed with him, as a matter of fact, it was almost pleasant, but the money was more pleasurable. New clothes, some good meals at decent restaurants, and a present for Linda, the girl she was hustling. It had to be something sexual and intimate, a negligee . . . maybe she'd try it on for her. Sooner or later the young girl would yield to Carol's advances. The thought alone excited her.

Hank watched Carol fondle the money. Now was as

good a time as any to approach the delicate subject. He steered her to a vacant bench and began his pitch. "I've never known anyone who liked money as much as you. Some people will do anything for money. A prostitute I know makes two hundred dollars a night, and she's cheap."

"I used to charge that an hour . . . when I was younger. You didn't know I was in that profession. Almost two years. Then I discovered that some men would pay that much to have me all to themselves."

"What did you have to do for them?"

"Uhm, wouldn't you like to know?"

Hank wasn't after a description of her antics; he wanted to penetrate her potential for violence. He continued to probe and Carol continued avoiding the issue. His questions became more direct. "Some hookers enjoy beating up their Johns and stealing their money." A callous grin on Carol's face unwittingly disclosed her answer. "Some Johns have died from the beatings. If there was enough money in it for you, would you kill somebody?"

Carol's left eyebrow arched but it was far from an offensive reaction. "How much money are we talking about?"

"A few thousand."

"Precisely how much?"

"Three thousand. Aren't you gonna ask who I want killed?" Hank blurted out.

"I know who, but I'm more interested in the money. Joe's worth at least five . . . if I do it. On the other hand, if I tell Joe about this he might pay me more to kill you."

Hank grabbed her by the hair, yanking her head back and banging it against the back of the bench. "If I even suspect you told Joe I'll kill you. Do you understand?"

"I was just kidding." Her voice showed signs of

panic.

Hank released her, although his hand hovered about her face in a striking position. "I gave you a choice, now you don't have one. Either you kill Joe or I'll kill you. And don't think I wouldn't." He pressed his index finger into her cheek and ran it across her face in warning. "I want it done within the week." Hank's hand moved to her thigh. "Let's go back to my apartment." It was not a request.

She'd been with too many violent Johns to know when or when not to resist. Carol obliged.

Near the corner of the park, hidden by the bushes, Joe watched them. The yank of Carol's hair told him Hank wanted her to do something against her will. He had a hunch what it was. Hank was running out of time.

On the racquetball court Paul followed the bouncing ball off the wall, then smashed it back. Barry lunged to his right and half hit the ball. He was exhausted from the day's legwork and disappointed at finding nothing. The crack of Paul's racquet striking the ball reverberated in the court. Barry hustled forward, tapping the ball so it would just graze the front wall. Paul positioned himself and swung his entire might into the shot. Barry watched the ball sail out of reach.

A bell rang, signalling their time. Barry flopped down on the bench, tossing his racquet into the locker. Both men were worn out. They showered, dressed, and then went across the street to their usual restaurant.

"You mad at me, Paul?" Barry asked, still trying to catch his breath.

"No, why do you ask?" His hands ached. He shouldn't have played racquetball so soon after the fire.

"The way you tried to smack the ball through the wall tonight. You're mad at somebody. I know priests receive confessions, they don't give them, but as a friend I would like to help if I can." A woman dressed in shorts and a tee-shirt snared Barry's attention. His eyes followed her out the door, yet curiously, Jenny came to mind.

"I'll never get used to the way you stare at women. Don't they mind?"

"Nah, they enjoy being admired and I enjoy admiring. Besides, there's no harm done."

"The woman who marries you will have to paste blinders on your eyes."

"Me get married? Paul, I thought you knew better than that. Marriage and police work don't mix." He ran his hand through his still damp hair. "I couldn't subject my family to the strain of my job. Hell, I barely survive it myself." Dave and his family entered his thoughts. Barry hadn't heard from him since that night. Not a good sign.

"You need the *right* woman, that's all, Barry. God intended people to be fruitful and multiply. Marriage, love, trust, children . . . it's God's will."

"Then how come priests can't marry?"

"Why do you ask such questions?"

"Why do you pray so much?"

"To give me the strength to answer your questions."

Their grins turned to laughter.

"Well, maybe the Pope will issue an edict and let you off the hook. I mean devotion, poverty, prayers—I could live with that, but celibacy, in New York City. . . ." Barry ended his sentence with a cringe. "You know sex invigorates the soul, and makes it happier. Look at Abraham: everyone in the world's related to him."

"Could we talk about another subject?"

"Sure. Life without sex is like eating lobster without melted butter, it's enjoyable but it could be fantastic. Take Mary for instance; charming, bright, generous, self-assured, and a great figure."

"You're interested in her?" Paul asked nonchalantly.

"Nah, she's interested in somebody else."

"Oh? I didn't know she had a boyfriend."

"Paul, teenage girls have boyfriends, thirty-year-old women have relationships. File that fact for future reference. Actually, Mary doesn't have a relationship. She likes the man but the man has not reciprocated."

Paul shrugged. "He's probably a doctor."

"No, the man she's interested in works for a non-profit organization, and his salary is at the poverty line. It must be love."

"Probably."

Wrapped in that one word was frustration, depression, confusion, and hostility for Paul, just like his game tonight. It was so obvious to Barry that Paul cared for Mary, and it was tearing him apart inside. A cop and a priest, two careers mutually excluded from the American Dream. No wonder we're friends, thought Barry. And friends help one another. Barry zeroed in on the problem directly. "How long have you been in love with Mary, Paul?"

Paul reacted like a kid who had been caught by his parents doing something wrong. Quickly he composed himself. "What kind of a question is that?"

"A sincere one, from a friend who wants to help. It's obvious, Paul."

Barry's honesty released the plug on Paul's suffocating feelings. "Dear God, I don't know what's happening to me, Barry. I have certain urges for a woman I shouldn't have, and contempt toward Rhoades that I shouldn't have. I feel like an imposter when I'm in Church or celebrating Mass. It's unholy."

"Love and hate aren't unholy, Paul; they're human. And you're human."

"I'm a priest. I'm not supposed to have feelings like that. But the worst part is that I can't control them."

"You really do love Mary."

"Yes," it embarrassed Paul to admit. "I'm always eager to see her, and when I'm with her I'm scared, but I don't want to leave."

"You've got it bad. What about the priesthood? You can't have both, but I guess you realize that. Instead of a priest, you should have become a rabbi, then you could have had both." Barry's comic relief was ineffective.

Paul's face hardened as he spoke. "Trying to choose between two things I love is driving me insane. Sometimes I wish I had never met Mary and other times I wish I hadn't entered the priesthood. The damnedest thing is that I wasn't looking to fall in love."

"That's when it happens." Jenny flashed into Barry's mind. "You've only known Mary a short time, Paul. Don't rush any decision. I don't understand why, but things will work themselves out as they usually do."

"Policemen aren't supposed to be optimists."

"And priests aren't supposed to be pessimists. Come on, I'll drive you back to the Church."

Paul continued discussing his problem as they drove. But the discussion was more between Paul and Paul then between Paul and Barry.

"I don't understand, Barry. How can you date so many women and have no feelings for them?"

Barry slowed in front of the Church and shut the motor off. "I've liked most of the women I've dated but I end the relationship when it gets too serious. I guess it's easy because I've probably never really been in love with any of them. I don't know. But the idea of divorcing someone I once loved, or might still love, that's inconceivable to me."

"So you just avoid it?"

Barry curled his lower lip. "I guess so."

"One final question, since we're being so confidential tonight. This man Mary is interested in, is it you?"

"No."

"Honest?"

"Honest. Besides, he's not your problem, *that* is," said Barry pointing to the church.

Paul stepped out of the car and looked at the church. A flash of light from the far corner and a figure partially hidden in the darkness caught his attention. Excitedly he whispered to Barry, "Remember that day the man was murdered by a Molotov cocktail and I saw a shadowy figure in the alleyway across the street?" Paul pointed to the small cluster of bushes at the far end of the churchyard. "That's the same figure, I'm sure of it."

Ordering Paul to remain in the car, Barry unholstered his gun and advanced on the stranger. He examined the ground ahead for anything that might alert the figure to his presence. Tightening his grip on the gun, Barry leaped out, shoved the gun onto the stranger's back and warned, "It's the police! Move and you're dead!" He dragged the intruder out of the shadows. "Oh hell! Father Rhoades! What are you doing here?"

Rhoades' voice resounded with fear even after the gun was lowered from his back. "We have mice. They're more active at night. I was trying to find their burrow." He switched off his flashlight, and held up a bag and shook it. "I was going to stuff some broken glass into the holes." Rhoades' breathing returned to normal and so did his personality. "Do you always point a gun at people?"

"When they're in the bushes at night, yes. From now on chase the mice during the day, Father. It's safer."

"It might be safer if you didn't carry a gun," admonished Rhoades, his face taut. "Not everyone is a criminal!"

"It's all a misunderstanding," Paul interceded. "No one was hurt. So let's forget about it."

Rhoades shook his head. "No, I don't like a gun shoved in my back." He brandished his flashlight at Barry. "Your superiors, Detective Martin, will hear about this." Rhoades stormed into the Church.

"I'll talk to Rhoades," said Paul. "It was my fault anyway. But it sure looked like the same shadow. Sorry."

"Don't worry about it. Give me a call tomorrow."

Paul entered the Church study. Father D'Angelo was sitting alone, a glass of cognac resting on his desk. "Father Rhoades told me what happened. He's after your friend, Paul."

"No, I think he's after me, but I don't know why. I'll go talk to him."

"Be careful, Paul. Father Rhoades, God forgive me for saying this, has an evil way about him."

"I'll be careful. Goodnight, Father."

"Oh, Paul," said Father D'Angelo detaining him with an afterthought. "Tomorrow morning I promised Mrs. Weaver I'd stop in to see her. She believes she's dying again. Would you please handle confession?"

Paul thought a minute. "I haven't seen Mrs. Weaver in a long time. Would you mind if I went to see her tomorrow instead of you?"

Father D'Angelo consented.

"Another favor," Paul added. "Father Rhoades needn't know where I am."

Paul went upstairs and knocked on Rhoades' door. Rhoades came out and shut the door behind him. Paul realized he'd never been in Rhoades' room, and he had a sudden curiosity to inspect it.

Rhoades continued his verbal assault on Detective Barry Martin, threatening to inform his superiors about his brutality. Paul had no chance of convincing him otherwise. The one-sided argument abruptly ended with Rhoades slamming his door in Paul's face.

"That bastard!" Paul muttered.

* * *

The following morning Paul visited Mrs. Weaver. *Ridiculous, Paul considered, but I have to be certain if Rhoades really saw her the night he said he did.* Paul couldn't decide if it was because he disliked Rhoades so much or because his suspicions were valid.

"Come in," came Mrs. Weaver's fatigued voice in response to Paul's knock. Mrs. Weaver, arms folded across her chest, was lying on a couch that looked as old as she did. A badly patched worn blanket covered her upper body. Knee-high stockings were crumpled midcalf. Her face confessed every year of her age. Yellow patches of hair offset the white.

"Mrs. Weaver, it's Father Tobin." Paul held her hand in his and felt a steady pulse. *Another false alarm. He suspected it would be. All she ever wanted was companionship.* "Mrs. Weaver, open your eyes and look at me. Come on."

Mrs. Weaver's eyelids gently fluttered open. "Father Tobin, am I dying?" she pleaded.

"No, Mrs. Weaver, you're going to be just fine. Perhaps a cup of tea would make you feel better." He knew the routine.

"Oh, that would be nice, Father Tobin. Would you stay with me for a while?"

"Of course. Where are the teabags, Mrs. Weaver?"

"I'm feeling much better, Father. I can make the tea."

Father Tobin helped her to the kitchen, sat her at the kitchen table and poured the already boiling water into the two waiting cups.

"Now be careful, it's hot."

"I will," she said blowing into the steaming tea as a child would do. "I thought Father D'Angelo was coming over."

"He was, but when I heard you were feeling poorly I asked if I could come instead. I hope you're not disappointed?"

Mrs. Weaver smiled her pleasure.

"We haven't seen each other in a long time, Mrs. Weaver. How is your family?"

"Very well, thank you. I have some pictures of my grandchildren." She pulled out an album from the drawer behind her, turned the pages and stopped halfway through. "These are the most recent ones. Look at Peter, isn't he adorable? He'll be seven years old soon. Of course the Mickey Mouse hat makes him appear younger." She folded her hands over the pictures and lamented, "I wish they hadn't moved to Florida. A grandchild should be near his grandmother."

"Well, perhaps you can fly down there."

"Oh, Father Tobin, I just returned from there. I don't want them to get tired of me."

"When were you in Florida, Mrs. Weaver?"

"Let's see . . . I got back last Wednesday. I was there for three weeks."

"Mrs. Weaver, when was the last time you saw Father Rhoades?"

"Father Rhoades? Oh, not for quite some time. Maybe five months. I never request to see him."

Paul promptly reviewed the situation: Rhoades said he was here two weeks ago when he was supposed to be delivering my paper. "It can't have been that long, Mrs. Weaver."

"Yes it was. My memory is still in working order. Father D'Angelo is the only one who visits me regularly. I look forward to his visits."

Her memory was not faulty. But why would Rhoades lie? Not over a forgotten article. The checks made out to cash sprang to Paul's mind.

"I must have been mistaken. By the way, some of

our elderly parishioners are having difficulty keeping up with inflation. We can't give much, but if you need any assistance with rent, medicine, or food, we'll do all we can to help."

"Thank you. And thank Father D'Angelo too; it sounds like one of his ideas. But I don't need any help—not yet anyway. My dear husband belonged to the Teamster Union, and his union benefits and my Social Security are enough. My oldest son helps out too." She paused and held up a framed photograph of her husband. "He was a marvelous man. I miss him terribly."

Before leaving Mrs. Weaver with her memories, Paul confrontingly reassured her that her husband was in God's care.

On the way back to the Church Paul attempted to make sense of Rhoades' blatant lies, but he could not. Maybe I'll just ask him straight out. No, too obvious. Too incriminating. It's best to let Rhoades reveal his own lie, with some prodding.

Scattered parishioners watched Father D'Angelo busying himself behind the new pulpit Paul had constructed.

"Father D'Angelo."

The simple greeting startled him.

"I didn't mean to frighten you," apologized Paul. "Do you know where Father Rhoades is?"

"He just left a few minutes ago for a meeting." He continued to rearrange the religious objects on the pulpit. "There, everything's in place. This new pulpit is so much better than the old one. You're really a talented craftsman, Paul."

"What sort of meeting?"

"Huh. He tells me nothing and I no longer bother asking." Father D'Angelo began rearranging again.

"Is there anything wrong, Father? You seem

nervous."

The aging priest leaned on the pulpit, his hands clasped in prayer. "Cardinal Alden telephoned me. A Father Inness from the Vatican is coming to stay with us. He should be arriving within the next few weeks."

"For what purpose?"

"To examine, first hand, why the Catholic Church of America is failing. And it is."

"I read the article. Did he mention anything else?"

"Father Inness will also observe the way we conduct Mass and examine our methods of gaining new parishioners."

Paul sat down in the front pew. "I don't get it. Our methods of gaining new parishioners is the same as other Churches': socials, old age clubs, AA meetings . . . As for the way we conduct Mass, there's no difference there either."

"I'm the difference," Father D'Angelo confessed. "I still say Mass in Latin."

"Only to those who request it." Paul stood up. "It just doesn't make sense."

"Cardinal Alden also restated his edict: no Last Rites or religious ceremonies for those whose lives are devoted to criminal activities. He stressed that we make it known to our parishioners that there is no salvation for such people. Their destiny is Hell." Father D'Angelo crossed himself and prayed, "May God have mercy on our souls, for we are now the judges of good and evil."

Paul aided him down from the pulpit and into the study. "What happens if we disagree with the Cardinal's new edict? I, for one, will not be intimidated as to what I can or cannot say. It's against the Bill of Rights."

"You are first a servant of God and the Church, Paul. Our law has precedence."

"You're agreeing with the Cardinal?"

"God works in mysterious ways, Paul. Cardinal Alden knows what he is doing."

"Father D'Angelo, in a house of our Lord and in a room with only my ears, you tell me if you believe Cardinal Alden's right."

"All mortal men are subject to error, Paul."

"Diplomatically stated, Father. Why haven't other priests spoken against this edict?"

"Cardinal Alden's not only a holy man but a politically powerful man in the Church. The prospect of a parish in a far-away desolate country makes a priest thankful for his present parish."

"Blackmail, that's all it is. And I suppose Rhoades was glad to hear that this edict is to be thoroughly enforced."

Father D'Angelo sighed. "One of the nuns at St. Patrick's informed me that Father Rhoades and the Cardinal had a lengthy meeting yesterday. Apparently Rhoades' influence over the Cardinal is even greater than I suspected. And before I forget, the telephone bill was delivered today. Over ninety dollars."

"Did you check the calls on the bill?"

"I only saw the computerized part, not the listing of numbers and places. Father Rhoades said he required those portions for his records. Oh yes, your sister called. She wants to meet you at noon tomorrow under the archway at Washington Square Park. Forgive me, I forget more things lately." He got up and headed toward the pulpit murmuring, "I must get ready for tonight's services."

Paul remained in the study contemplating what had transpired, and at every turn there was Father Rhoades. It was time to either prove or disprove his suspicions.

On questioning the billing department of the local telephone company, Paul was informed that duplicate copies of past bills would take three to four days, and they had to be picked up in person with proper identification. Using his priestly position, he was able to reduce the waiting time to two or three days. Soon he would learn the truth.

Barry read the scribbled note on his desk and hurried into Captain Adams's office. The police chaplain was also present.

Captain Adams took a deep drag on his cigar before speaking. "I received a frantic call this morning from a Father Rhoades and Cardinal Alden, plus a visit from our chaplain. They maintain that you almost blew Rhoades' head off last night while he was searching for *mice*. Is that true?"

"I did not almost blow his head off. It was dark and I spotted a man creeping in the bushes . . ."

"You pulled a gun on a priest! Jesus Christ! Oh, sorry, Chaplain," Adams said with a fake grin that disappeared when he addressed Barry. "What the hell's the matter with you, Martin? That's all we need, a dead priest on top of the dead boy," he sputtered before returning to the problem at hand. "I can put you on limited suspension for what you did!"

"Yes, sir. But it didn't go down the way they told it."

"Now you're telling me that the priests and a Cardinal lied? Priests don't lie, Martin. They don't do anything wrong, that's why they're priests. Now I want you to apologize to this priest, what's his name?"

"Rhoades," supplied the police chaplain.

"Yes, Rhoades. Apologize to him and to Cardinal Alden, today. That's an order!"

"Yes, sir. Does this mean I'm not on suspension?"

"You're damn lucky we're short of manpower, Martin, or else you'd be out on your ass. Now get going." After Martin left the office, Captain Adams explained to the police chaplain in a most sincere tone, "I'm hard on my men when they deserve it, but they respect me more for it."

Barry reluctantly drove to see Cardinal Alden first. He could understand Rhoades's rage over the incident, but he didn't have to complain to the Cardinal. An over-reaction, typical of Rhoades.

Barry entered the foyer in the rear of St. Patrick's Cathedral and waited to be announced. It did not take long. A nun escorted him into a room that resembled a small chapel. Magnificent statues and crosses adorned the wood panelled walls. An antique desk with a red upholstered chair that looked more like a throne spelled importance. Barry took a seat in one of the smaller chairs.

A side door opened and Cardinal Alden came in. He was a short man in his mid-fifties, although his priestly apparel and purple collar gave him an air of distinction. His heavy, thick-rimmed glasses constantly slipped down his nose.

Barry leapt to attention. "Cardinal Alden, my name is Barry Martin, I'm a detective at the Sixth Precinct."

"Your name is quite familiar to me, Mr. Martin. Please sit down."

"I came here to apologize for my actions concerning Father Rhoades. It was a regrettable mistake, and I'm thankful nobody was hurt." That sounded sincere, Barry thought.

The Cardinal pushed his glasses higher on his nose. "Your apology is accepted, Mr. Martin. Now I must apologize to you for Father Rhoades' lack of under-standing. There are times when understanding is easier to teach then to express, even with priests. As for my telephone call to your Captain, there are things a man in my position must do, whether he agrees with them or not. I hope you understand."

Barry tore his eyes away from the Cardinal's intense stare. "Yes I do. And I'm glad you realize I was only doing my job, sir. Thank you." Barry walked to the door relieved that the confrontation was over.

But before he could leave Cardinal Alden said, "The police chaplain informed me that you are investigating those dreadful murder cases." As the Cardinal spoke he advanced toward Barry. "Some of the victims were parishoners at Our Lady of the Shrine Church. May I inquire as to how the investigation is progressing?"

Barry felt uncomfortable being so close to the Cardinal, but he stood in his place. "Poorly. We have one suspect but no positive identification on him. But sooner or later he'll make a mistake."

"I'll pray that it be sooner. But for what reason are these men being murdered?"

Motive was the easiest part of this case, Barry thought before answering, "The victims have all been criminals, and the killers are their judge, jury, and executioners. It's not a new idea."

"I see. I am surprised the media have not covered this story in more depth. Violence always attracts people's attention, unfortunately."

Candidly, Barry explained to the Cardinal that the media were intentionally not being informed. "We don't like to advertise self-appointed vigilante groups. It produces a false sense of security, and it gives other people the same idea. There's already an over-abundance of weapons on the street, no reason to add to it."

"I wish you well in your investigation. God bless you, my son." The Cardinal removed his glasses and wiped them as Barry left.

Proceeding to his next destination, Barry couldn't help but think what a decent man the Cardinal turned out to be. It was a pleasant surprise. And he was so straight-forward about Rhoades and the position he had been put in. Well, he mused, I guess that's how you get to be Cardinal.

Nearing the Church, Barry spotted Father Rhoades getting into a taxi. He was not wearing his collar. Out of curiosity, Barry followed.

Paul walked through Washington Square Park toward the graffiti-covered archway. Three teenagers muttered "Loose joints, loose joints, good for the head," to the passers-by. Roller skaters, joggers, bike riders, and excessively loud stereo radios entertained the tourists while disturbing the neighbors.

Jenny, wearing dark glasses, leaned against the archway, her cane tapping to the beat of the music. People stared at her, some children pointed. She looked totally helpless even though she was smiling. "Dear God," Paul whispered to himself as he approached her. "Jenny, it's Paul."

She jumped. "You startled me, Paul. I was day-dreaming. The music and smell of grass reminded me of college. I had a lot of fun there. Too bad it had to end." They sat down on a bench. "I spoke to Mom and Dad last night. They've finally accepted the idea that I can take care of myself and be on my own. They're even leaving for a vacation today, the first one since my accident. I'll stay at the house while they're away. They get so paranoid about leaving the house empty. Dad told me three times to make sure I turn the lights on."

"Mary was right about your moving out of the house. Your improvement is miraculous. But she also told me that the nightmares haven't stopped. Is it still the same nightmare?"

Jenny tensed while her mind conjured up the image of Jimmy, the young man who was killed in the car. They had been such close friends in college, though nothing romantic developed, at least not on Jenny's part. He was the big brother she never really had. Someone she could confide in. But most importantly, he was there when she needed him, not like Paul imprisoned in that monastery.

Jimmy was so shy during college, she remembered. Wouldn't even pledge a fraternity. As for girls, if it wasn't for Jenny's social arrangements, he would never have dated. His longest relationship lasted a few months until graduation and, like so many relationships, became lost in distance.

After abandoning New York for two years to receive a Master's Degree in Computer Science at Georgetown University, Jimmy returned a new person: confident, businesslike, and with a special girl in his life. They were to be married at the end of the summer. The day of the accident was to be a private celebration between two dear friends. Jimmy promised Jenny that the marriage would not interfere with their friendship. Even his fianceé, whom Jenny had previously met and approved of, was adamant that close friends should remain as such. Life was being generous to Jimmy. Then came the accident.

Jenny shared her recurring nightmare with Paul. "I see Jimmy's body crushed beneath the steering wheel. My face is splattered with blood, and I can feel the broken glass in my face. But I'm conscious and always looking out my side of the window. Then I wake up."

"How can you see Jimmy if you're looking out the passenger window?"

"I don't know why I'm doing it or what I'm looking at. Mary believes I'm subsconsciously suppressing something." Jenny shook the nightmare out of her thoughts. "That's not the reason I called. I have a favor to ask. Actually it was Mary's idea."

"Name it."

"First promise that you'll do it."

"I don't think I'm going to like this. But I'll do it if I can."

"I want you to ask Barry to ask me out on a date."

The left-fielded request caught Paul off-guard. His thoughts abruptly shifted to Barry's active sex life and non-committal relationships. Jenny could wind up as a number. Worse, she could wind up hurt. Paul wouldn't let that happen. He thought of saying something like, 'You and Barry are like brother and sister. I don't think it's wise to change the relationship.' No, that wasn't a sound reason. His mind raced over names trying to come up with an alternative. The only single men he knew were other priests.

"I know what you're thinking, Paul, that Barry dates many women and he can't settle down, but it doesn't matter to me. Barry treats me like a person, not a handicap; he makes me laugh and he tells me I'm beautiful. I'll never again get enough courage to ask you to do this, so please say you will."

"Jenny, Barry's my best friend, and I'd do anything for him as I would for you. But he's not right for you. For one thing he's so much older than you are—"

"Eight years is not a lot."

"It's enough. And after all these years of living alone, he probably has terrible habits that he can't break, and—"

"I don't want to marry him, Paul, just go out with him."

Paul suspected that the first part of that wasn't quite true.

"Paul, at night I lie in bed trying to imagine what those lines in his face look like, and his ears and his broken nose. I've never wanted so much to be able to see anyone. He's the only one . . ."

"I wasn't aware you were in love with him, but lately I'm unaware of a lot of things. Okay. I'll speak to him first chance I get."

"You're a sweet brother, Paul."

He kissed Jenny on the cheek, but he was thinking of Barry. I'll have a long talk with him, he promised himself.

Paul accompanied Jenny back to the Institute. He had to talk to Mary before he spoke to Barry.

Mary interrupted her work when she saw Paul at the door. He explained, "I had lunch with Jenny, but I came back to see you. Your abrupt departure during lunch the other day has been bothering me. Whatever I said that upset you, I certainly didn't mean to."

"You said nothing wrong, Paul. Let's just say it was a strenuous day at work for me and I was wound up. Tonight Jenny is staying at your folks' home while they're away on vacation. Would you like to have dinner at my apartment tonight?"

"I'd like that very much."

"Eight o'clock."

Paul forgot all about Barry.

Rhoades' cab stopped at the corner of 98th Street and First Avenue. He got out and walked two more blocks. Barry parked and followed on foot from a safe distance. Rhoades glanced up and down the street, then ducked into an unassuming two-story building. Barry approached the door behind which was a small anteroom with a man in a theatre ticket cage.

"Five bucks, mister," the man grumbled without looking up from his newspaper.

Barry slipped the money through the bars, then went through the only other door. Beer and liquor permeated the darkened room. At the far end, on a makeshift stage, two topless but flat-chested women danced to recorded music. That horny bastard, Barry snickered, maneuvering his way deeper into the crowded room. Men stood gawking at the women on stage. Barry caught sight of Rhoades going through another door. He followed. The room was totally dark. Barry stood still, afraid to move for fear of tripping. Now I know how Jenny feels. Someone leaned against his shoulder as a strange hand rubbed his crotch. A faceless voice wheedled "Want a blowjob?"

Barry whispered back to the stranger, "I have herpes." The strange hand left. So did Barry. "A transvestite place," he huffed in the privacy of his car. "Son of a bitch, Rhoades is gay." Then he thought, no wonder Rhoades is so paranoid about where he goes on his free time. And there goes Paul's suspicion of him. Wait till I tell Paul. Or should I?

Barry drove back to the office to catch up on his paperwork. Still behind him was the Oldsmobile sedan.

Brooding on his bed, Paul eyed his limited wardrobe. He rubbed his clammy hands together. His stomach felt queasy. "I sure have plain taste in clothes," he commented to himself, "but then all priests do."

It was seven o'clock. Another hour before he was to be at Mary's. Paul selected a camel-colored shirt and tan pants. "A walk, that's what I need."

Downstairs he encountered Father D'Angelo, who gave a curt look at Paul's attire.

"I'm visiting a friend," Paul said defensively. "I am.

Really."

"I don't remember asking."

"Oh. Well, it was the way you looked at me."

"I was just wondering. From the way you're dressed I thought you might be going out with Father Rhoades. He's been wearing street clothes the entire day. Another meeting, he said. Two in one day. . . ."

"When did Rhoades leave?"

"Just now."

Paul hurried outside and saw Rhoades get into a cab. He hailed another one. "That cab up ahead, with the Town Monument advertisement on it—follow it but not too closely."

"You puttin' me on, mister?" snarled the cabbie.

"An extra five dollars says I'm not."

Minutes later the first cab stopped in front of a loft building in Soho. Rhoades got out. Paul had the driver stop the cab a block away, got out, and proceeded on foot the rest of the way. As on so many streets in this section, old attached warehouses lined both sides. Some were being gutted to be remodeled into expensive lofts for artists or people who just sought extra living space. At night, though, many side streets like this one were deserted.

Rhoades surveyed the street and infrequent pedestrians before entering the building. Paul rushed to the side of the doorway and saw the elevator doors close. Atop the elevator carriage, lights indicated the floors: two, three, four, top floor. Paul stepped back to the edge of the sidewalk, looked up at the outside of the building, and noticed that only the top floor lights were on.

The staircase. Paul began the slow climb. One inadequate naked bulb per level heightened the eeriness of the stairwell. Second floor. Creaking accompanied every step. Only cobwebs seemed to support the shaky banister. Third floor. Moaning sounds emanated from all directions. Paul felt as though some ungodly creature was watching him, waiting for him. Fourth floor. The air was dank and stale. He continued his ascent. His foot touched something on the stairs sending a bolt of cold through his spine.

"Hey!"

Paul leaped back almost losing his balance, his eyes focusing on the unnoticed derelict sprawled across the stairs.

"Watchya doin' steppin' on me, creep?" came the slurred voice.

"I didn't see you," Paul whispered.

The bum rotated his body into a more comfortable position, his hands protecting his pint bottle. "Hey, man, ya got some spare change?"

His voice echoed slightly through the stairwell Paul wonder if others might not have heard it. As a bribe to silence the bum, Paul handed him some coins, stepped over, and continued, stopping at the rear door of the top floor loft. Pressing his ear against the rotted wooden door he recognized Rhoades's voice but couldn't distinguish what he was saying. A beam of light escaped through a hole in the door. Paul squatted down and peered through. The smell of dried urine made him gag, but still he watched. There were four men sitting at a table. Rhoades faced in Paul's direction. Paul maneuvered to get a clearer look. One man had silver hair and beside him was a thin man. He couldn't see their faces.

The fourth man sat out of view behind a post. Paul's legs ached. He compressed his ear against the hole but still he couldn't hear clearly.

A hand latched on to Paul's shoulders. Paul

wrenched backwards, his body slamming against the door. "Hey Mister, ya got another dime?"

Altered footsteps from inside the room charged toward the door. The elevator motor switched on. Paul scrambled to his feet but the bum held on to his arm. "C'mon, Mister, how about some more money?"

The elevator began its descent. Paul pried the bum's hand off his arm, shoved him away, and scrambled down the stairs. Wood snapped as Rhoades and his associates broke through the door.

"There he is!" one of them blared.

The staircase quivered under the trampling weight. The elevator was ahead of Paul. The fourth floor. Paul leapt two stairs at a time. Terror made him move faster. He held onto the banister for balance.

"Third floor," one of the men reported for all to hear.

Paul was even with the elevator. Echoing footsteps made it impossible for him to judge how close his pursuers were. Second floor. Paul was ahead of the elevator. Anticipation of being tackled from behind played with his mind. He resisted looking over his shoulder for fear he might see someone. Paul could see the bottom of the elevator through the shaftway. He hurdled the last few stairs. Street level. Bolting through the front door precisely as the elevator motor snapped off, he fled down a side street as a voice barked "Down there!" He zigzagged in all directions trying to lose them. He didn't stop. His chest burned and all he could hear was his heart beat. An abandoned building up ahead. He vaulted through an empty window space and crawled into a dark corner, listening for frantic footsteps that he prayed weren't there. His breathing was exaggerated and too loud. There was a rustling in one of the other corners. Rats. Paul folded his hands across his chest. He could not recall ever being this frightened. Waiting minutes seemed endless.

Inching his head out the window opening, he saw that the immediate vicinity appeared safe. An available cab stopped for a red light. I have to chance it. Sprinting from his hiding place and lunging into the cab he ordered, "Drive! Hurry up and drive!" The cabbie sped through the red light and continued straight until Paul gave him Mary's address.

Paul arrived at Mary's apartment at nine o'clock. She glimpsed is disheveled clothes and said, "Oh my God, you've been mugged!"

"No, no. Nothing like that. I'm not hurt at all, just exhausted." Mary tactfully prevented him from resting on the white Haitian couch. "I'm that dirty, eh?"

"You can take a shower. Are you sure you haven't been hurt? Your hand is all red."

Friction burn from grasping onto the banister. It didn't hurt until she mentioned it. "Let me take a shower before I explain. You have a robe or something?"

"Your Father's. Jenny wears it around the apartment. A semi-security blanket."

The warm pulsating water cleaned Paul of the nervous perspiration and calmed him down. It was a lengthy shower. Finally he felt safe and secure. "I've never seen a bathroom that neat," he commented to Mary as he entered the livingroom. "Every towel is folded uniformly. As a matter of fact I've never seen such a neat apartment."

"Habit," she replied from the kitchen. "When you have a blind person in the family, neatness is of utmost importance. Everything must have a permanent place."

Paul had forgotten that her father was blind. As he sat down at the diningroom table he noticed an oval silver tray of toothpicks proportionately placed between the two candlesticks. Even those had been patiently arranged.

"Would you like a drink before dinner?"

"A double scotch."

"Can you tell me what happened tonight?" Mary asked as she served the food.

In between bites, Paul recounted the night's bizarre events. "It just doesn't make sense. There's no reason for a priest to be in on a secret meeting. And the way they chased me. I'm positive they would have killed me if they had caught me. Damn, I wish I could have seen the other faces."

"You're over-reacting and too suspicious, Paul. There's probably a logical explanation for the meeting. I suggest you simply ask Father Rhoades."

"Can't do that." Paul told Mary about the excessive telephone bills, the large amounts of money Rhoades had spent, and how he had lied about visiting Mrs. Weaver and lending her money.

"Without knowing the motives behind his actions, it's difficult to make a judgment. What are you going to do?"

"I'm getting copies of the church's telephone bills. I'll call the numbers and see who answers. The only problem is that I can't use the church phone. I was wondering if . . ."

"Of course you can use my phone."

"Thanks. I'll do it some time this week. There's something else: Jenny asked me to fix up a date for her with Barry. She said it was your idea."

"They make a nice couple. You disapprove? I thought he was your best friend."

"He is. I just don't think it's a proper match. They have nothing in common."

Mary's perfume seemed faintly exotic to him. Paul

gushed like a teenager on his first date. He didn't really want to discuss Barry and Jenny.

"Jenny's been in love with Barry for a long time," Mary said clearing the dishes off the table. "One date with Barry would be more beneficial than a number of psychological sessions. I just hope he'll agree to do it."

"He will, I'll make sure of it. But I'm worried that Jenny could be hurt." They adjourned to the livingroom and relaxed on the couch.

"Now I know where Jenny gets her negative outlook. If she gets hurt, that's what she has to face. We all do."

Paul sensed the last sentence was directed toward him. Say something, and stop being so childish, he reprimanded himself. His stomach had that butterfly feeling. Do it! He touched her hand. "You're a beautiful and talented woman, Mary." Her hand tightened around his. Leaning toward each other they kissed briefly but at the next kiss their arms wrapped around each other. Their bodies merged, their lips became more impassioned.

"I'm scared too," Mary faintly voiced.

Paul let out a sigh of relief. "I don't understand how this happened, but I've fallen in love with you."

"I tried to deny my feelings too, but I couldn't." She leaned her head against his shoulder. A disquieting laugh preceded her saying, "My clinical mind warns me this is wrong . . . falling in love with a priest. And I don't know how to handle the situation."

"Slowly," Paul answered, "for both our sakes." He pulled away. "I'd better leave. Can I see you tomorrow night?"

"Every night, if you wish."

Paul dressed and following a lingering goodnight kiss, headed home to the Church. It was well past midnight by the time he entered through the side door of the Church. Night lights guided his way into the main chapel where he knelt down in front of the alter and prayed.

"Dear Lord, I have devoted six years to the Church and I have lived by its principles, but now I have arrived at an impasse. In my heart I would like to be both a priest and a husband, yet, admittedly, that is impossible. Priests are allowed to be only priests, and so I must choose between the two loves, neither of which I want to lose. Please Lord, help me make the proper decision."

Standing, Paul tiptoed back to the hall and up the stairs when suddenly his ears perked up. He stopped and turned full circle. "Is somebody there?" Paul softly called. "Hello?" silence. He gave one last look before retiring to his room.

Stairs creaked as Father Rhoades descended back into the darkness of the cellar. Positioning himself in the middle of the room, he held aloft, as if it were an offering, a long thin leather strap stained with his own blood. His bruised naked back ached with pain, but it was insufficient for absolution of his crime. His fingers tightened around the braided handle, his hand arched forward and then sprang back as the strap crackled in the air before striking the scarred red flesh of his back. Traumatized muscles relayed confused signals awkwardly contorting his body. Sweat mixed with his blood.

"Dear Heavenly Father," came his warped voice, "again I succumbed to the will of the flesh." The strap cracked through the air again. "This is my penance. I do it lovingly for You." His hand rose, halted, then came down with more force, the strap almost falling from his grip, his legs buckling at the knees.

Rhoades straightened his racked body, his head

tilted back, and in the darkness his mind saw a bluish white vapor hover above. "It is You, Father." Letting go of the strap he sank to his knees and cupped his head in his palms. "I gratefully accept the curse as a test of my obedience to You. My penance serves to strenghten me so that I might carry out Your Will. For I am Your servant, O Lord. I am Your Servant . . ." Each tear that fell into his palm brought back the reality of pain. "Sweet Jesus," he pleaded, "help me. Please help me."

The next morning Barry, at Paul's urgent request, arrived at Mary's apartment. Paul informed him of the incident in Soho and asked Barry to search the place for evidence.

Barry noticed a far-away look on Mary's face and wondered if Paul had spent the night with her.

"Barry, are you listening to me?"

"Yes. You want me to scout for evidence. But evidence of what?" Barry decided not to reveal his own encounter with Rhoades. "It's not illegal for a group of men to meet privately. Although there are times . . ." he quipped to himself. "Besides, it's against the law to search a place without a warrant, and to get a warrant I need probable cause."

"What if the doors had been broken down and we could walk right in?"

"Okay if the door's open."

"It will be."

"I have to go to work," Mary announced.

"Isn't Jenny going with you?" Barry wanted to know.

"She's staying at her folks for a week," Mary answered. She and Paul eyed one another. The corners of their mouths arched into smiles. They kissed good-bye.

Barry shied away trying to make believe he didn't see what he saw. Well, scratch celibacy.

On their way to Soho, Paul felt compelled to relieve Barry's suspicions. "I guess I should explain that kiss."

"It was self explanatory."

"We only kissed. I mean nothing happened last night. I'm glad it didn't. I'm so anxious all the time I'm with her." Paul faced Barry. "Would you believe that I've had sexual intercourse only once in my life? Don't look at me like that, it's the truth. My junior year in college at a fraternity party. We were all high, and the next thing I knew we were in bed. It was over so soon. I can't remember if I enjoyed it."

"You did, she didn't. Paul, you have to realize that sex isn't a sin; especially if the two people love each other. If anything it's natural."

"Not for a priest."

"It is for a man. And you are after all, even with your vows, still a man."

"I know, I know. It's obvious when I'm with Mary. But the urge is so damn strong—barely controllable at times. Even my nights have become restless. I've never read so much in my life. I just don't understand. One day your life is simple and arranged and then, boom," snapping his fingers, "it's chaotic." He faced Barry. "What was it like for you—the first time?"

"Painful," Barry grinned. "I was a senior in high school. This girl, Peggy, you had to wait in line to date her. We went up to this lake and in the front seat of my father's 1955 Chevy we made love. Unfortunately my leg got caught in the steering wheel. While I was trying to maneuver out, Peggy heaved forward, I lurched back, fell off of her, and broke my leg in the steering wheel. After I got untangled and dressed, which took half an hour, she drove me to the hospital. I was in a cast for six weeks. My father never questioned how it happened, especially when he had to have a new horn installed the next day. For months all he did was snicker and shake

117

his head every time I hobbled by. He knew."

"I should have expected one of your weird stories," Paul sported before turning serious again. "But it still comes down to the physical, doesn't it?"

"All the time. And if love is involved, you'll be happy it did." He tapped Paul on the shoulder and with a wry look added, "No, you can't borrow my car." Their laughter temporarily eased Paul's predicament. When they reached their destination. Paul led the way up the staircase. Sure enough, the rear door had been busted open. Barry knelt down and examined the streaks in the dust. "This place has recently been swept." He surveyed the room. No tables or chairs, but he could see faint marks where they had been. "Somebody sure cleaned this place out. The question is, why? Paul, check the hallway for any container with garbage in it."

Barry continued his examination of the loft. Not a damn shred of evidence.

"What do you think, Barry?"

"Rhoades and his three cohorts did everything but vacuum. They're taking no chances, which means that their unknown Peeping Tom is driving them nuts." He emphasized, "Whatever you do, don't even hint to Rhoades that you're the one they're looking for."

"I won't. What do you think they were doing here?"

Barry figured that Rhoades had met some of his gay acquaintances there. It was time to tell Paul the truth, not here but in the car, just in case unknown ears were listening.

Paul's expression continually vacillated between shock and incredulity as he listened to Barry's saga concerning Rhoades' secret life. "Now you can understand why Rhoades is no mysterious and paranoid, Paul."

"It's unbelievable. Rhoades gay? He's so

masculine." Paul thought a minute. "I'm not doubting what you've said about Rhoades, Barry, but this meeting was something more. From the tone of their voices, it was serious and important." Barry pitched his head back, his eyes blankly focused on the car ceiling. "You don't believe they met there for sex, do you?"

"It's the way the room was so well cleaned. Nobody in his right mind sweeps an empty loft, meeting or no meeting. On the other hand, maybe they wouldn't have cleaned if you hadn't happened along. We'll never know."

"That's it? You're not going to investigate further?"

"Investigate what, an empty room?"

"What about the Forensic Department? Maybe they can find something."

"No crime has been established, Paul. I can't have them come here without cause. Listen, I'll check out the owner of the building and see if that leads anywhere. It's the best I can do for now."

"You need more evidence."

"Don't play hero, Paul. You're a priest, not a cop. If you pick up any information give it to me and I promise to check it out. You have my word on that. Is it a deal?"

"It's a deal."

"You agreed too fast, Paul. I don't believe you. I'm not going to try and talk you out of whatever you're going to do; I have a feeling it would be useless, but be very careful and keep me posted on what you find out."

"I'll agree to that."

Barry turned the ignition key when he caught sight of the front portion of the Oldsmobile sedan in his rearview mirror.

Paul swivelled about. "What are you looking at? I don't see anything."

"Hang tight," Barry warned as he threw the gear in

reverse and skidded backwards. He wasn't halfway down the street before the sedan veered out of sight. "Somebody's been following me lately and I hate being followed."

"The Crossbearers! Maybe you're on to something."

"They think I am, whoever they are. I just wish I knew what it was." He shifted back into drive and headed toward the Church.

"Too bad we couldn't see the license plate."

"I got the number a few nights ago. The plate's off a rented car that's still in the lot. They probably rotate license plates when they follow me or else we would have spotted them by now."

"Intriguing. Detectives probably thrive on cases like this."

"You're a child of television, Paul. My caseload fluctuates between eighteen to twenty-five, which means that the more time I spend on one case the less time I devote to the others, not to mention that my caseload continually increases. The faster I solve a case, the better off I am. It keeps the brass off my back."

"You make detective work sound like any other work."

"It is. We have to produce just like everyone else who works for a living."

"Are you sorry you became a cop?"

"Depends on what day you ask me. I always wanted to be a lawman. Wyatt Earp has been my hero since I can remember, but since Dodge City was cleaned up, I was stuck with New York. Dodge City was easier to clean up."

"It's amazing how almost every job simply turns out to be just another job. I wonder how many people are satisfied with what they do."

"Dictators," Barry joked as he pulled up in front of the Church. "Not to get off the subject, but the past few days I had the computer list all known unorthodox religious groups. You have a lot of competition."

"The Church is well aware of the problem. The tragic part is that these groups have acquired substantial followings. Last week Rabbi Cohen told me that seven of his young people had left the synogogue and joined some whacko sect. We're all losing to these groups."

"What's the Church doing about it?"

"Initially we tried to stop them through the courts, but we lost badly. Freedom of choice, the judge proclaimed. Next we tried a media blitz but it had a reverse effect on those who had left. It was like crying wolf only we couldn't produce the wolf. Sermons and encounter groups didn't work either. Our last resort is prayer."

"That won't work."

"When you're dying, you don't ask to see the doctor any more."

4

Joe Ricart picked up the receiver on the first ring and listened as the voice asked, "Are you a believer?"

"Yes sir, I am. We are all believers," looking at his group and checking to see if any strangers were near the telephone booth.

"The police have distributed a composite picture of you to the street people," the voice warned. "You'd better stay out of sight for a while and let one of the others handle the next sacrifice."

"I've seen the picture, sir. They're searching for a blond man, not me. Besides, God will protect me. What's the mission?"

There was a pause on the other end of the line. "God protects all of us, but the evil ones are devious and so must we be. I therefore order you to send another member on this surveillance until it is carried through. do you understand?"

Joe could feel his groups' eyes on him. "Leave it to me." The unknown voice hung up but Joe continued to talk. "Another meeting . . . yeah, I'm free that day. Same time and place? . . . Oh, thanks, sir. I'm glad the Crossbearers liked my plan. See you soon."

The artificial conversation impressed the group. It always did. Carol inched herself beside Joe as he spoke. "As you heard, the Crossbearers have agreed to my plan." He handed the manila envelope to Hank. "The next sacrifice is yours. Watch him closely and pick the best time and place, but check with me first. Is that understood?"

"I don't need your approval for anything I do. I'm competent enough. That means I'm smart."

"I'm smart too, and you ain't the leader, I am. So you check in with me."

"Ha, this sacrifice will be easy. And it will be quality work."

"You check with me, Hank. That's an order. If you don't, I'll report you. And they listen to me."

Hank draped his arms around Doug and Roger. "How would you two like to join me for some ice cream?"

Like children they jumped up and down with enthusiasm and almost dragged Hank with them as they left.

Carol ran her tongue inside Joe's ear and cooed, "You really do know the Crossbearers. I like men in charge."

"What about Hank?"

"Nothing happened between us, Joe, honest. It's you I've always wanted. Let's go to your place . . . our place."

"I ain't decided if I want you back. You stay with me for a while, then you stay with Hank. How come you ain't screwed with Doug and Roger yet? Or maybe you did."

"Please, Joe. I won't leave you."

"Ah, I don't want you," he tossed out, flipping his

hand at her. "Go back to Hank or that young girl at Palmer's Church you've been trying to seduce."

Dogging him she pleaded, "Joe, I'll do anything you want, just take me back."

"Anything I want?"

"Anything."

Joe clamped his hand over hers and gently squeezed. Suddenly his grip tightened, discoloring her fingers into a bloodless white. "It's nice that you're coming with me," he said in an easy tone while thinking she'll either tell me what she and Hank discussed in the park the other day or else she will die. He released her. Another thought crossed his mind. For the first time Hank had accompanied Doug and Roger for ice cream, and it wasn't to become friends with them. I have to be careful of everyone. And Hank is a dead man!

Like little kids, Doug and Roger slobbered the ice cream into their mouths. The cold drippy dessert made them giggle while it stained their faces and shirts.

Retards, Hank thought, and stupid enough to do what I want just in case Carol doesn't.

"Can we have more?" Doug pleaded as the tip of the cone disappeared into his mouth.

"We want another one, we want another one," Roger pestered, stamping his foot.

Hank handed them more money and once again watched their greedy mouths devour the treat. "We should do this more often," Hank said. "That's what friends are for, to do each other favors. I'm surprised Joe never treated the two of you to ice cream, I thought you were good friends."

"We are, we are," Roger said. "Aren't we, Doug?"

"Yah," he answered licking the last drop off his fingers.

"If you say so, but it seems strange that he never

does anything for you. Now if I was the leader I'd do things for you, like buying you ice cream, letting you carry out some of the sacrifices, sharing Carol with you." Their eyes lit up. "But if Joe's your friend then I guess we can't change anything."

"You'd really give us Carol?" Doug asked, his expression already showing his imagination at work. "We could screw her any time we wanted?"

"Why not? But let's forget it." Hank walked away but he didn't get far before the two were at his side begging to know what to do. "Joe won't leave the group voluntarily. He's just like Miller and Frederickson, bad. There's only one way to get rid of Joe. Sacrifice him."

Doug and Roger exchanged confused gazes. It was useless to think they could make a decision on their own. Hank stopped, faced them, and said, "There are five of us in the group. I say Joe is no longer the leader, I am. Do both of you agree?"

They both raised their hands.

"That's three votes for me. I win. My first order is to kill Joe. The two of you will do it. And the sooner it's done the sooner you get Carol."

"How do we do it?" Roger asked.

"Knife! Then dump his body in the river or some place where it won't be found for a long time; maybe an abandoned building. And I want it done fast."

Barry showed up at Mary's apartment for his date with Jenny, who had come over for Mary's advice on how to dress. The more he thought about the date the more he liked the idea, in spite of Paul's warnings of damnation if he got out of line with Jenny. It had taken Paul less than a minute to explain the fix-up, followed by twenty minutes of rules and regulations. Oh well, that's what big brothers are for. He adjusted his sports jacket before ringing the bell.

Paul opened the door, his eyes showing approval of Barry's attire. "Jenny will be ready in a minute. She and Mary spent the entire afternoon shopping. What a waste of a nice day." Paul drew Barry closer to him. "I want you to remember our talk. You promised."

"Paul, we're going on a date, I'm not taking her to a volcano as a sacrifice. Relax."

"I am, but I want you to relax. Be calm. She's vulnerable and naive. She doesn't know about the real world."

"Paul, go back to what you were doing," Barry pointed to some papers on the table.

Mary stuck her head out the bedroom door. "She'll be ready in five minutes, Barry."

"No rush," Barry answered curiously flipping through Paul's paperwork. "Paying your telephone bills?"

"No, these are the ones I told you about. Look at 'em. The same long distance numbers every month. I got the copies this morning. I don't want Rhoades to become suspicious, so I'm doing the work here."

"And how you're going to call each number and see who picks up. Clever. Except that if they're business numbers nobody will answer because it's seven-thirty at night."

Paul frowned. "Boy, am I dumb. Oh well, I'll try anyway."

Mary came out of the bedroom, and in an over-animated manner asked, "Are you ready for your date, Barry?"

"This is just like the Dating Game," Barry quipped. His laughter was cut short as Jenny made her entrance. She wore a light pink chiffon dress that flowed with her every movement. Make-up just slight enough to enchance her natural beauty. Her black hair curved about her shoulders. The ominous dark sun glasses had been replaced with stylish tinted ones.

"You look fantastic!" Barry said giving her a kiss on the lips. "Jesus! Oh, sorry, Paul."

Paul couldn't believe his eyes. This was not his little sister. "I've never seen anyone as beautiful as you," he marveled.

Jenny shied away as she held on to Barry's arm. "Do I really look all right, Barry?"

"I've never lied to you, Jen. You're gorgeous. But we have to get going; they won't hold the motel room forever. Just kidding, Paul."

"Have a great time," Mary directed to Jenny as they left. "Your kid sister has matured into a beautiful woman, Paul."

"It's too bad my folks couldn't see her like this. They'd be proud of her. Oh well, back to the mysterious telephone numbers." Mary joined him and read off the first telephone number coming from Los Angeles.

Paul waited. "Uhm, sorry, wrong number," he said, then hung up.

"What's the matter, Paul?"

"It was the Church of Our Savior. You sure you gave me the right number?" He looked at the number again. "Let's go on."

He repeated the routine six times, with unexpected results. The Church of Our Savior in Los Angeles; St. Paul's Cathedral in St. Paul; Church of the Ascension in Dallas; St. Matthew's Church in Chicago; Our Lady of Grace in New Orleans; St. Ann's Shrine in Boston; and the Transfiguration Catholic Church in San Francisco.

All Churches. That solved part of the mystery.

"There's nothing suspicious about one Church being in contact with others," Mary said.

"Not a damn thing!"

Arm in arm, Barry and Jenny strolled down the street

as male passersby gave her the once-over. He felt proud to have such an attractive woman next to him, but at the same time he objected to the silent thoughts he knew were running through their heads; the same carnal thoughts that accompanied his once-overs.

"You're mumbling," he said to Jenny. "What are you mumbling about?"

"I count the number of steps to various places to determine how far I've gone. For instance, it's one hundred and twenty-one paces per city block going East and West; North and South the blocks are one hundred and fifty-six paces; and street crossings are fifteen or thirty-two paces depending upon the direction. I didn't realize I was counting. Sorry."

"No problem."

"Smell that? Fresh bread baking. You're walking so slowly, we've gone only a block and a half. Have you been injured?"

"No, just pooped. The last few days I've canvassed the city visiting certain religious sects. Talk about an A.P. problem, those religious sects have their own."

"What's A.P.? Associated Press?

"Asshole Population. It includes everyone you'd never want to meet. Bums, derelicts, drug addicts, pimps, prostitutes, mental cases, lawyers."

"Lawyers? Why lawyers?"

"They have to belong to some group."

"I'm sorry I asked," she said with a smile. "Does any of this have to do with the case you're working on?"

"The Crossbearers?"

"You name your cases?"

"No, that's what they call themselves."

"You're right, I don't want to meet them." Jenny tilted her head from side to side. She pinched Barry's arm and whispered, "The last two days I've been hearing the same footsteps following me; metal taps on the shoes, and I'm hearing them again."

"Play along with me," Barry said in a subdued voice as he guided her to a store window. In a normal tone he remarked, "That's what I need, a new television. It's time I bought a color set." Through the reflection in the glass he saw, and recognized, the man who quickly crossed the street and entered an all night drug store. They began walking again. "Jenny, why did you pick this restaurant?"

"They have delicious roast beef and it's nearby. Why? Did you see who was following us?"

"Yeah. Listen Jenny, I'm sorry but I think it's wise to cancel tonight's dinner."

"Why? He's gone, isn't he?"

"I can't explain now." Barry reversed directions.

"Is it going to be dangerous?"

"No, nothing like that. It's more of a conference."

"But why would they follow me?"

"To get me in a sociable atmosphere . . . with no bugs attached." They're being overly cautious, he decided.

"Well, if it's not dangerous and they're expecting us to be together, why disappoing them? Besides, I'm starving."

"I don't know. . . ."

Jenny reversed their direction. "You've seen me at work, now I'll get to see you at work."

He was eager to find out what they knew. Yeah, why not. "Just remember that there's nothing to be frightened of, Jenny."

"I'm not frightened when I'm with you."

Before entering the restaurant Barry transferred his gun from his hip holster into his jacket pocket. Experience had taught him to be prudent. Once inside the restaurant they were promptly seated, the maitre d' escorting them to the table Jenny always occupied. One of the waiters greeted Jenny. Barry now understood why she came here; it was another secure place for her. He bet she even memorized the menu and daily specials.

"Are you having roast beef or would you like me to read off the specials?"

"Roast beef, please. Thursday specials aren't to my taste."

She's still a long way from being independent, Barry surmised, but she's trying. Barry inventoried the customers. The room was crowded, mostly couples. Nothing out of the ordinary. At least not yet.

After dinner they lingered over a liqueur, mixed with personal conversation. Jenny did most of the talking, or rather reminiscing, especially about her college years. She did too much of that, Barry estimated. Underlying her conversation, the present and the future did not excite her, but why should it when you're blind. Only her memories gave her pleasure. Barry felt helpless.

Jenny interrupted her reminiscing with "Why haven't you asked me how it feels to be blind? Everyone else does." It sounded like a challenge.

"To be candid with you I don't think it would help. I can't imagine being blind, no sighted person can. However, I have found myself being more aware of things: details on buildings, people's faces, I even looked at the sky the other night and saw a star. Pretty daring for a New Yorker."

"Did you make a wish?"

"Yeah, but the Captain was still in his office the next day, and my name wasn't on the door. Anyway, that night I did wonder what I would miss most if I were blind, and it was a sense of location . . . being lost."

"That's why I count as I walk. Once your location is established then you can determine what you miss seeing the most. For me it was easy; the faces of my family and friends, although most of them are stored in my memory. It's primarily my new friends, the ones I can never see, that bother me, such as you and Mary, Father Crowley and the people at the Institute. For the past year I've been exploring your face with my hands and still get no clear image. The simplest way to explain is to say that before I was blind the world was a motion picture, now it's a tape recorder."

"Nicely said."

"I've had plenty of time to think about it. During college I was an art major and I was trained to use my sight more efficiently than most people. Maybe that's why I miss seeing faces so much; they're never the same. But I'm trying to get back into art, at least into clay sculpture."

"You can do that?"

"Not well. If I lose my tactile sense of direction, the nose winds up on the forehead. I did that last week."

"You should have left the house there and called it modern art. I'd like to see some of your work."

"It's not very good, but I do need a subject. Are you willing?"

"Sure, but I don't pose in the nude."

Jenny held up her glass of liqueur. "Barry, thank you for tonight. Thank you for making me laugh."

Barry put her drink down, leaned across the table, and kissed her.

"What was that for? And can I have more?"

"For being so beautiful and yes, later on." Barry monitored the people in the restaurant. Only two other tables were occupied, both by men only. Eleven-thirty. The shades in the restaurant had been drawn. What he suspected was going down now. "Jenny, I want you to listen to me and do exactly as I say. First of all, put your smile on. That's it. There's no danger, it's just that some men want to have an unexpected pow-wow with me."

"Are they included in the A.P.?"

"Leaders of it." Barry inconspicuously moved his hand into his pocket and gripped his gun. The other men at the tables stood up and moved to the front door. "It's about to begin, Jenny."

Two business dressed men entered the restaurant and surveyed the place. One of them nodded. An older, balding short man entered, sporting very expensive clothes. He looked directly at Barry, then approached him.

"Detective Martin, what an unexpected surprise! Mind if I join you?"

"Yes, I do."

The man sat down. "A bottle of your best champagne for my friends," he ordered, snapping his fingers at the waiter. "You have a beautiful looking lady. Jennifer Tobin, correct?" he said, bowing to Jenny. "My name is Robert Stoner. Detective Martin and I are old acquaintances." The waiter poured the champagne. Stoner guided Jenny's right hand to the glass. "How about a toast?"

Barry raised his glass toward Stoner and toasted, "May the rest of your life be short."

Champagne spilled out of Jenny's shaking glass. Stoner's body guards advanced toward Barry but the boss waved them off. Then in a threatening voice he intoned, "Nobody pushes me, Martin, especially a goddamn cop."

"Somebody is, and they're pushing to kill. Word's out that you can't protect your own people. That's bad for business. Your *family* must be upset."

Stoner reached into his breast pocket and threw a piece of paper at Barry. It was his own DD5 form he had given to the Captain.

Barry brushed it back to Stoner. "I know what I wrote, and now you do. So why the meeting?"

"My sources tell me that you keep more information

in your head than you write down in your reports. I want that information."

Stoner's voice was more desperate than authoritative. He knew nothing, Barry surmised, not even about the poetry or the telephone calls, meaning he knew nothing about the Crossbearers. And Barry was not volunteering information. Time for a white lie so Stoner and his comrades wouldn't disrupt his investigation. Barry geared his deception to Stoner's unspoken suspicions. "The killer is an import or else he'd be dead already. That yields two theories: First, revenge; second, somebody's trying their level best to make you appear incompetent, perhaps to entice other members into another syndicate. It's been tried before."

Stoner slid his index finger around the rim of his glass. "What else?"

"Nothing. We have no idea who it is. Do you?"

"As you said before, if I did he'd be dead."

"If that's it we'll leave."

"I hope you're not keeping anything from me, Detective Martin."

"You've been following me, you should know."

Stoner shook his head. "No one in my organization is following you."

"But you were following Jenny."

"It was only temporary. We just had to make certain arrangements with the owner of whatever restaurant you were dining at. Meantime, I might want to see you again, and you will come."

Barry took Jenny's arm and they left the restaurant. Jenny's pace was fast. Barry stopped and gave her a hug. "It's okay, it's all over. You're shaking."

"I thought men like that existed only in the movies. Doesn't he scare you?"

"All the time. But I know how far I can push him and stay alive. Come on, we'll walk for a while." Barry condemned himself for subjecting Jenny to such an ordeal. It wasn't necessary. Nobody should have to meet people like Stoner. Barry gave Jenny's hand an extra squeeze. He enjoyed being with her, but that episode proved once again that a cop's life is best left to the unmarried. His thoughts rambled to Dave, whose family had to suffer as only a cop did. It's not fair to the family.

"Why such deep thoughts?" Jenny asked picking up on the silence. "Is somebody behind us?"

"No, we're safe. I'm having second thoughts about the meeting. I shouldn't have involved you. It was dumb."

"It wasn't that bad, Barry. I was scared, but I knew you wouldn't let anything happen to me, and I was right. By the way, I picked up on what Stoner said, that his men weren't following you."

"I could have sworn it was them. One of my informants told me that the syndicate wasn't having an all-out pursuit after the killers, so I got to wondering why. As Stoner admitted, it's bad for business when you can't protect your own people. The next logical step was to see what the police had, including my reports. Jesus, I don't know who the hell's following me."

"Paul told me you're a resourceful detective. I have confidence in you."

"You sound like my mother. Whatever I do is great. Even when I failed she was always sure there was a legitimate reason for it. When I was twelve years old I read about the Nobel Peace Prize. I was devastated when my name wasn't on the list. But what's even worse is that I actually threw the newspaper away so my mother wouldn't find out my name had been omitted. I even considered breaking the television so they couldn't watch the news, but I chickened out. My father would have killed me."

"You tell unusual stories, Barry."

"It helps if you've had a weird life. One day I'll tell you about the old lady who babysat for us when my folks went on vacation. You know what happens to a person's face when they can't find their false teeth for a week; their mouth becomes a suction cup. You ever seen eyes right above the upper lip? It's gruesome."

Barry halted, caressed Jenny's face and kissed her. "I'd like to go out with you again, Jenny, although I can't promise the same entertainment as tonight."

"Then I accept, although you must promise me more stories."

"I promise."

"I have to ask another favor. Paul and Mary are getting to be more like my parents—over-protective. Don't tell them about tonight's escapade."

"I had no intention of it. Come on, let's go inside."

Mary did not have to ask how their evening went. Jenny's radiant smile said it all. Anticipating everyone's request, Mary and Jenny brought out the already brewed coffee.

"Did you have a good time?" Paul asked Barry.

"We had a marvelous time." Paul's paperwork still cluttered the table. "What happened to your mystery?"

Joining Mary and Jenny in the livingroom for coffee, Paul answered, "It turned out not to be a mystery. Here's the list. The telephone numbers were all churches."

"Makes sense. It certainly covers most of the country, and each one in a major city. Well, you gave it a try, Paul."

"But Rhoades lied to me and it's not the reason you think, Barry." Paul divulged Barry's encounter with Rhoades and his theory concerning how Rhoades' sexual preference was the reason for the meeting in the loft. But Paul could not be swayed from his suspicions. More bantering followed until Barry got fed up with it.

Jenny escorted him to the hallway. She was fidgety.

"Barry, we both know how this date was arranged, and even though we've made plans to go out again, I don't want you to feel you have to." Her tone anticipated the worst.

"I know you're blind, but I didn't think you were that blind. I had a great time tonight; we both did, that's why we're going out again tomorrow night."

"I'd like that."

"Then it's settled. And before I forget, I owe you a second helping." Their arms encircled each other as their lips met. Neither one wanted to stop. Barry felt an ease he had never experienced before. No raw passion. He felt comfortable and Jenny felt good next to him. It was difficult saying goodnight.

Alone in his car, his thoughts lingered on that last kiss. Her lips were so smooth and soft, they were made for gentleness. I enjoyed that kiss more than going to bed with Ann. That's foolish, it was only a lousy kiss. No, it wasn't lousy, it was anything but lousy. What's happening to me? He checked the rearview mirror as he drove away. No sedan tonight. I wonder why.

Jenny eased into slumber, a satisfied glow swept over her face as she dreamt about Barry. Her sleep deepened, the glow drained and was replaced by rigidity and distortion, the dream succumbing to the nightmare of the accident. Beads of perspiration dripped across her forehead. She twisted to and fro. Her fingers clutched the sheets as if she were holding on to a ledge while some force exerted from below. Her body quaked. Her right leg kicked out again and again. "Nooo," she moaned, her nostrils flaring. "Watch out for the car! Jimmy! Jimmy!"

Mary rushed into the room and cradled Jenny in her arms. "It's okay, Jenny. You were having another nightmare. You're safe."

"Why won't it stop!" Jenny beseeched her, sobbing. "Why? Why?"

"Shhh, go back to sleep. I won't leave you. Go back to sleep."

5

Father Rhoades, casually dressed, entered the Park Lane hotel and went directly to Room 333. A camera slung about his neck added a touch of authenticity to his touristy appearance. As arranged, he knocked three times and announced, "It's Number Four."

The door opened and closed quickly. The same three men who had been at the loft were present. Rhoades took his seat commenting, "This is a much safer meeting place."

The Leader, Number One, agreed. "Any news about our eavesdropper at the loft?" His voice was demanding.

"I questioned the Bowery bum," Rhoades reported. "He saw nothing and remembered less. He couldn't even recall his own name."

"How unfortunate," scoffed the Leader, "but our plans will not be interrupted. My patience is wearing thin."

"Perhaps we should wait," cautioned Number Two,

his gray hair almost silver from the sunlight streaming through the window. "Our intruder at the loft was too agile in escaping; he was not a bum. I have a feeling one of us is being watched, and until we expose that person, we should cancel, or at least delay, our plans."

The Leader deferred to Number Three for his comments. Number Three straightened his thin gangling body, preparing to speak. "If we cancel our meetings then we'll never discover who the intruder was. The more meetings we hold the better the chance of catching him."

"And him catching us," added Number Two. "Can we take that chance?"

"We have no choice," replied Number Three. "We discover who it was and we kill him."

"Our attention should be focused on young agile people, someone in good physical condition who could run down five flights of stairs and more," the Leader re-emphasized.

Rhoades could think of only two people close to him who fit that description: Paul Tobin and Barry Martin. He immediately ruled out Martin; there was no reason he would follow Rhoades. Same goes for Tobin. He was curious about those telephone bills and checks, playing matchbook cover detective, but he's more meddlesome than harmful. Still, I'd better be careful of him. If anything goes wrong with our plans, I don't want it to be because of me.

"Are there any questions?" the Leader continued in his normal crescendo tone. "Then on to the next order of business. Number Two, your progress report."

The other two subordinates, having previously discussed the contents of the report, watched Number Two scroll the white hair of his sideburns between his thumb and forefinger as if any delay might miraculously change the facts, but it was an empty wish. One of them, although they didn't want to remember who, had suggested that the conclusions of the report be compromisingly altered, even overlooked to spare the Leader undue anguish. Perhaps a few months of intense work could amend this report, they argued, so why release the findings? Yet their overriding loyalty and obedience to the Leader, their respect for truth, and their absolute allegiance to the cause annulled all else. Everything and everybody was extraneous to the New Order. That was the word. It could be no other way.

Number Two began his oral report following a firm rap on the table by the Leader. "Certain divisions in our organization are reaching their goals on time while others—through nobody's fault—are lagging behind. This can easily be corrected given a little extra time and attention to details which were ignored due to lack of manpower in specific areas. My proposal is that we—"

The Leader held up his hand. "Your words, Number Two, are carefully chosen yet they say nothing. Which divisions are lagging?"

"Finances, Sir."

"I see," the Leader said, as Number Three, the budget director, mentally readied himself for his report. "And precisely how far behind schedule are we?"

"Six to eight months. A year at the outset. It's not that long a delay, Sir."

"Number Three. Your report!"

"Sir, our expenditures are out-pacing our incoming resources. The treasury now has less than four million dollars, whereas we had forecasted eight to ten million at this time. Between traveling, recruiting, and lack of private donations, not to mention the overhaul of our building which has already exceeded its original estimate, we simply cannot replenish the treasury as fast as we hoped. In regards to our other source of money, we must be careful, Sir. Any audit would devastate us."

"Number Four, can we cut recruitment?"

"No sir," Rhoades forcefully stated. "Granted their prices have increased, but all of our recruits are necessary. To eliminate some or stop recruiting altogether serves no purpose. If anything, it would hurt us in the future."

Leaning on his elbows, the Leader's shoulders rose while his head appeared to sink deeper into his neck. "No . . . no, no, no! I cannot do this by myself. I require your perfection, anything less is intolerable. Last night I was given the word again and I swore to obey it. I have contacted our brothers. Our internal arrangements are all but complete, and each day brings new converts. There is no more time for delay. Our final battle has now begun—there will be no mistakes." For no reason his fist relentlessly, uncontrollably pounded the table top. "The world can no longer wait. I can no longer wait. We continue as originally planned."

Number Two knew the Leader's statement concerning new converts was false from his recent telephone calls to the brothers. If anything the opposite was true. Yet he withheld the correction, for he was witnessing history repeat itself, and he was an integral part of it. The word had been given—the future was certain.

Number Three hesitantly motioned to be heard. He waited until permission was granted. "Next month we are scheduled for a full meeting; is that still on?"

"It is," replied the Leader. "And everyone will be present, no exceptions."

Rhoades raised his hand. "You haven't told us what this meeting will be about. There have been inquiries."

"You will all find out at once. That is all for now."

The three disciples stood, bowed, and took their leave. Alone, the Leader drew back the curtains and looked upon the man-made structures of Manhattan. His crippled mind envisioned the skyscrapers as Man's outstretched arms beseeching the Lord to help them in their hour of moral demise. I can help them, Lord, but not by myself. My disciples falter the closer we come to success. Give them strength, Oh Lord My Father. Allow them to feel Your Greatness and to know my Greatness so we may deliver the New Order to the world.

6

Dave swung his eyeballs upward and met Barry's scrutinizing leer. I'm fine," he volunteered to Barry. "I saw the shrink this morning. He okayed my going back to work."

That's ridiculous, Barry thought keeping his opinion to himself. It was late and the protestors had gone home, but during the day they were still here. Doesn't the psychiatrist know that? And as for Dave being better. . . . "You've been working on that report for over an hour and you haven't written one word yet. A cop can fool everyone but another cop. Take a leave of absence, Dave, you deserve it."

"My caseload's too big."

Barry squinted over the feeble excuse. "Why aren't you home, Dave?"

Dave's fingers played with a pencil until it splintered apart. "Goddamn reporters are swarming all over my house and my neighbor's houses," came his bitter statement through clenched teeth. "One reporter asked me if I'd killed any other black kids. That son-of-a-bitch! My wife won't leave the house and my kids aren't going to school. They got into a fight with some black kids. Nobody had to tell me what it was about." His face was masked in tragedy. "The shrink said once the media coverage dies down, things won't seem so bad." The whites of his eyes enlarged. "Ha, I wish I hated blacks, then maybe I wouldn't feel so bad. That's what some other cops have told me: Long as it wasn't a white boy you killed things will be all right. It's amazing, isn't it?" But it wasn't; not for self-preservation. Being black did make a difference. It had to, he tried to convince himself. They're not like other kids—like white kids. Stealing. The kid shouldn't have done it, should have known better. Black bastard! Dave covered his face. O God, he was only a kid! And his color didn't make a damn bit of difference."

Barry reached over and pried Dave's hands away from his face. "I'm almost through, Dave. Why don't you and I go for a beer? My treat. Better yet, we'll go to a topless bar."

"Nah, I gotta watch myself on the eleven o'clock news tonight. It's not every day I'm on television." His voice choked.

He resembled Father D'Angelo as he walked away. But it wasn't age suffocating his body, or even the shooting. It was the pressure his family was under that was really killing him. Dave's home life was crumbling and so was his career, Barry suspected. He and his family needed a long vacation. Barry dialed Dave's home number and got a busy signal. His wife probably had the receiver off the hook.

As Barry hung up, his phone rang. "Jenny. Oh, oh, I didn't realize it was so late. How about a late night snack? Pick you up in half an hour."

Barry stacked his paperwork into neat piles, threw

out the half-full cup of stale coffee, and was ready to leave when the phone rang again.

"Martin here."

"How are you tonight, Badge 5746?"

"Well, if it isn't the blond man. Isn't it past your bedtime?"

"Oh, Badge 5746, you're pissed off at me, not because of my sacrifices, but because you can't catch me. And you never will because God is on my side. He told me so Himself."

"What did God do, send you a singing telegram?"

"You shouldn't joke about it. My soul has been saved, even guaranteed, but yours, Badge 5746, yours will go straight to burning Hell. But that ain't why I called. Another sacrifice is about to take place. He's waiting at Lincoln Center." The line cut off.

Jeeze, he's setting up his own man. Before leaving, Barry contacted central dispatch to have the Lincoln Center area cordoned off and, if possible, to apprehend the suspect alive. But Barry had doubts about that. All the killer has to do is kill one innocent bystander and the police would be forced to shoot. A perfect location for a murder—and for a potential disaster.

The attendants at Lincoln Center swung the large glass doors open as the Philharmonic Symphony filled the halls with a final burst of music.

Elegantly dressed men and women began leaving. Their metered chatter reiterated what their ears had just heard. Hank, wearing his best grey suit, leaned against the bus stop eyeing the outpouring patrons. Methodically his mind rehearsed the plan one last time: Shoot, proceed at a quick pace down the street being careful not to run, keep head lowered, drop the gun into the sewer, turn right, sprint toward Joe and the car. Trial runs put the elapsed time at under thirty seconds.

Murder did not take long.

The target emerged. Hank crossed the street mixing with the crowd on the sidewalk. Purposely he bumped into the distinguished-looking gentleman.

"Please get out of my way," the man responded, letting go of his wife's arm. Hank didn't move. In one swift motion he pulled a gun from his pocket, shoved it into the man's stomach, and squeezed the trigger twice.

Screams assaulted the air. People dashed for cover, all but the dead man's wife; she stood in shock, frozen, her mind rejecting the image of her husband's slain body.

Hank, trembling with success, his instincts urging him to run, proceeded at a quick pace down his pre-determined escape route. Sirens! Hank's feet moved even faster. More sirens. The corner. Hank turned right. No car. No Ricart. That bastard! Het set me up! Hank's mind exploded with the need for revenge.

Police cars squealed toward him from all directions. Hank reversed direction and headed back to the crowd. Only one thing mattered to Hank; kill Ricart.

"Stop or I'll shoot!" warned a cop.

Hank whirled and fired. Bystanders crouched and crawled along the sidewalk, one man covering his wife and daughter with his own body. Hank fired again. The cop grabbed his shoulder in agony and collapsed to the pavement. Hank jumped into a doorway where a man and woman had taken refuge. A hostage. He yanked the woman towards him. "Leave her alone, you bastard," shrieked her husband. Hank aimed at the husband's chest and fired.

"No!" the wife cried hysterically, her hands flailing in the air.

Hank let her fall back into the corner, then sprinted toward a car. Police called out, warning him that he was surrounded, but Hank knew they couldn't shoot for fear of hitting innocent people.

Hank opened a car door but somebody forced it shut from the other side. With all his strength, he flung the car door open and came face to face with a young girl.

"Gimme the keys!" he said in desperation.

Fumbling, the girl searched her pocketbook.

"Hurry up!" Hank fired two more shots in opposite directions. "You're coming with me, lady. Find those fuck'n keys!"

Panic-stricken at the thought of going with a maniac, the girl tossed her pocketbook out the driver's window.

Erupting rage overcame Hank as two bullets from his gun shattered the girl's head. A shot whizzed by Hank's head from the side. He jumped up toward a better hiding place when a flurry of shots rang out, each bullet blasting into him. Hank was dead before he hit the ground.

Police swiftly roped off the area and aided the injured as spectators eerily made their way around the bloodshed.

A rookie cop stood over Hank's body. "Jesus Christ! One . . . two . . . three . . . Shit, twelve holes in him." He gazed around at the other strewn bodies. "My God!"

More sirens, more ambulances, more police arrived. Black bags were unfolded and laid next to the casualties. Chalk marks littered the sidewalk. Medics rushed from one victim to another.

Barry wedged his way through the crowd and blockade. It reminded him of a war zone. "Which person was shot first and who did the shooting?" he asked the rookie cop who was still in a state of shock. He repeated the question. Barry followed the hand signal. Doc was examining one of the corpses. "Who is it?" Barry asked.

"Charles Fino, syndicate owned and first victim."
Doc completed filling out the bag tag before okaying the
body to be removed. He stood and brushed some dirt
off his pant legs. "Some fuck'n mess. I had Mrs. Fino
taken to the hospital, severe shock. That's the alleged
suspect over there. Young, well-dressed, well-groomed;
he looks more like a victim. All these bodies—the
media's going to go crazy with this. The larger the body
count the more attention there is. Bizarre, isn't it?"

"Doc, do me a favor, handle the autopsy on the
suspect yourself. He's my only lead so let's make him
talk. Either from his insides or from on him, get me
something.

"Will do." Doc suddenly covered his mouth. "Your
friend's here."

Captain Adams stormed into the scene. "What the
hell happened here?" he asked Barry and Doc. Then,
yelling across the way he ordered, "Hey, keep those
reporters outta here; they'll get a statement later on."
He spat on the ground.

"I warned you about innocent bystanders," Barry
declared to the Captain while Doc quietly eased away
from the confrontation. "You didn't listen. And now
look!" his hand waving over the crime scene.

"Don't imply that this was my fault, Martin, 'cause it
wasn't. Nobody could have prevented this." He glanced
at the reporters who were pressuring some of the police
for details. "Hell, I'd better make a statement before
somebody says something they shouldn't." He turned
toward Barry. "I'm gonna tell them that, for reasons
unknown at this time, it appears that the dead suspect
simply went berserk. Meantime, I want these goddamn
Crossbearers, and I want them fast." He left in a huff.

Barry cursed the Captain under his breath as Doc
joined him on his way to the suspect's body. "Every

time you have words with the Captain, you look like you've been sucking lemons."

Barry halted and pointed to the chalk marks. "You've still here and the suspect's body isn't."

"I'm leaving, I'm leaving. Christ almighty, can't even take time out to breathe around here without getting chewed out."

Barry inspected the dead killer's personal belongings spread out on the hood of a police car. "Wallet, one mailbox key, one bent apartment key, a white enamel crucifix, two rings, and a handful of bullets." He opened the wallet. "Hmm, no money, no tokens, no credit cards, no pictures, no nothing. Just what I needed, a John Doe. Why the hell would somebody carry an empty wallet? And no car keys either. How was he planning to escape?"

Feeling obliged to answer Barry's thinking aloud, a uniformed officer shrugged. Barry ordered a few officers to make a check of the cars in the vicinity and see if anyone looked like they were waiting for someone.

Barry, still bothered by the empty wallet, re-examined it again, sliding his finger between the fabric lining and the leather. "Ah ha. I got something." He pulled out a crumpled library card that had been issued five years ago. "Henry Wynn. 137 Hudson Street. Isn't that a shitty neighborhood?" he asked a policeman who agreed. "Look at his suit. It doesn't fit this address, if he still lives there. Let's take a ride. He ushered two uniformed officers and a Forensic man to accompany him.

"Should I inform the Captain where we're going?" asked one of the officers.

"Fuck 'im!"

The Hudson Street address was an old decaying apartment house, now used as a single room occupancy place. The desk attendant, wearing a torn undershirt, continued wolfing down his pizza even after he saw the uniform and badges.

"Hank Wynn's apartment," said Barry.

"Ain't in."

"The number of his apartment."

The attendant gulped some beer, and belched. "Gotta warrant?"

"It's easy enough to get one."

"Guess you gotta wait, cop."

Barry, thanks to Adams, was in no mood for snide remarks. He drew out his pistol and gently laid it on the counter. The barrel faced the attendant. "The trigger of this gun fires with one pound of pressure. Example," Barry raised his fist in the air. "If I strike the counter top hard enough the gun will go off." His fist moved slightly.

"4D." The attendant tossed the key on the desk.

Barry handed the key to the two other policemen, then turned his attention back to the attendant, his fingers now caressing the gun. "Tell me about Wynn."

"A loner, didn't say much."

"Did he have a job?"

"If he did would he live here?"

"How did he pay the rent?"

"He did, that's all I care about."

"Any lady friends?"

"Hookers. Cheap ones."

"Any particular one?"

The attendant took a bite of pizza. Sauce and cheese dribbled from his mouth as he answered. "Some dirty bitch."

"Give me a name."

"Hey, what do I look like, a telephone book?"

Barry picked up the gun.

"Her name's Detroit."

"She still working this neighborhood?"

"Nah, got transferred to 42nd Street. If she does good there maybe they'll make her Queen of England. Ha!"

One of the officers ran halfway down the stairs and called Barry. "You're not going to believe this guy's apartment! It's weird!"

All stood in the doorway of the apartment. "Holy shit! I don't believe this. But I know who should see this." From the hallway phone Barry called Paul at the Church and told him to rush over to the address. During the wait, the Forensic expert examined everything.

Paul finally arrived. His eyes traveled around the room. "Sweet Jesus!"

Every inch of space was covered with pictures of Christ, the Virgin Mary, the Pope, various Saints, and printed prayers. Huge gold painted crosses lined the walls and ceiling. Crucifixes dangled on cords everywhere. Behind the bed was an enormous picture of the crucified Christ. There were four Bibles on a small dresser.

"Now you know why I called you."

"I've heard of people like this. Religion gone haywire. Who lives here?"

"Hank Wynn. At least he did. He just killed five people before he was killed. His original target was Charles Fino, another syndicate man. Have you ever heard the names before?"

"No." Paul continued to roam about the small room.

The Forensic man gave Barry the go-ahead to search the room.

Paul continued talking, unable to comprehend such madness. "How can people go so crazy? Is this what we do to people? God help us." He opened a Bible to a bookmark. "Listen to this, Barry," he said reading from the bookmark: " 'Peace and order are from God. Anything less is evil and must be eliminated from His universe. God's word is law and I am His interpreter.' It's signed Prescott Palmer, Founder and Holy Master of the Church of the Interpreter."

Barry examined it. On the back was the Church's address. "Well, I guess I know who I'm seeing tomorrow. It should be interesting. It also makes sense, using cult members—easy to manipulate them. The rest of the Crossbearers are probably cult members too. But which cult?"

"Can I go with you?" Paul asked. "I've heard of people like Palmer, but this is the first chance I've had to meet one of my so-called competitors. I'll stay out of your way."

"Not this time. Besides, I also have to visit Wynn's family out on Long Island. We ran Wynn's name through our computer; he has a list of offenses a mile long, and not minor ones either. I'm gonna stay here a while longer. Why don't you go home."

"You'll let me know how it goes with Palmer?"

Barry agreed. It was already past midnight. Before inspecting the room he called Jenny, canceling their date for that night. He was really looking forward to seeing her, but the job . . . always the job.

Across the street from Hank's address Joe, Carol, Doug and Roger watched the goings on. "I don't understand what went wrong," Carol lamented as she watched the police got about their business. "Hank planned it so well. He should have gotten away."

Doug, clutching his white enamel cross, offered, "His time was up. God wanted Hank by his side."

"He's in God's hands," Roger concurred, his eyes cast upward. "Police were everywhere before Hank could even make it to the car."

Joe rubbed his fingers over Carol's neck and peered

at her breasts visible through her sheer blouse. There were no bruises on her and she did not reveal any of the conversation she had had with Hank. Joe had not even asked. He wanted to but he was afraid that the answer could have sentenced her to death, and he didn't want that. He needed somebody like her . . . like his mother. Somebody had to love him.

"Last week I had a revelation," Joe informed his friends. "God Himself spoke to me and told me that my enemies would die. From now on anyone who disobeys me will be punished. Hank was God's message to the three of you. I am the sole leader of this group now and forever."

"You can trust me," Doug said. "I'll never go against you, Joe. Never."

"Me neither," said Roger.

"And you, Carol? Am I the true leader or will God have to send us another message?"

Carol headed the threat. "I'll show you my obedience, Joe. I'll bring in new members for you, any way I can."

Roger lagged behind close to Joe as the group departed. "Did I do good, Joe? Did I?"

"Excellent." He placed a hundred dollar bill on Roger's palm.

"I'm your lieutenant too, eh, Joe?"

"Of course you are, Roger. You and Doug go get some ice cream now. I'll be at my apartment with Carol."

"Can we have Carol tonight? Can we?"

"We'll see," Joe said, knowing that he'd kill either one of them if they ever touched her—just the way he'd had Hank killed. Carol's mine and so are the Crossbearers.

7

Morning found Barry stuck in traffic heading toward Long Island to meet Hank Wynn's parents. He was already twenty minutes late thanks to Doc's autopsy and forensic reports. According to the reports, all identifiable foreign particles found on the decedent's clothes were traceable back to his apartment or surrounding neighborhood. Internally, partially digested food found in his stomach—pizza with anchovy and mushrooms—meant he had eaten at one of a thousand pizza joints in the city shortly before the shooting spree. As for the .22 caliber pistol, the registration number had been filed off and then acid applied to it, leaving nothing to trace. Fingerprints all belonged to Wynn.

Doc, cranky from his all-night scientific probing, was disappointed that nothing substantial had been found. For Barry however, the total absense of traceable evidence underscored one thing: the clumsy emotion and blatant bragging of the telephone caller seemed contrary to the meticulous staging of the killings and to

Wynn's clueless corpse, as if there had been anticipation of being caught. Barry's conclusion: the caller was not the leader of the Crossbearers. But if not him, then who? This case was becoming very annoying.

A few turns off the Long Island Expressway brought Barry into suburbia and his destination. The Wynns' house, on what Barry estimated to be half an acre, was a contemporary design surrounded by similar homes. It appeared that money was not a problem for this family.

The front door opened before Barry reached the house. The parents stood waiting, both with puffy red eyes. Mr. Wynn thoroughly studied Barry's credentials, explaining that the press had been badgering them for a story and he was taking no chances. Entering the drawing room, Barry noticed the way they clung to each other, and in Barry's line of work such clinging usually signified a tragedy.

The room was elegant: a thick wall housing an enormous fireplace, a built-in bar, modern furniture, and glass doors opening onto a ground level patio leading to a swimming pool. Barry estimated the couple to be in their late fifties, although he wasn't sure if it was age or stress. Barry had never found any diplomatic technique to interview parents who had just lost an offspring, and under these conditions it was even worse.

Barry extended a courteous apology before tackling the subject head on. It was the quickest way. "Your son belonged to a group called The Church of the Interpreter, headed by a Prescott Palmer. Did he ever mention this Church to either of you?"

The father answered as his wife struggled for self control. "A few times. He told me he had made a lot of friends there, that he felt wanted."

"Last night I ran your son's name through the computer. He did not fare very well."

"We know. Kicked out of three colleges, arrested for

attempted rape and theft . . . Not a son to be proud of, but still we loved him and tried to help him."

"Henry was never convicted of rape," the mother stated defiantly, clinging to a counterfeit memory of her son.

Her husband furnished the truth. "The courts released him because the girl showered after she was assaulted, so there wasn't any evidence. But we knew Hank had done it. In fact, he confessed to us. His lawyer ordered us to keep quiet. We did, but we shouldn't have. Anyway, after that he moved into Manhattan and he'd call every few weeks."

"Did you send him money?"

"No. Money would keep him out of jail but I wanted him in jail before he hurt anyone else. I never want to make a decision like that again."

"Did he ever mention his friends by name?"

"Only one. Joe. I don't know his last name."

"Any girlfriends?"

"Prostitutes. No other girls would go out with him."

"When did he become so religious?"

The mother excused herself as the reality of her son's existence began to accumulate.

"After he moved into the city. Hank wasn't religious but his friends were, so he went along with them. He was always treating them, spending money on them. That was the only way he could sustain a friendship."

"For someone who didn't work, he spent a lot of money. I inspected his apartment and found no drugs." Barry leaned forward. "Mr. Wynn, who sent him money?"

Mr. Wynn gave a quick look toward the hallway. His voice lowered. "His mother. No matter what Hank did, he was still her son. I tried to have him committed once, but there was no available room for him. The doctors even warned us he was prone to violence." Mr. Wynn's head bowed. "Every day I expected the phone to ring with the news that Hank had hurt somebody else. Thank God it's over."

"Mr. Wynn, can you tell me anything else about this guy Joe? Would you know if he had blond hair?"

"Hank only mentioned him in passing, and I never met him. My son did mention one thing concerning Joe: that they were of the same mold."

"What's that mean?"

"Violent. Very violent."

"I see. A final question, Mr. Wynn. Did your son ever mention a group called The Crossbearers?"

"Yes, yes, he did. That's the name of the group Joe is the leader of. Hank wanted to become a member so badly, but I never knew if he made it."

"He did. Thank you, Mr. Wynn, and I'm sorry I had to upset you and your wife."

"After what we saw on television last night, I expected somebody would be out to see us. Now all we have to do is try to live with it. We gave Hank a great deal of love and understanding and discipline, Detective Martin, but nothing we did helped him. How do you convince yourself that your own son was born bad and is better off dead? How do you do that?"

"By looking at what he has done." Barry left and headed back to the city and his rendevous with Prescott Palmer.

Paul and Father Rhoades entered the study at Father D'Angelo's request. "You're both here. And it's not even a holiday. I've received another telegram from the Vatican. Father Inness will arrive at the end of this week. His stay at our Church is indefinite. He will be in the room next to you, Paul." Father D'Angelo put the telegram down. "While this visitor is here, I think it most appropriate that you two spend more of your time *in* the

Church. And Paul, wear your clerical collar and hide your jeans and sneakers."

Father Rhoades sat down and scratched at the chair's upholstery like an angry cat. "It's obvious why Inness is coming here. To spy on us, all of us."

"What do you mean? asked Paul. "We haven't done anything wrong."

"Not us," Rhoades pointed to Paul and Father D'Angelo. "All priests in the United States. It's because of that report."

"Another report? What did this one allege?"

Father D'Angelo answered Paul. "Over the past eight years the Vatican has declared that the churches of the United States are on the verge of collapse."

"That's right. And this visitor wants to see how close we are."

"Is the report accurate?" Paul asked.

"There is no reason to lie. Even our parish membership has declined over the years. But our Lord will not foresake us, Paul, and their report fails to mention that."

Father Rhoades jumped up and raised his hands as if imploring Heaven to listen to his indictment of his two fellow priests. "You two are the cause of our dilemma and you don't even realize it." He directed the next remark at Paul. "You were unaware that the report even existed, and," pointing to Father D'Angelo, "your solution is to pray. This church *is* in collapse. We're fighting for our survival! Can't you see that!"

"You're over-reacting, Father Rhoades," Paul said trying to calm him down. "Reports always stress the negative, it's almost inherent in the writing of them. Religion moves through cycles. In a few years the church will bounce back to full strength. It always has."

Father D'Angelo added, "God will not allow His church to die, Father Rhoades."

"Neither of you can see the truth. No one can but me

and . . . Ah, what's the use of talking?" He left in disgust.

"Wow, I think Rhoades has been sniffing too much incense. He's beginning to believe his own propaganda," said Paul.

"He is a tormented man, Paul. May God have mercy on his soul." Father D'Angelo looked at Paul. "You have something to tell me?"

"Are my expressions that revealing, or are you psychic?"

The elder priest answered with a smile.

"I made an appointment with Cardinal Alden," Paul said, "to see if I could change his mind regarding your retirement."

"You made three appointments," Father D'Angelo corrected. "I am not without my sources, Paul."

"Obviously. Then you know that all three appointments were cancelled by the Cardinal. I get the feeling he's avoiding me."

"The Cardinal's a very busy man, Paul. This is a large diocese with many problems."

"That's bull. He just doesn't want to see me and I don't know why. What else have your sources told you?"

"Nothing."

"I've been hearing rumors. Quite a few prelates are retiring lately."

"Age."

"Then you have heard. Is it true?"

"Old age and ill health accompanies these positions, Paul."

"Rumor has it that their successors will be younger, in their thirties and forties. That's unusual."

"You disapprove?"

"I look at Rhoades who's young, and you who are old. That's my answer. Can you imagine Rhoades as a Cardinal, or higher? What's left of the Catholic parish would thin out even more. And what if there were others like him? No, God's infinite wisdom wouldn't allow for two mistakes, would He? Would he?"

Clustered among a row of small neighborhood stores was an unassuming building with a sign above the door that read: Church of the Interpreter. Barry entered a small room which led to a more spacious one with rows of folding chairs facing a pulpit. The interior was dreary except for a huge white enamel cross hanging behind the pulpit.

All other hangings were enlarged photographs of Prescott Palmer. Bingo! Finally a lead, Barry thought, with a touch of self-congratulation on finding something the computer couldn't.

A young girl, neatly dressed yet far from stylish, approached Barry. Her hands were clasped in prayer position, as were the others who milled about. And there was no talking between the people. Barry corrected himself, there was a murmur, but without depth of feeling, almost artificial. On one observation he was dead right though: there was no laughter. A lot of smiles and grins, but no laughter. This girl, like the rest, wore a contented expression that never changed as she spoke. "Welcome to the Church of the Interpreter. Have you come to meet God's interpreter to find peace of mind?"

"Among other things." The white enamel cross around the girl's neck was identical with the one Wynn had been wearing. They were all wearing them.

"You must wait until the Master's door opens; that means his meditation is over."

"How long will that be?"

"Probably another few minutes. Would you like to sit down? My name is Linda. I am one of the Master's disciples. You may ask me questions if you wish; the

Church is for everyone."

"What's your last name, Linda?"

"Last names, like all names, are meaningless. You may call me Linda."

"Okay, Linda. How long have you been with Mr. Palmer?"

"My life began when I met the Master. I have therefore been with him for my entire life."

"And your parents, do they know where you are?"

"If they loved me they would have found me by now."

"Did you tell them where you were going?"

Linda turned up her nose. "What would that matter?"

Her answer signalled it was her first run from home. Barry wanted to convince her to call home before being lost to the streets. "Living with parents is often an ordeal," he began. "Don't look at me like that. I was much younger when I was born." A genuine smile came to her face. "I ran away a few times. At first it was thrilling and exciting, but after a few weeks it got scary. I can't remember why, maybe it was an anniversary, a birthday, or a holiday, but I called home. Their voices sounded so comforting."

"Not my parents. They were always yelling and screaming at me."

"Maybe they had reason to." She was weakening, but there wasn't enough time to work on her, especially here with all these followers watching. "I believe what you're saying, Linda, but you still have real parents, and they're probably very worried about you."

"I belong to the Master. I am the Master's child. I need no others."

"Do you have any money, Linda?"

"Our Master says money is sinful. And he is righteous enough to safeguard us from it."

"In other words, you gave him your money." Barry reached into his pocket and handed Linda a five dollar bill and his card. "The money is to call your parents and to come to me if you need help."

"I would never leave the Master," she said loud enough for some eavesdroppers to hear. She handed the money and card back to Barry, but he refused to take them.

"Linda, how old are you?"

"Eighteen."

"And you love your Master?"

"Of course."

"How do you show your love to him? Do you sleep with him?"

Linda's face twitched at the question.

"You haven't answered my question, Linda. Do you sleep with him?"

Linda grasped her cross and muttered a prayer. Her body weaved back and forth. "You are a sinner come to test me, but I will not fail. My Master is my life; my life is my Master's."

Linda's intense denial brought Joe Ricart into the room. He froze on seeing the owner of Badge 5746 standing before him. In a controlled voice he asked, "May I help you, sir?"

"I've come to see Palmer." Barry noticed the same kind of white enamel cross around the man's neck. "May I know your name?"

"Names are unimportant here," Joe said as he gave Linda a comforting smile. "Why did you upset Linda?"

"I didn't mean to. I'm sorry, I forgot your name . . ."

Joe glanced into the other room. "The Master's door is open. You may go in now," Joe said to Barry before leading Linda up the staircase.

Barry knew one thing from his conversation with Linda: he already detested Palmer, that self-proclaimed interpreter of God.

Sitting on what looked like a throne was Prescott Palmer. He was in his forties with dyed black hair that curled to a point above his forehead. He looked like a middle-aged groupie. Palmer's obviously tailor-made clothes fit him perfectly. Everything about him looked impressive, except for his excessively large ears which stuck out from beneath his hair. Dumbo, Barry mocked.

Barry showed Palmer his badge and sat in a chair facing him.

"Police? In my house of worship your earthly authority is not recognized," stated Palmer with choreographed hand gestures. "My temple is sacred. No one violates it."

"I wouldn't want to do that," responded Barry, unlatching his handcuffs and letting them swing on one finger. "To avoid the problem you will accompany me to police headquarters where my authority *is* recognized." He stood up. "Shall we go?"

Palmer momentarily hesitated before motioning Barry to retake his seat. "Ask your questions."

"Hank Wynn was a member of your Church. Last night he murdered five people."

"I have heard about that and I prayed for all the victims' souls. But I hope that his individual actions do not reflect upon my Church. That would be a grave injustice. You see, the members of my Church seek to comprehend each word of the Bible, and in so doing we may glimpse into the wonderment of God's ominipotent mind. It is truly the way to be one with God."

"Very nice, but back to Hank Wynn. How long was he a member here?"

"Approximately a year. He was spiritually depleted upon his arrival, so I personally instructed him through God's words, but alas, I was unsuccessful."

"May I have the names of his friends?"

"I am only concerned with people's eternal souls, not with their mundane names. Whatever a person is or may have been, I can turn his soul around and point it in Heaven's direction. That is my only concern."

"Did Hank ever hang around with a blond man of average build, first name Joe?"

"More earthly description of which I have no concern."

Palmer was beginning to grate on Barry's nerves. "I want a list of all your members. I can get a court order."

"It will be of no use. I keep no written list of my members, their souls are my only concern." Hands clasped, he stood up. "Will that be all?"

Barry stepped to Palmer's side. "You have a disciple named Linda. If I hear that you've laid a finger on her I'll come back here and send your soul to eternal Hell—prematurely."

The door slammed behind Barry. Palmer had turned out to be a less than prime suspect. His Church meant too much to him to be involved in murder, although Barry isn't that sure about involvement in sex. Palmer was too good an actor. What would be Palmer's motive? Barry was more concerned with trying to save Linda.

That night Barry had another date with Jenny. For convenience sake they met at Mary's apartment. Paul was there too, telling them about their forthcoming Vatican visitor and how Rhoades was so distressed by it. Barry figured the visit could be related to Rhoades' sexual activities, but he kept his opinion to himself.

Paul ended his tale of woe with an inquiry about Prescott Palmer. It wasn't until Barry mentioned Linda's desperate situation that Paul's ears prickled to attention. A young displaced runaway in the throes of being swallowed up by a religious cult leader. And God only knew what they'd do to her, mentally and physically.

She needed saving and Paul needed someone to save. Immediately his mind began scheming on ways to infiltrate the cult to rescue her. So engrossed was he in thought that he didn't hear Barry and Jenny leave. Not until Mary nudged him into conversation did Linda slip to the back of his mind.

Barry and Jenny drove toward a restaurant of Barry's choice. "I'm sorry about last night, Jenny. Emergencies are the rule in police work, but at least it's time and a half in my paycheck."

"Mary and I listened to the television report. All those dead people. And judging from Mary's gasps the pictures must have been more grisly than the reporters' descriptions. I didn't mind missing that part. But it still made me sick. I guess it doesn't bother you anymore, does it?"

"Yes and no. Yes, I don't like to see people killed; no, I can't afford to mourn every victim. Curiously though, and maybe this just occurs with cops, I don't know, I've found myself more concerned with the murderer than with the victim. Maybe that's the impetus that makes us want to catch him quicker. Does that make sense to you? I don't want you to think that I'm a monster without feelings."

"I'd never think that. And I guess police have to view death differently . . . as a doctor does."

Jenny's statement severed Barry's built-up prejudices like an ax. She was agreeing with him, or at least understanding him. No woman had ever done that before. Violence, they always contended, was violence and they wanted no part of it. *Have I misjudged Jenny?*

Jenny turned about in the front seat and faced Barry. "When you're investigating a case, are you ever afraid?"

"Afraid of what?"

"Death."

"No, not death, I can live with that. But being

crippled . . . severely crippled . . . There was a patrolman who was shot in the spine, leaving him totally paralyzed below the neck. I saw him some months after the accident. There were always visitors at the house, or should I say people making condolence calls. Only the dead person was still alive and sitting with them. You could tell from the patrolman's eyes, the way he operated them, narrowing or expanding his pupils, blinking his eyelids, that he understood everything that was being said and how utterly phony and awkward the conversations were. But through it all, I saw his eyes pleading, begging for death. I don't know how I would have accomplished it, but I never would have lived like that for that long. He didn't want to."

"There are times when death is more appealing than life," Jenny hauntingly admitted. "Lying in the hospital bed after the accident I felt that the Jennifer Tobin I had known had died, and that some freakish unknown stranger had trespassed into my life. And I hated her. Death seemed the only way I could become myself again—a sort of transfiguration. It would have been so easy with all those drugs around."

"Why didn't you?" Barry asked flat out.

"I lied to myself. Always in the back of my mind was hope that my blindness wasn't permanent, or if it was, that medical science would find a way to reverse it, and all I had to do was hang on and wait for that day." Jenny expelled a heavy sigh. "I no longer wait for that day."

Barry noted her avoidance of the word "suicide." There was one more question he needed to ask; and it was necessary because he loved her. "Do you ever think about suicide anymore?"

Silence. Jenny turned her back to Barry as if by not seeing her face the words would not be hers. "During the day I'm kept busy remaking my world so it's not bad. But at night, alone, abandoned, enduring a life I didn't choose and that no one would want, I wonder if it's worth the effort. It's not that I want to die, not anymore, it's that I'm so tired from living; of always having to overcome something. I feel as though I'm constantly training for a race but I'm not allowed to compete to see if I could win. I wouldn't mind losing, Barry, but I can't even qualify."

Steering with his left hand, Barry reached over with his right hand and drew Jenny closer to him, her head nestled against his shoulder. The pain and suffering she felt, he now felt. He understood her loneliness and desperation, and he wanted to protect and care for her forever. He wanted to help her fight.

Suddenly the moment was broken when Barry spotted the Oldsmobile sedan in the rearview mirror. He pushed Jenny back to the passenger's side.

"You've got that strange quiet again, Barry," Jenny said quickly composing herself. "That means trouble. What is it? And don't tell me it's nothing."

"It's the Olds sedan, they're tailing us. If I could just get a look at who's inside. One lousy look! I've got an idea." If Jenny could have seen his devious smile she might have guessed his wild scheme involved her. "Jenny, we're gonna switch places. You're going to drive the car half a block while I jump out and backtrack."

"Yeah, sure! Are you mad?"

"I'm serious."

"And I'm blind!"

"So are half the drivers in Manhattan." Staying in the right hand lane Barry slowed the car. "When I stop the car, move to the driver's side. You're going to drive fifty yards, stop, shut of the engine, and snap the warning lights on." He guided her hand to the steering wheel. "Are you ready?"

"What about pedestrians?"

"They're used to it. Let's switch." With difficulty,

they maneuvered over each other. "Okay, go ahead slowly. Go straight, straight. You're doing fine."

"I can't believe I'm doing this."

"Don't talk, just drive. Okay, stop!"

She slammed the brakes on, rocking the car. Barry, hunched over, jumped out, and, maintaining a half-erect position, waddled toward the Oldsmobile. He mainly wanted to see the passenger, reasoning that the man in charge would not be driving. He was three cars away. The Oldsmobile squirmed out of the lane. They'd spotted him. Horns honked. A green light. Barry held his hands up to stop the traffic, as he darted between the cars. One car's length away. For an instant, before the unwitting stranger ducked and the car swerved away, Barry caught a glimpse of a man with a pronounced cleft lip.

Across the street, horns were blaring and people were leaning out their windows, cursing at the stalled car. Barry sprinted back to his car, hurriedly pushed Jenny to her seat beside him, and turned down a side street.

"You were great, Jenny. I knew you could do it."

"I didn't run over anybody?"

"Not a one."

"Only because the pedestrians are fast in the city."

Barry impulsively leaned over and kissed her. The more he was with her the more he didn't want to leave her. "We must celebrate your driving lesson. How about picking up a pizza and beer and eating at my apartment?"

"Do I have to drive?" she laughed as Barry joined her laughter. But she was still frightened. Being alone with Barry was worse than driving. It had been a long time since she had been alone with a man in his apartment, and never before with Barry. Fool, she reprimanded herself. I'm blind. All he wants is a quiet dinner, not me. At least I'm the right person to have a quiet dinner with.

Barry flicked on the apartment lights and led Jenny to the leather couch. At her request, Barry described his two-bedroom apartment. Fine art work decorated the walls and coordinated with his modern furniture. It was a comfortable apartment, affordable because it was rent controlled. Unfortunately some of the tenants were pressing to convert the building to a cooperative, and Barry wasn't certain if he could afford that. "I really dread losing this place. My accountant thinks buying it would be a wise investment, but I'm the one who has to pay for it. I hate talking to people who can afford things, it's depressing as hell."

"Ask for a raise," Jenny said naively.

"Ha! A public employee getting a raise during an inflationary period! No chance unless I get a promotion, and that seems unlikely."

Reaching for another slice of pizza, Jenny knocked her shin against the glass coffee table in front of the couch. "I'm sorry."

"You apologize too much. Why don't you get a Seeing Eye dog? It would help, wouldn't it?"

"I'd love to get one, but it wouldn't be fair to Mary." As she spoke she felt the length and breadth of the table to avoid the mishap again. "Mary's a marvelous friend, but she doesn't like animals inside. Besides, I've learned to tolerate more pain over the past year. I'll stick with the cane." Her fingers touched two metal frames on the table. "Family pictures?"

"My parents' picture is on the right, and the other is my sister and her family. They have two boys and live in California. Her husband is an astronomer. To this day I can't figure out how he makes a living. All he does is gaze at the stars. I did that when I was a young kid, and they used to call me a daydreamer."

"Have you ever thought about moving out there?"

"My sister has suggested it to me but I have a distaste for being on ground that moves."

"So you stay in Manhattan with all the noise and dirt and crime. At least you have a choice. Me, I'm relegated to the Institute. Who else would hire a blind person?"

"I don't buy that."

Jenny rested her head against the back of the couch. "After college I took a two-week retreat to the beach all by myself. The house was situated on a hill, and at night I'd relax on the terrace, looking into the darkness and listening to the water. No people, no cars, no noise, just the water. And I thought, this is the place to live." She sat up straight. "If I were in that house now I'd be scared to death. I need the noise of people, it's my security blanket."

"Would you be afraid if I were in that house with you?"

"No."

"I was hoping you'd say that." Barry stroked her cheek. "I've known you for over a year, yet it's only the past few weeks that I've known you as a woman. A beautiful woman." They kissed. "You're blushing."

"I know." Jenny pressed her palms against her cheeks. "I can feel it."

The next kiss was passionate. Barry's hands caressed Jenny's body and she responded. Barry picked her up, carried her into the bedroom, and laid her down on the bed. Jenny removed her shaded glasses. Barry's hands continued to roam. She tensed.

"I'm not going to force you, Jenny. Say no and I'll stop."

"I'm frightened. But I don't want you to stop, Barry."

Lingering kisses and gentle caressing followed as Barry's nimble fingers undid the buttons and belt. Jenny's

173

hands fumbled. Finally their naked bodies pressed against each other. Jenny's both swayed under Barry's touch and shivered as his tongue kissed and explored. Barry was rock-hard and ready. Like that, he would usually plow into his woman. But not this time, not with Jenny. He moved slowly, carefully, adorning her body with kisses. For the first time in his life, he was getting pleasure by giving pleasure to someone else.

Jenny reached out and pulled him onto her. He eased himself into her, stopping when she winced. He didn't want to hurt her. Again he pushed forward. Jenny's legs opened more, her hands firm on his back as their rhythm synchronized. Their lips met, then parted. Barry began to shudder but he resisted thrusting hard. Jenny smothered his mouth and neck with kisses as her own bodily movements climaxed.

"You okay?" Barry asked out of breath. "I didn't hurt you, did I?"

"No, but I was too tense. I'm sorry I spoiled it for you."

"Apologizing again when you didn't do anything of the kind." Barry rolled her on top of him. With the light on he could see the faint scars around her eyes. "You don't know how much I enjoyed it, and I'm not saying that just to say it."

Jenny stretched her body over his and held on tight as if the dream would be over soon.

Barry desperately wanted to tell her how he felt but he couldn't. The relationship, his feelings toward her . . . everything had progressed too fast. It was out of control. I have to break this relationship, he thought. She snuggled closer to him. I love having her next to me. Do I take the chance? He switched off the table lamp.

With their arms wrapped around each other they fell asleep, dreaming their own dreams. But Jenny's contented slumber shattered and surrendered to the violence of the past. Her sleeping body twisted free from Barry's arms, waking him. He switched on the lamp. Perspiration covered Jenny's forehead. Her irregular movements became aggressive. He controlled himself so as not to waken her. Her hands flailed. He'd heard about her nightmares and he wanted to see her through one. Suddenly her body was overcome by a jerking spasm as she cried aloud, "Jimmy, look out! Look out!" Her head ducked as her body momentarily curled into a fetal position before twisting out in all directions. Her fingers picked at her left cheek as her slurred mumbling became understandable. "Wire! On his face!" she screamed. Her hands moved to the sheets, clawing at them and then, just as quickly, moved to cover her eyes. Her breathing deepened. Her body became limp as her spasm subsided into a gentle rocking motion. It was over.

Barry pulled the covers over her and switched the light off. He had personally never experienced nightmares. It was as if Jenny was possessed by the car accident. But the wire? What did that mean? And on whose face? It didn't make sense. She was probably remembering things out of context. Or maybe not. First chance he'd go over the police report of the accident. Whatever you're trying to remember, Jenny, I'll help you, he promised her.

Ten a.m. The Vatican visitor was arriving late this afternoon. That still leaves me plenty of time, Paul estimated, foregoing shaving and dressing in his oldest jeans, sweatshirt, and sneakers. He took a cab to Prescott Palmer's Church of the Interpreter. He had already made two brief appearances at the church and had met Linda and some of the others. Strangely enough, he had not yet met Palmer, and Paul decided to keep it that way, although he would have loved a one-on-one dialogue with this man. But his mission was to rescue Linda from the grip of this cult.

Another surprise upon entering the church was the ease with which he had been accepted by everyone. No questions about why he was there, where he came from, what he did. Palmer had made it too easy for lost souls to get caught up in his cult.

Paul entered the Church of the Interpreter and found Linda engaged in a small group discussion on how wise and godly a man the Master was. Paul accepted the invitation to join them and purposely sat next to Linda. For almost an hour he listened to the laurels heaped upon the Master. The adjectives were the same, the monotone voices were the same; it was redundantly boring yet terrifying. Their individualities had been stripped away, and all that was left was Palmer's dictates. Names of other religious and political leaders came to Paul's mind. This was how they all started; that was the terrifying part.

Palmer's door opened and the group discussion ended as a line formed outside his private chamber. "May I speak to you for a minute, Linda?" Paul asked, leading her to the back row of chairs. "We don't know each other very well, but I feel as though I can talk to you . . . that you'll understand."

"I'll help you any way I can," she said with a genuine spark of concern.

For effect, Paul spoke in a remorseful tone. "At seventeen my wife and I eloped, and a year later we had a baby girl. We were so young, so naive. All we did was yell and scream at each other until, over the years, it became our natural way of communicating. We didn't realize the damage it had on our daughter until she ran away from home last month. I finally found her two days ago. She belongs to a Church like this. I tried to explain to her that our fighting had nothing to do with our love

176

for her, but she wouldn't listen. She even told me to come back. I don't know what to do."

Linda's hands covered her face as she struggled to fight back her emotions. Nobody was allowed to lose control in this place.

"I didn't mean to upset you, Linda. I'm just scared that I'll never see my little girl again. Every day my wife sits by the phone, and when it does ring she's afraid to answer it for fear it might be bad news. We love her so much and we want her home."

Linda ran her fingers over Barry's card and the money in her pants pocket. "Tell her what you told me and she'll go home with you. If you'll excuse me I have to make a telephone call."

I did it! Paul congratulated himself. Finally I feel like a priest!

A black limousine pulled up in front of Our Lady of the Shrine Church and Cardinal Alden got out with another priest. The stranger was in his early fifties, on the short side, and had a cleft lip that contorted his face. Cardinal Alden formally introduced the three parish priests to their Vatican guest, Father Inness. Across the street Paul spied a bunch of kids encircling Bobby. More drug selling. Father D'Angelo nudged Paul as their guest entered the church.

Father Inness paused every few feet to inspect and admire the church's interior beauty. With curiosity he inspected the electric candle machines and shook his head in bewilderment at the technological intrusion into the church.

"Strike one," Paul whispered to Father D'Angelo.

Father Inness leered at a drunk sprawled along one of the pews. "Strike two," Paul whispered. "Rhoades' attitude will be strike three. We don't stand a chance."

"Shhh," Father D'Angelo admonished as they took

their seats in the study and listened to Father Inness' rehearsed explanation of why he was here.

"I am on a six-month tour of the Churches in America." The Vatican visitor spoke slowly and with a distinctly Italian accent. "As you well know, the Church is caught in the struggle between faith and innovations, and we are losing. Priests are leaving the Church at a high rate for marriage; high and middle income parishioners have rejected faith in God for faith of money; and the young people are gravitating toward dangerous cults and drugs. At our last International Synod of Bishops, His Holiness asked us to recommit ourselves to the Church and its laws against contraception, abortion, and divorce."

Father D'Angelo glanced at Paul in reference to the visitor's last sentence.

Father Inness continued: "My task is to observe how American priests are attempting to obey His Holiness' commands."

Father D'Angelo motioned to be heard. "May I inquire why you chose this humble parish as one of your observation places?"

"All choices were made by computer."

"What specific conditions are you looking for?" asked Paul.

"There has been a sharp split between American and European churches regarding the way they view the function of the Church. Over the past few years at least three million Americans have been involved with so-called religious cults. There has also been a drastic decline enrollment at American seminaries. Indeed, I'm sure you are all aware of the report concerning the Church's declining influence in the United States. We want to know why. No doubt Cardinal Alden is familiar with this situation."

All eyes focused on Cardinal Alden, who was busy cleaning his eye glasses.

"Cardinal Alden," Father Inness repeated.

Rhoades tapped the Cardinal on the knee. He looked up, slipped his glasses back on, and apologized for his lack of attentiveness on the grounds that he was running behind his schedule. Rhoades helpfully reiterated the remarks their guest had made.

"Your statistics are, unfortunately, quite familiar to me," affirmed the Cardinal. "However, I might add that world-wide the Church's spiritual religion is being incorporated into so-called religious cults. It is therefore unjust to separate us from the rest of the world, Father Inness."

"There is one distinction," Paul added. "As Father Inness indicated, money is more popular than religion and we have fewer poor people in the United States than in European countries. The truth is that religion is a poor person's money, and to many money is salvation."

"God is within everyone," Father D'Angelo professed. "Some people simply forget He is there, but in time they will rediscover Him."

"And if they don't?" Rhoades snapped. "God is losing the fight against man's greed because man enjoys and profits more from the greed than he does from God. Maybe it's time someone helped God fight this evil."

Paul held up three fingers signalling strike three to Father D'Angelo.

Cardinal Alden interjected with, "I am sure God does not require our help on anything, Father Rhoades." He stood up and shook Father Inness' hand. "I am sure that my priests are open-minded enough to explore the many possibilities of adjustment and compromise. After all, we were all put on earth to do God's will. I foresee no problems." His gaze fell on Father

Rhoades. "But now I must excuse myself and attend to other duties. I will be in touch."

After the Cardinal had left, Father D'Angelo escorted their guest to his room, leaving Paul and Rhoades alone in the study. Paul wanted to hear more of Rhoades' helping hand for God.

"I'd still like to know what you meant about helping God fight man's evil, Father Rhoades. It's a unique theory, your New Order."

"You wouldn't understand."

"Try me."

"No."

"Why?"

"Because your belief in God is not strong enough."

"And yours is, eh? Well if you're that strong a person then why are you afraid to tell me your theory? You should be able to convince me."

"Everyone must bear his own cross. Yours is weakness. Mine is having to contend with people like you and Father D'Angelo."

He made a move toward the door but Paul blocked his path. "Father Rhoades, sometimes continuing to worry about the same problem can transform itself into a obsession. When that happens, professional help should be sought."

"You think I'm crazy? I'm not. I'm just a priest doing what must be done." He sidestepped Paul and left.

Paul stared at the small crucifix on the wall and asked it, "What is he doing in Your name?"

Barry read the police report covering Jenny's automobile accident. It wasn't very helpful. Apparently Jimmy had lost control of the car and smashed into three parked cars. His chest had been crushed by the impact of the steering wheel. Jenny had a mild concussion. If it hadn't been for the particles of flying glass that had ricocheted into her eyes, she would have been all but unhurt. Hmm, Jenny was apparently facing Jimmy in a squat or bent position because she didn't hit the passenger door or the dashboard.

Barry moved his chair away from his desk and pretended he was Jenny sitting in the car. He turned to his left, bent his head down, and crouched.

Dave watched the unusual antics. "I know you and the Captain are feuding, but that's no reason to hide behind your desk, especially when your back faces his office." Dave meant that as a joke, but his limp tone of voice eliminated the punch. Dark circles under his eyes made him appear sickly. From outside the chanting of Dave's name and slogan referring to police brutality echoed in the office. Dave strained not to look, but his stomach churned with hurt. "Go away! Go away!" The words had slipped out. He looked up to see other heads turn away. Barry looked directly at him. "Guess I made a fool of myself, ah?"

"No more than usual," Barry teased. "They have a right to be out there, you know." Although, for Dave's sake, he wished they weren't.

"Naturally. Everyone has rights up the kazzoo. Everyone but cops." Dave glanced toward the window. "I hope it pours."

Barry jumped up. "Can you imitate what I just did?" Maybe this will bring a gleam of life to his face. Barry pulled Dave's seat away from the desk. "On the count of three. One. Two. Three."

Dave ducked.

"Hold that position," Barry ordered. Dave had unconsciously brought his hands over his face for protection just the way that Jenny must have done. Barry's mind stalled a minute as he arranged events in sequence. An impending crash might cause a person to revert to that position, but it wasn't likely. Not enough time to react. Bracing for a crash would be the reaction. No, that's wrong. Jenny said she was ducking from the man with the wire on his face, not from the impending accident. Hmm, why would she duck from a man in a car beside her unless something was being aimed or thrown at her? Aimed. A gun? Why? And what's the significance of that wire?

"Can I get up now?" Dave groaned.

"Yeah. Thanks. I hope you didn't hurt your back or your wife will have my head."

"She's staying with her brother—temporarily. We had a small spat," Dave disclosed in answer to Barry's questioning look. "Want some coffee?"

"Dave, we have to talk. Name the time and the place and I'll meet you. For old time's sake."

"I'll think about it," he said walking away.

I wish he'd let me help him, Barry thought, before his career goes down the drain. I'll keep on bugging him until he agrees. Meantime, back to Jenny. Barry noted the location of the accident. Seventh Avenue and Forty-Second Street. Nothing around there in particular. Seventh Avenue heads downtown so they must have been coming from uptown or midtown. Shrewd deduction, he jibed at himself as he contacted the Records Division and had them find out whether any major crime had occurred on that day in that area. Even with his priority rush it would take a few days to get the information—a result of increased crime and fewer personnel.

Barry's phone rang. An undercover cop had a lead on the prostitute Detroit. It's about time, Barry thought. I'll tell Paul.

Paul sat in the confessional booth as he listened to the high squeaky voice of the boy repeating for the third time, "Forgive me, Father, for I have sinned."

Paul, when requested, held private confessions for the kids; somehow the anonymity afforded them courage to confess. Nobody sins at such a tender age, Paul thought, then said aloud, "There's nothing to be afraid of, my son. Tell me what you have done." He avoided the word sin.

"Father, I didn't mean it. I was reading a book and my hand was suddenly going up and down against my . . . against my, uhm, thing. All of a sudden there was a spurt . . ."

"Oh yes," Paul cut him short recognizing, what the boy had unintentionally done. "What you did is called masturbation, a self-stimulation of the sexual organs."

"A what?"

Paul searched his mental card catalogue for the slang terms. "You played with yourself. You beat off. Do you understand?"

"Yeah. I mean yes, Father." There was a pause. "I'm a pitcher for the Little League, Father. The next game I'm the starting pitcher. Uhm, will I be blind by then?"

Oh Lord! "No! Masturbation will not make you blind or give you pimples or grow hair on your hand, or condemn you to Hell. Masturbation is part of growing up; there's nothing wrong with it."

"Really?" The boy responded with enthusiasm. "Then I can do it some more?"

"Well, perhaps you should limit yourself."

"Limit? You mean there's a limit to the spurt? Oh God, how much have I used up?"

"No, no, there's no limit." There was an audible sigh from the boy and silent one from Paul. It was time for the truth. "You can do it as often as you want, but in *private*." Why don't parents teach their kids these things?

"Thank you very much, Father."

"Don't go yet. I have a question for you. Is Bobby

still selling drugs to you kids?"

Silence.

"Answer me."

"Yes, Father, he is. But I don't take drugs. Honest."

"What's he selling? And don't tell me just grass."

"Everything."

"LSD?"

"Yes."

"Pills?"

"Yes."

"Heroin? . . . Yes or no."

"Yes. And coke. Can I leave now, Father?"

"Go ahead." Paul listened against the confessional wall as he tried to think, of a new approach to reach those kids and convince them that drugs could ruin their lives. He often thought how he'd like to get his hands on all those celebrities who joked about their drug habits.

The adjoining confessional door opened and closed. "Paul, you in there? It's me, Barry."

"Just the person I wanted to see." His tone was abrupt. "Mary called. Jenny didn't come home last night. What the hell did you do to my little sister?"

"Nothing. Let's talk face to face, I'm getting claustrophobia." Once outside the booth, Barry said, "I never did like those confessionals. They make you feel guilty even if you haven't done anything wrong."

"My sister. What did you do to her?" His loud voice brought stares from some parishioners.

"Let's talk outside."

Paul took a deep breath and started again, waving an accusing finger at Barry. "She stayed at your place last night. Did you sleep with her? No, I don't want to know. I can't believe you took advantage of her like that. And I thought you were my friend."

"I am. And your sister is not the little girl you make her out to be. She's an attractive woman whom I find very lovely. You look surprised. Good Lord, Paul, do you really consider her helpless and hopeless?''

"I'm realistic!" he defended himself. "Jenny's blind and will be for the rest of her life. Oh, it's nice the way Jenny and Mary speak of independence and self assurance, but it's not the real world."

"And that is?" Barry pointed to the church. "I'm not going to argue with you, Paul, but if you want to see the real world I'll show it to you. I just got a lead on that prostitute, Detroit. Tonight we'll visit her. Be ready at 9:30."

"Where are we going?"

"To the real world, Paul. To hell and back."

What's that supposed to mean, Paul wondered as Barry drove off.

Paul glanced at his watch for the third time in as many minutes. 9:32. Barry drove up and off they went.

"You look nervous," Barry observed. "Relax, it's going to be a long night."

"I want to apologize for yelling at you today, Barry. I don't know why I did it."

"Maybe you feel guilty about Jenny being blind."

"Why do you say that? Did Father D'Angelo tell you something?"

"Don't get so defensive. It's just that your parents felt guilty about Jenny's accident, so I figured maybe you did too. Guess I was right."

"Unfortunately. I thought I had overcome the feeling but it sneaks through every now and then. You should have seen me eighteen months ago. Talk about a cross to bear . . . I simply have to remember that she's more of a woman than she is my sister. Now I know how parents feel when their children leave home."

"All *Fathers* do."

"That's a terrible pun, Barry. Ah, Broadway."

185

"Not quite. Forty-Second Street and Eighth Avenue, known to the professionals as the Minnesota Strip. Our destination." Barry parked in a gas station lot and waved to the owner.

"Paul, welcome to reality," Barry extended his arm toward Eighth Avenue. "It's nice and hot; they'll be strolling tonight." He gestured to a drunken black man sprawled on the sidewalk. "He's the one who gave me the tip; our best undercover cop. Would you believe he has a Ph.D. in Criminology? If only his parents could see him now!"

The drunk rolled toward them, his dirt-encrusted hand outstretched for money. Paul stepped back. Barry flipped a quarter into the bum's hand and whispered, "She still at the same place?"

"I don't know. Ever since we got word where she was, she hasn't been seen."

"Somebody got to her?"

"Haven't heard anything. Check the place out anyway, but be careful, it's slimy." His voice grew louder. "A lousy quarter! Give me some more money!"

"Dirtball!" Barry retorted walking away.

The dazzle of lights reminded Paul of an amusement park, only this one was for adults only. Each colorful neon sign signalled the message that sex was for sale: Nude! Explicit! Bizarre! In the flesh! Live! Raw!

"Stop gawking; you look like a tourist."

"I am. It's the first time I've ever been here." Paul tried to take in all the sights.

Mixed with the roving tourists were prostitutes hustling any male who looked like a potential customer, bargaining for their trade. They were all so casual about it, Paul noticed as he passed by one discussion in progress. The prostitute's eyelids were smeared with purple eye shadow that matched her lipstick and fingernail polish. Her revealing shorts and clinging jersey amply displayed her product. In the back-drop was a class of people who just hung out along the sidewalks.

Barry directed Paul's attention to a prostitute across the street. "The one in the green shorts. How old do you think she is?"

"Mid-twenties?"

"She was picked up two weeks ago. I saw her in the precinct up here. She's fifteen. Ran away from home a few months go . . . parents aren't eager to have her back."

Paul took a long hard look. Fifteen? A child. He couldn't believe it.

"Around here reality is a fantasy, the only way to survive," Barry commented putting his hand in his jacket pocket where his gun was. He slowed their pace. "You're about to meet our unwilling tour guide. The chunky one up ahead."

Paul focused on the girl. Hair so caked with spray that not even the breeze moved a single strand. Bright red lipstick and fingernail polish. Tight leopard shorts and a halter that showed her pendulous breasts. They were closer to her now and Paul found her singularly unattractive. Her eyes were glazed and bloodshot. The heavy make-up couldn't hide the furrows in her face. She looked more like a grotesque doll than a person.

"Betsy, Betsy, Betsy," Barry greeted her in a friendly tone. "How's business tonight?"

"Get off my ass. I'm waitin' fer my boyfriend; it's the only reason I'm hangin'."

"Sure, just like we came down here looking for Snow White."

"Well I'll be goddamned if she ain't playing across the street with the seven little perverts."

Paul chuckled.

"Who's he? A rookie cop?"

"Where's your man? I wanna make a deal."

" 'Bout what?"

"I don't talk to the help."

Betsy gestured to a baby blue Cadillac with the rear window molded in the shape of a heart. Paul and Barry walked over. The interior was covered with white fur. Paul wondered about the double antenna until he spotted the color television in the back seat.

A good-looking black man stepped out of the car. He was wearing a dark green suit, no tie, and a beret. Half a dozen gold chains hung around his neck. Paul couldn't help but notice the gold crucifix among the chains.

Barry and the pimp eyed each for a minute before the pimp said in a reserved voice, "Whatcha all doin' here, man? Ya didn't come to give Whip a bad time, did ya, man?"

"Friends don't hassle one another; you know that, Whip."

"Shee-it man. Didya hear that, woman? We'se friends now. Shee-it!" A strikingly beautiful black woman, sporting elegant clothes and expensive jewelry, climbed out of the car and draped an arm around Whip's shoulders. "My newest acquisition to the stable," Whip announced with pride. "She don't talk unless I tell her to. Ain't that right, woman?" Tilting her head back slightly as if she were striking a pose for the camera, she smiled. "Hey, man, who's yer silent partner?" asked Whip, pointing to Paul.

"Another friend," Barry answered.

"Shee-it, ya gotta lotta fuckin' friends. I got me a lot too."

"That's their problem."

Whip's jovial manner vanished. "Hey, I don't take no insults from nobody. Dig! Now why don'tcha just take Mr. Talkative there and go find some fresh young meat. Looks like he needs it."

Barry pushed his jacket pocket against Whip's crotch. Whip's startled expression conveyed that he felt the gun barrel. "On this street a pimp without a pump is unemployed. Isn't that right, Whip?"

Whip sucked in his lips. "Hey, that ain't no way to treat a friend. Whatchya want, man?"

"Detroit. The girl, not the city."

Whip motioned to his female companion to take a walk. "Detroit, like she's corporately owned. Know what I mean? Heavy trouble, man."

"Where do I find her?"

"Arms Hotel. But ya need a ticket, and you ain't got one."

Barry pointed to Betsy. "You'll loan me a ticket, won't you . . . friend?" He pushed his pocket even closer.

Whip glanced down at the bulge in the pocket, then summoned Betsy. "Get'em into the Arms Hotel," he ordered Betsy, who was not pleased at losing so much valuable time on such a warm night. The three stalked away when Whip yelled, "Only one favor per friend, man. Dig?"

Three blocks later Betsy turned the corner and stopped in front of a seedy looking building. Written on the door, in blue faded paint, was Arms Hotel. Betsy lifted the dented mail slot on the side and pressed a button. A buzzer rang, and Betsy opened the door. A putrid smell stung Paul's nostrils as he and Barry entered.

Long fluorescent lights lit the foyer. They proceeded up the narrow wooden staircase. Phone numbers and obscenities were scratched into the stairway wall. Paul scanned the alien surroundings. Dust and dirt covered everything but the well-traveled stairs. Paul could taste the musty smell mixed with the other smells, body smells. At the top of the stairs, in a corner, was a pile of beer cans, pint bottles, contraceptive wrappers, boxes, newspapers and torn clothes.

Paul tugged at Barry's sleeve and asked, "Are all whorehouses like this?"

"This is clean compared to some I've seen." Since entering, his eyes had been glued to their guide. And with good reason; you never trust a hooker. "But it's more than a house, Paul. You'll see."

Betsy hesitated as she took the last step. "What room do ya wanna try first?"

"The show," Barry answered knowingly.

Betsy opened the first door on the right in the hallway.

Thick smoke hung in the unventilated room. Small rows of collapsible chairs lined the walls. Most of the seats were occupied as the all-male audience gawked at the two young naked girls on stage grinding to the disco beat. Other girls roamed through the heavy-breathing audience trying to score, as customers' hands grabbed at their bodies. The girls made no attempt to stop them.

"Do you see her?" Barry asked their guide.

"Nah, I'll check the place."

"You okay, Paul?"

"I never imagined such a place could exist. The girls are so young and unconcerned about their nakedness." He focused on their faces. "They're all drugged up."

"Probably heroin or speed. When I was a rookie cop, prostitutes were professionals; today they're teenagers and children, not professionals. It's called satisfying the customers, giving them what they want. And as you can see, there are plenty of customers."

A naked young girl approached Paul. Above her left breast an infected red sore oozed pus. A burn. She must have been cute at one time, but no more. Her body looked worn, used.

"You're cute, Sweetie, real cute." Her hands

massaged her supple breasts as she spoke. "Ten dollars for a hand-job, twenty for a blow-job, and thirty for whatever you want." She reached for Paul's groin but he nervously jolted back.

Barry grabbed her away from Paul. "What's your name?" he asked in a muted voice.

"Whatever you want to call me, Sweetie."

"How old are you?"

"Young enough to be good. And I am good. Wanna try?"

Barry pointed to the sore on her breast. "Strange place for a cigarette burn. Why don't you go see a doctor and have it treated?"

"Don't tell me what to do, you ain't my father." The hostile response conveyed the reason she had run away.

Betsy circled back. "She's not here, left last week. Nobody knows where she is. Let's go."

Paul and Barry followed Betsy into the hallway. Unexpectedly, Barry flung Betsy against the wall, locking his hand around her throat. "You have five seconds to tell me where Detroit is or I'll break your neck."

Paul controlled his urge to intervene, praying that his friend knew what he was doing.

The count began. Five, four, three, two . . . "Upstairs . . . in the recovery room."

Barry released her and shoved her toward the staircase that led up to another narrow corridor. There were five doors, but only one had a key in it. That was the room. The locked door kept people from leaving, not from entering.

"Stay here," Barry ordered them both as he cautiously proceeded toward the door. He turned the key until the lock clicked open. A door behind him flew open and a burly man jumped Barry before he could react.

"You're dead, mister," growled the guard, bouncing his weight over Barry's straining body. "You're gonna die, man. Die!"

Barry butted his head against the man's face a few times, and the massive arms loosened enough for Barry to slip free. He twirled and drove his foot toward the man's groin but caught his thigh instead.

"Ahhh!" the guard shrieked, but the pain subsided all too fast. He raised his hands, his thick fingers curled like claws.

Barry drove his foot into the man's groin, this time hitting his mark. Again his foot burrowed into the target doubling the guard over. He wouldn't go down. The guard's protruding jaw looked too dense for Barry's fist. The guard began to straighten up, his eyes blazing. Taking a running start, Barry grabbed him by the hair and rammed his head into the wall once, twice, three times. Blood splattered the wall as it cracked. The guard sank to the floor.

Barry breathed deeply, calming his body.

Paul ran toward Barry. "Are you okay? I froze! God, I wanted to help, but I froze."

"It's over and I'm fine." Barry's breathing was near normal. "If you had helped, I would have had to save both of us, and I don't know if I could have done that. It was easier this way. Take my word for it."

The consoling remark meant nothing as Paul repeated, "I should have helped."

Before opening the door, Barry suggested that Paul wait in the hall.

"No, I want to go in. I've come this far into your reality; I might as well go all the way."

Hall light crept into the dark room. Beckoning Paul to enter, Barry grimly said "Welcome to Hell."

Seven cots cluttered the small square room. Three lamps cast unnatural-looking shadows on the dingy walls. The room was deathly quiet. Paul sniffed the stale antiseptic. "It smells like a cheap clinic."

Barry checked the cots. Only three were occupied. He moved a lamp closer to the first patient, a young girl. She was sleeping. As he rolled the sheet off her, roaches scattered from the light. A long row of fresh stitches on her abdomen jutted out against her pale flesh. "Knife wound," Barry commented.

Paul gulped the air. Betsy shied away.

Barry moved to the next cot. The woman's face was covered with black-and-blue marks. Her eyes bulged. She was so still, so quiet. And her flesh was so white. Barry felt for a pulse. He pulled the sheet over her head.

In slow motion, Paul made the sign of the cross above her body and uttered a quick prayer for her soul.

The last girl was Detroit, Betsy confirmed. Barry knelt beside her and felt a faint pulse. Gently he shook her. "Detroit. Detroit, wake up, it's a friend." Barry brought the other lamp closer as he held her arm up for examination. It was so thin, almost deformed. The skin was puckered into bunches with red and blue streaks.

Barry checked a large infected area on her arm. "Betsy, got a tweezer?" She handed him one. Barry placed the tweezer on the infected area and tugged. The girl moaned. He pulled again and drew out a needle that had broken in her arm. "She's half dead. Let's get out of this hole."

The fresh air was a blessing for Paul but it was too late. He ran to the side of the building and vomited the nightmare out of his system.

Barry patted him on the back. "You feel better?"

"I'm sorry," Paul said still gagging.

"Don't be. It took me years before I could stop gagging. I called Vice and they're going to raid the place tonight. I don't want to be here when they do. Are you able to walk?"

Paul nodded as he slowly straightened up. "Where's Betsy?"

"She took off." Barry steadied Paul as they walked back to the car.

Paul, vowing to himself never to return to this part of the city, took a final look. It was all a fake—the smiles on the hookers, the bright lights, the ogling customers— Barry was right, this place *was* Hell, and the only escape was death. It consumed his thoughts all the way home.

"You haven't said a word since leaving Forty-Second Street. You okay?"

"Still in shock. That should give me nightmares for the rest of my life. I just can't believe that people and places like that exist. I mean that's not prostitution, that's . . . that's depravity. Good Lord."

"I'll add another kicker to tonight's episode. The so-called hotel was once owned by your righteous parishioner Mister Arnold Frederickson. Last year the Vice Squad was investigating him and they were able to trace him to the ownership of the place. He sure had that racket sewn up from beginning to end."

"You sound as though you're glad he was killed," Paul moralized.

"You saw what went on there and what Frederickson was involved in. What do you think the answer is?"

"If I answer the question honestly I'll sound like Rhoades, and I don't want to do that. But it does seem wrong for a man like Frederickson to go to Heaven. No, my thinking is off, I'm tired."

"You look it. Go to bed."

"I will, after a long prayer. What's going to happen to Detroit, if she lives?"

"Depends on how old she is. We'll contact her parents, they'll say they don't want her, we'll hold her for a while, maybe put her in a house of detention. Then she'll be back on the street. It's a vicious circle because nobody wants the children.''

"But you'll try to talk to her and help her, won't you?''

"Somebody will. I'll let you know what happens.''

Paul went straight to his room, sat on the bed, and with his Bible in hand prayed aloud: "Dear Lord, there is a young girl far removed from Your sight and mind . . . Detroit . . . I don't even know her real name. But she needs Your help more than anybody I have ever met. I am sure she will not even accept Your name into her heart and she will return no goodness unto You. But let her at least live. That's all I ask. Give her one more chance at life. Please.''

8

Father Inness waited until Father Rhoades was alone in the study before entering and engaging in talk, he hoped, would be useful. "Buongiorno, Padre. I am disturbing you?"

Rhoades's head snapped up from his paper work. "Not at all. I was just auditing the church's monthly bills. We're in much better financial shape since I took over. Father D'Angelo does not have a head for figures."

"It is a wonder he kept the books so accurately before you arrived." The Vatican guest relaxed in a chair. "Does not Father Tobin assist you with the church's finances?"

"He's too busy playing detective."

"I have heard of these murders. Terrible. Was not the first victim a parishioner here?"

"For his entire life. How did you know about Mr. Miller?"

"Some of your parishioners speak in loud voices. There have been other murders too. These are the ones

197

Father Tobin and his detective friend are investigating. Yes?"

"They are, although it's a strange hobby for a priest. Father Tobin should stick to his architecture; it's safer."

"Everyone must have a hobby, even priests. Your hobby, Padre, what is it?"

"The Church is my hobby and my work, Father Inness. That is the way it should be."

"Even God rested from His work, Padre. Rest gives one a better . . ." he paused, searching for the proper word in English. ". . . A better perspective on what one has done. Reflection. Is that not true, Padre?"

"I know exactly what I'm doing."

"Do you? I have noticed that Father D'Angelo is close to the older parishioners, Father Tobin concentrates on the younger ones, but you concentrate on none. That is not right, Padre."

"I was taught that our parishioners are like sheep, they depend upon the shepherd—the priest—for guidance and salvation. But isn't it wise to make sure that the shepherd is strong enough to protect the sheep from the wolves before turning the flock over to him?"

"And the wolves, Padre, who are they?"

"As always, anyone who would divert the righteous from the path of God." Rhoades discreetly checked the time. He was running behind schedule and talking too much. "You must excuse me, but I have a great deal of paperwork to finish." His gaze lowered and remained there until he heard the study door close. He looked up; his eyes squinted. I don't trust him and I don't like him. What does he know?

Rhoades hurried upstairs, changed into street clothes, and took a cab to the hotel, Room 333. He went through the usual security procedures before he was allowed in. The same group of men present at the previous meetings sat around a small table. Their arched eyebrows noted his tardiness.

Rhoades's prepared excuse was silenced by the raised hand of the Leader, who began, "Our last incident was a fiasco. All those people dead. Unnecessary."

"The police arrived too soon," stated the white-haired man. "It was bad luck."

"Was it?" queried the Leader. "I wonder."

"About what?" asked Rhoades. "It was almost inevitable that the police would stumble on one of the targets."

"It was a bad location," assessed the tall lanky man, "and it was badly planned."

"Perhaps," the Leader said, still showing his pessimism. "Our problem now is, do we replace our lost man?"

Except for Rhoades, who did nothing, the other two gestured no. The Leader tapped his fingers on the table as he waited for Rhoades to respond.

"Is there something wrong, Number Four?" the Leader asked, seeing Rhoades's lips move but hearing nothing. "Speak up, Number Four."

"The Vatican envoy," he shouted, then lowered his voice. "He's suspicious of me; I can feel it when he talks to me."

"What has he asked you?"

"He knows too much about the murders. For someone who just arrived from Rome he knows much too much. I don't trust him."

"He knows nothing," the Leader asserted, "unless you inadvertently told him something. Have you?"

"No, I haven't told him anything. I swear."

"Be sure you don't," the white-haired man admonished. "Now is no time to become clumsy, especially when things are going so well in the other areas."

"I said I'll be careful, but I think we should slow down our pace." Rhoades's voice was jittery. "There are just too many people around me who are interested in the murders. I say we stop for a while."

"It's only what I say that counts, Number Four," the Leader emphasized. "And I say we continue as scheduled." The others confirmed his decision. After ending the meeting he beckoned for Number Two to remain behind and warned, "We must be careful of Number Four; he's growing weak. Whenever possible, have him watched."

"Yes, sir."

Prescott Palmer opened his door to receive his followers. Linda was the first to enter. She bowed before his presence and spoke in a demure voice. "I telephoned my parents today. They were crying and begged me to come home. They said my running away was mostly their fault and if I came home, they'd try to change. My mother called all my friends to find out where I was. They really were looking for me. And my father, I had never heard my father cry before."

"You want to return home, Linda?"

"Yes, Master. I really miss them, now that I know they love me."

"No one has ever left my fold, Linda. Nobody." He stood up, walked toward her, and gently laid his hands upon her shoulders. His voice was sympathetic and fatherly. "When you first came here, Linda, you were without friends and parents. Now you have both, yet you're willing to desert us for those who originally abandoned you. My child, your family is here."

"You've been very good to me, Master, but my father . . . he cried because I wasn't home. I have to go back." She wiped the tears from her cheeks.

Prescott returned to his seat, gripped the arms of the chair, and just stared at the girl for a moment. "I am your Master, Linda. I gave you life when you had none, and now you repay by leaving me. But even if I let you go, how would you get home? Ohio is a long way from here, and you have no money."

She reached into her jeans and pulled out a card. "That Detective Martin said I could call him if I needed anything, even money to get home."

Prescott held out his hand for the card and crumpled it. "Nobody helps my followers but me. You want money to go home, I'll give it to you." He directed her to the door behind him. "Go upstairs to my private office while I make arrangements."

"Thank you, Master," said Linda acknowledging her obedience with a bow. The upstairs room was a combination office/bedroom. In one corner stood a desk and a few chairs while in the opposite corner near the window was a queen-size bed. More self-portraits of Palmer draped the walls. Awkwardly, Linda stood in the middle of the room, her arms crossed in front of her. Palmer entered with Carol. Palmer sat behind his desk while Carol positioned herself next to Linda. Palmer signaled Carol to begin.

Taking hold of the frightened girl's hand, Carol, in a warm and understanding tone related "The first time I ran away from home was when I was your age, Linda. My parents never had any time for me. My old man was always at work or talking about work, while my dear mother was worried about all the injustices in the world and joined one committee after another. They had time for everything and everybody but me." Her voice was coarse and bitter. "I was like one of my own childhood friends—invisible. Fifteen years was enough. I ran. I stayed away for a year, but returned home because my parents always cried when I spoke to them over the phone. Fakers, both of them. I discovered that their grief wasn't because I was gone, but because I had disgraced them socially. The neighbors blamed them for being incompetent parents and they couldn't stand that. I lasted two months."

"My parents aren't like that," argued Linda. "They cried because they love me and miss me."

"No they don't, Linda." Carol faced Palmer. "The Master is the only one who really loves us, and we should do anything he commands." Carol sensually traced her fingers over Linda's moist lips, and tenderly whispered, "We love you. I love you. I love you very much and you love me." She kissed Linda on the lips. The months of teasing preparation and breaking down her inhibitions were successful. Linda had found the love and attention she so desperately desired. Willingly she submitted.

Carol took Linda's hand and placed it on her breast, then moved her own hand to Linda's breast, and massaged it. "We're your friends, Linda. We love you." Carol's hands unbuttoned the young girl's blouse as she spoke. "Unbutton my blouse, Linda. Show me you love me." She leaned forward and kissed Linda. Linda responded. Their lips opened. Their tongues sucked at one another. Their blouses fell to the floor.

Prescott leaned forward licking the saliva off his lips. His right hand rubbed against his groin. He swallowed loudly.

Carol brushed her nipples against Linda's. Carol's head swayed. Their hands feverishly undid their pants until they both stood naked. Linda momentarily resisted. Carol forced Linda's mouth against her breasts. She was not about to let Linda back down now. "Lick it," she moaned. Linda's tongue darted over and about Carol's breast, then she kissed her again.

Prescott's hand was moving quickly over his erection. Carol moved her mouth down Linda's body. Prescott let out a sigh of relief. Another one who wouldn't ever leave him. Then, quietly, he opened the drawer and pulled out a camera.

Jenny entered Mary's office. "I was told you wanted to see me." She counted the paces to the chair and sat down.

"I'd like to have a talk with you, friend to friend."

"It sounds ominous."

"The past few nights you've been staying with Barry."

Mary's opening remark stung Jenny's hypersensitive emotions and she lashed back. "Paul put you up to this, didn't he? Well, I'm tired of having other people dictate my life. Nobody can read my mind, so whatever I do is my business; nobody else's."

Without thinking, Mary angrily returned the fire. "First, nobody 'puts me up' to anything, so don't ever again accuse me of that. Second, I said I wanted to talk to you as a friend, so allow me the courtesy of finishing."

Jenny was taken aback by Mary's unexpected retaliation. Even Mary was surprised at herself. Rarely did she let herself fall prey to her unchecked emotions; it was totally unprofessional. Yet there were times she tired of always being the professional, always being in control. Nobody would believe she had problems, but she did. All the feelings her patients felt, she felt too. But her job was to listen. Desperately she wanted to confide in a friend, but the roles couldn't be reversed, she thought.

Suppressing her own anguish, Mary resumed her proper role. "Since your involvement with Barry, your personality and outlook have improved dramatically, and that makes me feel good, professionally and personally. But yesterday and today there's been a regression. You sit at your desk pouting and slamming the typewriter as if it were your enemy. Why the backslide?"

Jenny's hands moved about as though she didn't know what to do with them. "I've loved Barry for a long time and the past few days are better than I ever dreamed they could be. I think he loves me too. But I'm worried that I'll saddle him with my handicap."

"Be more specific."

Jenny ignored the inquiry and dismally stated, "Tonight I'm going to tell him that I don't want to see him any more."

"And poof, it's over just like that? I don't understand. A year ago this self-doubt might have made sense, but you have progressed too far for what you're proposing now. I can help you only if you tell me the truth, Jenny."

Jenny drew a deep breath, then let the air out slowly. "It must be obvious that Barry and I have been sleeping together."

"Well, it's not obvious but it's easily assumed. What was Paul's reaction?"

"So far, I've avoided the issue with him. He still thinks of me as his virginal little sister."

"I'm sure he knows."

"Probably, but I feel if I don't tell him then there's still that doubt in his mind. This way I won't feel guilty and he won't be angry." In a half laugh Jenny added, "That sounds dumb."

Mary guided the conversation back to the original problem. "You still haven't explained why you're backing out of the relationship."

"I'm not backing out, I'm facing the facts. Sex is only one aspect of a relationship, and it's usually done in the dark. But everything else is done in the light: traveling, going to the movies, to shows, museums, cooking . . ."

"Has marriage come up?"

"No."

"But you're afraid it will."

"Scared to death. Marriage, children, how can a blind person be a good wife and mother? I couldn't do it."

"My father was the best father anyone could have, and his being blind never prevented him from loving and enjoying his children or his wife. He refused to let it happen. There's no doubt that being blind drastically alters your life, Jenny. My father could never enjoy a movie or the scenery or our summer trips, but he did enjoy our love all the time, and that's more important than a movie or a mountain. Allow Barry to love you, Jenny. I'm sure that's what he wants."

"When I listen to you everything sounds nice, like a fairytale, but when I think about it all I see is disaster. The last few days have been so great I feel like I'm living somebody else's life. He hasn't said it, neither of us have, but we love each other. But the thought of marrying Barry frightens me. I feel as though I'm being unfair to him."

Mary carefully calculated her next move. Sympathy was not the answer; forcefulness was. "Jenny the martyr. Involved in love yet willing to make the ultimate sacrifice that will free her man from future hardship. It sounds more like a cancelled soap opera. The truth is that you're scared he might want to marry you, blindness and all. You're making the decision for him and you're going to lose because *you're* scared, not him. If you walk away from this problem, you'll walk away from others. And then you *will* be handicapped."

A sullen look overcame Jenny as she listened to the truth—something she didn't necessarily want to hear.

Mary shifted to a sympathetic tone. "Jenny, don't walk away from Barry or yourself. After the four of us have dinner tonight, explain your fears to Barry. But don't let a chance for happiness slip away just because one of us is different."

"Us?"

"I meant one of you."

"Freudian slip," Jenny charged, eager to change the subject.

It was and Mary knew it. She wanted to talk and welcomed Jenny's intrusion into her private thoughts.

"I'm different and Paul is different," Jenny said. "Are you going to follow your own advice and take a chance for happiness? I know you and Paul love each other. It's in your voices."

"So is fear," Mary found it difficult to confess.

"You, afraid? I don't believe it."

"Everybody's afraid of something, Jenny. I've devoted most of my adult life to understanding people and their problem. But it's always been other people's problems, never mine."

"And the problem is that Paul is a priest."

"No, not that he's a priest, but that he truly loves God. I don't think I can compete with that. If there was another woman I'd know how to handle it, but vying with God—and maybe winning? My frailty is showing."

"Strange, isn't it? We're both afraid of obtaining what we want. With one exception: love can disappear over time, blindness doesn't."

"You're going to tell Barry it's over, aren't you? You're making a mistake, Jenny."

"It'll be my mistake, then. I'll see you tonight."

Darkness encased the eastern seaboard and with it came more of the Crossbearers. Boston, Chicago, St. Paul. The three lone men, separated by distance yet linked by a common purpose, began their hunt.

Commonwealth Avenue in Boston hummed with the constant flow of traffic into and out of the city. On the sidestreets, beautiful old townhouses stood beside new luxury buildings. A youngish man watched the doorman at one of the buildings as he greeted Sam Baker, one of the tenants out for his nightly stroll. His wife thought it was marvelous that a man Sam's age could walk for hours, and how much happier he was since his walks began.

An anticipatory smile of excitement was evident on Sam's face. Having a young mistress will do that, especially when she lived only two blocks away. His bodily juices, which he presumed had given way to age, were already stirring. He hadn't felt this vibrant in years. It was a little after eight o'clock. Sam would spend a few tantalizing hours with his mistress, go to the Ice Cream Emporium for his usual soda, and return home. Suddenly he realized, too late, that there was a presence behind him. Sam turned to face the unknown stranger, the last person he'd ever see.

Chicago. The wind intermittently gusted down the corridor of Lake Shore Drive. Jerry Hayward, a large bulky man, exchanged trivial conversation with the doorman as he waited for his car to arrive from the underground garage. Across the street, the hunter took out a small black box from his knapsack, extended the antenna to full length, placed his thumb against the red detonator switch and waited until Hayward's car moved onto the street.

St. Paul. The rowboat hovered in one place as the tranquility of the lake invited many nighttime fishermen. Whirling sounds of fishing lines being cast, followed by dull splashes of lures striking the water, made up the only unnatural sounds. One rowboat headed toward another at a fast pace. The rower had a fishing rod but no bait or tackle box. He eased up on the oars as his boat slithered closer to the other boat.

"The fish aren't biting tonight," the stranger commented to Rusty Garwood, outfitted in a fisherman's jacket and hat. "My lures don't seem to work. Mind if I borrow one of your lures for awhile?" Garwood muttered something that sounded belligerent as the stranger spoke again. "I'm sorry to disturb you but I promised my kids fresh fish for tomorrow night and I don't want to disappoint them." He reached across and held the two boats together as Garwood rummaged through his tackle box, still mumbling about the intrusion.

The stranger slipped on a pair of heavy gloves, wrapped a piece of rope between his two hands and gave it a few sample tugs, then leaned forward.

But it had not ended yet. Three more Crossbearers waited for nighttime to cover Dallas, Los Angeles, and San Francisco. Six before the night would end. That would complete the plan.

Barry was late in arriving for dinner at Mary's, but for a good reason. He waited until dinner was over before revealing his startling discovery. "Do any of you remember where you were on May 3, 1981?"

"That's easy," Paul answered first. "I was on the Indian reservation in New Mexico. I remember because on May fourth I received the telegram about Jenny's accident, which occurred on May third. News travels slowly out there."

"That's funny," Jenny fretted, "I don't even remember the exact date of my accident. I don't think I want to. Guess that puts me in the hospital on that day. Where were you, Mary?"

"Bermuda. Warm, glorious Bermuda. It was my first major vacation. Blue-green water, sand so fine and warm you could curl up in it. I must go back there. But I see no relevance to Jenny's accident."

"There is," Barry guaranteed. "On the afternoon of May third, 1981, at approximately 2:30, Cardinal Beck was assassinated as he was leaving the side entrance of St. Patrick's Cathedral."

Paul and Mary concurred in unison. Then Paul said, "Of course, I remember, but Jenny's accident was all I could think about. The day of the Cardinal's funeral I was at Jenny's bedside. Even with that excuse, I got holy hell for missing it. It never entered my mind that Jenny's accident occurred on the same day as the Cardinal's assassination."

"I heard about the assassination when I returned home," responded Mary. "I can recall a discussion one of the psychologists was holding. He noted how upset the older people were compared to the younger ones, because the younger generation was used to assassinations." As an afterthought she added, "It's amazing what you can get used to."

Barry unfolded a piece of paper and passed it around. "That's a copy of Jenny's accident report. Her accident happened on the same day about twenty minutes after the assassination."

"I don't understand," Jenny said, uneasy over this entire discussion.

Barry produced another piece of paper. "This is how a witness described Jenny's accident. 'I heard a car backfire, I turned and saw the car crash into the parked cars.' Later on in his statement the witness recalled '. . . a dark-colored car speeding down the street after the accident, but I don't know if it caused the accident. I'm sure there were four men in the car.' Unquote."

Barry produced more official papers. "This is the report on the assassination. I'll give you only the highlights. One shot, fired from a rifle with a silencer, emanated from an angle across the street." Parenthetically Barry added that the Cardinal's body went undiscovered for five or ten minutes due to the concealment of the private entrance, and that it was his daily constitutional where he could be alone with his thoughts. "Some witnesses recalled an alleged white male suspect, dressed in black, running west. Most likely he escaped by car."

"I've got it," Paul said as if it were a game. "In his fast getaway, the assassin caused Jenny's accident."

"Let me give you more information," Barry added. "One shot killed Cardinal Beck, and one man was seen running. Ten or so minutes elapsed before the police blockaded the area and stopped any car driven by a single man. The assassin escaped only to be killed two days later by the police."

It was Mary's turn to conjecture. "So if the assassin got into a car with other men waiting for him, the car would not have been stopped."

"He could even have had a change of clothes in the car," Paul reflected. "But where does all this lead us?"

"It leads us to connect Jenny's accident with the assassination," Barry offered, "something the police didn't do and with good reason."

"According to the statements from Jimmy's parents," Barry continued, "he and Jenny were going to Rockefeller Center that day. Let's assume that Jimmy was cruising around searching for a parking space when a man dashes from nowhere. He sees you and Jimmy, and you see him. Still insignificant, unless the man unintentionally reveals a weapon. Then it all makes sense. That was how it began; now let's skip to the end. From the impact of Jimmy's car he was travelling at a high speed. The question is why? If the stranger did accidentally reveal a weapon, Jimmy could have driven away to safety. But why continue to speed if he had already driven away to safety? Answer: he wasn't safe yet, he was being chased. When Jenny has her nightmares, she constantly ducks as if somebody was throwing something at her or shooting at her."

"Shooting?", Paul repeated with surprise. "The police never mentioned anything about a shooting. Besides, there would have been bullet holes in the car."

"Not necessarily. It was late Spring and the car windows were open. I checked the photographs of the accident. Also, the temperature that day was eighty-one."

"And Jimmy had no air-conditioning in the car," Jenny recalled. "The bullets missed us and travelled through the open windows."

"That would also explain the witness' hearing what he thought was a backfire," Barry ventured.

"Jimmy ducked, lost control of the car, and crashed. I can't remember that or your supposed stranger. I don't want to either," said Jenny.

Mary brought her hands over her mouth as her mind unearthed Barry's true reason for all of this. "What you're really saying, Barry, is that the assassin killed by the police was not the only one involved, and that Jenny saw the others who got away."

"It's a possibility."

"These would-be conspirators wouldn't try to hurt Jenny after all this time, would they?" Mary inquired.

"No," Barry off-handedly replied, in an attempt to squash any of his friends' fears. "But there is a possible explanation for why those other men haven't tried to kill Jenny. Not only is she blind, but she's blocked the accident from her memory."

"How would they know that?" Paul asked Barry.

"They've been watching her. Somebody *close* has been watching her. But I don't know who."

"I've read you thoughts, Barry," Jenny relayed to the

others. "They're still watching me. So as long as I can't remember the accident, I can stay alive. Isn't that right, Barry?"

"Something like that."

Gently touching Barry's cheek, Jenny chided, "You have this uncanny habit of scaring me to death. I'd like to go home."

"I'm sorry I upset you, Jenny, but I thought you'd want to know the circumstances surrounding the accident."

"Not really. Please take me home, Barry."

Alone, Paul and Mary relaxed on the sofa, reviewing Barry's theory. After awhile, the conversation edged toward their own relationship and whether or not there was one. Stilted ambiguous talk shadowed their true feelings for one another, but what they couldn't say they expressed by what they did. Holding hands they walked into the bedroom.

"You haven't said a word since we left Mary's apartment." Barry remarked to Jenny as he drove toward his apartment. "I'm not good at reading other people's thoughts the way you are. Mind sharing them?"

"It's strange. As you were talking about the accident I wasn't shocked. I wish my subconscious would tell my conscious mind what it knows: then maybe I could sleep better at night."

"One day something will jar your memory."

"Yes, but do I really want to remember if those men are still out there watching me? I wonder how much a bodyguard costs?"

"You mean I'm being replaced?"

What a perfect opening to tell him it's all over, Jenny resolved. I love him so much, but I must let him go. No, not tonight. Yes, tonight. Right now or never. "Barry, you are being replaced. I'm moving back with my parents. I've given this a lot of thought, and it just won't work between us. There'd be too much strain." She slanted her head toward the car window to hide her tears. "Please drive me to my parent's house."

"I've been waiting for you to say that, Jenny, and you're probably right. When I feel this way I usually break it off with the woman, but I can't with you. The only thing I can say is that detectives don't usually get shot at. Of course there's always that possibility, but I'm an excellent shot, I know some hand-to-hand combat, and I've learned not to bring my work home. Yeah, there will be times I'll be late and I won't call, but I'll try my best not to have it happen often. As for my age, thirty-nine isn't that old."

"What are you talking about?"

"What do you mean, what am I talking about? What are *you* talking about?"

"I'm blind."

"What does that have to do with us? I'm talking about the divorce rate among cops. It scares the hell out of me."

"And my blindness scares the hell out of me when I think of *us*."

Barry swerved over to the curb and shut off the engine.

Jenny continued. "Being blind would limit me from doing a lot of things with you, and I don't want to be a burden. That's what I meant when I said it won't work between us."

Barry grabbed Jenny by the shoulders, and exclaimed in a loud authoritative voice, "Now listen! You're the only woman I've ever met that I can't drop. Do you realize that the nights we've made love I was deeply concerned about how *you* felt. That's never happened before! And as for your being blind, sure it'll be difficult. So's my job. But Christ almighty, we have to take the chance. I'm not going to lose you, Jenny." He flung his arms around her and held her tight. Sounding more like an order than a question, Barry said "Marry me. And don't say no. I can't deal with rejection."

Amidst laughter, tears, and excitement, Jenny answered "Yes. Yes. I love you Barry. I'll marry you."

Barry held her at arm's length. "Are you sure? There's no doubt in your mind? Even if there, is we can work it out. We belong together, Jenny."

"Barry, stop trying to convince me. I said yes."

"I'm nervous. This is the first time I've ever proposed to a woman. What about our age difference? I mean, you're thirty-two and I'm thirty-nine. Hell, I'm forty."

"Forty? I thought you were thirty-nine?"

"I must have overlooked a year. Does it matter?"

Jenny burst out laughing. "I don't care, Barry. I love you. Wow, I wasn't expecting this tonight."

"Well, I have another surprise for you at my apartment. Don't ask, you'll find out in a minute."

When they entered Barry's apartment, Jenny tilted her head as she heard something prance across the floor. "A dog!" she correctly guessed. She knelt down and the dog snuggled into her arms. "What kind is it?"

"The trainer said it was a German Shepherd, but it's closer to a horse. Damn thing eats two cans of food a day. Yesterday when I took the dog out for a walk it scared the hell out of Mrs. Tarrings' little creature. She's the yenta of the building. Actually, she's a nice lady, but her dog looks like a hairy rat. Not like this beast." Barry scratched the dog's powerful neck, which made its tail wag faster. "This dog is very special. It's a Seeing Eye Dog and a protector for you."

"You're worried that the assassins might still be after me aren't you?"

"Let's just say I'm cautious."

"When do I go to school to learn how to use this dog?"

"You're not. The trainer owes me a favor. He'll train you around the neighborhood." The real reason, however, was to keep Jenny close to him . . . just in case. "The dog's name, oddly enough, is Cyclops."

"Cyclops? Accurate but weird." She wrapped her arm around the dog. "We're going to be a good team, Cyclops. Wait and see." She found Barry's hand and vowed. "We'll be the best threesome ever."

Paul sat at Mary's kitchen table, staring, forgetting to drink his morning coffee. Mary poured herself a cup, then joined his silence. Paul was deep in contemplation. We should have waited, she despaired. Although she wanted to discuss last night, and the conflicting feelings she had, "Paul" was all she could force out.

"I had forgotten how good sex felt," he revealed meeting her eye level.

"No guilt?"

"Not enough to make me stop."

"You did for a while."

"Yes, I know." His eyes lowered, then rose. "Sex has become more varied and women have become more liberated while I was regressing in the monasteries. I was just shocked, you caught me off guard with that . . . that . . ."

"I won't do it again."

"Oh no, I want you to, I mean if you want to." He gritted his teeth. "You'll notice I have trouble talking about sex. Can I ask you a personal question? Except for when you caught me off guard, how did I do?"

Mary laughed. "A classic case of role reversal. Paul, that's the question everyone thinks the virgin female asks of the experienced male. But you were very good last night. Really." She took hold of his hand.

"I'll get better with practice," he said half heartedly, then glanced at his watch. "I have to get back to the Church and you have to go to work."

"See you tonight?"

"I hope so." After a passionate kiss, Paul headed back, his mind racing through various lies to tell Father D'Angelo of why he had stayed out all night. None of them sounded plausible.

Father D'Angelo, wearing alb and cincture, was speaking to some early morning parishioners on the church steps when he spotted Paul. Excusing himself from the conversation, he cornered Paul half-way up the stairs. "Are you all right? When you didn't telephone last night . . ." Father D'Angelo allowed the sentence to end, finding Paul's intent nervous expression more revealing. Paul fought making eye contact with him. "She must be a very special woman."

"What? Uhm, yeah, Jenny's fine. Fine."

At Father D'Angelo's insistence, they made their way, side by side, down to the foot of the stairs away from the uninvited ears, as the elder priest recalled, "I had that look once, a long time ago."

"I don't know what you're referring to, Father," Paul replied too quickly to be convincing.

"Only those who have wrestled with the problem can identify the look. I wasn't sure until now." He looked over his shoulder at his parishioners and smiled before relaying to Paul. "I was twenty-eight when I encountered my special woman. I had been a priest for five years, and I wanted nothing else, but it is when you are not expecting something that it happens. We met at a tea social. They had those when I was young. She was more charming than attractive, and imparted a sensitivity that drew me to her as honey draws a bee. For a while I fought seeing her, even at social occasions, but I knew I'd see her again. I wanted to see her again. We saw each other more and more until my thoughts were more of her than of the Church. That was the look you have had lately." His voice took on a soulful tone. "We agreed to wait two months until I decided which road of life to take. I never decided. She moved away. I often wondered whether doing nothing was my decision or the decision my friends forced me to make. Your expression tells me you are at the decision stage."

"Her name is Mary Evans . . . and I love her. But I also love the Church, and you're right, I am at that stage. Any recommendations as to which way I should turn?"

"That decision is yours, Paul, although I can offer you some wisdom. After you decide, leap. Don't walk and don't look back. Either way, commit yourself." Father D'Angelo held onto Paul as they ascended the stairs. "I was hoping one day that this humble parish would pass into your hands. Our parishioners are good people, Paul; they've just been temporarily sidetracked from their Lord. They require understanding and a good listener, not a zealot."

Paul recognized the last word as another way of referring to Rhoades. "I tried to see the Cardinal again and failed, but I'll keep on trying."

"I have a feeling the good Cardinal is as upset about our Vatican visitor as everyone else is. Speaking of whom, Father Inness was extremely eager to know where you were last night. I told him you have a sister who is blind. That was not a lie."

"Thank you, Father. Has our guest been a bother?"

"He questions everything we do or have done. If he were not wearing a clerical collar, I would judge him to be a detective. He especially likes conversing with

Father Rhoades, although the feeling is not mutual. Following their tete-a-tete, Father Rhoades always appears agitated."

"What's your opinion of Inness?"

Father D'Angelo's voice fell to a hush. "He's a Judas Iscariot. Be careful of him, Paul."

"I will." Leaving Father D'Angelo with the parishioners, Paul hurried through the church. The study door was ajar and he could see Father Inness near the file cabinets. Paul's first impulse was to sneak by, but then he had second thoughts. I'm the only one left he hasn't interrogated. Maybe it's time, and I'm prepared. Paul entered the study casting a friendly greeting at the visitor. "Have you been enjoying your stay, Father?"

"Si. Pardon me—yes." His cleft lip contorted his face as he spoke. "Padre D'Angelo informed me of your sister. She is well?" He gestured for Paul to sit.

"As well as can be expected. I see you're going over the Church account. Are we being audited?"

"No," he answered with that crooked smile that contradicted his word. "I have heard you are helping the police with those murders. Is that not unusual for a priest?"

"I believe a priest should help his community in any way he can, even if it is slightly unorthodox. Do you disapprove?"

"Not at all, Padre. It is a noble gesture. The investigation, it is progressing well?"

"Not really. How is your investigation going?"

"Priests in America are very different from European clergymen. More involved in non-Church business, such as yourself. Do the police know who are commiting these murders?"

"It is a fanatical religious group, but which one they don't know yet."

"Ah, such groups are plentiful today. You have

many such groups in your country. We are aware of all of them."

"All of them?" Paul repeated. "Then perhaps you know which group is responsible for the killings."

"We know of their beliefs, leaders, and number of followers, that is all. Perhaps if you tell me which group you suspect, I could be of some help."

"I don't have that information," replied Paul. "It seems odd that you would be so interested in such cults. That's not exactly Church business either, is it?"

"Oh, it is, Padre Tobin. Many of their followers were once our parishioners, or more precisely, the children of our parishioners. In your country the Church is dying, and that is of grave concern to us. Do you understand? The Church is fighting for its survival."

Where have I heard those words before? Rhoades, of course. Paul revealed his minor discovery. "You sound exactly like Father Rhoades."

"That is bad? Padre Rhoades realizes what is happening. Many clergymen do not."

"I have no doubt that the Church will be around a lot longer than all of us, and to be fanatically pessimistic about its decline or demise is nonsense. People will always need God and the Church; more so in some ages, less so in others."

"It is good to hear you speak so positively, Padre Tobin. I pray that what you say is true."

"It is, Father Inness. It can be no other way. Now I will let you get back to work while I do some of mine." For a Vatican priest, he certainly is pessimistic, Paul reflected as he left. The telephone in the hallway rang. It was Barry, and the message was short and tragic; the young girl, Detroit, had died. "I just got off the phone with her father. He refused to claim the body. He said, 'We're not going to bury our daughter a second time.' I'm sorry, Paul."

Paul, head lowered in defeat, moved down the aisle and stopped in front of the altar. Another prayer gone unanswered and another life uselessly lost, he told himself. Lifting his head, he gazed at the statue of the Virgin Mary cradling the infant Jesus in her arms. "Why are our prayers always for the dead when it's too late? It's wrong. Everything is wrong." Almost in slow motion, he turned and left the Church.

Barry's investigatory report on the mail clerks revealed nothing conclusive. That didn't automatically rule them out as suspects, but it did move them to the bottom of the list. The question remained, who was watching him?

Barry's concentration subsided as his mind noticed what his eyes were looking at: Dave's empty chair. Jesus, I forgot all about him—I hope he's all right, he thought as he dialed. His family must be torn apart. There was no answer. It was early; time for a visit.

"Detective Martin," a uniformed transit officer interrupted his departure. "Word has it that you're looking for a young male Caucasian with blond hair."

"You've arrested somebody like that?"

"No sir, but there's a victim who might be able to identify him. A few nights ago a blond assailant grabbed ahold of this guy's arm when it was caught between the train doors. The train began to move and the blond guy wouldn't let go."

Hank Wynn's father's comment on how Joe thrived on violence came to mind. "It could be my suspect. What took you so long to tell me?"

"The victim's been in a coma all this time—until last night, that is. The hospital placed him on the stable list this morning. He's at St. Vincent's."

"I appreciate it," Barry said shaking the officer's hand. His visit to Dave was set aside for the time being.

The doctor on duty at St. Vincent's, reviewing patient charts with the head nurse, allowed Barry only a ten minute visit on the condition that Mr. Redden would not be subjected to stress.

Barry consented to the doctor's orders, then entered the last room on the right. Mr. Redden lay motionless on the bed, with tubes running into his body as if he were an experiment. Bandages covered his skull and nose; the rest of his bruised face was still swollen, particularly the area around his eyes. His left hand was also bandaged and in a splint; broken fingers and missing fingernails testified to his futile attempt to escape.

And now Barry had to add to the cruelty. Gently rousing the patient to consciousness, Barry identified himself before asking Mr. Redden to go over the details of the incident. "Take your time, Mr. Redden. Easy and relaxed."

Struggling against physical and mental pain, the victim recounted bits and pieces of the horror, but supplied very few details.

"Were there any distinctive features about your assailant other than his blond hair?"

"His smile. God, he enjoyed it."

The victim was becoming overly excited and Barry knew his questioning should end, but he needed more answers. Against his better judgment he continued. "Was he wearing a white enamel cross around his neck? It's important. Try to remember."

"A cross?" Mr. Redden repeated. Pain etched deeper into his face, and a hysterical laugh broke out. "You ask me about a cross?" He raised himself on his elbows. "What kind of an animal would do this?" Balancing on one elbow he grabbed Barry's arm and began to jerk it back and forth as the tubes in his arms swayed the attached bottles of fluid. "Why can't you catch scum like him and lock them up?" he shouted.

221

"Kill 'em! Kill 'em the way he tried to kill me!" One of the bottles fell from its hanging position and splattered onto the floor. "They should all burn in Hell!"

"Take it easy, Mr. Redden," Barry implored, trying desperately to get him to lie down. But hysteria took over and suddenly Barry was battling a thrashing body. Barry applied more pressure as Redden continued his screaming and bucking.

Two nurses ran into the room and positioned themselves on either side of the bed. While one held the patient's arm, the other administered an injection. In seconds Redden's body went limp.

Barry let out an audible sigh of relief as he felt the stares of the two nurses. Giving an it-wasn't-my-fault shrug did no good either.

"You were told not to get him excited," the head nurse said. "If anything happens to this patient, I'm holding you personally responsible." She walked around the bed closer to Barry. So close he could feel her breath on his face. "You can't protect the public on the streets and now you're making it unsafe for them in a hospital. Get out of here. Get out, get out!" She shooed Barry out of the room like an annoying fly, and watched him until he was out of sight.

Barry leaned against his car and tried to shake off the moronic episode. Years of experience had covered him with the skin of a reptile when it came to hearing about things of the police department. But even when said in rage, it still hurt when coming from an average citizen. They're the ones we want to help yet somehow we've become their enemy; it's all screwed up, Barry thought.

The hospital came into focus and so did the problem at hand. There was no way to prove it was the same blond man, but Barry sensed it was. A man who enjoys violence. Barry unconsciously touched his gun. If Barry and this blond man ever met—and that was almost inevitable—Barry would need more than his police revolver. He made a mental note to switch guns at home and carry the .44 magnum. When we meet, the blond man is dead, he promised himself.

He got into his car and pulled out a handful of crumpled notes from his jacket pocket to search for the addresses of two other cults that Hank Wynn had been associated with, according to evidence found in his room. One scribbled note read "Braille book." Barry snapped his fingers thinking his memory was getting as bad as Father D'Angelo's. For Jenny's comfort, Barry wanted to learn to read Braille. On the way home tonight he'd stop at the Institute and pick up a book on Braille and a novel in Braille. To help him remember, he left the note sticking out of the ashtray.

He read the other two notes Barry chose the one with the closest address. This is gonna be good, he joked to imself. Donald Drury, God's doctor, who with the laying on the hands can cure anything from acne to depression to cancer. Sure beats Blue Cross, Barry snickered.

Drury's clan met in a dreary-looking store front building on the East Side. As Barry approached the building he could hear the singing of hymns. A pleasant clean-cut man greeted him at the door and escorted him into a small room filled with people. Incense permeated the air. Two immense candles stood burning on either side of the pulpit. Drury, outfitted in flowing white robes, thrust his hands skyward beseeching God's magical light to touch his all-too-human hands and once again bestow the power of miracles on them.

The audience, mostly poorly dressed older people, clapped and shouted their praise for their last desperate hope.

Drury tapped his finger against the podium microphone, which intermittently went on and off, and jested, "My hands are ineffective at fixing sound systems, my friends." As he spoke two gentlemen holding wicker baskets positioned themselves in the aisles. Drury continued. "God has granted me a gift which I freely give to anyone, because we are, in His eyes, all one. Never will this gift be sinned against by the acceptance of money. No, my friends, while those so-called doctors cut and rip your bodies apart in the name of medicine, we know they really do it in the name of money. But not my gift! Miracles are always free, yet, alas, not this place where I perform them. We must pay rent here. So I ask you, brothers and sisters, to help me continue my mission. I care not how much you give or whether you give at all; my miracles still belong to you."

People twisted about in their seats reaching into their pockets for whatever they had: most of it in the form of dollar bills. Some searched another pocket hoping to find more. Eagerly they gave and humbly their offerings were accepted.

A basket hovered in front of Barry. He shook his head. The man held the basket stationary. Barry made eye contact and shook his head again. The basket was removed.

Drury stepped from behind the pulpit and walked into the audience. A man, about sixty years old, jumped up and grabbed at Drury's cloak. A large lump protruded from the nape of his neck.

"Do you remember me, sir?" the man asked Drury. "My lump has gotten bigger and the pain is terrible. Please help me!"

Drury spoke into the hand microphone. "Did you follow my instructions, friend? Your eyes say no. What did you do?"

"It grew so big and the pain . . . My wife rushed me to the hospital and—"

"And undid what I had done for you." Drury faced the audience and pointed to the man's lump. "When this friend first came here the lump was large and painful. I made the lump shrink and took the pain away, but see what the doctors have done! They polluted his body with drugs!"

The audience clamored their disapproval of the medical profession.

Drury held up his hands silencing the audience. "All is not lost, friends. God not only heals, He also forgives."

Drury placed his left hand on the lump, tilted his head back, and cried, "Release this brother from his pain, Lord. Remove this growth from his body!"

In unison the onlookers shouted their praise of Drury who wavered back and forth as if he were in a trance. His voice resonated with suffering. "I will take his pain! Give *me* this growth, Oh Lord, but release this friend from torment!" Drury's hand shot into the air proclaiming, "It is done!"

One of Drury's aides broke into song with the audience quickly following, making it seem entirely spontaneous.

Another hour of such antics passed before the session ended. Barry waited until Drury was alone in the room, then approached the healer and showed him his badge. Drury's face remained expressionless. It was not the first time he had seen a police badge, and Barry knew it.

"How can I help you, officer?"

"Detective Martin." Barry showed Drury the coroner's photograph of Hank Wynn. "We found a pamphlet of yours in his room."

"I remember him. Hank Wynn. He tried to seduce some of my female followers. He was discharged."

"Anything else? Friends?"

"There was a girl. I forget her name and I never met her."

"How about a blond male friend?"

"Not that I know of. Hank didn't work here too long."

"After Hank left your employment he went to work for Palmer."

"No, he went to work for Wayne Wilkins. He has a church uptown."

A new name. Barry jotted it down. "Same type of church as yours?"

Drury noted Barry's skepticism. "Detective Martin, the laying-on of hands has been proven effective in many cases. Don't judge what you can't understand."

"My understanding is extremely comprehensive. Wilkins' Church?"

"Wayne Wilkins has stigmata marks on his hands, you know, the same sores Christ bore because of the crucifixion."

"And of course, they're real."

"People such as yourself will never believe in miracles, and for that I feel sorry for you."

"I feel sorry for that man with the lump on his neck, and all the other desperate people who give you money. I'm sure the American Medical Association will be interested in you."

Drury's hand flew up in the air. "Get outa here. You cops are all alike! Get out!"

"I might want to see you again, so don't plan any pilgrimages in the near future."

As Barry left he heard the crash of chairs against the floor. An unholy temper. He drove to Wayne Wilkins' establishment, but it was closed for the day. Good, Barry thought. I couldn't take two of these characters in one day. He returned to the office, filled out a priority report on Drury, and sent a copy to the New York chapter of the American Medical Association. That should take care of the medicine man.

A smoldering cigarette reminded Barry of the note he'd half-way stuck in the car ashtray. Off to the Institute. As his key clicked the car door latch open Barry felt heavy breathing on his neck. From both sides, two pairs of abrasive hands pinned his own hands to his sides. "Mr. Stoner wants to see you," said one of the men.

"Kidnapping is a federal offense," Barry responded.

The hands left. "Mr. Stoner requests your presence," the younger man rephrased.

Barry turned and faced Stoner's two envoys. Both men opened their sports jackets. No guns. And a request? Something's happened, and Barry wanted to know what it was.

"Do I follow you?" asked Barry.

"Mr. Stoner has provided transporation," the collegiate one replied, looking toward a black limousine with tinted windows parked down the street.

"You expect me to get into that car in front of the police station? I'd be up on bribery charges in three minutes. I'll follow in my car."

Both men agreed and walked away. Barry suddenly noticed how quiet it was outside the police station. No more protesters. Maybe they came to their senses and realized the truth about the shooting. Or maybe it was just late in the day and they had gone home. Barry had a feeling it was the latter. He pulled up behind the limo and off they drove.

The trail let to a high rise condominium on Central Park West, with a doorman outfitted like one of the Queen's guards. The two men accompanied Barry into a private elevator which took them to the penthouse on the forty-eighth floor. Barry noticed the camouflaged camera in the upper right corner of the elevator. As the elevator doors slid open, three more men greeted Barry and escorted him inside. The place was nothing less than exquisite. A wall of picture windows provided a breathtaking view of Central Park and the East Side of Manhattan. To the left, a spiral staircase led to an upper level. The furnishings in the livingroom were mostly antique in design; a couch with a low back, puffed pillows, and hand-carved wood trim looked expensive but uncomfortable. A marble bar ran the length of the livingroom. Barry calculated that it would take three lifetimes for him to afford a place like this.

It was easy to understand how honest cops and citizens could be induced into this way of life. He often wondered what his bribe price would be. It would have to be an amount that would set him up for the rest of his life. And if he was caught? Those who had been somehow managed to survive. But could he live with himself? the bitter truth was, he'd hate to be tested. Maybe that's why his price was so high.

From another room came two luscious-looking Oriental women, dressed in revealing black peignoirs. They were followed by Stoner. "How do you like my possessions?" he asked Barry, referring mainly to the women, who trailed behind him like trained dogs. "Not bad for a kid who grew up on the lower East Side, wouldn't you say, Martin?"

"Did you ever wonder how many people had to die and get hooked on drugs to pay for all of this?"

A flick of Stoner's hand emptied the room of nonessential personnel. He strolled over to what looked like the most comfortable chair in the room and sat down, gesturing to his guest to do the same. "I'd offer you a martini, but the gin is imported; it's far beyond your taste."

"If you like it I'm sure it tastes like piss!"

Stoner jumped up. So did Barry, drawing his gun.

The doors burst open and four men aimed their revolvers at Barry.

Barry's gunhand didn't budge. "I'm aiming right at your head, Stoner. And at this range I can't miss."

"Leave us," he ordered his men then sat down again.

Barry took his seat and reholstered his gun. "Is your game finished, Stoner?"

Stoner gave a quizzical look.

"You let me in here armed, and then you try to antagonize me. The question is why?"

"You're a smart cop, Martin. You're also one of the few cops I trust. Last night six of my acquaintances were murdered around the country." Reaching into his jacket pocket he handed Barry a piece of paper. "Six men killed in six different cities. Naturally the police are viewing them as isolated incidents or chalking them up to a syndicate feud—but there ain't no feud, and they ain't isolated. You know that."

Barry hadn't heard of these murders yet, but he knew what Stoner was after. "You're trying to connect these murders to the ones I'm investigating, eh?" As Barry talked his mind clicked off the cities: Boston, Chicago, St. Paul, Dallas, Los Angeles and San Francisco. Why are these cities ringing a bell? he questioned, then said aloud, "These murders are out of my jurisdiction. Besides, there's no hard evidence to connect them."

"I'm telling you there is!" Stoner stated, as though his words were the evidence. Barry believed him. Stoner gulped the martini down. "A few hours following the Boston murder we got a lead on the murderer."

"That sounds positive. When you apprehend the suspect, I'd like to interrogate him."

"We did catch him, early this morning."

"But . . . ?"

229

"He died during our interrogation."

"He probably punched himself to death with his hands tied behind his back."

"Something like that."

"And then his body fell off the chair into the river. Your people aren't very smart, Stoner. Assuming there is a connection between the murders, you blew the only lead."

"There's one chance left. His apartment. We've had it under surveillence, nobody's been in or out. And I've ordered my people to stay out; all they'd do is mess things up. But you'd know what to look for, Martin."

"Can't do it, Stoner. It's out of my jurisdiction and due to the budget crisis all travel has been halted. Have the Boston police—"

"Fuck the Boston police. Fuck the budget crisis. I want your help, Martin." Stoner was running scared. He was getting pressure from above and pressure like that meant either success or death. "I'll fly you up to Boston in my private jet and have you back home before dinner."

"What makes you think I want to help you, Stoner?"

"I didn't get where I am today by being stupid, Martin. It's called a mutual exchange. The sooner you find the killers, the less likelihood of another Lincoln Center. That's your gain. My gain is that my people stay alive." Stoner anticipated a follow-up question. "I'm not going to make you do this by force or bribery; it'll be an even trade. I'll owe you one, payable at any time. Deal?"

Barry had nothing to lose. "Deal."

Stoner summoned his men. "They'll take you to the airport. I'll arrange everything from here." With no "thank-yous" the two men parted.

On the way to the airport and during the flight, Barry reviewed the familiar names of the six decadents. Boston's victim was Sam Barker, owner of a dozen or so nursing homes, two of which were closed due to un-sanitary conditions. The rest weren't far behind. A lot of money for little service to those too fragile to fight back. Jerry Hayward was a union boss in Chicago who took his orders only from the syndicate. He was also overseer of the union's pension fund, a major portion of which found its way to the development of a Nevada casino. In St. Paul, Dr. Russell Garwood was the victim. Owner and operator of a string of abortion clinics; something necessary cheapened by its backers. Dallas was Everett Dane, a prominent banker who laundered syndicate money. Los Angeles was Gil Arby, owner of an an import/export company that allegedly also imported drugs. Last was San Francisco, and the victim there was Ralph Robinson, the West Coast's syndicate accountant. All respectable men with good businesses that had been overtaken by the syndicate, most of them probably terrorized into the ranks.

Barry gazed out the porthole of the private jet, still deliberating on those cities. Paul! Paul's list, the telephone list from the Church, or more precisely, from Rhoades. A connection between Rhoades and the Crossbearers? Perhaps, but Stoner didn't mention any-thing about letters or telephone calls such as Barry had received. On the other hand, maybe the police had received letters but were keeping them under wraps. Barry made a mental note to get that information when he returned home. But even if that turned up empty, he still felt it had to do with the Crossbearers.

Conspiracy. That was the new operative word Barry had to deal with. Conspiracy put everything into perspective. And since the killings began in New York, it was logical to assume that that's where the orders originated. But from whom?

Barry slipped the list back into his pocket. Reading was making him ill, and he felt hot although his forehead was covered with cold perspiration. Only one thing reminded him of death: flying. He closed his eyes and tried to concentrate on something happy. Jenny . . . sex with Jenny. It didn't work. Another twenty minutes left. Oh God, please don't have us circle. He closed his eyes and began counting. Just counting.

In one of the many busy lounges at John F. Kennedy International Airport, a lone man sat at the bar checking his watch every few minutes and belting down double scotches as if they were water. "The only way to fly is when you're bombed," he slurred to the uninterested bartender who in turn told the nervous customer to take a bus or train next time.

In a far booth, Father D'Angelo anxiously awaited the arrival of his long time friend, Cardinal O'Toole from Chicago. The Cardinal's last minute call to have the two meet during a short layover would have been more pleasant if Father D'Angelo had not detected an urgency in his friend's voice. And that the Cardinal was traveling without his usual entourage was also strange.

"My dear friend," came a raspy voice. Father D'Angelo stood and motioned to kiss Cardinal O'Toole's ring of office, but was stopped by a handshake and then an embrace. "It is so good to see you, my friend," Cardinal O'Toole strained, his voice heavy and wheezing from a life-long asthmatic condition. He wore a suit and his thinning hair was dyed brown, making him look much younger than Father D'Angelo, who was actually three years his senior.

Sitting down to a glass of the Cardinal's favorite port, Father D'Angelo lifted his glass for a toast. "To the memorable experiences of two young seminary students, and a third who was sinfully taken from us." Their glasses met.

"Those were joyous times," Cardinal O'Toole

reflected, "and I'd like nothing more than to sit around with you one day and relive them. But not today."

With concern Father D'Angelo inquired, "Are you in ill health, Your Eminence?"

"My medical staff doesn't allow me to get sick." The corners of his mouth briefly curved upward. "But I do have an affliction, one that regrettably might involve other priests. I know you have not been in touch with our peers recently or else you would realize that what is happening to you is also happening to many of us. Retirement. It's like a plague upon our generation. Priests, Cardinals, Bishops, all are being put out to pasture."

"I have heard rumors of that sort, yet I was told that because we're all approximately the same age it's reasonable that our retirements would come at the same time."

The Cardinal refilled both glasses. "A logical conclusion until you read this confidential report which was sent to the Vatican." He handed Father D'Angelo the two-page report. "Notice the words used to describe me: loss of memory retention, unable to handle work load, lack of communication, faltering guidance. . . ."

"Who wrote this?"

"If I knew, he'd be conducting Mass for the snakes in the Amazon," he stated humorlessly, his breathing becoming heavier from the aggravation. "I was able to get hold of two other reports. Here is yours."

Father D'Angelo read it. "Forgetful . . . continues to conduct Mass in Latin . . . unable to control the priests in his parish . . . severe loss of parishioners . . . church accounts in disarray . . . moments of senility . . ." His fingers curled the pages as he finished. "Statements without context."

"Making them sound like valid accusations. The other report is on Bishop Edmunson in Dallas. Others retiring are Father Garret in Boston, Cardinal Hartley in Los Angeles, Bishop Montierie in San Francisco, and Father Randall in St. Paul. All our contemporaries."

"But no reports on them?"

"Not that I'm aware of or they're aware of. When I asked them why they were retiring, they answered that it was that time."

"Just like me," Father D'Angelo bemoaned.

"I felt the same way, my friend, even to the point where I thought my retirement was *my* decision; that is, until I saw this report. Without knowing it, we are all being forced to retire."

"I don't see how, Your Eminence. My decision to retire was made without the knowledge of this report, the same as our contemporaries."

Cardinal O'Toole checked the time. "My plane will be leaving soon. Father, you are known as a holy man who seeks no great power. I, on the other hand, admittedly enjoy my position. The priests I mentioned fall mainly into my category. They all exude a great deal of influence or power upon the American clergy—and all are retiring. Four years ago I took under my wing a young priest who displayed leadership potential. He was a fast learner, and before I realized it, he was carrying out many of my duties. Only after I saw this report did it dawn on me that this priest had been prompting me to retire for some time. At present he has more influence than I have. I did not ask the others about this for fear they would make known my suspicions. I now ask you: Is there such a priest in your parish who has been spurring you into retirement?"

"Father Rhoades," answered Father D'Angelo automatically. "God forgive us for what we're thinking."

"I must go now. My good friend, you cannot retire. No matter what anyone says, you must fight to retain

234

your position. I am convinced that if these new priests gain too much power there will definitely be a split in the Church, and it could be disastrous."

They walked toward the departure gate. "Will I hear from you soon, Your Eminence?"

"As soon as possible, but first I must contact others. Stay well, Father, and may the grace of God continue to shine upon your life."

Father D'Angelo remained until well after the plane took off. Confusion filled his thoughts. The Reformation and the Protestant Revolution were history. Priests were devoted to the Church, to its solidarity. But there was Rhoades! Dear God, Father D'Angelo prayed, I am a simple man. If what the Cardinal says is true, give me Your guidance to understand it and Your strength to fight it.

The seat belt light flashed on and the private jet began its descent into Logan Airport. Following a three-point landing the aircraft taxied to a reserved area where a black limousine awaited. In the car was a chilled magnum of France's best champagne, a small color television set, and, lying on top of it, a manila envelope bearing Barry's name. Opening it he pulled out a photograph of one of the younger new rising starlets who was going through a promotional blitz, endorsing everything, appearing on walk shows, making movies. What a beauty! Attached was a note that read: "She belongs to us. If you want, she's yours for the night. This has nothing to do with what I owe you." It was signed Stoner.

Barry replaced the photograph and note back into the manila envelope and placed it on the television. Sometimes it seemed like the syndicate owned everybody, Barry thought. The guard in the passenger seat buzzed Barry through the car intercom to ask if he was interested in meeting the actress. Barry politely declined. And as he wondered how such people became entangled with Stoner he reopened the envelope, shredded the picture and note, and tossed the pieces out the window. No sense leaving incriminating evidence, especially the sentence ending with ". . . what I owe you." He wouldn't want to explain that to the Chief or to the District Attorney.

The limo stopped in front of a rundown apartment house in a section known as the Combat Zone. Three other men in a parked car joined Barry as he followed them inside. One of the men unlocked an apartment door and allowed Barry to enter by himself, closing the door behind him.

Deja vu. It looked as though Hank Wynn's apartment had been transported to Boston. The hovel was covered with religious pictures, crucifixes, and crosses. Uneasily Barry moved about the room feeling as though an exorcist should be present. A mattress lay on the badly warped bare wooden floor. The only other objects in the room were a tattered leather chair, a small folding table with a black and white television set and a hot plate on it, and, on the floor next to the bed, a clock radio. The lone narrow closet had an assortment of worn jeans and dress shirts with frayed collars, some shoes with holes in the soles, and a pair of sneakers. In a corner was a stained sink and a bureau, minus one handle, that contained underwear, socks, porno magazines, a white enamel cross and, tucked away in the back, a manila envelope. The address was a post office box number probably belonging to the murderer. Inside was a news clipping and picture of Sam Barker, the victim. If this is the way the Crossbearers learn about their intended victims then there's a good chance that the ones who pull the trigger have never met the ones who give the orders. Very efficient, Barry thought, as he folded the envelope and tucked it into his pocket.

Investigation of books and pamphlets in the room turned up no known names, although a new religious cult was uncovered. Barry checked the time. It was still early. He ordered Stoner's men to drive him to the cult's residence on Beacon Street. On the way he read the cult's pamphlet. This time the leader professed to be Jesus Christ. Unbelieveable, Barry thought. How can so many young people believe such garbage? Besides the Crossbearers who belonged to such cults, Barry was hoping to strike a familiar name, a tie-in.

The address turned out to be a beautiful ranch house on the outskirts of Boston. There were no visible indications that this was anything more than a suburban home, with nicely mowed lawns, pruned shrubbery and a Mercedes parked in the driveway. Answering the doorbell was a young woman dressed in a toga. Traces of marijuana seeped through the dense smell of incense. Surrounded by other males and females outfitted in Roman togas was the star of the show. He had thin long blond hair with matching beard, wore sandals, and was smoking a joint that was laced with more than just marijuana. After five minutes of sporadic conversation with the Messiah, Barry knew this cult was far from being religious or helpful. Sex and drugs were the only things on their minds, and from the amount and assortment of both, Barry ventured that the leader was just a bored rich kid who had nothing better to do than this. The idle rich. I wouldn't mind trying it for a month or two, Barry thought as he left the house and had the men drive him to the airport.

Oh well, at least the trip was not a total waste. There were other Crossbearers around the country and Rhoades, or somebody at the Church, was connected to them. He'd have to revise the theory he had mentioned to Stoner about another syndicate trying to move in, but he still wouldn't say anything about the telephone calls and letters. One thing was obvious: there was a conspiracy at work. The question was, who was in control? Rhoades? Or somebody else who just used the Church phone? There was one more possible answer to the match-up of telephone numbers and the killings: coincidence. Barry immediately dismissed that notion. Connections in an investigation are like the answers in a crossword puzzle; they fit only because they are supposed to fit.

9

Father Rhoades sat at he desk in the study going over the church account books. The latest balance showed close to twelve hundred dollars. He wrote out a check to cash for seven hundred dollars. That should cover everything, he figured, stretching his hands above his head to loosen his sore back muscles. Since that night of penance he had had no more urges of the flesh. I am strong, he thought with self satisfaction. I have driven the demon temptation out of me forever. He brought his hands back down and, clasping them together, offered a prayer of thanks and renewed obedience to Jesus.

Glancing through the previous telephone bills, he noticed they were out of monthly sequence. "Paul," he mumbled with contempt, thinking, Every time I turn around he seems to be watching me. And if it isn't him it's Inness. Why don't they leave me alone! His hand crumbled a piece of paper. Inness knows nothing, but Tobin, he's curious enough to stumble onto something. Him and his companion, Martin, playing detective, following people . . . Following people?

He picked up the telephone bills. Out of sequence, eh? He wondered how curious Paul had really been. The fingers of his right hand drummed against the telephone receiver. He had to find out. He dialed the telephone company to relieve his apprehension. After speaking to three different people, his fears were confirmed as the woman read the name of a Father Paul Tobin who had requested copies of previous telephone bills to Our Lady of the Shrine Church.

Rhoades slammed the receiver back into the cradle. His mind seethed with anger as he repeated Paul's name in disdain. He rubbed his sweaty palms together. I have to call the leader, he thought. No, I can't; they'll blame me. Oh my God! He pounded the desk top, tumbling a photograph of Father D'Angelo's family. Has he followed me other times? Did he hear anything? How much does he know?

Rhoades paced about the room, lecturing himself to calm down and think clearly. No one in the group must know. I have to do it by myself. How? The answer was all too clear. Eliminate Tobin. He opened the back door for a breath of air and spotted Paul walking toward the corner. It was time to turn the tables and discover what Paul was up to.

The trail led to Mary's apartment house. For two hours Rhoades tarried across the street. It was 7:30 p.m.

''Who the hell is he visiting?'' he asked himself out of frustration. Then Barry Martin arrived. Rhoades withdrew into the shadows but took notice of the girl he was with. Dark glasses at night and a long thin cane. It must be Paul's sister, Jennifer. Barry draped his arm around her waist and they entered the building. Fifteen minutes later Barry and Jenny left in the car. Standing on the corner were Paul and a young woman Rhoades did not recognize. He watched as the two strolled down the street hand in hand.

Rhoades approached the doorman, pointed at Paul's female companion, and asked, "Is that Sandra Wellings? She used to be one of my parishioners. I haven't seen her in years."

The doorman eyed Rhoades' collar, then the girl. "No, Father, that's Mary Evans."

"Really. Well, they say everyone has a double. Thank you, my son. Have a pleasant night."

Rhoades proceeded in the opposite direction from Paul and Mary, but quickly doubled back. They were still holding hands. They kissed.

Rhoades breathed erratically. Paul had probably told her, Barry, and his sister about the telephone bills, he thought. No, maybe he hadn't. I can't take the chance. If Paul disappears, his three friends would be suspicious. I can't have that. First it was only Paul, now it was the four of them. It was snowballing and Rhoades didn't like it, but it had to be done. All four had to be eliminated. He rationalized about it more. Four lives versus his cause. Four lives to save his group. Four lives for God. I'll do it, he decided. It's God's will. The New Order demands it.

Sleepily, Barry rolled over, shut the alarm off, then rolled back to find Jenny's naked body pressing against his.

"This is better than an alarm clock," he whispered in her ear, his left hand moving to her breast.

In between yawns, Jenny replied, "I can feel which part of you wakes up first." Barry nudged himself on top of her. "Wouldn't you prefer to brush your teeth and have some coffee first?"

"Nah," he moaned sliding his hips forward. The bed

creaked on the downstroke. There was a muffled laugh.

"Am I doing something wrong?" Jenny asked, still half asleep.

Barry pulled out. "Cyclops is licking my feet."

Jenny scrambled out of bed fast before he tried a second time. Brushing her teeth and drinking coffee were the only things on her mind at seven o'clock in the morning.

Cyclops leaped on the bed and snuggled next to Barry. "You don't like sex in the morning, do you?" he shouted, to be heard over the running water. "People usually have sex at night. It's so planned that way. People should do it whenever they have the urge."

"Nobody has the urge to have an urge at seven in the morning," she drolled as she made her way to the kitchen. The automatic coffee maker had already finished brewing. Jenny swallowed the coffee as if it were a magic elixir.

Barry joined her. "I meant to ask you how the lessons are going with Cyclops."

"Your friend has the patience of an angel and Cyclops is really smart, almost human sometimes in the way he obeys commands. Today's our first attempt at walking all the way to the Institute, with teacher of course. Do you have time for some eggs? Take only a minute."

"No, I'll grab something at the precinct. Nobody makes powdered eggs like our vending machines."

"You were restless last night. The Boston trip?" Jenny squeezed Barry's hand. "I can't hear a nod. Maybe you ought to tell the Captain about it. Just to protect yourself."

'It crossed my mind."

"So you're not going to tell the Captain. But can you trust Stoner?"

"As much as I trust the Captain. I can't investigate

this case properly if all these people are butting in and following me. I'm better off working it out by myself."

"Speaking of being followed, what ever happened to that sedan that was following you?"

"I haven't seen it in a week."

"That's good," Jenny said, pouring another cup of coffee. "It was making me nervous that some unknown creature was stalking you."

"The only problem is, I never figured out why they were following me. I hate that. By the way, I might be late tonight. The Captain and the Chief want this case solved, as if I'm not trying to do it."

"You should make them honorary A.P. members."

"They're already earned permanent membership. Do you have an art class tonight?"

"Every day you ask me that question and I know why, but I wish you wouldn't. You're making me paranoid about someone watching me. The other day I was so intent on listening for repetitive footsteps that I tripped on the curb."

"There's nothing wrong with being cautious."

"It's going on two years, Barry. They've probably forgotten about me."

"Take Cyclops with you tonight."

"I will, I will. And you be careful today too."

"I always am. See you tonight."

Lingering over her coffee, Jenny thought about those faceless assassins and Barry's apprehension. Was the case of the Crossbearers related to Cardinal Beck and her accident? Barry's evasiveness told her he suspected they were. The daily sounds of apartment life suddenly took on a foreboding nature.

Cyclops rambled over and laid his head on her lap. "You'll protect me, won't you, Cyclops?" she said, kissing him on the head. "I just wish somebody would protect me from Barry's bizarre theories." The telephone rang, startling her. "See what I mean?" And then, into the telephone, she said with surprise, "Father Crowley. Is there anything wrong?"

"Not at all," answered the detached voice, "and I'm sorry for disturbing you at such an early hour, but your parents said you would be awake. You're a hard girl to find, Jennifer. I spoke to your parents who referred me to a Mary Evans who referred me to this number. Congratulations on being on your own."

Diplomatically Jenny answered "I have a roommate, but the independence does feel good. It has been a long time since we've seen each other, Father Crowley. You must join me for dinner one night; there's a person I'd like you to meet."

"I'd be delighted to. From the sound of your voice you seem well and happy, Jennifer."

"I am, Father. I really am. When you come for dinner we'll have more time to talk, but right now I'm late for work. Thank you for calling, Father, and I'll be in touch with you soon."

Sweet man, Jenny thought.

Barry checked in at the precinct but was detained along with the other detectives for another punitive lecture on the excessive use of firearms by the police, a result of Dave's killing of the young boy and the media attention it still attracted. Dave was conspicuously absent from the lecture.

Vocal opposition to Captain Adams' lecture was fast and furious. The retorts ranged from prejudices on the media's side against the police to gun control. One officer announced, "I don't care who it is or how old he is, if someone points a gun at me I'm gonna kill him first. Fuck the media!"

A round of applause and whistles followed. Barry just listened. He'd been through these lectures before and knew that no cop in his right mind took these lectures seriously. They were held mostly for public relations purposes. For Barry, they were a waste of time.

Barry didn't arrive at Wayne Wilkins' establishment until eleven o'clock. From the foyer he heard the distinctive evangelical voice booming from behind the closed doors.

"Can I help you?" inquired a husky voice.

Barry turned. The voice was in accordance with the man's stature. "Police," he said showing his badge. "I'd like to see Mr. Wilkins."

"Mr. Wilkins is busy. Will be all day."

"I'll wait."

"The man said he's busy all day," came another voice from the left. "This is a private meeting, buddy, and you weren't invited."

"How do you know?"

" 'Cause I do. Why don't you leave?" He gestured toward the front door.

Obviously they'd been warned by Drury. But he boldly restated, "I'll wait," and managed to keep both men peripherally in sight as they circled about. There wasn't enough time to draw his gun.

One of the men dashed forward. Barry kicked his foot up into the man's abdomen, stopping him in his tracks. The second attacker's fist was already in motion. Barry ducked the first punch but couldn't escape the second; it caught his right temple, looping him backwards to the floor. The first man was beginning to get up as the one who had just struck him moved in. A few years ago Barry could have taken both of them in a fight, but now he wasn't so sure. Forty wasn't old unless you had to fight two men simultaneously.

Barry's legs wobbled slightly as he rose to his feet, his clenched fists ready for another attack. The charging man's arm swung around from his body like a boomerang. Barry's left forearm intercepted the shot. From the corner of his eye he spied the second attacker closing in. He had to defeat this one before both of them overpowered him. Hauling back with his right, Barry swung from his hip upward, catching the man's jaw. The attacker stiffened, then collapsed to the floor in a heap.

Barry instantly whirled around and, with both hands clasped together in one over-sized fist, struck the other man's nose, staggering him. Before the man could fall, Barry grabbed him by the arm, spun him around, and hurled him through the closed doors into the meeting room, his body sprawling to the floor.

The alarmed audience scattered to the sides.

"What's the meaning of this!" bellowed Wilkins, attired in vibrant red robes.

"The door was stuck," muttered Barry, walking down the aisle feeling the effects of each punch his body had absorbed. Then in a deliberately loud voice he broadcast, "My name is Detective Barry Martin from Homicide Division. I'd like to talk to you in private about a murder."

There was a rustling in the crowd as they scurried to leave.

Wayne Wilkins jumped off the stage and faced Barry. "What do you want here? And make it fast. I have no time to waste." His voice was belligerent. He was not about to be helpful.

Barry sized up the evangelist. It was amazing how they all looked alike. His eyes were drawn to the blood-stained wounds on Wilkins's palms. "Aren't you worried you'll bleed to death?"

Wilkins hid his hands behind his back "This is an invasion of my privacy," he intoned articulating each syllable. "My lawyers will hear of this. They'll have your badge!"

Barry returned the threat. "Lawyers? I hate lawyers. I

hate people who have lawyers. Just the word 'lawyer' makes me violent. And you know what happens when I get violent?" Barry seized Wilkins by his robe and yanked him closer. His accentuated breathing created a whistling sound through his clenched teeth. "I hurt people. I hurt them badly." If the Captain saw me doing this, he thought, I wouldn't be able to get a job as a janitor in the police station. But he won't find out—I hope. Barry twisted the robe for added persuasion. "My patience is running out."

Wilkins held up his hands in surrender and Barry released him.

"That's better," said Barry. "Now tell me about Hank Wynn."

Following a moment of thought, Wilkins replied "He was employed as a handyman, but lasted only a few months. He was caught stealing money. Not much, though. He was a petty thief."

"What about friends?"

"A girl named Carol, that's all I know. I never met her. He wasn't the type that made friends easily. Weird, know what I mean?"

"How about a blond male friend named Joe?" Barry wished he could give a fuller description of the culprit, but when there's more than one eyewitness, there's more than one description—and it seems as though they never match.

"Not that I can recall," Wilkins answered in a bored voice.

"After he left your fold, did he go straight to Palmer?"

"Yeah."

"Did you warn Palmer about Hank stealing?"

"Sure, but Palmer loves people like that; turn their souls around so they can go to Heaven. The worse a person is, the better Palmer likes them. I guess it's a

247

challenge. Me, I can do without challenges like that."

"You ever hear of a group called the Crossbearers?"

"No. Is that all?"

"For now, but I might want to talk to you again."

The two guards, having regained consciousness, blocked Barry's path.

"Mr. Wilkins," Barry said not taking his eyes off the two men, "if these gentlemen don't get out of my way, those wounds on your hands will be for real."

Wilkins flicked one of his hands in the air and the two guards moved aside.

Barry drove to Prescott Palmer's establishment. If Palmer knew of Wynn's menacing traits from Drury and Wilkins, as he obviously did, then why harbor him in his congregation? To send his soul to Heaven? No. For a special project? Possible.

Inside Prescott Palmer's place, a small entourage had already formed, waiting for their Master's door to open.

A whispered "Detective Martin" made him turn. "Remember me? I'm Linda." She was huddled in a corner.

"Of course." Barry observed her hands rubbing against her pants, her eyes darting from side to side. "How can I help?"

"Get me outta here. They've made me a prisoner." She stopped and smiled at other members walked by. "I'm watched all the time. I'm scared and I want to go home." Barry held her arm and made a motion toward the front door but Linda retreated back into the corner.

"I'll protect you," encouraged Barry. "Just walk out the door with me, Linda. That's all you have to do."

"No, they'll come after me, I know they will." She was on the verge of hysteria.

"Okay, there's another way, Linda. I can obtain a court order and arrest everyone here and take them downtown for questioning. From there we'll send you home and you'll just disappear. Nobody will know, you have my word. It'll be about an hour. Don't leave this place."

Linda's relief was momentary as her eyes fixed on a presence behind Barry. Barry turned. He didn't know he was looking at Carol. She walked next to Linda and placed her hand on Linda's neck in a friendly manner, then pressed her nails into the flesh, still smiling. Linda's expression remained nervously unchanged.

"May I help you, sir?" Carol asked graciously, detecting something vaguely familiar about this stranger.

Other members encircled Barry from behind. He needed a reason for being there and a way to get out without provoking suspicion. "My car broke down and I need a telephone to call for a tow truck. I tried the one on the corner, but it's out of order so I came in here. She," pointing to Linda, "said you don't have a phone."

Carol loosened her grip on Linda's neck. "That's correct, but there's a gas station two blocks North."

"North? It's my first time in New York. Which way's North?"

"Straight up the street. You can't miss it."

"Thank you," Barry said making a fast exit before Palmer spotted him. Immediately he telephoned for the necessary court papers and then waited in his car. Each minute seemed like ten and he wondered if Linda could hold out that long.

Carol marched Linda upstairs into Palmer's private chamber. She pressed her hands against Linda's breasts and kissed the nape of her neck. Linda pulled away begging, "Please don't."

"You liked it the other day."

"I was confused. Please leave me alone." Her voice sounded desperate now.

Carol grabbed Linda by the hair, arching her head backwards. "You'll do what I say, Linda. Do you understand?" The frightened girl's tears had no effect on Carol. "You belong to me, Linda, don't forget that!"

The office door swung open and Joe entered. "I have to see you, Carol. It's important." Carol released Linda reluctantly joined him in the hall. "Detective Martin is outside in his car watching this place. I snuck in the back way. I don't like this."

"Describe him."

"Curly brown hair, six feet, brown sports jacket."

"Cocksucker!" Carol gritted between her clenched teeth, glancing at Linda. "Stalled car, eh? I knew he looked familiar."

"What's going on?"

"He was talking to Linda. I have a feeling that as long as Linda is here, Martin will be here. He's too close to us. We have to get rid of Linda before Prescott finds out about us too."

They re-entered the room and Joe, flashing his knife, forced Linda to accompany them out the back door.

An hour later three patrol cars arrived; one with the warrant, the other two as back-ups. Two officers stationed themselves at the front door and two more were sent to the rear doors to make sure no one escaped. Barry handed Palmer the search warrant as his men began herding the members into the meeting room.

"That's everybody," a patrolman announced.

No Linda and no Carol. Barry knew he blew it.

"How long is this police harassment going to continue?" Palmer censured at Barry. "Or will I have to contact my lawyer?"

"A girl named Carol. Describe her."

Palmer obstinately remained silent. Barry was in no

mood for a convenient lapse of memory, but he had to be careful, there were too many witnesses roaming around for him to use physical force. Barry slung his arm over Palmer's shoulder, feigned a smile to the other officers who were still interrogating the cult members, and in a subdued tone stated, "You know, Palmer, in my line of work I meet a lot of characters who wind up owing me favors because I've helped them out of certain sticky situations. There's this one guy, he's a chemist, of course he's not licensed anymore since that bottle of sulphuric and accidentally fell onto his boss' face . . ."

"Okay, okay, what do you want?"

"First, Linda's address."

"The East Village, 41 Saint Mark's Place."

"Now describe the girl named Carol."

"Good looking face and body. Short black hair—"

Barry swung his fist through the air. I had her and I didn't even know it, he reprimanded himself. "Where does Carol live?"

"With a man named Joe Ricart. 117 Houston Street."

"Joe?" Bingo. Finally a last name. "Does he have blond hair?"

"No, brown hair."

That doesn't make sense. It has to be the same guy. Blond . . . blond *wig*. Shit! I should have guessed. "You'd better not be lying, Palmer," Barry warned, and headed for Linda's apartment. He prayed she was there, alive.

It was an old tenement painted a depressing gray. A thin Puerto Rican superintendent unlocked the apartment door. The tiny studio had one small, barred window, but a young female's touches were obvious. Two fluorescent lights hovered over a dozen healthy plants while on the wall was a large poster of a rock group Barry had never heard of. A square framed picture of a middle-aged couple, most—probably her parents—and some makeup cases on a round table next to her bed. The most expensive item in the apartment was the stereo equipment, but there was no television and no telephone. A handful of paperback books ranging from best selling novels to the Bible were stacked on top of one another. Pamphlets concerning Prescott Palmer lay under the books.

In one of the drawers was her high school yearbook. Judging from the inscriptions she was apparently well liked, yet nothing suggested why she had run away from home. Next to the yearbook was a small tan leather address book. Barry flipped through it quickly. He found no Carol, no Joe Ricart. He put the address book into his pocket for further investigation, then headed for Ricart's apartment on Houston Street.

The address was another tenement with graffiti scrawled on the outside and the inside. The handwritten directory showed Ricart in Apartment 2D. Barry inserted his credit card between the door lock and went upstairs to 2D. No sound came from within. Using a special tool he unlocked the door and, with gun drawn, entered the empty apartment. He locked the door behind him. A huge crucifix hung over the bed; smaller crucifixes hung from the walls.

"Bingo!" he said as he began searching. The sink was alive with roaches crawling over encrusted plates. A color television, a new stereo, and a closet full of expensive clothes clashed with the cheap apartment. Barry found a brown paper bag beneath four pairs of shoes in the closet. One fell a blond wig. "Double bingo!"

A key jiggled in the door lock. Barry squatted behind a chair. Carol entered. As she turned her back to close the door, Barry grabbed her by the arm and shoved her against the wall, spread-eagled. Disregarding her nonstop string of four letter expletives, he identified himself as the police and searched her. She carried no weapons. He handcuffed her hands behind her back, then turned her around to face him.

Her arched eyebrows and open mouth showed recognition of Barry. "Well, I see you got your car fixed."

"Where's Linda?"

"Linda who? Oh, that Linda. I don't know. Hey, you got a warrant to be in here?"

"Only people who have been this route before ask that question. What were you in for?"

"I don't know what you're talking about. Besides, I don't have to answer you, I got my rights."

"They've been temporarily suspended. Where's your boyfriend Joe Ricart?"

She shrugged.

"We're going for a ride." He held her by the arm.

"Let go of me, you cocksucker!" she squealed, twisting free and kicking him in the shins.

Barry grabbed her by the throat and pinned her shoulders against the wall. "I don't play games, little girl, so don't fuck around any more." He spun her around and guided her to the door.

"What's going on in there?" questioned an old man standing in the hallway. More neighbors peered through their half-open doors.

Barry displayed his badge to the onlookers. "Wha'd she do?" asked a man while another said, "You sure you're the police?" A woman cried out, "Somebody call the police."

Barry, with Carol in tow, eased his way through the small group of spectators and took his first step down the staircase.

Suddenly, Carol shrieked, "Don't push me!" ripped herself from Barry's grip, and flung herself down the stairs.

Barry leapt after Carol's tumbling body as did one of the spectators, who screamed, "I saw him push her." Another yelled, "Police brutality," and an old lady cried, "She didn't do nothin'; why did you push her? I'm calling the police!"

"Call an ambulance," Barry ordered, feeling a still fairly strong pulse in Carol's wrist. He unlocked the handcuffs. So young, he grieved, to be filled with so much hatred.

Sirens screeched and uniformed policemen converged on the scene. The witnesses continued heaping obscenities on Barry. What a disaster, he thought, as fingers pointed accusingly at him.

Joe Ricart watched the proceedings from the corner. "Carol," he muttered as she was wheeled out on a gurney and lifted into the ambulance. Barry came into view holding the brown paper bag.

"My wig!" Joe said in terror. Concern for Carol vanished. He glanced at the car trunk. Time to move fast. Joe drove toward the docks, a contented smile smothering his face. I'll call Badge 5746 tomorrow. Jeezus, will he be surprised! Joe burst into a cynical laugh, tuned the radio louder, and sang along.

The other detectives watched the Captain pace around the chair Barry was sitting in. His hands flailed in the air and his mouth gnawed at his cigar as if he were a hungry rat with a piece of cheese. The onlookers did not need to hear what was being said. The gestures were enough.

Barry sat quietly waiting for Captain Adams to finish his tirade. Twelve years on the force and even after a computer check had spit out Carol Lynch as a shoplifter and prostitute, the brass was taking her word over his. Unbelievable!

Captain Adams's pupils contracted into small pellets. "You didn't read her her rights. You didn't explain the nature of your interrogation or what charges she was being arrested for. You threw her against the wall and for an encore you pushed her down the stairs." He slapped the papers against the desk. "You didn't do one goddamn thing right, Martin. Basic police procedures, and you missed all of them. Jesus Christ! The P.C. is on the Chief's back, the Chief is on my back, so I'm on your back. They're calling for your suspension pending a formal investigation, Martin, but I can't afford to lose a body when there are no replacements available." The Captain sat on the desk top. "Carol's lawyer is after your ass too, and you know how lawyers love to stick it to cops."

"I'll say it once more, Captain: She threw herself down the stairs and I don't give a shit what those witnesses say."

"Can ya prove it?"

"And waste my time? At least I kow who the blond wigged assassin is, and isn't that what we wanted?"

"Martin, you're a good detective, but Jeeze if you don't give me hemorrhoids. Why is it that every case you work on you break the law at least once? Can you explain that?"

"All of my major arrests have been solid and you know it. Let me get back to work."

Captain Adams stood up, his hands wringing the papers. "How long's it gonna take to find this guy. . . ."

"Ricart. He was probably waiting outside his apartment for Carol and saw everything. I don't know. I put out an A.P.B. on him, but he'll just hole up somewhere. I'll have to talk to Carol again."

"No way. You can't go near her."

"I have to. She's a member of the Crossbearers. I have to see her."

"No, and that's an order."

"Captain, she can help break the case. That would make a lot of people happy."

The Captain rolled his cigar in his mouth as he mulled over the situation. "Let me put it to you this way, Martin. You're still on the case but you do not have my permission to see her."

I feel like a boa constrictor's next lunch, Barry thought. But at least the snake's giving me an opening. "I understand, Captain." Barry's tone acknowledged the double interpretation as he mentally moved the Captain and the Chief to the top of the A.P. list.

He headed for the hospital. The doctor's report listed Carol in satisfactory condition with multiple contusions and a mild concussion. A few days for observation was all the doctor required. But Barry didn't have a few days, not if there was going to be another murder.

Barry glanced down the white sterile hall of the hospital. There was no security guard outside Carol's door, as he had ordered. He sprinted into the room and found the guard lying unconscious on the bed, a bloodied spot behind his ear. Ricart! Dammit! It was back to Ricart's apartment to conduct a more intensive search.

More religious books and a handful of pamphlets concerning Palmer were everywhere. There were no personal touches anywhere, giving Barry a sense of Ricart as a habitual wanderer. Only the necessities to get through life on a daily basis were here, and they were in poor condition. A plastic yucca tree gave a simulated semblance of life. One tree? It was out of place. Gripping the stalk, he twisted the plant out of the large clay bowl and unearthed three small plastic envelopes containing a white powder. He knew what it was even before he tasted it. Heroin. A larger bag contained plastic explosives. Lining the bottom were three manila envelopes. Each one contained newspaper pictures and profiles of the people the Crossbearers had murdered so far—the same as in Boston. This proved there was a conspiracy. But still puzzling him was the absence of letters and evidence of telephone calls to the other cities. There was one possibility, but that could only be proven once the case was solved.

First things first. I gotta find this crazy bastard fast. Only two avenues were open: Palmer and Linda's address book. It wasn't much. But the manila envelopes substantiated his theory: Ricart, Carol, and whoever else was in the group were only puppets, probably not even aware of the other murders. Somebody else was controlling the strings, and with great skill. A bunch of madmen controlling another bunch of madmen. The only difference being that the controllers were quietly mad: People appearing sane yet harboring a concealed madness . . . and just as ruthless. And Barry had no evidence to prove who it was.

10

The whistling of a cheerful tune drew Paul to the study. "Father D'Angelo. You're in a good mood today. Did our guest leave?" There was a rustling of papers from the corner of the study behind him. He didn't want to turn but he did. Breezes from an open window fluttered a bunch of papers on top of the file cabinet. He let out a sigh of relief, then crossed the room and took a seat.

"Paul, over the past few weeks church attendance has increased almost fifteen percent and our visitor is greatly impressed."

"It's probably your sermons."

"That is a pure guess, since you're never around to hear them. That goes for Father Rhoades too, although he's not as bad as you are."

"I realize I've been neglecting my church duties, Father, but, as you well know, I've had other things on my mind."

"Yes, of course. I'm sorry for being so abrupt with you, Paul. Older people tend to forget the problems of younger people."

"And vice versa. What are you reading?"

Father D'Angelo handed Paul two mimeographed sheets explaining. "Father Rhoades' updated list of television shows to be avoided, and their advertised products to be boycotted."

"My God, the only shows he missed were the news."

"Look on the next sheet."

"Ah ha, that takes care of the new television season. Wait a minute . . . Space Ranger? What's wrong with that?"

"Evil communications corrupt good manners. Corinthians One."

"That can be applied to the news, but not to Space Ranger. It's mindless dribble."

"If you're Father Rhoades, it can be applied. Beings from other planets that do not look like us, that were not created in His image, and that are omnipotent. Father Rhoades is also trying to have this book banned from libraries."

"And I'll bet he has some community support," Paul guessed.

"Some Church support too," added Father D'Angelo. "This is God's way," he said, holding up the two lists, "of telling me to retire because my aged mind cannot comprehend such extremism."

"Your age has nothing to do with it, Father, only your insight. Speaking of Rhoades, I haven't seen him for a while."

"He is a troubled priest. I offered him confession the other day but he refused. Perhaps solitude will help where I could not. Over the years I've watched him become more isolated from those around him, and I've never been able to get through to him." Father D'Angelo crossed himself. "That's not quite true. The past year I haven't even tried."

"You can't like everybody, Father."

"God expects it of me."

"Except for Rhoades. Toleration is sufficient." They both laughed.

Father Inness entered the study, silencing the conversation. "I am not intruding?"

"Not at all," Father D'Angelo lied graciously.

Father Inness eyed Paul's sweat suit and sneakers. "Is this not inappropriate dress for a man of the cloth, Padre Tobin?"

"I'm playing racquetball with my friend today. He should be arriving any minute," Paul said checking the time.

"Your activities are quite varied, Padre Tobin. I hear you are also a professional builder—an architect. Padre Rhoades showed me your workshop downstairs. The rocking chair you fashoned is quite a work of art."

Paul shook his head at the untimely comment. Addressing Father D'Angelo, Paul explained, "It was meant to be a surprise for your birthday, but since you know about it now . . ." Father D'Angelo stammered his surprise and gratitude. "I'll bring it up to you tonight when I get back. Do you want it here or in your room?"

"No one has ever before given me a gift made with his own hands. I am . . . I . . ."

The study door opened and Mrs. Rodriguez, a long-time volunteer at the church, announced that Detective Martin was in the vestibule.

"Would you like to meet my friend?" Paul asked Father Inness politely.

"No!" replied Inness, wide-eyed. "I mean, you go, I do not want to hold you up."

"No bother, we have time."

"I must really finish writing my reports. I will leave by this door," he pointed to the rear exit, "and pick up some fruit."

"Strange behavior," Paul commented to Father D'Angelo. "Very similar to Rhoades. Paranoia." Paul greeted Barry and rode off with him.

As Barry's car pulled away from the church, Father Inness watched from the side of the building.

Barry's police radio signalled his number and gave a location down at the docks near Morton Street. Barry replied and the car accelerated.

"What is it?" Paul inquired.

"A female body was discovered near the Morton Street piers." His voice slumped off and his lips mashed together. "I know who it is, goddammit!"

Paul said nothing. There was nothing to say. Once again he saw the by now all too familiar scene: an ambulance, flashing lights, crowds of policemen and spectators, and the black plastic bag—the body bag. He even knew the name of it. Paul remained in the car as Barry approached the crime scene. He lifted the sheet from the body. Linda!

"Pull the sheet down all the way." Doc ordered. Barry obeyed. Carved on Linda's naked torso were the numbers 5746.

"If it's any comfort to you, that was done after she was dead," Doc offered.

Barry found no consolation in the words. "How did she die?"

"A knife wound between her shoulder blades. Death was instantaneous. But she did have some grease smudges on her clothes and arm, and rope burns on her wrists. My guess is that she was in the trunk of a car. I'll give you a full report in two days." Doc paused, looked at the body being lifted into the ambulance, and observed, "People don't just kill any more; they mutilate."

"Anything on the blond wig I gave you?" Barry asked.

"We know where the glue was made, where the hair came from, and who the manufacturer is. As for the person wearing the wig, we found small strands of brown hair."

"That's all?"

"It's a cheap wig, Barry. In the city alone there are over three hundred stores that carry that brand."

"With all your knowledge and modern scientific equipment why can't you give me one good piece of evidence?"

"Barry, if there's nothing there, there's nothing there. I can't invent evidence!"

"Go over this area again. I want *something*!"

Doc consented. This was no time to argue.

Barry checked with other uniformed policemen who also came up empty-handed in regard to witnesses. He returned to the car.

Paul had overheard much of the conversation and felt compelled to discuss his visits to Palmer's place and his talk with Linda. "I was trying to save her from Palmer's brainwashing, to get her to go back home Another failure."

"Yes, but it was mine, not yours. I should have taken her out of there by force instead of playing conservatively. I should have listened to my instincts, dammit."

"That guy you mentioned the other day, Ricart. Did he do this?"

Barry nodded.

"Maybe you can catch him on this murder charge. People like him deserve to be put on public trial."

"He'll never make it to trial," Barry unconsciously mumbled aloud.

"Barry, we don't have to play racquetball tonight."

"Maybe you don't, but I do."

And he did. Vollies became hits, hits became slams,

slams became wicked attacks. The ball flew against the walls even harder than they had done on Paul's night of frustration. Paul allowed his friend the time for vengeance on the ball.

By the end of the hour, Barry's arm was sore but his mind was calm. They went back to Barry's apartment where Jenny, with Mary's assistance, was preparing dinner for them. This would be the first full course dinner Jenny had attempted since the accident.

"Do me a favor, Paul; don't mention tonight's incident. I promised myself I wouldn't bring my work home with me. It's going to be hard tonight."

"Are you all right? That was an ugly sight."

"I hate to tell you, but I've seen worse."

"I've read about them in the papers. Perhaps Mary and I should skip dinner tonight, give you a chance to relax."

"Jenny's been working on this dinner all day; we can't disappoint her. Besides, I'm feeling better." But he wasn't.

As Barry turned the key to enter, a menacing growl came from the other side. This being Paul's first visit to Barry's apartment since Jenny had moved in, he explained, "It's Cyclops, Jenny's Seeing Eye dog. He won't bite, I don't think." Paul entered behind Barry.

"How was your game?" Jenny asked, kissing both Paul and Barry.

"Useful," Barry answered.

"Paul, Barry, I'd like you to meet Father Crowley," Jenny said extending her hand toward the livingroom. "He stopped over tonight to see how I was."

Father Crowley stood up. Just as Jenny had described him. Mid-forties, portly, a cigar in his hand, and, surprisingly, snow white hair. Jenny had never mentioned that. But she couldn't have, Barry remembered, she had never seen him.

Barry extended his hand. "Nice to meet you, Father."

"So you're the reason for Jennifer's smile. A pleasure. And Paul, finally we meet. I spoke to your parents recently; I'm pleased they're doing well and in good health."

"Thank you, Father. And now I can thank you in person for your help and prayers during Jenny's convalescence. It meant a great deal to all of us."

"I just happened to have been at the hospital visiting another patient when I heard Jenny's name mentioned. I'm glad I could be of help." Barry took note of the reason he was at the hospital while Father Crowley continued. "Tell me, how is Father D'Angelo? I heard he's retiring."

"He's thinking about it, but I'm trying to talk him out of it. I've also heard some other priests are retiring; even some Cardinals."

"Unfortunately many prelates are in the same age category and so it seems that they all retire at about the same time."

Jenny interrupted. "Barry, your presence is required in the kitchen. It will only take a minute."

"Paul will help you." Barry nodded to Paul.

"Barry, it's impolite to ask a guest—"

"I don't mind. Honest." Paul replied.

"Jenny can show you where everything is," added Barry, wanting to be alone with the priest.

Paul almost had to yank Jenny away.

Father Crowley initiated the social conversation with Barry. "Jennifer told me you're a detective. An interesting occupation."

"It has its moments. Have you known Father D'Angelo long?"

"Many years. He's a fine man. You know him also?"

"The church is in my precinct. I know everybody there."

"Then you must also know Father Rhoades. He and I attended seminary college together. I don't see much of him anymore. People think a priest's life is full of free time, but it's usually just the opposite."

"I didn't know you and Father Rhoades were classmates. Where did the two of you graduate from?"

"Boston Seminary College. A beautiful city, Boston. Not as hurried as New York."

"Nothing is," Barry light-heartedly responded, trying to maintain a casualness in their conversation. "Paul hasn't adjusted yet, but at least we can complain to each other. It's a good outlet. I complain about crime and he complains about the lack of young men entering the priesthood. Did you have a large graduating class?"

Father Crowley thought a minute with the aid of his fingers. "Eleven. And Paul's right; today it's probably much lower than that. As for our parishioners, the Day of Judgement can no longer compete with worldly intimidations. I'm afraid the Church in the United States is fighting its last battle for survival."

"That sounds ominous, Father. But if it's true, how do you resurrect it?"

"Priests can be resourceful, Detective Martin. People simply don't give us enough credit for being imaginative. We can be very imaginative if we have to be."

"I'll bet you can, Father. But not all priests have that trait. I'd guess that the priests you're most friendly with are like yourself, imaginative and innovative. Am I right?"

"Since all priests are brothers, I try not to be selective, Detective Martin. You can understand that."

Father Crowley conspicuously checked his watch. "I didn't realize it was so late. Tell Jennifer I said goodbye, and to the others."

"I will. By the way, you'll be happy to know that Jenny has overcome much of the trauma of the accident. Every day she remembers more and more."

"That is good news. But I recall her parents' saying she still had nightmares."

"On and off. Once she remembers everything the nightmares will disappear. Good night, Father."

Paul, Jenny, and Mary entered from the kitchen. "What's going on here?" demanded Jenny, with Cyclops sitting at her feet. "Paul kept us in the kitchen as if we were prisoners while you're out here interrogating Father Crowley as though he was a common criminal. If it wasn't for Father Crowley I might never have recovered. What you did is disgusting!" With a stamp of her foot Jenny went to the bedroom.

"I'll look after her," offered Mary.

"I've never seen Jenny so mad," Paul commented.

Barry had other things on his mind. "You still have that list of churches from the telephone numbers you called?"

Paul took the list out of his wallet and handed it to Barry. "What are you thinking of? Just because Crowley has white hair doesn't mean he was the one I saw at the loft."

"Your initial expression says he was." Barry glanced at the list. "Seven churches plus Crowley and Rhoades makes nine plus the other two men you saw makes eleven. Eleven. And Crowley said there were eleven in his graduating class. A match."

"It doesn't make sense. So it's a match. Big deal. You still have priests talking only to priests. It's absurd to think that they're involved in your investigation, Barry."

"Listen to the facts, Paul. The entire case revolves around religious fanatics, and there are fanatics in all groups. We also have the meeting in Soho with Rhoades, a white-haired man who closely resembles Father Crowley; the shadow turned out to be Rhoades; murders in cities corresponding to the telephone list; Cardinal Beck's assassination; and Jenny's accident."

And now Barry also knew who was watching Jenny's progress, but he kept that to himself. "That's quite a bit of circumstantial evidence to be ignored."

"Granted, but still no proof to connect priests with the murders yet or to the Crossbearers."

"So far. Maybe there isn't a connection, but something's going on and it's not right. The only two men not accounted for are the thin man you saw at loft and my cleft-lipped man in the Oldsmobile. I wish I knew why he disappeared so suddenly."

"Cleft-lipped?" Paul repeated uneasily. "Can you describe him better than that?"

"A round freckled face but not fat. Wide nose, small mouth . . ."

"How tall?"

"Don't know. He was sitting in a car. Why the questions?" Barry put his hand on Paul's arm. "You know him. He's another priest, isn't he?"

"My God, yes. A visitor from the Vatican. But he arrived only last week. I wanted to introduce him to you but he suddenly had reports to write out. No! Dammit, you can make anyone look suspicious."

"They do it all on their own, Paul. I think I'll join you for breakfast at the church tomorrow. What time is it served?"

"Father Inness has breakfast at 8:45 every morning."

Mary joined them in the livingroom. "Jenny's really upset, Barry. I can't calm her down. You try. Paul, we should leave."

Barry went into the bedroom where Jenny was curled up on the bed with Cyclops. He sat on the edge of the bed. "I'm sorry I hurt your feelings, Jenny. It's just that something clicked in my mind and I had to pursue it. I know how much Father Crowley means to you—"

"No you don't. Nobody does. You don't know what it's like to wake up in a hospital room, open your eyes, and see . . . nothing. No matter which way I turned, I saw nothing. Then I felt the bandages around my eyes, and I thought, Thank God, it's only the bandages that are keeping me from seeing. Sometime later I overheard two people talking about the young girl in the accident who was blinded. I knew who they were talking about and I knew what I had to do. If my eyes couldn't see I didn't want them at all. I took hold of the bandages and began to rip them off when suddenly two soft and gentle hands touched mine and a voice that seemed to come at me from all sides said, "Your eyes are now like the eyes of God. Don't hurt them."

"For a moment I thought it was God Himself who had touched me and talked to me. Of course it wasn't, but that day Father Crowley was God for me, because God could have done no better."

Barry lay down, gathered Jenny in his arms, and held her.

"You're silent again," she said. "You still believe Father Crowley's involved with the Crossbearers, don't you?"

"You can't help the way you feel, but I can't help the way I feel, either."

"What do you want to know about him?" Jenny asked.

"Did you know Father Crowley before the accident?"

"No, but then again I wasn't very religious before the accident. Tragedy is the quickest road to prayer and

God. I speak from experience.''

"If you and your folks didn't attend Church regularly, then why—assuming Crowley was actually visiting another patient at the time—why would your name be familiar to him? Anther thought: Cardinal Beck had just been assassinated, yet Crowley was at the hospital visiting another patient and then took time to see you rather than rush to the Cardinal's bedside or to St. Patrick's.''

"I don't know . . . I don't know,'' she said. Her hero was becoming tarnished.

"Jenny, speaking from experience, if the same people continue to pop up in an investigation, it's for a good reason. There's a connection all right, but I don't know what it is yet.''

"I honestly hope you're wrong, Barry. Father Crowley's a good man, and he'd never be involved in anything like you imagine.''

Barry did not counter her last statement; only proof would convince her otherwise—and sometimes that didn't work. He'd seen this before; the suspect who was so nice to his family and friends that when the truth was revealed, nobody believed it. That was the saddest part.

As far as Jenny was concerned, Crowley was the epitome of the priesthood; for Barry, Crowley's attentiveness was all a charade. And in the end, Jenny could wind up being hurt the most. It seemed that the innocent always got hurt.

Mrs. Rodriguez scurried to the bottom of the stairs calling "Excuse me! Excuse me, sir. You're not allowed upstairs, that's only for the priests of this church.''

Barry held up his hands in a gesture of innocence. "I must have gotten lost. My sense of direction is terrible. Father Paul Tobin is expecting me for breakfast.'' He turned and headed toward the diningroom.

The woman gallantly attempted to block his path. "You must be announced; it's my job, sir. Sir!"

"I tried to stop him, Father," she apologized to Father D'Angelo.

"That's quite all right, Mrs. Rodriguez, Detective Martin is always welcome here."

Before leaving, Mrs. Rodriguez slanted her body toward Barry and sputtered something in Spanish that, even without understanding the language, he knew was not complimentary.

Barry extended a general greeting, then transfixed his stare on Father Inness, whose expression revealed a combination of surprise and panic.

Paul stood up. "Barry, you know everyone except Father Inness, our guest from the Vatican."

Barry shook his hand and pulled up a chair beside him.

"What's that detective doing here?" Rhoades asked Paul. "We have a right to our privacy."

Barry answered before Paul could, all the while staring at Father Inness. "I just came by to tell Paul that Jenny's feeling much better and that Dr. Booker thinks the hypnotism will solve everything."

"That's good news," Paul answered. He had no idea who Barry was talking about, but instinctively played along.

Barry shook his finger at Father Inness. "You look very familiar."

"I just arrived last week," Father Inness responded, his cleft lip twitching. "It is my first visit to America." He pushed his half finished plate of food away. "It was nice to meet you, but I must now get back to my report."

As he stood up so did Barry saying, "I have to use the phone. It's in the hallway, isn't it? I'll walk out with you, Father." The Vatican guest was not pleased with his sudden, and unwanted, companion.

"Are you enjoying your visit, Father Inness?" Barry asked as they entered the hallway. "Manhattan is a very exciting place, you've probably seen a lot of it in the three weeks you've been here."

"I have only been here a week."

"No you haven't. You've been in this country for at least three weeks. You and another person were following me around in an Oldsmobile sedan. I want to know why!"

"You must be mistaken."

Barry flicked his finger against the priest's cleft lip and stated, "That makes you a liar. I saw you that night and you saw me. Now why were you following me?"

"I can only repeat myself, Detective Martin. I have been in your country for one week, and if we did see each other it was purely accidental, for I do not recall seeing you before today. And may I also inform you that I resent being called a liar."

Barry grinned, reached into his pocket, and handed the priest his passport.

"This was in my room!"

"Underneath your shirts to be exact." Barry offered it back to Inness. "The date of your arrival is fifteen days prior to your story of arriving last week. That makes you a liar again. It also makes me think that you might not even be a priest."

Inness opened his passport and held the picture next to his face for verification. "That is me. I am Father Inness."

"Photographs are easily switched. For all I know the real Father Inness is no longer in this world. That would make you worse than a liar; it could make you a murderer."

272

"The priests inside can identify me," Inness pointed to the diningroom. "Also the Cardinal."

"None of them had ever seen you before, so they wouldn't know the real from the fake. I must warn you that murder or conspiracy to commit murder commands a penalty of life imprisonment." That should shake him up.

"I can prove who I am. Father D'Angelo, I need his help. In the study."

Barry summoned Father D'Angelo into the hall, and the three entered the study. Father Inness pointed to a photograph over Father D'Angelo's desk and asked him to identify it.

Father D'Angelo took down the photograph explaining, "This was taken six years ago when Cardinal Beck and I had an audience with His Holiness." He handed the photograph to Barry.

"What does this prove?"

Father Inness pointed to a priest standing behind Cardinal Beck. It was Father Inness, *this* Father Inness.

Father D'Angelo left the room. "You are now convinced, Detective Martin?"

"You're still lying about the length of time in this country, and don't tell me it's Church business. And you were also following me. So you see, no matter what you say, I won't believe you. I don't know what your game plan is, Father, but now that I know who you are, the rest should be easy."

"The rest?"

There was a knock at the door. Father Inness repeated, "What do you mean by the rest?" But Barry said nothing and opened the door. Paul whispered to him and they both left the study.

In the dining room was a new visitor, Father Crowley. This place is swarming with priests, Barry mused as he greeted the new arrival. The small table talk remained small. Barry focused on Father Rhoades who maintained a perpetual smile no matter who spoke or what was said. A forced laugh. His fingers picking at each other, his eyes jumping from person to person, he stared at Inness when he entered. Barry glanced at Crowley who was studying Rhoades. Crowley knew Rhoades was panicky too, and everyone was anxious with Inness around. It was Big Brother watching Big Brothers. A great place to catch paranoia. Figuring he couldn't elicit any more information with so many ears around, he left the Church with Paul.

Once outside, Paul asked, "What did you mean about Jenny and the doctor? Is she all right?"

"Fine, fine. It's a trick of the trade; don't worry about it."

"You still believe priests are involved in a crime and Jenny knows something about it?" Paul's face flushed with anger; he shook his head in disbelief. "That trick of the trade, suddenly it makes sense. Boy, it took me a long time to catch on. But everything fits. You're setting Jenny up. That's what you're doing, you're setting her up. How the hell can you do that? I thought you loved her."

"I do, and I aim to keep her alive."

"Oh yeah, so you make her a target! Why don't you just leave her alone!"

"Paul, I'm trying to save her. I don't know all the answers yet, but when I do I'll tell you. 'Til then, trust me."

"I can't, not when you're using my sister as bait. And I thought you were a true friend. But you just want to solve this case and get a promotion. I wouldn't be surprised if you falsified evidence to get your promotion." The huge door of the Church boomed shut.

It wasn't true what he said, Barry reflected. For the first time in my life, I love somebody and she loves me. Paul just doesn't understand that sooner or later those assassins will decide that Jenny's a risk they can no longer tolerate, unless I can get to them first, and to Jenny's subconscious. Barry released a grunt over Paul's insinuation about falsified evidence. In this case it wouldn't matter, but in that other case . . . No . . . Maybe. He drove back to the precinct for conferences with the computer, the Medical Examiner, and two-year-old autopsy reports.

Joe Ricart made his daily trek to the post office box and brought another large manila envelope back to Roger's apartment. Inside the envelope was a plastic vial containing four small white pills. A note gave instructions to be at the usual telephone booth at noon. Carol, still recuperating, had stayed behind, as Joe, Doug and Roger hurried to the booth. Joe picked up the phone on the first ring.

"Are you a believer?" asked the voice.

"Yes, sir, I am. We all are and we want to do your bidding."

"I assume you have perused the folder, Joseph."

"Yes, sir. Uhm, are you sure about this sacrifice, he's a little—"

"Absolutely. Just make sure he takes all the pills enclosed in the vial. Any more questions? We'll speak again soon."

Joe hung up. "There ain't no mistake," he related to Doug and Roger, interrupting their comic book reading. "We have until the end of the week. Let's check him out."

Doug shoved the comic book into his back pants pocket and pouted like a child. "We never done a kill,

Joe. Give it to one of us, please, Joe. You can trust us, Joe."

"Yeah, Doug's right," Roger said. "Me and Doug can do it. We've watched ya. Let us have some fun."

"Not with this one," said Joe. "It's gonna be tricky. You can have the next sacrifice, promise."

They smiled and shook each other's hands in mutual congratulation, then followed Joe to spy on the next victim.

The distinct odor of formaldehyde invaded Barry's nostrils as he walked down the bleak white corridor of the newly revamped morgue. Behind the glass-enclosed cubicles, men and women carried on the newest form of police investigation, Forensic Medicine. Millions of dollars worth of equipment and personnel were housed here, yet Barry still referred to it as the slaughterhouse.

Doc ran after Barry and tapped him on the shoulder. "I thought that was your brown sports jacket. What are you doing here? If you like, I'll give you a tour."

"Tours are for museums, thank you. I want to go over the autopsy reports on Miller, Frederickson, and Tora. I seem to have misplaced my copies."

"I'm so glad I rushed them for you," he said in a sour tone before giving directions. "End of the corridor, take a left and take the elevator to the third floor; the Records Room. Will you need my assistance?"

"I'll call you if I do. And Doc, those rushed reports were valuable to me," he said with sincerity.

At the desk in the Records Room Barry signed in, identifying his badge number and the case numbers of the reports he wanted to check. The woman behind the desk pointed to aisle 22. "The right top shelf," she directed in a bored voice.

"Thank you. By the way, I might require a case

report that happened eighteen or nineteen months ago. Where would I find it?"

"You have an identifying autopsy number?"

"No," he lied, not wanting anyone to know he was investigating this closed case. "It was 43 something, something, something."

"I need the precise number in its entirety."

"Okay, but for future reference where would the 43000's be?"

The woman ran her finger down a list of numbers. "Aisle 87, near the window there. But if you need it, you must sign for it."

"Absolutely." He walked to aisle 22, found the reports, then casually sauntered over to aisle 87. He took a piece of paper from his pocket. Number 43791. He found what he was looking for. Concealing the unsigned report inside the signed one, he sat near the window and read. Ogden, Lucius. Male. 48. Caucasian. Cause of death: Bullet wound in left ventricle. Three more bullet wounds about upper torso. Barry skipped down. Newly fractured upper second sternum; chest tapped. Multiple contusions over upper torso and right clavicle. Injuries prior to death. Barry read the last sentence again. Injuries prior to death . . . Hmm. He skipped down to the bottom. Victim suspected of Cardinal Beck's assassination. Case closed. It was signed by the then Lieutenant Adams and Captain Westen.

Barry copied more information, replaced the files, and headed for Lucius Ogden's last known employer. The Manhattan Cast and Dye Company on Eighth Avenue near Fourteenth Street. Twenty minutes passed before Barry could see the personnel director.

"Detective Martin, I'm Alex Smith. I'm sorry to have kept you waiting, but corporate meetings have a tendency to turn into personal accolade." He pushed up the sleeves of his white shirt, inadvertently displaying large discolored sweat stains under his armpits.

"A year and a half ago a Mr. Lucius Ogden worked here. Were you employed here at that time?"

"Unfortunately yes. I was the one who interviewed and hired him. How the hell was I supposed to know he was going to kill Cardinal Beck?"

"Nobody is blaming you."

"Tell that to my boss. You are who you hire. It's still thrown at me, those bastards."

Barry felt sorry for the struggling middle management man, but he had his own problems. "Did Ogden have an accident of any kind a week or two before the incident?"

"Yes he did. How'd you know that?" Smith swung his chair around to the files and pulled out a folder. "That's what I thought. This accident happened three days before. He wasn't watching where he was going, and he bumped into a steel pipe that was lying on a work bench. As you can see by this report we observed all safety regulations. It wasn't our fault. He should have looked where he was going. It was his fault."

"Take it easy; I'm not your boss. It says here that Ogden saw your company doctor."

"Correct. We have a full medical staff. The doctor's on call, of course. He's affilated with St. Vincent's Hospital."

"It doesn't mention anything about a follow-up call."

"No, the patient went to Doctor Dale's office following the initial examination. The doctor's office address is at the bottom."

Barry handed the folder back to Smith. "What kind of worker would you say Ogden was, and what you say goes no further."

Smith's eyes flashed to the closed door before answering. "Ogden worked here for over a year and he was one of my best workers. No fights, no calling in sick, no getting drunk on the job. He was reliable."

"That doesn't coincide with what his fellow employees stated on the police report."

"I know, and it's a damn shame too. He was always a quiet man, never socialized with anybody. When his wife died, she'd been sick a long time, he became more reclusive—and religious, real religious. He wore an over-sized silver crucifix and on his coffee breaks he'd read the Bible. That's why nobody was surprised when we heard the news about Cardinal Beck. We just assumed he flipped."

"Do you think he did?"

"Yes I do, but I don't know why."

"One last thing, Mr. Smith. You've given me more information now that you did to the investigating officers a year and a half ago. How come?"

"They didn't ask me anything. As a matter of fact they told me to remain silent; that all statements concerning Ogden would come from them. They even confiscated my personnel reports on him."

"Do you remember who the officers were who ordered you to do this?"

"No, but one always had a cigar in his mouth and the other one was a big brute."

Adams and Westen. Barry headed for Doctor Dale's office two blocks away. Apparently his badge had more authority here than at the other places, since Doctor Dale came out of one of the examination rooms almost immediately and led Barry to his private office.

"Detective Martin, how can I help you?"

"Lucious Ogden." That was all Barry had to say. In minutes the nurse handed the folder to the doctor who handed it to Barry.

Aloud, Barry mentioned the few major points. "First visit March Third at 2:00 at the plant. Second visit was

March Sixth at 4:00 at this address. Are you sure about the time and date of the second visit, Doctor?"

"My nurse has been with me for almost twenty-five years and she excels at keeping accurate records."

"A final question, Doctor: Did the police ever contact you in reference to Mr. Ogden?"

"No, why should they? I wasn't his personal doctor."

"Thank you for your time, Doctor." Barry leaned against his car and rehashed the new information, especially the second visit—March Sixth at 4:00. And Cardinal Beck was assassinated on March Sixth at around 4:20. No way could it have been Ogden. We killed the wrong fuck'n guy, and it was worse than lousy police work that did it. Adams and Westen knew exactly what they were doing. A cover-up. And now I know it . . . and I know why. Dammit, I wish I didn't. And another answer fell into place. That's why the true assassins didn't go after Jenny—they were in the clear. Her blindness and loss of memory insured that fact. But when can they no longer risk her being alive? He headed directly home.

Lying atop scattered newspapers on the living room rug was a large heap of gray something. Barry cocked his head toward Cyclops who sat next to the papers, his tail wagging. "Hey, Jen, does this gray pile belong to the dog? Because if it does, I'm shooting the dog."

"It's clay. Haven't you ever seen clay before? It comes from soil."

"We don't have soil in Manhattan, just dirt and garbage." Jenny came out of the bedroom. "What's this clay for?"

"That's the medium I use in sculpture class. The teacher wants us to do a bust of someone we know. I'm doing you."

"You have a good taste in choosing your subject matter. And I've thought it over, I'll pose in the nude."

Jenny showed no reaction. "What's the matter?"

Jenny led Barry to the couch. Cyclops shadowed close behind her. "Paul called me today. I felt your hand twitch. I guess you know what he said. I want the truth, Barry. Are you using me as bait to solve your case?"

"Sort of. Don't turn away, Jenny. Listen to me. You have to learn one thing about me right now: No matter what I do, no matter how it appears, I never do anything without a good reason."

"Getting promoted is a good reason."

"You're right, only you have the wrong person. A man named Lucius Ogden was killed by the police when he resisted arrest for the assassination of Cardinal Beck. Today, I discovered that Ogden could not possibly have been the assassin. The police killed the wrong man, which means the assassins are still free and still watching you."

"As you keep reminding me. But how could the police kill the wrong man, Barry?"

"Not how, why. Two police officers' promotions depended on that case. They falsified, or rather ignored, the evidence, solved the case fast, much to the delight of the media and the public, and were rewarded with promotions."

"Your theories are growing stranger all the time, Barry. First you suspected priests and now you suspect other cops."

"But I have the evidence on the two cops." His tone of voice showed no pride in his discovery, only disappointment.

"This evidence you have on the two policemen, is it conclusive?"

"One hundred per cent."

"Who are the two policemen?"

"Captain Adams and Chief of Police Westen."

"My God, you do get the top echelons. What are

you going to do?''

"Turning in fellow officers is not my favorite sport, except, maybe, for Adams."

"What's the name of the department that handles those matters?''

"Internal Affairs."

"That's the one. Give it to them. Don't involve yourself."

"Don't involve myself," Barry answered in a half laugh. "I'm a cop, I'm supposed to be involved. Besides, everyone always knows who turns who in."

Jenny knew he was wrestling with a moral dilemma and decided not to sway him one way or the other. It would have to be his decision, although privately she hoped he would consider his future on the police force. For all his moaning and groaning about his work, Jenny knew he still enjoyed being a detective. But no matter what his decision, she'd stick by him, there was no doubt about that.

"Not to change the subject, Barry, but I still don't understand what Cardinal Beck's assassination has to do with the Crossbearers."

"It could be a combination of two things. First, maybe he knew something he wasn't supposed to; and second, there's politics. If you want to move up the ladder of power fast, you eliminate your opponent. In this case, Cardinal Beck. And I believe those involved in the assassination are now pulling the strings of the Crossbearers."

"God, you don't give up. A priest would not murder another priest, let alone a Cardinal, would he?''

"There's madness in every profession, Jenny. It's just that the public doesn't read about it in the Church because the stories are squelched—protecting your own, it's called." A thought occurred to him. The public might not know, but what about those on the inside? "I'll bet Inness knows what's going on. Maybe that's why he's really in this country. It's something to consider."

"Inness? The priest from the Vatican? Barry, you're talking about holy men. Priests. Men of God. You're going too far."

Barry knew he was right, but he couldn't convince Jenny. Or anybody for that matter. Nobody could. Religious men are godly men. That's all their lawyers would have to say to a jury. And the public, they'd never stand for it. Immoral politicians, yet, but immoral clergymen? Heaven forbid. A perfect cover. But he knew he was right. He just needed a missing link to bind it all together.

With evidence mounting, and Jenny in the middle, Barry pressured her to forgo her sculpture classes at night and to avoid direct contact with strangers as well as with Father Crowley. "I mean it," he emphasized.

"Barry, for one year I didn't leave the house because I was scared to death. I overcame that with a lot of encouragement, but I'm still not that strong. If I begin to hide again, I might never stop. That would be devastating for both of us." She leaned against his chest. "You really believe someone will, in time, try to kill me. Will setting me up as bait catch these assassins?"

"Yes."

"I'll be able to walk the streets and have to worry only about tripping or getting lost?"

"Yes."

"Barry, I don't want to die . . . not any more." Her body snuggled closer to his. "You're in charge."

Barry realized he was carrying out a basic police procedure, but he was still apprehensive. It had taken forty years to find Jenny and he wanted forty more with her. He had a personal reason to solve this case fast now, and nobody was going to divert him from it.

* * *

The following day Barry's theory of the priests became sharper. He had obtained the graduating list from the Boston seminary college and it took three hours and close to eighty telephone calls before he tracked down the present residence of each priest. He took out the list of churches Paul had gathered from his investigation of the telephone numbers. A perfect match except for two priests: one who was stationed in the Vatican and a second who had been killed by a hit-and-run driver a month after graduation.

Barry ran down the list. There were three priests in New York City: Rhoades, Crowley, and Johnson—a new name. That would account for three of the priests Paul saw in that Soho loft. And the fourth, Barry guessed the fourth man was the leader of this group, but there was no other New York priest on the list. So what was the identity of the fourth man? And what exactly was this special graduating class of priests up to?

"Martin! Get in here!"

Barry strode into the Captain's office. Chief of Police Westen and the Police Chaplain were also present. Their expressions were far from friendly. Barry had a feeling that Father Inness was responsible for this gathering.

Captain Adams was the first to speak, although the others were obviously eager to have their potshots. "I received another call from Cardinal Alden. Some of his priests are complaining that you're needlessly harassing them. Is it true?"

"Which priests complained?"

The Chief of Police leaned forward. His huge forearms bulged as they strained to support his bulk. "Detective Martin, police harassment is a problem the Department strongly frowns on. Your current case involves a group calling themselves the Crossbearers.

Do you have any supportive evidence to suspect this group of being associated with priests?"

"No, sir. I do not."

"Do you suspect these priests of any unlawful conduct?"

With no hard evidence, Barry could only answer no.

"Then why, may I ask, are you harassing them?"

"I'm not, sir. Father Rhoades and Father Inness are paranoid about something, but it's not me."

"Priests are not paranoid!" the Police Chaplain stated in defense of his associates.

"Why were you at the church, Martin?" the Captain asked.

"To visit my friend Father Paul Tobin." Barry was waiting for them to mention his illegal search of Inness' room.

"Detective Martin, Captain Adams has informed me that on a previous occasion you drew a gun on Father Rhoades. Your explanation was accepted, but it appears that there might have been some underlying circumstances. Do you have any personal vendetta toward these priests or against the Church?"

Barry controlled his temper at the insinuation. "No sir. I believe the problem lies with the priests, not with me. If they feel I'm harassing them then it's because they have something to hide, not me!"

"Priests never have anything to hide," Chief Westen responded. "I'm ordering you to stay away from those priests. Is that clear?"

"It is."

The Police Chaplain spoke. "Cardinal Alden would appreciate it if this matter went no further. He asked us to confer with you, Barry, and we have done that. The incident, as far as we are concerned, is closed."

Captain Adams, taking it upon himself to speak for

everyone, reassured the Chaplain it would not happen again.

"One more thing, Detective Martin," Chief Westen said, delaying Barry's departure. "I want this case on the Crossbearers solved, and solved quickly. Now that we've had this talk, I'm sure you'll find more time to devote to the case. It would make the Commissioner happy, which in turn would make me happy." He ended with a phony smile.

Barry was busting to divulge his findings on the Ogden case, but for Jenny's future well-being he remained silent. At least for now.

The Chaplain accompanied Barry out of the office, apologizing for things getting out of control. Barry was only partially listening; another piece of the puzzle suddenly had fallen into place. A chaplain is a priest. It was time for an educated guess. "Chaplain, you knew Father Rhoades in seminary college. Can you tell me why he would be so hostile toward me?"

"Not really. He was a loner. Nobody knew him well."

Bingo! The connection was made. Barry had just discovered who his informer in the precinct was and maybe even the fourth man in the loft in Soho. But why wasn't the Chaplain's name on the graduating list?

Barry pursued the matter. "Maybe Rhoades changed after graduation. Did anything happen to him or his family that might have made him bitter toward the police?"

"Not that I'm aware of. I contracted hepatitis during my final semester and didn't graduate with my class, so I lost contact with them."

"Too bad," Barry said as he applied Paul's description of the third man in the loft to the Chaplain. No match, although he could be the man Paul didn't see. That seemed unlikely; a police chaplain doesn't have enough political clout. As for the third man, Barry required a thin person. What was that other priest's name? Johnson, that's it. Time for another educated guess. "Perhaps Father Johnson knows. I met him only once but I remember him mentioning the fact that he had graduated with Father Rhoades. Is Father Johnson still as thin as ever?"

"Oh yes, he's always been thin, and it makes no difference what he eats. I envy him."

"Me too," Barry agreed, his voice falsely despondent in an effort to maintain a purposelessness to the conversation. "I gain weight just looking at food and it always ends up right here," his hands jiggled his midriff bulge. "It's good that you keep in touch with your classmates. Do you ever have alumni reunions?"

"No, we're spread all over the country and traveling is so expensive nowadays, not to mention finding the time. Shortly though, I might be traveling since I now have a pilot's license. I am being reassigned, flying prelates here and there. It will be a good opportunity to see more of the world."

"You'll be leaving us, then?"

"Within the next few months, maybe sooner. I've already informed the Captain. If you want to know the truth, I've enjoyed my assignment here and I don't want to leave, but orders are orders."

"Can't you decline?"

"A Vatican order? Never. Oh well, no job is perfect. Listen, I'm truly sorry about the predicament you're in. If I can be of any further assistance come see me."

Two-faced priest, Barry thought as he assumed his thinking position, feet on the desk, hands intertwined behind his head. Four priests, four men at the loft, all graduated together, and perhaps all murderers. I wonder if my theory on Beck's assassination is correct. It sounds logical and the motive is there. But are these same men really connected with the Crossbearers? And who's their leader? Or is one of them the leader? God only knows, and He's not about to turn His own kind in.

Joe Ricart stood near the benches in the square and watched the young kids play stickball in front of Our Lady of the Shrine Church. At the side of the Church, Bobby, sporting his designer jeans and a monogrammed shirt, carried out his business dealings.

Joe, keeping his head bent so no one could have a clear look at him, approached the kid. Without his blond wig he felt too conspicuous. As he closed in, the other youngsters moved to the other side of the street and milled about, waiting for business to commence again.

In a whisper Joe said, "I know you're the pusher in this neighborhood. Don't get excited, I ain't no cop." He pulled out a small vial containing the four pills. "I want you to push for me. Same percentage as the others give you." He handed the vial to the kid. "These are for you. Samples."

"What's in 'em?" Bobby asked inspecting the pills.

"A little of everything, and I can make them any strength. These are weak. Take the four, see how you like them. I'll be back tomorrow, same time."

"No deal," said Bobby, "unless I see some bread up front. Like right now, man."

"Then give the pills back. You ain't the only one I can deal with around here." Joe held his hand out.

Bobby put the vial in his pocket. "Bring some bread with you tomorrow, in case I like your product."

Joe nodded and walked away. Bobby went into the church lavatory for a cup of water and swallowed all four pills. After an hour of more transactions outside the church, he went home and lay down on his bed. Goddamn pills were shit, he thought. They don't do nothing. Goddamn rip-off. Well, I'll get him tomorrow, take his money and run.

Bobby's father called him down for supper. Bobby hadn't eaten anything all day, yet he still had no appetite. He picked at his food, then went up to his room, switched on his stereo, took off his shirt and pants, lit up a joint, and lay down. He was exceptionally tired. Even the grass didn't help. Bad stuff that jerk gave me. A numbness took over his body. The joint fell from between his fingers. A trickle of blood seeped out of his ear. His eyelids narrowed. He could feel the air in the room press against his body as if he were in a vise. Blood oozed out of his nose and eyes. He couldn't move, couldn't scream. All he could do was die.

Barry pulled up in back of the ambulance and patrol cars. From outside he heard the victim's parents, the police, and Father Paul Tobin. Doc, leaning over the banister, summoned Barry upstairs.

The boy's body lay in a pool of blood. Sheets, covers, and pillows were red. Dried patches of blood encrusted his nose, ears and mouth. There were even scattered blood stains covering the rest of his body.

Barry let out a groan at the disgusting sight before turning to Doc for an explanation.

"The kid must have taken an overdose of some type of blood thinner."

"Blood thinner?"

"Patients with obstructed or hardened arteries use it. The drug thins the blood so it can flow easier."

Barry pointed to the body. "We're talking about a fifteen-year-old kid, and you're giving me a lecture on hardening of the arteries. C'mon, Doc."

"I know it sounds crazy, Barry, but that's my preliminary diagnosis. Maybe it'll change after the autopsy, but I doubt it."

"Then tell me why a fifteen-year-old kid would take blood thinner?"

"I don't know. The kid couldn't have gotten the drug, you need a prescription. Okay, okay, he still could have gotten it."

"Does it get you high?"

"Nope."

"Maybe he took it by mistake. What is it, liquid or pill?"

"Comes both ways, but the quantity he took was excessive to say the least."

"Possible suicide?"

"I wouldn't rule it out."

"What about the parents? Does either of them use this type of drug?"

"They said no."

"The hell with what they said; check with their family doctors."

A uniformed cop signaled Barry over to the closet, and handed him a shoe box. Inside were packets of marijuana, pills, heroin, rolling paper, hypodermic syringes, spoons and matches. Another cop uncovered two more shoe boxes filled with the same buried treasure. Barry estimated that there was about ten thousand dollars worth of drugs. Pretty good business for a fifteen-year-old kid.

Barry ordered one of the uniformed officers to get the names of all the boy's friends and added, "Be discreet. Don't tell the parents about the drugs; they've had enough sorrow for one day."

The telephone in the dead boy's room rang. From downstairs somebody called Barry Martin to the phone.

"Martin here."

"Badge 5746. I knew you'd still be there. How do you like my work?"

Ricart! Barry glanced at the bloody sheets and wondered how anyone could be proud of this. "As

CROSSBEARERS

usual, Ricart, your work is thorough. But I am pleased to report that you weren't as thorough with the man in the subway. Why did you do that to him? He's a high school teacher who never hurt anybody in his life. Why?''

There was a prolonged pause. Joe's mental disconnection surfaced. ''I don't know. Sometimes I do things . . . I'm glad he lived.'' Then, as if the mental short circuit corrected itself, Joe stated. ''Did you like the way I snatched Carol from the hospital? You almost had her.''

''I almost had you too.''

''Never. You'll never catch me. What I did to that girl's chest, that was to let you know that I can kill anyone I want, and nobody can stop me.''

''Isn't this victim a little young, even for you?''

''I am a soldier for Jesus, and a good soldier doesn't question orders.''

I wonder who's worse, Barry momentarily evaluated, the people who give the orders or the ones who carry them out? The ones who give the orders, he decided. ''I saw the news clipping of Frederickson in your room. That's how you get your orders. Aren't you worried that one day one of those envelopes will contain your name? After all, soldiers are expendable.''

A disturbed laugh accompanied Ricart's reply. ''Everybody is. Good-bye Badge 5746.''

Barry stood in front of the bedroom window and gazed at the city veiled in its night illumination. From this limited perspective there were hundreds of thousands of hideaways that Ricart could find refuge in. He could disappear in the underground for years; it had been done before. The only way to catch Ricart was to lure him out into the open. Easier said than done.

Barry recalled the computer check on Ricart, or more specifically, on his family. His father dead from an alcoholic liver, his mother dead from the strain of life, and a son who was the victim of his drunken Father's rage. Ricart never had a chance to be anything else. But still he had to be stopped.

Barry's thoughts shifted to Rhoades. He was the weak link in this unknown chain, but to break him meant harassing him, and maybe jeopardizing his own job. One more complaint to the Captain or the Chief could be the end. What does a forty year old ex-cop do—a security job. Shit!

Eleven-thirty. Barry closed the boy's bedroom door and telephoned the church.

"Our Lady of the Shrine Church. Father Rhoades speaking."

Without disguising his voice, Barry pressured, "Father Rhoades, this is the police. I know about your graduating class from seminary school. I know about the meeting in Soho and who the other priests are. I know you're one of the Crossbearers. And I'm watching you." Barry hung up. That should do it.

It did. Rhoades locked himself in his room, grasped a crucifix, and anxiously pondered his next move. The voice on the phone was vaguely familiar. It had to be Martin. I can't delay any longer. Dear God, I have to do it. He lay down on the bed and rested the crucifix on his chest. "Give me strength, dear Lord, my God. Know that what I must do is for You."

Morning found Barry across the street from the Church in his car. Father Rhoades appeared and another car with Father Crowley at the wheel pulled up and both priests drove away. Barry followed. They drove around the neighborhood for nearly thirty minutes in no special direction. The privacy of the car was apparently all they wanted. Rhoades was dropped off in front of the church.

Barry waited until Crowley's car was out of sight before he approached Rhoades. Rhoades' hands were clenched into fists. His right foot unrhythmically tapped against the pavement. Oh to have been a fly in that car, Barry thought.

"Father Rhoades," Barry called stopping him halfway up the stairs. "How are you this morning?"

Rhoades' eyes shot toward Barry as if they were weapons. "Paul's in the study," he said in an acid tone. Desperately he wanted to ask Barry why he had called, but he knew he could incriminate himself by doing so.

"I came to see you, Father."

Rhoades stopped in midstride. "I'm a very busy man. What do you want?"

"You seem upset, Father. Anything wrong?"

"I have much on my mind, Detective Martin. If you'll excuse me." He turned his back on Barry and fled into the church.

Barry wondered who had upset Rhoades more, he or Crowley. No matter. Rhoades was cracking fast. Perhaps he was getting pressure from two sides. A few more visits, Barry reckoned, and I'll have him, and hopefully everyone else in his group.

Joe, Carol, Doug, and Roger continued arguing as they waited at the usual corner for the telephone to ring. "I'm telling you there's something wrong here," Carol advised. "The letter is different from the others, using the words 'emergency call,' and look, four sacrifices, especially this one. But no photographs of the victims. We shouldn't be here, Joe. The cops could be watching us. It could be a trap."

Roger and Doug momentarily interrupted their comic book reading.

"Nobody knows about the post office box. We wait

for the call," Joe stated in a tone ending the discussion.

Still, the break in the pattern made it seem like a long time before the phone rang.

"Are you a believer?" asked an unfamiliar voice.

Joe hesitated. "Say that again."

"Are you a believer?"

"You ain't the one I usually talk to. Who is this?"

"I am the Leader's assistant."

"Prove it," Joe demanded.

"You and your group belong to the Crossbearers. We send you pictures and information of specific people and you carry out the sacrifices."

"A cop could know that." Joe paused to think of a question only his superiors could answer. "How did you recruit me?" He held the phone out so Carol could listen too.

"A private party was held in a Soho loft with a group of people. You were and still are a member of Palmer's Church. We chose you, Hank Wynn, Roger and Doug Mollahan, and Carol Lynch to be our swords of Jesus because you believe as we do."

Carol okayed the response.

"I am a believer," Joe replied, according this stranger the same respect as he gave to the Leader. "What's the emergency?"

"The names and addresses in the letter, they must die, but not like the others. Jennifer Tobin, Paul Tobin and Mary Evans must disappear forever."

"How? We don't know how to do that, we just kill the people and leave 'em."

"Kidnap them!"

"Yeah, right. What about the other name on your list, the most important one?"

"Him you can deal with only after you deal with the others."

"Too bad, I enjoyed our telephone conversations. Poor Badge 5746. Hold on." Carol whispered something to Joe. "O yeah, how do we recognize the three people you want us to kidnap?"

"Ask the people or doorman at the addresses, they'll point them out to you. Kidnap the three first, then Detective Barry Martin is all yours."

"When do you want all this done?"

"As soon as possible. This is an emergency, a secret emergency. Do not even mention this to the Leader because he'll be testing you for loyalty. I wasn't supposed to tell you this but you have served us well and I trust you."

"Thank you, sir. I won't let you down." Joe turned to his group. "You heard what we have to do. Carol, you find out who these broads are; Doug, Roger, and I will take Paul Tobin."

Carol asked, "What about Martin?"

"Me, me," Doug huffed excitedly. "Let me do it."

"How 'bout me too?" added Roger. "You promised us the next sacrifice. You promised."

"Yeah, you promised, Joe. Let us do it. Please."

"We'll see." Joe said putting them off for the moment. "First we have to find out who these people are and whether we can kidnap them tonight. The man said they're all friends and hang out together, so it shouldn't be hard."

"I have an idea," Carol voiced. "We'll watch all three and see if they meet regularly at one place, then we'll watch only that place and wait for the proper time. The best time is night."

"Sounds good. We'll start tomorrow. After we kidnap them we'll hold them at Roger and Doug's place until Martin's taken care of." Joe folded the list and stuffed it in his pocket. The corners of his mouth arched into a menacing grin as he meditated on how much pleasure he'd derive from killing Badge 5746.

"I'm getting tired of looking at the grimy soles of your shoes," Dave joked to Barry as he took a seat. "Can't you sit like a normal person?"

"You look refreshed. I tried calling you but you weren't home. It's nice to have you back permanently, Dave."

"It's good to be back. And I *was* home. Sometimes being alone is the best medicine. I straightened out my head, gained two pounds, and I didn't have one drop of liquor." He thumbed through the accumulated pile of paperwork on his desk. "Well, back to business."

Barry wondered if his one-time partner was really psychologically well enough to be back on the job. Outwardly he looked composed, but his recovery had been awfully fast. I guess the shrink knows what he's doing, he concluded. At least the protesters finally disbanded, that must have helped.

Back to his problem. He put his hand on a stack of folders and counted. Twenty-three cases and I haven't started any of them. And the Captain hasn't said anything; he really wants me to solve the Crossbearers so he can have another feather in his cap. He thought of the senseless killing of Lucius Ogden. Man, I'd love to turn in the Captain and the Chief and see them try and squirm out of that case. But what would be the use? The case is old and forgotten, they'd be reprimanded or forced to take an early retirement, and I'd still be here. Barry remembered his first patrol as a rookie and the advice his seasoned partner had given him: Police work consists of staying alive and getting promoted so that you can retire with a larger pension; it has nothing to do with law and order. He must have been right because everybody does it but me. Damn fool!

A tap on Barry's shoulder whisked him out of his daydream. "This just came over the teletype for you," said an officer, handing Barry the printout.

It read: Boston, Mass. June 4, 1966 Father Thomas Brice critically injured in hit and run. Died June 5, 1966. Case unresolved.

Barry referred back to his notes. Father Brice was a member of Rhoades' graduation class at seminary school. Graduation was on June 1, 1966, and Brice was killed a few days later. Bad luck or did they want to get rid of him for some reason? It had to be the latter. He knew something. What the hell did that graduating class learn? It was time for another visit with Rhoades.

As Barry drove up to the church, he saw Rhoades and Crowley come around the corner. Before he had a chance to duck or drive away they spotted him. They sure are seeing a lot of each other lately, he thought, getting out of the car to exchange greetings. Crowley stayed but a minute before driving away. Rhoades, displeased at being stranded with Barry, continued walking past the church as if he were headed for some place else.

Barry walked stride for stride beside him. "How are you this afternoon, Father?"

He stopped. "Fine, thank you. If you're looking for Paul he's probably downstairs in his workroom. Do you want me to show you there?"

What the hell's going on, Barry wondered. Why's he being so pleasant? "I came to see you again. An old case was just reopened and I discovered that the victim was in your graduating class at seminary school. His name was Thomas Brice. Do you remember him?"

"Certainly I do. I believe he died from a hit-and-run accident shortly after graduation. I was in New Jersey visiting my parents when I heard about it. He had strong faith.''

Barry noted the voluntary alibi and his uncharacter-istic helpfulness.

"Have you found out who the driver was?" Rhoades inquired further.

"There's a suspect," Barry lied, then decided to drop the subject to see if Rhoades would press him on it. But he guessed wrong.

"Whoever it is, I do hope you catch him. Is there anything else?"

"Not at the moment, but I know where you can be reached.''

Rhoades gave an accepting nod and continued on his way.

Rhoades' casual attitude in contrast to yesterday's abrasive encounter baffled Barry. It was as if all of his problems had been miraculously solved overnight. He was up to something.

"Barry," Father D'Angelo called as he carefully made his way down the stairs. "Barry, I must talk to you. Walk with me." He took hold of Barry's arm for support. "The last few months things have happened that I cannot understand. Father Rhoades acts more unlike a priest with every passing day. We have a Vatican visitor who interrogates us, and Paul has entered into a bad state of depression. God teaches us to love everyone but I have failed Him in that respect. I am ashamed to admit that my concern is for Paul only, regardless of my ulcer.''

"How can I help, Father?"

"You're his best friend, Barry. He informed me you two had had a disagreement, and on top of his other problem of being in love with a woman—yes, I know all about it—he's being torn apart."

"What have you said to Paul concerning Mary?"

"Whatever I said did not help. He's afraid of his own feelings; somebody must talk to him in a language too harsh for me to use. Please, go talk to him, Barry. He's downstairs in his workshop."

Barry ducked his head below the slanted ceiling above the basement staircase. Paul was at his desk, his head bowed, his hands just resting on the diagrams.

"Paul. It's Barry."

"What do you want?" Paul didn't move.

"I don't like talking to the back of somebody's head." Still no movement. Barry leaned against another table and said, "Have it your way. You remind me of myself when I was ten years old. Sulking in a corner, thinking nobody loved me. My upper lip would quiver and I'd suck it into my mouth to dramatize my anger. But it never worked; my parents would still punish me. My father even began to call me Louie the Lip."

A faint smile broke through on Paul's face. He turned toward his friend. "I'm still angry about what you're doing."

"I know, but Jenny's not, and she's the only one that counts. She realizes that what I have to do is for her own good."

"And if she gets killed?"

"If I don't do anything, she will be killed. Being an eyewitness to a murder is not the way to grow old. But my way, at least she has a chance."

"Maybe you're right, I don't know. I don't know anything any more."

"There's trouble between you and Mary?"

"No, there's trouble between me and me. Mary and I, we ahh . . ."

"And you enjoyed it." Barry finished the thought. "Most people do. So what's your problem?"

"I'm afraid to leave the priesthood. It's a very safe life, Barry. Free room and board, no time cards, no real bosses, automatic good standing in the community, a place to retire. What if I can't make a living as an architect? I've never done a job for money, I wouldn't even know what to charge. And on top of that, becoming a husband, maybe a father. I could fail out there, and then where would I be? And where would Mary be?"

"And I thought Jenny was the only one in your family with a handicap. But you're right, you could fail, many people do. You already have. You're not a priest anymore, Paul, and you know it. So you see, this place isn't that safe either. No place ever will be." Barry's voice turned gentle as he added a peace offering. "Everybody's scared of life at some point, Paul. It's nothing to be ashamed of."

"When I saw Linda's body I knew then that being a priest wasn't enough for me. I'm not sure yet what will satisfy me, but I'm going to find out." Paul crossed the room and shook Barry's hand. "Thank you for being my friend, Barry."

Barry nodded, but his mind was on Linda. One of his fatal errors. What he wouldn't give to turn the clock back and have another chance of getting Linda home safely.

"What's going on between you and my sister? My parents are beginning to wonder why Jenny's never home when they call at Mary's. And I'm not getting in the middle of this one."

"There's nothing to get in the middle of. We're going to get married, although we haven't set a date."

"*You're* getting married? And they say miracles don't happen any more! That's great. Congratulations." His smile turned to concern. "Jenny's not pregnant, is she?"

"Not that I know of, but even if she were, what

difference would it make? As a matter of fact, it's not a bad idea. Yeah, a little baby girl."

"I thought men always wanted sons."

"Little girls are so much cuter. And when she grows up she'll be the first female police commissioner, and she'll hire me as a consultant for $85,000 a year."

"To interrupt your fantasy for a moment, what about those characters stalking Jenny?"

"I'll take care of them. Meantime, go upstairs and talk to Father D'Angelo; he's very worried about you. And tell him the truth."

"I will. How about the four of us getting together this week? A sort of celebration, now that I know which way my life is going."

"Make arrangements with Jenny, and when you speak to Mary, have her keep an eye on Jenny at work, just to play safe."

Outside the church, Barry spotted Rhoades, Crowley, and a tall gangling thin man whom he took to be Father Johnson, get into Crowley's car and sit there. From the way Crowley and Johnson were facing Rhoades in the back seat, it looked more like a cross examination than social chatter. They also knew Rhoades was the weak link. I'll definitely pay Rhoades another visit today. Two cross examinations should have some effect on him.

Father Crowley knocked on the apartment door.

"It's Father Crowley, Jennifer."

"What a pleasant surprise, Father." Cyclops growled at the visitor. Jenny clamped her hand around the dog's snout and apologized, "He gets rambunctious when I come home from work. Now behave, Cyclops. Let's sit in the living room, Father." Jenny kept Cyclops by her side as she recalled Barry's suspicions. "May I get you something, Father?''

''Nothing, thank you.'' Father Crowley's concentration shifted between what he wanted to say and Cyclops' tightly drawn lips and huge white teeth. ''I must say that your dog is devoted to you. Uhm, the reason I'm here is that your parents are still concerned about your nightmares. I was wondering if I could be of any assistance. I know some doctors who specialize in cases like yours. Naturally they cannot guarantee anything but—''

''You never stop trying to help me, Father,'' Jenny said, thinking how utterly insane Barry was to be suspicious of him. ''Between Barry and Mary's help I'll be fine.''

''Do you remember anything more about your accident?''

''The other night at sculpture class I was molding a clay bust of Barry when suddenly my hands began to change the ears, to make them smaller and the face thinner. I don't know why I did it.''

''A face from the past?''

''Maybe.'' She shook her head to get herself out of her trancelike state. ''I'm sorry, Father. I must have been daydreaming.''

''Most of my parishioners do that during my sermons. If you don't mind my asking, how can you do sculpture?''

''At the moment not well, but there are some blind people in my class who can, according to the teacher, recreate life-like images from their memories. It's difficult, but not impossible.''

''That's marvelous,'' Crowley said with concern. ''I'd like to see some of your art work.''

''When I finish you can see it.''

He rose. Cyclops stood up, positioning himself

between the two. "Your dog is extremely aggressive for a Seeing-Eye dog."

"Cyclops is also a trained watchdog. It was Barry's idea."

"And a good one. I must be going now." Cautiously he made his way to the front door. Cyclops' eyes followed him. "If I can be of any help at any time, Jennifer, just telephone me."

"I will, Father, and thank you again." Jenny could feel the erect hair on Cyclops' neck soften after Father Crowley left. "You and Barry ought to be ashamed of yourselves, mistrusting Father Crowley like that." As she spoke, Cyclops's tail wagged faster and faster. "You're forgiven and so's Barry. Come on, I'll give you a biscuit."

11

The next few days were busy ones for Joe and his cohorts. All their targets had been visually identified and some interesting discoveries emerged. Jennifer Tobin was not only blind but living with Badge 5746. Paul Tobin was a priest seeing a lot of Mary Evans, and not on a business level judging from the way they held hands.

Carol concluded that the most likely meeting place was Barry's apartment, because of the blind girl. The problem was Barry. Joe wanted to make sure that Barry was out of the way the night they'd make their move. There was a simple solution. A telephone call to Badge 5746 announcing another murder by the Crossbearers, in a far part of the city, would take care of him at least temporarily. Joe would have another chance later on to eliminate Martin premanently. He was looking forward to it.

While Doug and Roger gleefully watched a cartoon show on television, Joe and Carol plotted the kidnapping for Thursday night. The problem was how to bring the three victims together. Joe, impersonating a fellow officer, would telephone Jennifer Tobin to say that Barry had left a message to have her call Paul and Mary and meet them at his apartment at the proposed time, although the officer did not know for what purpose. Simple yet effective. And tomorrow was Thursday.

To celebrate their plan, Joe made a trip to the liquor store for a bottle of wine. On hearing the front door shut, Doug and Roger silently signalled each other and moved from the floor to either side of Carol on the couch. Doug awkwardly slid his hand on Carol's knee and panted, "You never pay any attention to Roger and me. We're as good as Joe and Hank. Why don't you pay attention to us?"

Carol, using only the tips of her fingers, removed his hand from her knee as if it was contagious and scorned, "I choose who to make love to and I would never choose either of you. Now go back and watch your cartoon shows like good little boys."

Carol started to stand up but Roger yanked her back by her arm. She twisted free and raked her nails across his cheek, drawing blood. Roger, holding his cheek and screaming, "I'm bleeding, I'm bleeding," retreated in pain.

Doug threw himself onto her and slapped her across the face. She lashed out with her nails but his sheer bulk was too overpowering and the slapping continued. "You shouldn'ta done that to my brother!" The slapping stopped and Doug's knife snapped open. "Nobody calls us boys, we're men. We've fucked women before, lots of 'em, haven't we, Roger? You, you we ain't touched but you've wanted us to. Struttin' around here in shorts and a tee-shirt. You want it!" He held the knife high in the air. "And you're gonna get it! Now."

Carol spat in Doug's face and tried to thrust her knee into his groin but a fierce slap on her face brought her to passivity.

Roger crouched on the arm of the couch beside Carol and ground his hand into her breasts. "Oh, you got nice titties, Carol. Come on, let's play. We're better than your lezzie friends—and Joe. Two at once, we'll have fun, ah."

Hands crawled over her body, reminding her of the days she got money for this and why she hated men. Lips mashed against her body and face yet she remained detachedly motionless.

Consumed by raw passion the two did not hear the front door open, but they did hear it slam shut. They froze and without looking knew it was Joe. Roger leapt from the couch into the corner pleading, "It was Doug's idea. He made me do it. Don't hurt me, Joe, please."

Doug backed off Carol who ran next to Joe. Doug's knife fell to the floor. Joe opened his knife waving it at Doug's face.

"Cut'em," Carol demanded as Roger whimpered in the corner. "Cut the son of a bitch. Cut 'em both!"

Joe stepped forward. Doug's knees buckled as he fell to the sofa. Joe grabbed Doug's hair, wrenching his head back. "So you wanna play, do ya?" Joe pressed the knife's edge against Doug's throat. Slowly he moved the knife back and forth. Droplets of blood trickled down Doug's neck. "You swallow too hard and the knife will go in deeper. That's right, breathe easier . . . Oh, don't cry, Doug, you might not die. I said stop crying! You're not listening to me, Doug. Stick out your tongue . . . Stick it out! Can you feel the blade against your tongue? Cold, isn't it? And sharp. I don't like people who drool over my knife, Doug. Swallow! Now you're listening. You even stopped crying. But you ain't smiling . . . That's better. I bet you feel sorry for what you did . . . I thought so. Don't cry! Can you feel the knife touching your eye-lashes? Don't move your head back! If you can't see then you can't touch. But you're not gonna touch any-more, are you? But how can I believe you, Doug? I can't trust you any more . . . You wanna say something? Don't! You get one more chance, but if you ever do this again I'll dig out your eyes with my knife. That goes for your brother in the corner." Joe backed off. Doug's face was death-white.

Carol hit Joe's shoulder. "Why didn't you cut the cocksucker?"

Joe transferred his knife to the other hand, then reared back and smacked Carol in the mouth flooring her. For an instant Joe imagined his mother's face instead of Carol's, but before he could make a move to help her up, the dream vanished and only Carol was there. No one could ever love him like his mother had. "That's for the way you tease them, you slut! Now you're all square."

Barry impatiently sat in the luxurious waiting room of the Police Commissioner's office. On the walls hung photographs of previous Commissioners and special citations commemorating fallen New York policemen. Barry plucked some lint off his jacket. He had met the Commissioner only once before and that was with a group of other detectives being honored for out-standing police investigation. Dave had been honored too. They had broken the case together. It was nothing special; some psychopath decided to unleash his fury on derelicts and eight were killed in two nights. What the clues and leads lacked in quantity they made up for in quality. Everything fell right. Not like the Crossbearers where nothing was going right.

That was two years ago, and he had known what to

expect, but not this time. He hated surprise meetings like this, although he had an inkling as to the reason. Now it was the Commissioner's turn to apply pressure to break the Crossbearers' case. It was inevitable. Barry knew how the Commissioner had started out as a patrolman, got his college and law degrees at night, worked his way up the ladder, then entered the political arena. Everyone agreed he was honest and truly had the betterment of the Police Department at heart, but once a lawyer always a scoundrel.

The secretary announced, "He'll see you now, Detective Martin."

The private office was finished in oak wood panelling and thick leather furniture. The Commissioner stood up to greet his guest. He was in good shape for someone in his mid-fifties. Dark brown hair, brown eyes, and glasses.

"Detective Martin, I'm glad you could make it. Please sit down. I believe the last time we met was two years ago at a very special ceremony honoring you and some of your fellow officers. I enjoy ceremonies like that, although it seems lately I'm honoring more policemen postumously." Solemnly he shook his head, then rubbed his hands together, signalling a change in mood and subject matter. "I've been reviewing your reports on this group calling themselves the Crossbearers. You've devoted a lot of time and energy with little results."

Barry mashed his fingers against the leather arms on the chair. This was the reason he disliked people in authority: they think they know it all and don't care to remember what it's like to investigate a case. But I don't want to be a security guard yet, he resolved. In an authoritative voice he rebutted, "They're amateurs, but extremely efficient. The lack of evidence proves it."

"So I read. Even our Forensic Department hasn't faciliated the investigation. Most unusual. These Crossbearers plan and execute extremely well."

"The killers don't do the planning, sir; they get their victim's identity through the mail."

"Ingenious. So even if you apprehend one of the murderers you still wouldn't know who the brains are. Truly ingenious." He flipped through more pages of the report. "I've heard that you've had some confrontations with priests. Not your usual suspects, wouldn't you agree?"

"Yes, sir."

"Is that your honest answer?"

"Sir?"

"That priests are not your usual suspects."

"Not usually," Barry answered playing the word game.

"Was there ever a time during your investigation when you did suspect priests of being engaged in some illegal activities?"

"I'm sorry, Commissioner, I don't know what you mean," Barry avoided committing himself.

The Commissioner handed Barry a copy of a morgue record with Barry's signature on it. "You signed for one folder, and then surreptitiously took another folder concerning one Lucius Ogden. Following that you proceeded to reinvestigate this case after it had already been closed. And, I might add, without authorization from your superiors. With man power in such short supply, investigating old cases could be considered a waste of your valuable time, Detective Martin. Wouldn't you agree?"

Barry had an uneasy feeling about this so-called moral man he was speaking to. "It was peripheral to a case I'm investigating, sir." He could feel his career slipping away as he attempted to cover his tracks. Instead of a security guard, maybe I'll become a private detective, he thought, before adding, "I didn't unearth anything new and it didn't help my case. As you noted, it was a waste of time."

"Detective Martin, you should be in politics." The Commissioner stood up and tapped his finger against a plaque on his wall. "This is my citation for bravery. It happened five years ago. It seems longer. It was my day off and I went to the neighborhood market to buy some diapers for my baby. Two men were in the process of robbing the place. I waited for the proper time, and without a shot being fired or innocent bystanders hurt, I captured them. I became an instant hero and the politicians swarmed over me. Heroes are in great demand nowadays, probably because there are so few. My new-found friends transformed me into a politician, and I'm a damn good one. But I'm also an honest one, and my reputation means more to me than this plaque. I can accomplish more as Police Commissioner than I ever could as a cop, and the primary reason I can do it is my reputation." He sat on his desk. "Except for some liberties you take with the law during your investigations, I've heard your reputation is also excellent. You should be proud of yourself."

"I am, sir."

The Commissioner moved back to his chair behind the desk. "As you might well guess, being Police Commissioner is not a nine to five job. Usually I'm behind in my paperwork, and there are times I'm not as thorough as I'd like to be in reviewing certain cases. And sometimes I'm too late in acting. Lucius Ogden is one of those cases. You brought it to my attention."

Oh oh! Stay calm and lie. "I don't know what you're referring to, sir."

"An honest man doesn't lie, Detective Martin."

"It depends upon whom he's talking to, sir."

The Commissioner grinned. "If it wasn't for a certain female officer who saw you examine Ogden's folder, and who used that information to finagle a transfer out of that dull job, I would never have found the cover-up. I also spoke to the personnel director and the company doctor. I saw what you saw: falsified evidence, ignoring known evidence, a cover-up, two promotions, an innocent man killed."

"And you want me to testify against the Captain of Detectives and the Chief of Police?"

"No. I already have them by the balls and it will be my pleasure to squeeze."

Barry was greatly relieved that the decision to turn them in had been taken from him. "Then what am I doing here?"

"As I said, I reviewed Ogden's case closely, along with some of your other inquiries. The blind girl you are now residing with, Jennifer Tobin, was close to the assassination—a car accident. Before I start squeezing I want to know if it would interfere with your investigation of the Crossbearers."

"It would," Barry admitted.

"You'll let me know when I can begin squeezing?"

"If you need any help, I have large hands."

The Police Commissioner extended his hand in friendship and Barry complied. "You realize that your girlfriend's life is still in danger and we don't know who the assassins are."

"I know who some of them are but I can't prove it."

"Do you need any help?"

"Not at this point."

"If you do, call *me*. And just out of curiosity, who are the suspects?"

"As you guessed, Commissioner, they're not your usual suspects."

Barry headed back to the precinct feeling great. Finally an honest politician who's also a decent man. Too bad he's a lawyer.

Barry's police radio signalled him to call the station. Dave relayed the message that there had been a phone call for Barry from a man named Joe saying another sacrifice would happen tonight at Kennedy Airport, ". . . but Badge 5746 won't be able to stop us because he ain't smart enough to figure out the exact location."

Barry rolled the challenge around in his mind. Except for the time Joe had set up Hank Wynn, all other phone calls had occurred after the victim was dead. Why the sudden change?

"Dave, do me a favor. Watch Jenny tonight. I don't want her alone."

"I have a stake-out but it should be over by seven. I'll be at Jenny's by seven-thirty, eight o'clock."

"Are you sure you're up to it? I need you there, Dave."

"Don't worry, I won't let you down, partner."

Barry's skepticism mentally broke through. He's got to be better or the psychiatrist wouldn't have allowed him back on the job. Why do I keep on thinking that?

Barry arrived at the airport and immediately ordered all security people to full alert. Now it was just a waiting game. But something still nagged at his mind. It was five-thirty; Jenny would be on her way home from work. I'll call at six. I'll call every half hour too.

7:35. Joe, Carol, Doug, and Roger sat in the car across the street from Barry's apartment.

"There they are, Joe," observed Doug, pointing to Paul and Mary.

"We'll give them a few more minutes before going in." Joe directed his next remark to Doug and Roger. "Don't forget: no noise, no violence, and no first names."

"You can trust us, Joe," Doug said with a nod from Roger.

"Let's go," ordered Joe. "Carol, you're first."

Carol sauntered up to the doorman as the others waited at the side of the building. The doorman couldn't miss her tight jeans and sweater.

"May I help you, Miss?"

"I'm looking for a one bedroom apartment."

"Nothin' available. Here's the manager's card; you can talk to him if you wish."

"It takes too long that way or they have a waiting list, but I need the apartment now." Carol arched her back slightly. "I'd be extremely grateful to anyone who could help me. Very grateful."

The doorman scanned the empty lobby. "I'll have to check the records—in the back room." Carol took hold of his arm and followed him.

When the door shut Joe, Doug, and Roger dashed into the building and used the service stairs to the fifth floor. Apartment 518B. Martin. Joe rang the bell.

"Who is it?" Jenny asked.

"Doorman. You have a package."

Jenny opened the door and the three men surged into the apartment. Joe pressed his knife to Jenny's throat, warning her not to scream while the other two rounded up Paul and Mary. Cyclops bolted from the bedroom toward Joe, teeth bared.

"Call off your dog or I'll cut your throat!" Joe warned. "Call him off!"

Jenny's hands wildly searched about, finally nabbing him by the collar. The hair on his neck bristled. "It's okay, Cyclops." Jenny stroked his back, but still he strained against her hold as his frightful growl continued.

Roger and Doug dragged Paul and Mary to the entryway, knives at their throats.

"What do you want with us?" Paul asked.

"Shut up!" Joe ordered. "Nobody talks and nobody gets hurt." Then to Jenny, "Put that dog in the bedroom."

He let go of Jenny. Cyclops fought Jenny's every step, saliva dripping from his mouth. Jenny pleaded with Cyclops to relax and obey. It was no use. Cyclops ripped free from Jenny's grip, swiveled about and leapt onto Joe, smashing him to the floor. Cyclops's mouth and front paws dug into Joe's body as he screamed for help. Roger and Doug stood there and watched, their knives pressing even harder against Paul and Mary's throats.

Joe lashed out with his knife in a wild fury until he felt the knife plunge into the dog's soft flesh. Cyclops squealed and staggered to a half prone position.

"Cyclops," Jenny cried out running toward the sound of pain.

Joe lifted himself up and slapped his hand over Jenny's mouth, warning her to shut up. Overcome by rage, she wildly struck out against her abductor as he struggled to control of her flailing arms and legs. Twisting both of Jenny's arms behind her, Joe said, "We're going for a ride. Everyone smiles and no talking; our knives will be aimed at your backs. Move!" He felt the sores the dog had inflicted on his face and chest. There was time to stab the dog again. The telephone rang. The hell with the goddamn dog.

The six entered the elevator. Already in it was an older woman, her nightgown visible below her coat.

Slippers covered her feet. She noticed the fresh cuts on Joe's face, and the tense faces of the captives.

"Jennifer, my dear. It's Mrs. Tarrings. Your dog was barking again, and it scared my little Poopsie. I had to rock her to sleep. She's so cute when she's sleeping, I decided she needed a treat. She loves vanilla ice cream cones. Every time your dog barks my Poopsie gets an ice cream cone. My husband thinks I'm spoiling her. He says I treat Poopsie better than I treat him."

The elevator opened. Joe and the others hurried through the lobby to the car where Carol was waiting. Mrs. Tarrings waved good-bye to Jenny.

"Who's that?" asked Carol.

"Some old broad. Let's get out of here."

Mary sat on Paul's lap in the back seat between Roger and Doug; Jenny was stationed between Joe and Carol.

"What do you want with us?" Paul asked holding Mary tightly. "We have no money."

"He thinks we want money, Joe," Doug said with a laugh.

"Everyone shut up! Get us out of here, Carol."

The car jerked forward, crisscrossing through the traffic. Carol swerved and braked as a taxi cut her off.

"Slow down!" Joe warned. "We don't need any cops stopping us for speeding or reckless driving."

Jenny swayed to and fro with the car's movements. Her nails dug into the rubberized dashboard for balance. Normal traffic sounds brought new foreboding as they conjured up her nightmare. The same surge of feelings swept over her as on the day of the accident. Suddenly, like a flash of light illuminating the dark recesses of a cave, the accident Jenny had suppressed over the years flooded her mind. And as it slowly unravelled, she felt as though she was once again reliving it.

First came the unexpected. Jimmy slammed the brakes on as the stranger darted in front of their car. Startled, he dropped the long canvas bag exposing the rifle barrel and scope. Another car, seeming to appear from nowhere, skidded to a stop near them. A white-haired man was driving. Beside him was a younger man with a sickly-looking thin face. There was a third man in the back seat, his head turned away from them. But there was something on his face.

Jimmy pressed the accelerator down. Their car just missed hitting the stranger who then jumped into the other car. Safe. They were safe.

Sirens grew louder, closer. Jimmy's shriek signalled the panic. They were being chased. A police car shot across an intersection. Another. But they weren't stopping to help. The other car was gaining. Jimmy was crying, he was so scared. The car moved along side. A gun was aimed at Jenny and terror invaded her body. Muscles tightened, tears rolled down her face, her mouth opened to scream but was silent. The man moved his gun hand further out the window. The wire! The small white wire bounced against his cheek. A shot! Jimmy yanked Jenny down by the shoulder. Brakes squealed. The car swerved.

Jenny let go of the rubberized dashboard, covered her face, and the silent scream of years ago blasted forth in full frenzy.

Joe wrapped his arms around Jenny's convulsive body. "Shut up and be still," he warned. "Another move like that and you're dead. That goes for everyone."

Disregarding the weapons and Joe's threat, Paul asked Jenny if she was all right. She answered with a nod. Her body was still quivering from the full revelation of her past nightmare and the reality of her present one. But for the moment she was still living the past terror. She remembered Jimmy's car colliding into a row of

317

parked cars, her body uncontrollably hurtling about the front seat, the windshield shattering, and specks of glass shrapnel stinging her face like hundreds of needles. She recalled her eyes swelling with tears and that horrible sensation of her eyeballs bulging to the point where she felt they would explode out of their sockets. Suddenly there was darkness and bandages and the distant echo of her parents' voices.

The car jerked to a stop, interrupting her recollection. The three prisoners were herded into Doug's apartment, tied to chairs, and gagged.

"We did it!" Joe exclaimed with pride. "Doug, get me a beer."

"Sure, Joe."

Carol whispered to Joe, "What about Martin?"

"That bastard's mine, and, boy, am I gonna have fun with him." Joe watched Carol who was watching Jenny. He grabbed her arm. "You keep your hands off of her or I'll cut your face!"

"I wasn't looking at her like that, Joe. I've just never seen a blind person this close."

"Make sure that's the only reason."

9:15. Jesus, what a waste of time, Barry thought. And no answer from Jenny. She's probably out shopping with Mary.

A security man reported, "Everyone's checked in, no problems."

Barry dialed his home number again. Where was she? He tried Mary's number. Still nothing. He telephoned his precinct and asked if Dave had called in. Barry's call was transferred to Captain Adams.

"Martin here, Captain. I asked if Dave had checked in and I got you. By any chance have you heard from him?"

"Where are you, Martin?"

"Kennedy Airport. Another murder by the Cross-bearers was supposed to take place tonight, but so far nothing. I told Dave to tell you. He must have forgotten."

"Barry . . . I hate this. Barry, Dave was killed tonight, around seven. He was on robbery surveillance. The store was hit, Dave gave pursuit—"

"Killed? Dave killed?" Barry's voice was barely audible. "How could that happen?" His tone increased. "I know how it happened. He didn't shoot first, did he? Did he?"

"Some witnesses did mention he hesitated before firing, but we're still unsure. Martin, I realize he was your friend and your partner at one time—I'm truly sorry."

"You bastard! You and your goddamn lectures on trigger-happy cops." Barry slammed the phone down and headed home. Every derogatory word he knew he applied to Adams, the Chief of Police, the media, and the shrink. They killed Dave, not the criminal. If they had left his mind alone he'd be alive. Barry pounded his fist against the steering wheel. If outrage had not taken over, there would have been tears. Jenny! Nobody was watching her. He accelerated the car and attached the magnetic siren to the car's roof. He had a premonition. Forty minute later Barry jiggled the key into the lock of his apartment's door. There was no growl. The door slid open revealing Cyclops' bloodied body, his chest still moving. Barry lunged behind a chair and drew his gun. Now the airport episode made sense. He gave considerable attention to the bottom of the bedroom door to see if any shadows moved from behind it. Using the furniture as protection, he approached the closed bedroom door, and with one kick, sprung the door open. Empty. Just as cautiously he checked the rest of the apartment. They had her.

A gutteral cry came from Cyclops. Barry phoned the

Animal Rescue League, then Mary's apartment, and then the Church.

"Father D'Angelo, it's Barry Martin. Where's Paul?"

"At your place. Where are you?"

"Home. Did Paul see Mary tonight?"

"Yes, at your place. Jennifer telephoned saying you wanted to see them at eight. Is everything all right, Barry?"

"Where's Rhoades?"

"I don't know; he's been gone the entire day. Barry there is something wrong; what is it?"

The doorbell rang. "Talk to you later, Father." Barry admitted the Rescue Squad. One of the attendants examined Cyclops, cocked his head, and in an accusative tone stated, "This dog's been stabbed."

Barry showed the attendants his badge as if that automatically cleared him. "Will he live?"

"It appears to be a superficial wound but he's lost a helluva lot of blood and he might be in shock. We have to get him to the hospital quick."

There was a knock at the door and Mrs. Tarrings peeked in. "Mr. Martin. I saw the Animal Rescue—O my God!" One hand covered her mouth, the other pointed at Cyclops. "What happened? O my God!"

"Mrs. Tarrings, did you see Jenny at all tonight?"

"Huh?" her attention still fixed on Cyclops and the blood. "Jenny, yes I saw her a few hours ago. She was with some other people."

Barry described Paul, Mary, Joe and Carol to Mrs. Tarrings who acknowledged all but Carol, although she said there was a woman in a car they got into. She went on to describe the two other men who ". . . looked alike. Slow, retarded maybe. Both had comic books sticking out of their back pockets, and around their necks were white crosses."

Barry had no idea who the other two men were but he knew where he could find out. "Did Jenny or anyone say anything to you?"

"No."

"Can you describe the car at all?"

"Heavens, yes. It was tacky."

"Can you be more specific?"

"A 1976 green four-door Plymouth Valiant with terrible rust on the driver's door. The car's interior was a distasteful blue-green, and strung around the rear window were those tiny white cotton balls that foreign people like."

"Excellent, Mrs. Tarrings."

"I was born and raised in Brooklyn, plus I have two sons. I learned a lot of useless information that way. Cars and rock music were two of them."

"Did you happen to notice the license number?"

"I'm sorry, I didn't. I'll call you if I think of anything else, Mr. Martin. By the way, would you let me know how your dog is?"

"I will indeed, and thank you for your help."

Barry contacted the precinct and had them issue an All Points Bulletin on the car, but only to locate, not to apprehend. The next step was a visit with Prescott Palmer to see whether he recognized the two unknown men Mrs. Tarrings had described. Before leaving, Barry went into the bedroom, opened the second drawer of the bureau, pulled out his .44 magnum handgun, and replaced it with his police revolver.

Barry drove through the crowded night streets like a madman. He was furious at himself. He had set Jenny up, they took the bait, and now he had no idea where they were. He was also jeopardizing the lives of Paul and Mary. Sound police procedure that backfired. How many times had he baited innocent people? Six? Seven?

And not all of those had worked. Once the bait was killed. The Teamster official. Three years to retirement, that's all he had. We made him do it. No, I made him do it. I forced him into a no-win situation. Either help me or go to prison at age 62. The poor sap didn't even have a chance. Neither did Jenny. I set her up before she consented. Damn you, Barry!

It was past 11:30 when Barry arrived at Palmer's church. The front door was locked. He knocked for a solid five minutes, each hit increasing in power as his guilt and frustration grew. Taking a tire iron from his car, Barry snapped the door open and headed directly toward Palmer's private office. Another twist of the tire iron got him quickly inside. There was a rustling of sheets. Barry flicked the light on as a bare-bottom female fled into the bathroom.

Palmer, pulling the sheet over him, sat up and beat his hands on the mattress. His face cringed with rage. "You have no right to be in here. Get out!"

Barry slowly raised the tire iron above his head and walked toward Palmer. "Two men, could be brothers, both probably mentally slow, both read comic books. Where do they live?"

Palmer stammered.

Barry cracked the tire iron against the bed. "I don't have time for your bullshit, Palmer. The next time this will go through your head." The tire iron teetered.

"Roger and Doug," Palmer blurted out. "I don't know their last name."

"Address!"

"They live together somewhere downtown near Hudson Street."

Barry pressed the tire iron against Palmer's throat. "I want an exact address."

"I don't know it," his voice pleaded. "They

mentioned a science fiction bookstore near them, it's where they buy their comic books."

Barry knew the store he was referring to. "If you're lying . . ." Barry waved the iron weapon at Palmer huddled in the sheets, then left.

Barry got the bookdstore owner's name and home telephone number from the precinct computer files, and anxiously waited as the phone rang for the third time. "Be home! Be home!" he prompted. A sleepy voice answered the phone. Barry identified himself and then gave a description of Roger and Doug. "Do you know them?"

"The brothers grim. Yeah, I know 'em. They always buy used comic books. A few weeks ago—"

"Do you know where they live? It's very important."

"Can't help you there. They never speak to me; just come in, browse for a few minutes, buy the comics and leave."

"Would you guess they lived in the neighborhood?"

"I couldn't say either way."

"How about a last name for them?"

"I don't have the slightest idea."

Barry described Carol and Joe but he came up empty-handed again.

As the next logical step, Barry drove to the bookstore. Palmer said they lived near the bookstore. Barry figured "near them" included the five or so surrounding blocks. Proceeding North to South, he drove down each street, his spotlight shifting from one side of the road to the other as he searched for the car. It was a long tedious process, but he had no alternative. Hours passed. Barry's apprehension increased with the approaching daylight. Now they could spot him or the car could be on the move. He was distraught about Jenny and remembered he had promised Paul that nothing would happen to her. He was so damn sure of himself. The investigation of Jenny's accident and the Crossbearers would be close to a solution if somebody had talked or more evidence had been uncovered. But nobody talked and no solid evidence was found. He had underestimated the suspects and overestimated himself. Three lives were now at stake, and if Jenny died . . . Repeatedly he hit the steering wheel. He had solved so many cases that he believed he could solve anything, but is just wasn't true.

People began to leave the surrounding apartment buildings, trucks rolled by toward their deliveries, cars revved up, and restaurants and newspapers stands opened. Barry continued the search.

12

Joe Ricart walked to the post office, got the manila envelope from the box and headed back to Roger and Doug's apartment.

Roger looked at the photograph. "This guy's a priest, he's at the same church as Paul Tobin. I forget his name."

"You sure?"

"Yeah, Joe, real sure."

Joe read the accompanying letter. "They want him sacrificed immediately. They're gonna call us here at ten o'clock." It was almost that time. Joe said to Carol, "Feed those three, but no bacon, I want that."

The telephone rang. "Are you a believer?" asked the voice.

Joe responded in the usual manner, then asked, "Why are you calling here?"

"Too many people are looking for you and your girl-friend. I want both of you to stay out of sight. Have the other two Crossbearers carry out the sacrifice."

"But, sir, they're inexperienced."

"After today they won't be." There was a pause. "Following today's sacrifice there will be no more sacrifices for a while. I am sending you money."

"No more sacrifices? But what about—" Joe stopped. Was this the test the co-leader spoke of? He wasn't sure.

The unknown voice ordered Joe to complete his sentence. Joe faltered.

"Are you planning more sacrifices without my approval, Joseph? Answer me!"

"Sir—"

"I order you to answer me or the wrath of God will be upon you."

"Tell him," said Carol overhearing the Leader's command.

"Sir, we already have three sacrifices waiting to be carried out. They're here. We kidnapped them. It was on orders from your assistant. Don't be angry, sir."

"Who gave this order?"

"Your . . . your assistant. I don't know his name."

"Who did you kidnap?"

"Jennifer Tobin, Mary Evans, and Paul Tobin. He's a priest just like the guy's picture you sent today."

"Let them go, immediately."

"I can't, sir, they've seen us. Barry Martin is also to be sacrificed." Joe's voice shook with fear. "You gave the orders, it's not our fault."

There was a long pause. "Carry out all the sacrifices," the voice said uneasily. "First Rhoades, then Martin, then the others. Have Roger and Doug sacrifice Rhoades and Martin."

"No, Martin is mine. He was promised to me."

"Too many people are looking for you. Send the other two Crossbearers." Click.

Joe slammed the phone down, picked it up and

slammed it down again. "He's mine. You promised. He's mine, mine!"

Barry parked in front of Our Lady of the Shrine Church and found Father D'Angelo speaking to a small gathering. Barry dragged him to a corner of the stairs. "Where's Rhoades?"

"He went for a walk. Barry, Paul didn't return last night, and he hasn't called. I have this terrible forboding. Please tell me what is happening."

"I'll explain later. Which way did Rhoades go?"

"Around the corner to the fruit stand."

Barry hurried around the corner and saw Rhoades inspecting an assortment of apples. Out of the corner of his eye, Rhoades spotted Barry, dropped the fruit, and walked away at a fast pace.

Barry sprang after Rhoades, caught hold of his collar and jammed him against a building. "Tell me where Jenny's being held or I swear I'll tear you apart." As he spoke, Barry bounced Rhoades against the building.

"I don't know what you're talking about," Rhoades angrily denied, his hands fighting against Barry's grip. "And if you don't let go of me I'll see to it that you're thrown off the police force."

Barry clamped his fingers around Rhoades' throat and squeezed. "I'm out of patience. Where is she?" He squeezed harder before easing up.

"You're crazy! Leave me alone."

Onlookers gathered across the street wondering whether or not to get involved in the fracas. The fruit store owner joined Father D'Angelo as he hurried toward the two.

Barry applied more pressure. "You, Crowley, and Johnson assassinated Cardinal Beck. Tell me where Jenny is and I'll forget about the other thing." He meant it.

Father D'Anelo latched on to Barry's arm. "Are you mad, Barry? Let him go, he's a priest. My God!"

"Stay out of this!" commanded Barry shaking him off.

"Hey, you can't do that!" said the fruit store owner. Barry still retained his grip on Rhoades. "You asked for it buddy." The owner leapt on Barry's back knocking him down, allowing Rhoades to escape up the street.

"I'm a cop, you idiot." Barry scolded struggling to get free from the owner. "Tell him, Father."

Father D'Angelo restrained the owner confirming, "He's a policeman; let him go."

"No cop beats a priest," argued the owner laboring to stand up.

"This one does."

Rhoades was half a block ahead. A 1976 green four-door Plymouth turned onto the street. The car Mrs. Tarrings had described. Barry tore into a run calling out, "Rhoades, the green car. Take cover!" The car slowed as Rhoades drew closer to it. Barry's neck muscles strained against his skin as he hollered, "They're gonna kill you, Rhoades! Rhoades!"

Pedestrians nervously backed into stores and doorways as the two running and screaming men came at them.

Hearing Barry's screams, Rhoades glanced backward, saw Barry's frantic gesture, and ran faster. Guided by Doug, the green Plymouth slowed while Roger edged the rifle barrel out the window. The car stopped. Rhoades was parallel to the car. A shot. Smoke. Rhoades' body spasmodically snapped before collapsing. The car screeched toward a side street. Barry fired two shots at the car but couldn't stop it. Police sirens blared.

Father D'Angelo knelt beside the slain body of his fellow priest to administer the Last Rites.

Barry commandeered a car from a driver who had watched the shooting and took to pursuit. The car jetted onto Seventh Avenue as the normal traffic parted like the Red Sea. In less than a minute, there was visual contact between the pursuer and the purused. Both cars simultaneously accelerated.

Roger leaned out the window and fired aimlessly in Barry's direction. From behind Barry came the screeching of brakes. Pedestrians dropped to the pavement for cover.

Doug swerved left onto Fourteenth Street, sideswiped a few cars and careened off another, but still Doug kept the accelerator down. Two police cars zeroed in from opposite directions, cutting in front of Barry. Roger picked up the shotgun and fired both barrels. The first patrol car spun, skidded onto its side, sending sparks into the air, and leapfrogged over itself, smashing into a row of parked cars. More patrol cars converged from the side avenues, putting a greater distance between Barry and the killers.

Suddenly there was a rapid exchange of gunfire between cars. The first patrol car locked bumpers with the green car, twirling both cars to a halt. Doug and Roger, shooting recklessly in all directions, scrambled out of their car and hid behind it while the policemen escaped to a further patrol car. A shot rang out. Only one cop made it to safety.

Barry stopped his vehicle half a block away and sized up the situation. Shots were exchanged. Doug, still squatting behind the car, proclaimed, "We'll kill ourselves. For the glory of God we'll die!"

Fanatics, Barry thought. And they're dumb enough to do it. But I need them alive. He started his car and aimed directly at the green car. Doug and Roger fired at the one approaching. Barry crouched down, spun sideways, and plowed into their car. An agonizing scream ruptured the air. Doug stood up and with a gun in each hand fired at Barry, but missed. A barrage of gunfire was returned and Doug slumped to the ground.

Barry and the others surrounded the green car. A car tire was embedded in Roger's chest. Blood gushed from his nose and mouth.

Barry knelt at Roger's side. "Where's Jenny? Tell me what you did with the people you kidnapped? Where on Hudson Street are they being held?"

Roger never heard the question.

"Barry, over here," summoned a patrolman. "No I.D. but he's still alive."

"Find out who owns the car and get me an address," Barry ordered as he turned to the dying man. "Is Joe at your apartment?"

"Roger," Doug faintly whimpered.

"Is Joe at your apartment?"

"Yes," Doug mumbled, with not enough energy to move his lips. One of his hands groped for his cross as he uttered, "Roger?"

Barry placed the cross into his hand and said, "Roger wants a special crucifix from your apartment. He needs it to live. Help your friend, tell me where your apartment is."

"I'm going to heaven, Roger," Doug proclaimed with a final breath.

Barry stood up and said to the rushing paramedics, "Forget it, he's dead."

A patrolman handed Barry a piece of paper. The car was registered by Joe Ricart and the address was the same one Barry had searched. Shit! He kicked the car. Back to square one again. I have to catch a break sooner or later."

"You've had a busy day," Doc commented through the car window as he pulled up to the scene. "I just came from the first shooting." He got out of the car. "The priest is dead. I hope you're finished for the day."

"Two more," answered Barry. "Has the press showed up at the first shooting yet?"

"Hell yeah, they were there before me, and they're probably on their way here now. Heaven forbid they should miss all this excitement."

Assembling all police personnel in the area, Barry ordered them to keep the reporters far away from the crime scene, and to have the green Plymouth removed at once. He added, "No photographs of the car or the suspects. No comments to anyone, and that includes medical reports."

"I haven't received any such instructions," Doc remarked. "What's going on, Barry?"

"Just follow my orders, Doc."

Doc readily complied, then laid his hand on Barry's shoulder saying, "I meant to call you . . . about Dave. I'm really sorry, Barry." In the next breath he promised to have full reports on these victims as soon as possible.

Spectators lined the sidewalks. For all Barry knew, Ricart or Carol could be watching. There was no way to put the lid on these shootings. Ricart was sure to find out what had happened. The question was, would he retaliate against his prisoners? It was an easy yes. He couldn't let them live anyway; they could identify him. Time was running out.

Barry picked up his car at the church and drove back to the station. Another detective sitting at Dave's desk handed Barry a telephone number. "It's the Animal Rescue League. Call 'em back." The strange detective answered Barry's unpleasant look. "My name's Tom Sullivan. I'm taking Dave's desk, not his place." He held out his hand and they shook. "I heard what happened out there. You all right?"

"Yeah. There were a few cops hurt out there. Any reports on them?"

"Busted up but nothing serious. Listen, I got transferred from narcotics to homicide and since this morning I've done nothing but fill out forms and get calluses. You need help?"

Barry shook off the offer, offended at the quick replacement.

"If you change your mind, I'm right in front of you." As he eased into the chair, Tom mumbled, "Homicide's really boring."

Barry hesitated dialing the animal hospital. Would this be the first death, he wondered. An omen? No, it's only a dog, he forced himself to believe as he dialed, and it's not an omen. "This is Barry Martin. I'm calling about my dog Cyclops."

The call was transferred to the appropriate doctor. "Mr. Martin, Dr. Ross here. The operation on your dog was done as soon as he arrived here last night, but the loss of blood and oxygen to the brain was significant."

With a deep breath, Barry said, "Cyclops is dead?"

"Not yet, Mr. Martin. The operation was relatively simple, but the poor condition of the dog caused complications. At present your pet is in a coma and might never come out of it. If he does, he might have brain damage or paralysis or both; we just can't tell right now."

"What's the prognosis?"

"My recommendation is that we put the dog to sleep. It's a traumatic decision, Mr. Martin, but I feel it would be in your pet's best interest."

"What are the chances of a full recovery?"

"It's impossible to answer that question, sir, but the percentages would be against it."

"Seventy/thirty? Eighty/twenty? What?"

"In cases such as this, when we're unable to ascertain such things, putting an animal to sleep is the correct procedure. Now if you could come down here today and sign the necessary forms—"

"No! I won't put Cyclops to sleep. All he needs is more time to fight."

"Mr. Martin—"

"It's final!" Barry hung up. Everyone wants to give up so fast, I don't understand it. I'm not giving up and neither is Cyclops. He called the Medical Examiner's office to see if they had any preliminary work-up done on the two men and the car.

"You don't give me much time but I anticipated it," said Doc. "I finally have some information for you. We found chicken feathers on the soles of their shoes and in the tire treads. Hold on—Poultry blood too, Barry, and fresh. They must have lived near a live poultry market. The big markets are at nineth and fourteenth."

"Too far. There's one closer to their address. Thanks for the fast work, Doc." Three-thirty. Still enough time to canvass the neighborhood and plan his attack. Immediately he ruled out back-up units as too clumsy, too conspicuous. Or maybe he just wanted Ricart for himself.

Barry's phone rang.

"Badge 5746. It's 3:47, do you know where your friends are?" he asked with a conceited laugh. "I heard about Rhoades and my two men. You're good, Badge 5746, but not as good as me. And with Doug and Roger dead you still don't know where to look for your friends."

"Let me talk to Jenny."

"Oh, are you worried about your blind girlfriend? Don't be, Carol's taking good care of her. Ain't you gonna congratulate me on the kidnapping? I really burned your ass, didn't I? But the fun's over, Badge 5746. You see, my next sacrifice is you—and it's already begun. At any time, at any place, I'll be there waiting, watching, and shooting. You're as good as dead."

"I figured you'd take the coward's route," Barry said smoothly, trying to set up something. "Killing unarmed people and a young kid, you've accomplished nothing great. Coward!" Take the bait, you bastard!

"I'm good at what I do," Ricart replied, "and your death will prove it."

"No it won't, because you can't do it. I'm better than you are. I'm better than you'll ever be. If I was standing in front of you you'd probably miss." Even over the phone Barry detected Ricart's aggravated breathing. "Not one of your victims fought back, but if they had you would have been dead already. You slaughtered them like defenseless cattle. And the kidnapping? A priest and two women, one of them blind. A fool could have pulled that off. In fact, a fool did!"

"You're gonna die, Martin. I'm gonna kill you. I'm gonna kill you slowly, and I'm gonna enjoy every minute of it." His voice was volatile. "But I'm gonna make it even worse for you, Martin, since you think you're so goddamn good. I'm going to leave the address in my pocket of where I'm holding your friends. You kill me and you get the address. Then you just have to deal with Carol."

It was better than he'd hoped for. "How do I know you'll do it?"

"Nobody takes me alive, Martin. Nobody. Never. So you either kill me or I kill you and your friends. Whadayasay, Martin? Now you have a real reason to kill me."

"It will be my pleasure—and don't forget the

address. But just to make sure that killing you will be worthwhile, let me talk to Jenny to see if she's okay."

"I can't do that; you see I'm closer to you than to her. Good-bye forever, Detective Martin!" Click.

Every fiber, every muscle in Barry's body grew in strength from the pumping adrenalin. Every thought not connected to survival and total alertness was blocked out as he mentally and physically prepared for battle. The sun told him it was late afternoon. Window! Quickly but casually he moved away from what could be an easy shot. His first plan was to get out of the precinct undetected in case Ricart was watching.

"Martin!" the Captain called from his office doorway. "Martin, I want to see you. Are you listening to me?" Walking across the room, he nabbed Barry by the arm. "I said I wanted to see you."

Barry's eyes shifted from the grasping fingers to the Captain's eyes. "Get your hand off me."

All work and conversation in the squad room shut off like a motor.

Adams could feel his subordinates' eyes trained on him. The grip remained firm as did his voice. "I gave you an order. Now into my office!" Barry's crazed look overpowered Captain Adams. His grip loosened. "We'll talk when you get back." He returned to his office.

Barry went downstairs and inspected the assortment of derelicts detained behind bars. He tried to pick the cleanest one, but it was like trying to decide which rotten apple to eat. "You. Yeah, the one in the corner. Stand up." Too tall. He pointed to another bum and motioned him forward. "Trade clothes with me and I'll give you ten bucks."

The bum's bloodshot eyes lit up as he mentally converted the money into bottles. They exchanged clothes in a back room. Barry sprayed the crotch area of the pants with disinfectant before putting them on, but even that wasn't strong enough. Nestling his .44 Magnum revolver into the dirty coat pocket he had a patrolman escort him from the precinct for effect. Keeping his head down and the hatrim low, Barry began cruising the area on foot to look for Ricart. He had seen Ricart only that one time at Palmer's church, when he had come to Linda's defense, but it was enough to recognize him again.

Barry scanned the rooftops and alleyways as he staggered along. A bottle. I need a bottle. He entered a liquor store, bought a pint of wine, then sat on the curb and watched. He hadn't shaved for a day, yet he still looked too groomed for a dirtball. Barry reminded himself to keep his head bowed.

Sunlight was fading fast. There were two prime locations for Ricart to choose for the kill, Barry figured. Here in front of the precinct, swarming with cops, or at my apartment when I'm alone. Ricart's crazy, but he's not stupid; it's my apartment. On the other hand, he could be anywhere. Barry gave it another ten minutes before hailing a cab.

"Get outa here, you scummy bum!" threatened the driver.

Ten bucks shut him up. Barry had the cab stop three blocks from his apartment house.

"I'm keep'n the ten for deodorant," the cabbie sneered. Barry had no time to argue.

Head lowered, Barry staggered down his street, his senses alert to everything. Rush hour traffic increased. So did hurrying pedestrians. With one hand on his pint and the other gripping the .44 magnum in his pocket, Barry continued.

One block away, he sat down on the curb and surveyed the potential battlefield. Townhouses and apartments lined both sides of the street, with no alleyways between. That left the rooftops or his own apartment house. He dismissed that. No quick exit. The shooting had to be on the street.

Barry lowered his gaze to the basement windows. Too much of an angle for a clean shot. An open unobstructed space, that's what he'd look for. On the opposite side of the street was an iron gate leading to a backyard, which merged into another backyard and another street. That would be choice number one for Ricart. Barry, remaining on the opposite side of the street, staggered down the street parallel to the gate, stopped, faced the gate, pretended to take a swig of wine, and watched. He took another fake swig, shook his body, and leaned against the building. A head peered through the gate. Ricart.

The sealed padlock on the gate verified that Joe had entered from the back street, so that's where Barry headed. The lock on the corresponding rear gate had been pried open. Gingerly he inched the gate back, and slipped into the back yard. A three-foot high wooden fence separated the yards. Barry drew out his .44 magnum and crept up to the fence. Focusing between the slats he spotted Ricart cowering in the shadows at the base of the gate. An easy shot. Barry wanted to live up to the terms of the agreement and blow the bastard's head off—an execution more than a killing. But he didn't trust Ricart to have the address on him. Regrettably, Barry had to take him alive.

A window rumbled open and a woman leaning out screamed at Barry, "This is private property. Get out before I call the police."

Barry flattened himself against the ground as two shots splintered the fence near him.

"That you, Badge 5746?"

Barry back-pedaled along the ground, taking cover behind a tree. His enemy was no longer visible. He took stock of the immediate area. To his left, four parallel backyards, all squared off by wooden fences. To his right, connecting buildings. Ricart's only escape routes were to the left on Barry's side of the fence, and they both knew it.

"Who's there? Martin, if it's you answer me!" There was fury in his voice. "Goddammit, tell me who you are!"

The yard next to them had a shorter fence, easier to jump. He'll try for that, Barry deduced. There was no noise or movement from the other yard. Barry's gaze swept back and forth trying to detect something. A shadowy movement near the back stairs. Barry fired. A portion of the banister blew apart. Ricart bolted from beneath the stairs. Barry fired again shattering a bird-bath. Ricart jumped the fence. Paralleling Ricart's movements, Barry jumped the fence and took shelter behind a small brick barbecue pit. Both yards were partially visible to both men.

"I know it's you, Martin, even if you don't answer me. I was hoping it would end like this—face to face—to see who's really better."

Ricart's voice was coming from the right side of the yard. Almost everything was darkened by shadows. Barry still couldn't see him.

"Ya know your girlfriend's really got a nice body, Martin. After last night she'll never want another man besides me. Ya hear what I'm sayin', Martin?"

The staircase, it was on the right. He likes to hide in similar places. Fool. In front of the stairs was a pile of firewood. Barry gathered up some loose rocks and crawled along the fence, positioning himself at a cross-fire angle. Come on fool, jabber one more time.

Ricart obliged. "This is just like the old west, Martin,

a real shoot-out, but this time the lawman gets it."

On the silent count of three, Barry hurled the rocks, dislocating some pieces of wood. Ricart, half crouched, fired at the barbecue pit. Barry stood up, and with both hands holding the gun steady, rapidly fired four times. The .44 magnum slugs ripped into Ricart's chest with the force of a sledge hammer, propelling him off the ground into the staircase, then ricocheting forward to slump over the heap of wood.

Sirens. Barry leapt over the fence and shoved Ricart's body off the wood. Most of his chest had been blown apart. Barry heard the squeaky gate clank open. He dropped his gun, held his badge in the air, and repeatedly called out his name and badge number to avoid mistaken identity. Once safe from his own, he inspected the contents of Ricart's pockets and found a note addressed to him. It simply said, "I lied." Barry threw it aside and went through the contents of the wallet, finding a piece of paper with a telephone number scribbled on it. Barry handed it to the Sergeant explaining, "I want an address that belongs to this telephone number and an unmarked car fast."

Barry picked up his gun, brushed the dirt off, reloaded it an placed it back in his coat pocket as he waited for the information and the car, which arrived in jig time. The address was in the area of the science fiction bookstore and the live poultry market. He glanced at Ricart's body and said "Thank you." One more to go—Carol.

The red brick building was five stories high on a fairly decent street. Easily he jammed the front door open. There was only a staircase. Scraping some dirt and grease off the door, he smeared the goo on his neck and cheeks before going up to apartment 3F. He could hear the television. Taking out his pint and gargling, spitting it into a corner, he went into his drunken schizophrenic act as his other hand gripped the gun in his coat pocket.

Starting off in a mumbling voice as he conversed with his phantom friend, Barry argued "You always drink too much. It's my turn. Gimme that bottle." His voice grew louder. "Gimme that bottle! You're all alike, drinkin' more than yer share." Some doors inched open as the tenants looked out. Barry shot his hand in the air, the wine spilling over. "Rats! They've all over the place!" He jumped up and down.

A woman warned, "Get out, yah bum, before I call the police."

Barry lowered his head, scraped his feet if he were about to charge, and motioned to the woman to come closer saying. "You're the one. You're Mother Rat. They attack me on our command." Carol's door opened slightly. Barry kept his back to her. "I can feel 'em eatin' my legs. Goddamn rats. Can't get away from 'em." Backing up and slanting his body just enough, he saw Carol's hand clutching a pistol by her side. He heard other apartment doors close.

"I gotta get away from the rats! Get 'em away from me!" He spun around and threw himself through the open door, tackling Carol. Her eyebrows arched when she recognized her assailant. Furiously she beat the gun against him, her leg kicking incessantly. Carol's gun fired once, twice. Her body convulsed as she aimed her spit into Barry's face.

Barry struggled to capture her gun hand as it wavered between their heads. A bullet from her gun plowed into the ceiling. Barry pounced against her. He grabbed her gun hand, thrusting it against the floor in an attempt to dislodge it from her grip. The gun went off again. Carol's head snapped back and forth. Her body went limp. Blood covered her face and hair. Barry tossed the gun aside and entered the bedroom. His three friends were in chairs, bound and gagged, but alive and unhurt.

Paul and Mary's eyes glowed at seeing him. "It's Barry! Jenny, you're safe." He untied Jenny first. She flung herself into his arms and couldn't stop hugging him, smell and all.

"I thought I'd never hear your voice again, Barry. Thank God."

Barry freed Paul and Mary, who didn't know what to make of Barry's contaminated attire, but embraced him anyway.

"What about Joe and the other two?" Paul asked.

"They're all dead. And so is Father Rhoades."

"Father D'Angelo?"

"He's fine but very worried about all of you."

"I'll call him."

"No," Mary said. "Go see him."

"We'll both go," Paul replied, then asked Barry, "Was Rhoades involved with the Crossbearers?"

"Up to his collar. I'll tell you about it later on at the church. Don't leave until I get there." Barry sniffed the air. "I have to go home and take about ten showers."

Before leaving the apartment, Barry notified the precinct of what had happened, and then made another telephone call to Cardinal Alden, advising him to go to Our Lady of the Shrine as soon as possible. He'd explain at the church.

On the way home, after learning why Barry smelled like garbage, Jenny told her story of the car accident. "You were right, we did see the men who killed Cardinal Beck. I don't understand how I could have forgotten that. I guess being terrified can make you forget some things and remember others."

"Are you sure of those descriptions?"

"Yes and no. I've gone over them a hundred times,

341

and each time I remember another characteristic. But I don't know which man had which characteristic. It's like viewing superimposed images on a television screen."

"Forget about the others, concentrate on the man with the white wire over his cheek."

"I have, but it's no use. I recall the other men ducking from the gunshot, but the one who did the shooting didn't budge. And the white wire, I still don't know what it is. It just scares me to think that I waited that long to duck."

"You were damn lucky. Are you sure the man with the wire over his cheek did the shooting?"

"Absolutely. We were looking directly at each other. I remember both cars bouncing and the wire striking his cheek at each bump."

"You should write a letter to the Mayor, thanking him for the poor conditions of the streets. Anything else?"

"Yes, but not about the Cardinal's assassins." Jenny crossed her fingers on both hands for luck before asking, "What about Cyclops?" She held her breath.

"He's in critical condition, in a coma. The doctor doesn't know if he'll come out of it, and if he does he might not be normal."

"Can we go see him tomorrow, Barry? He protected me. I want to hold him once more."

"First thing tomorrow morning. But we're not finished tonight. We have to see somebody about a murder."

After his much-needed shower, he put on fresh clothes and made a quick telephone call to the Police Commissioner. Then Barry and Jenny headed for Our Lady of the Shrine.

They passed by a lone man sitting in the front pew and entered the study. Paul, Mary, Cardinal Alden,

Father D'Angelo, and Father Inness were all present.

Father D'Angelo embraced Barry and took Jenny's hand, pressing it to his heart. "It's Father D'Angelo, Jennifer."

"Father." Jenny kissed him on the cheek.

"I prayed for you all. God generously answered my prayers."

Paul escorted Father D'Angelo back to his chair and poured him a cognac. Paul looked at the gathering. "I guess I'll ask the questions," turning to Barry. "Why are we all here?"

Barry directed his opening remark to Father Inness. "You know everything, Father. You probably know more about this case than I do."

With an expression of mixed innocence and bewilderment, the Vatican priest replied, "I do not know what you are referring to, Detective Martin. But most of all, I am appalled that you would even consider my doing anything wrong."

"That's the trouble with priests; when they do something wrong nobody believes it. But the fact is that something was done wrong here, and by priests. Murder."

"Barry, you cannot speak to priests like that," sanctioned Father D'Angelo. "They are men of God."

"That may be true, Father. But there is a fine line between belief and extremism. A particular group of priests has stepped over the line."

"I do not like to criticize, Detective Martin," the Cardinal broke in, "but I fail to see your point."

"The point is simple and, I might mention, one that recurs throughout history in various forms. Two components are working here: Church membership is declining and crime is escalating. Crime pays; going to church does not. Statistics prove it. But there is a way to change the satistics—eliminate the criminals permanently. Use them as examples."

"To keep others from becoming criminals," said Paul. "Or at least, think twice about breaking the law."

"Precisely," Barry continued. "That's what a graduating class of radical priests believed. So they recruited a small band of religious zealots who pervertedly believed that these killings were God's orders, and they carried them out with the promise of going to Heaven."

"The Crossbearers!" Jenny declared.

"And I know which graduating class you're referring to Barry," Paul said, as a few pieces of the puzzle fell into place.

For the benefit of the others, Barry informed them of the various murders in other cities that Rhoades had been in touch with. "New York was the major testing ground; the others were one-shot deals just to see if multiple murders could be carried out at the same time. As for those churches Father Rhoades was in contact with, each priest in charge was a member of that graduating class. Two of the graduates do not fall into this category. One was killed, probably because he was going to inform somebody; and the second, Father Edmunds, was assigned to the Vatican or more specifically, to the Vatican bank." Barry read from a piece of paper from his pocket. "The Vatican bank is officially known as the Institute per le Opere de Religione, or Institute for Religious Works which, according to recent newspaper sources, is missing over one billion dollars. And it just so happens that Father Edmunds was the chief administrator of the bank. Six days ago he conveniently had a stroke and died. The Vatican uncovered the plan, and that accounts for Father Inness' presence."

"That's totally absurd," Inness defended himself. "You're making a mockery of the priesthood."

"Given the proper motive and indoctrination, anyone will kill." Barry sought Mary's professional approval.

"What Barry says has been tested, and the results support his propositions. Advertising agencies are the best known for using reinforcement/repetition techniques."

Barry continued. "These priests believed that the Church was dying in the United States. Even the Vatican was in agreement. Everybody held that view, and when everybody continually reinforced it, it had to be true, especially for those priests. To them this was war, and they were fighting the final battle for survival."

"Armageddon," Father D'Angelo proposed. "The decisive battle between the forces of good and evil."

"But only of man's forces of good and evil, Father."

"And my dear friend's death?" he asked Barry. "They killed Cardinal Beck. Why? He as a just and holy man!"

"That he was," emphasized Cardinal Alden, pushing his eyeglasses higher on the bridge of his nose. "Men such as he should live forever."

Barry directed his comments to Father Inness. "Father Crowley, Father Johnson, Father Rhoades, and one other man assassinated Cardinal Beck. The reason you're here is to discover who that fourth man is. Now I will tell you. At seminary school, as with every school, there are two types of people: students and teacher. We know who the students were, and the teacher...." Barry extended his hand toward Cardinal Alden.

Father D'Angelo crossed himself three times while the others rustled in their chairs to face the second.

In his usual stalwart voice, the Cardinal answered the

345

charges. "I was a teacher at the seminary and I did have those students in some of my classes, but so did other priests who taught there. As for your innuendo that I killed Cardinal Beck to obtain his position, it was the Pope's decision."

Barry gave an agreeing nod. "That's why your smartest student, according to his academic records, was sent to he Vatican. He politicked for you there while your other students politicked for you here. Pressure applied at all the correct posts, and it worked. You then appointed your studnets to higher positions in the Church, as their reward. As for Father Rhoades, it was obvious to his group that he was panicking. So the group must have had him killed for their own protection. It was all nicely arranged and very patiently executed."

"All those murders because you thought the Church would cease to exist?" Father D'Angelo asked. "God would not allow His own House to fall. It cannot!"

"I'm sure that's how it started," Barry added, "but Cardinal Alden's final goal was more grandiose. Your true intent was to form a new Church in the United States, with a new Pope. Yourself. That's why you killed Beck, and I'd guess that other deaths would have occurred as you expanded your control. The embezzled funds were needed to pay off the likes of Ricart, telephone bills, travel expenses, and perhaps a down-payment on a building that would be the headquarters for your new movement.

"Rhoades's New Order," said Paul. "It makes sense."

"Murder. Conspiracy. You are falsely accusing me of vicious crimes, Detective Martin, all of which are slanderous."

Barry put his hand on Jenny's shoulder. "Jenny witnessed the escape of Cardinal Beck's assassins. We already know three of the four men. Jenny, tell us about the fourth man."

"When the assassins were chasing Jimmy and me, they shot at us. The man who did the shooting had a small white wire hanging over his cheek."

"That's the full description?" Cardinal Alden taunted.

"It's enough to lead us to four other of your characteristics," replied Barry. "Staring and standing close to people when you talk, as you did during my visit. Your loud voice, and your glasses constantly slipping down your nose. A few years ago your glasses fell off during a bumpy ride, inadvertently exposing the white wire in the bow of your glasses. A hearing aid. And even with that, you still have to rely on lip reading. But that day you had to put your glasses back on so you could aim the gun at Jenny."

A disquieting hush enveloped the study. "Rhoades was the one who shot Cardinal Beck," Barry continued, "but it was all the teacher's idea. You're under arrest for murder and conspiracy to commit murder." Barry purposely omitted reading him his rights.

Cardinal Alden stood, his breathing intensified, his cheeks bloated. "I know what you're thinking," he challenged. His voice was strong but exaggerated as were his movements. "It wasn't for me. I did it to save the Church. God commanded me to do it. He spoke to me. His creation was crumbling, yet nobody cared, nobody did anything about it. So He chose me to bear the cross, so save the world, to save our God. And we must continue, it is His wish. Only a few more have to be sacrificed before the people realize that they must return to God. Purge the wicked so the righteous might flourish. Join my crusade. Help me. You must help me!"

"We will," Mary comforted him, recognizing the

signs of a highly charged body on the verge of shock and mental collapse. "Why don't you rest here for a while," she offered, helping him to a chair.

Cardinal Alden's eyes darted back and forth and his lips moved rapidly, making strange sounds. "You'll join me?" All of you? No, you won't join me. I didn't do anything wrong." His right hand flew forward. "Stop staring at me! Don't you understand, God spoke to me—to *me*."

Mary delicately touched the Cardinal's arm. "Why don't you pray; it will give you peace of mind. We won't disturb you. Yes—pray." Her voice and presence quieted him.

The study door opened and the Police Commissioner, holding a compact, but very sophisticated tape recorder, nodded to Barry.

"That tape recorder, is that not illegal?" Father Inness asked.

"It is inadmissible evidence," Barry replied.

"As I thought. And all the Crossbearers, they are dead. There is no evidence to support your theory," Inness recounted for Barry. "As for Cardinal Alden, obviously he is mentally disturbed. No jury will ever believe any of this."

Barry knew that was only the half of it. Between the police cover-up and frame-up of Beck's would-be assassin, the District Attorney would avoid this case like the plague. "But there is a solution, Father Inness," Barry heralded. "The Vatican knew about this. Your job was to discover who the top man was. The question now becomes: What would you have done once you uncovered the leader?"

Father Inness vigorously denied Barry's conclusion. "The Church had nothing to do with this ungodly tragedy. Were they not individuals acting on their own?"

"Don't be so defensive, Father; we're not in court. But now that you do know, what's your next step?"

"Solutions are more obtainable in privacy," he said without hesitation.

"You talk to both of us," the Police Commissioner demanded.

The others adjourned to the chapel except for Alden, who remained sedated in prayer.

Inness voiced his plan. "I can order all those priests involved in the conspiracy to gather in New York, put them on a private jet that will take them to the Vatican, and house them in a secluded building for the rest of their lives. Their families will be notified that they have been reassigned; no one will ever see or hear from them again. You have my word on it. However, none of this story must ever leak out. That includes handing that tape recorder over to me."

"How are you going to get the priests to obey?"

"We'll explain that the Pope is going to honor Cardinal Alden and the Cardinal has requested that his former students share in this honor. I can send the telegrams tonight. By tomorrow night they will be on a jet to Rome."

"It's a helluva scheme on such short notice," Barry commented with a smirk. "What do you think, Commissioner?"

"If we accept the Father's solution, we'd be covering up a crime."

"Do we want this crime to be known?" Father Inness stated. "The killers are all dead or captured. Displaying this case to the public serves no useful purpose. The knowledge of the case might be more adverse than the actual killings. Would that not be true?" Inness knew they would accept his proposal; there was no other choice. "Detective Martin, nothing can bring the dead back; we can only consider the feelings of the living—and they must not know of this."

Barry and the Commissioner adjourned to a corner for a private conference. "Dragging this into public would create more havoc than most politicians and lawyers would be willing to deal with," advised Barry.

"And everybody would have a field day with the police cover-up," the Commissioner somberly predicted. "It would utterly destroy the credibility we've regained. But another cover-up?"

"What's one more? At least we're doing it for a damn good reason."

The Commissioner approached Father Inness. "We accept your solution."

"That is wise. I will have the telegrams sent immediately."

Barry detained the priest for another moment. "There's a police Chaplain in my station you should also invite on the trip." Barry jotted down the Chaplain's name and handed it to Inness who put it in his back pocket. "Aren't you curious who the priest is?"

"Ah, yes," he answered taking a quick peek at the name. "He will be included. What do we do with Cardinal Alden until tomorrow night?"

The Commissioner answered, "A private room has been arranged for him. His personal escorts are outside. Detective Martin and I will see you off at the airport tomorrow night."

"It is not necessary."

"Yes it is."

"As you wish," Inness yielded, and with a gentlemanly bow, left the study.

Two plainclothes officers escorted Cardinal Alden to his temporary holding place, where, at Mary's insistence, a nurse would attend him through the night.

Barry and the Commissioner remained in the study for more private conversation.

"Detective Martin, you don't seem pleased over the outcome of this case. Granted it's bizarre, but it is, as far as we're concerned, over."

"Inness' plain is too neat."

"I agree with your suspicions that it was probably worked out long ago. It should be neat."

"It strikes me as peculiar that Inness isn't concerned about twelve priests just disappearing."

"As Inness said, priests are transferred all the time; go on missionary work around the world. I'm sure their families and friends are aware of that. Go home, rest, and call me tomorrow."

"Yes, sir. Good night." Barry joined the others in the congregational hall. He sensed their eagerness to be told what had transpired, but they respectfully remained silent on the subject. Loyal friends, Barry thought.

Mary planted a kiss on Barry's cheek. "Thanks again for all you've done."

"Why are you thanking him?" Jenny lightheartedly retorted, wrapping an arm around Barry's waist. "If it wasn't for him, you wouldn't have been kidnapped in the first place. Just me."

"What's the sense of living in New York if you're not kidnapped once in a while?" Barry joked. "I'm grateful to all of you, though, willing or not."

Paul, holding Mary's hand, directed a personal remark to Father D'Angelo. "The kidnapping confirmed the direction of my leap, Father. But it was not in the direction of the church. I'm sorry."

"You don't apologize for happiness, Paul. And you did leap in the right direction; the love you show for each other proves it."

Mary planted a kiss on Father D'Angelo's cheek as

Paul replied, "Thank you, Father. I'm also thankful that this parish is back in the proper hands."

Father D'Angelo shyly accepted the high praise. "A close friend of mine in Chicago will be pleased with the news I have for him and some others." He explained no further. Some things are better left unsaid, he decided. "And to you Bàrry, deep gratitude for bringing Cardinal Beck's assassins to justice. Now I must search my heart and see if I can forgive them. Bless you all."

Morning found Barry and Jenny anxiously waiting at the Animal Rescue League Hospital. Muffled barks and howls echoed like the cries of abandoned souls from the back rooms, imploring the animals' owners to take them out of this place of pain and fright.

Jenny tapped her tinted glasses against her knee. "You sure you told the doctor we're here?"

"Relax. He's a busy man."

"Now I know how Paul felt while I was in the hospital. Sometimes it's easier being the patient than the waiting family. At least you already know the outcome." She tapped her knee. "Where is he?"

Barry rubbed his hand over her back, trying to calm her, although he wished someone would do it for him. If Cyclops doesn't come out of this as his old self, Jenny might never forgive him. Maybe he should have had him put to sleep. Where the hell was the doctor?

"Mr. Martin?" a young man asked. "I'm Dr. Ross. Your dog came out of the coma late last night. First indications suggest he will recover, but there seems to be some loss of mobility in his right hind leg."

"But he's alive," Jenny exclaimed happily. "Thank you, Doctor."

"Remember, it's still too early to judge how full the recovery will be, but as you said, he is alive, thanks to

Mr. Martin. If it hadn't been for his insistance, I would have put Cyclops to sleep yesterday." The doctor chuckled. "My father was a vet and before I opened my practice he said, 'The marvelous part of being a doctor is that you get to witness the power of medicine and God.' And I must say they do work very well together."

"Is it possible that I could see Cyclops?" Jenny asked.

"I anticipated your request since it's a frequent one. My nurse will bring him out for a visit. But let me forewarn you that he is heavily bandaged, partially sedated, and he will be limping. Ah, here he is now."

A nurse guided Cyclops on a leash into the room. Bandages covered most of his midriff, his head hung, and his tongue stuck out, leaving droplets of saliva on the floor. The limp was worse than Barry had anticipated. One rear leg limped but the other one seemed to drag, giving an awkward list to his body. I'm glad Jenny can't see this, Barry thought.

Cyclops raised his head with difficulty. Suddenly his tail curled up from between his legs and began to wag. His wobbly legs moved him faster and closer to Jenny, who knelt down and hugged him. Cyclops excitedly licked her face and buried his head in her shoulder as though he couldn't get close enough to her.

"That's true love," observed Barry, listening to Jenny's giggling.

"Did you see the dog cross the room," said Dr. Ross, "the hind legs didn't limp once he saw the young lady. Cyclops will have to remain here for a few days. Is it possible that she could come visit him on a daily basis?"

"I don't think you could keep her away," Barry took another look at the two and knew Cyclops would make a full recovery.

*   *   *

At ten o'clock that night, Barry, the Commissioner, Paul, Father D'Angelo, and Fateher Inness stood outside a private lounge in the airport terminal and gawked at the reunion of the priests. Fathers Crowley and Johnson waved to the onlookers. All were smiles.

Barry gave a quick count. Two were not present. "Where are Cardinal Alden and the Police Chaplain?" he asked the Commissioner.

"The Cardinal was sent on an earlier plane so the others wouldn't become suspicious. As for the Police Chaplain, he's already on board."

"He is the pilot," Father Inness explained, "and is certified to fly such a plane. It saves us from paying a private pilot." Father Inness directed his next comment to Paul. "I have arranged for your immediate dispensation from your clerical vows. Much to our sorrow there is a backlog of over a thousand priests seeking dispensation, but considering all that has happened, I did not want you to wait."

"I appreciate that, Father. I was worried about the transition period. A long delay is always stressful. Now I can begin my new life." His thoughts turned to Chief Strongarm. I will offer my help to him, he thought, but this time as man to man.

Father Inness addressed Father D'Angelo. "We are truly sorry for the misery we have brought to your church and your life, but we had to know who was doing the killings and whether we could stop them."

Father D'Angelo replied, "The Church was created to worship our Lord. Priests are called by God to help those in need of help. You have confused this order. This chaos is of your own making."

"You still accuse me as if I were guilty, but—"

Father D'Angelo walked away. Father Inness turned to Barry. "He is accusing the wrong person. They," pointing to the priests in the room, "they are the wrong-doers."

"Who are you trying to convince, Father, us or yourself? Last night, with Jenny safety by my side, I rehashed everything more clearly in my mind, and I found I had made a mistake. I assumed you didn't know who the leader of the Crossbearers was. But you did."

"No, no. We did not."

"Yes you did. As an insider you couldn't miss it—young priests being promoted fast, old priests like Father D'Angelo being forced to retire, an assassination, pressure to select Alden as the new Cardinal, a significant drop in money that Alden and his group had to funnel off for their own cause, and consolidated voices caling for radical changes, even a split from the Vatican. All this over a period of years and no one noticed? No way, Father."

The Commissioner added, "The inner circle knew what was transpiring, but did not intervene because it was working. Unfortunately, violence and terrorism often work."

"I regret that neither of you believes *my* story, but it is the truth. Now I must leave with the others. Perhaps we will meet again under happier circumstances." After a gentle bow of his head, Father Inness joined the other priests.

"I'm still uneasy about these priests disappearing just like that," Barry thought aloud as he and the others made their way to the observation deck. The private jet taxied to the far end of the field and completed its take-off. In unison all four men gave a sigh of relief as the jet climbed higher into the sky.

Paul put his hand on Father D'Angelo's arm. "I'll give you a ride home."

"I'm not going home," he answered. "A very nice

young lady has invited me for a late dinner. Her future husband is an architect and she wants me to give him a job redesigning our school. I hope he's good." They walked to the elevator smiling.

"I hear he used to be a priest."

"You could never tell by the way he dressed." The elevator door closed.

"It's refreshing to see a case end on a happy note," remarked the Commissioner. "There are still some loose ends, though. This morning the Chief of Police and Captain Ames resigned and voluntarily forfeited their pensions. The position of Chief of Police has been filled, but I would like you to be our Captain of Detectives. That would give me two reliable men in key positions."

"I'm sorry, Commissioner, but what you want are spies to keep you informed. I'll pass."

"I already have enough spies, Barry. What I'm in need of are more forthright commanders. It also means more money and more prestige. Think about it and let me know Monday."

Barry remarked, "If I did accept your offer that would mean all paperwork, no cases to investigate, and hounding the other detectives. It sounds boring."

"If you wish, you could still be involved in certain investigations, but you would also be responsible for all casework and personnel in your department. It's a prized promotion, Barry, and they don't occur often."

They parted company outside the terminal. A group of polits and stewardesses mingled near the curb where their charted mini-bus was to pick them up. The wing emblems pinned to their uniforms brought the Police Chaplain to Barry's mind. Another coincidence—just when Inness needed a pilot there was one, Barry thought. And when I wrote down the Chaplain's name he didn't even look at it until I reminded him. I was right. Everything was set up, including me. Inness didn't overlook a thing. God, I hate being used!

Barry walked to his car, giving more consideration to the promotion. His whole life he had always had contempt for those in charge, and now he had a chance to join that impious group. "Admit it," he lectured himself, "It's not contempt but jealousy. I never thought I'd admit that." He got into his car. Me, Chief of Detectives. To be in charge—to do things my way. Hell, why not? He switched on the ignition key and headed home to Jenny. As he drove he repeated, "Barry Martin, Chief of Detectives. Barry Martin, Chief of Detectives."

The private jet taxied to a secluded part of Rome's Leonardo da Vinci Airport where Father Inness then shuttled the passengers onto the waiting bus. The long trip had quieted the guests, but their enthusiasm was rejuvenated as they undertood the final leg of their journey.

While the bus wound its way through the narrow streets, which were not designed for automobiles, Father Inness rose to address the priests who were busily pointing out and snapping photographs of the local sights. It took a minute to get their attention. Father Inness tried not to think of their fate and his role in it. It is something that must be done, he continually thought, hoping his guilt did not show through his feigned smile. "We will enter Vatican City shortly. So as not to disturb a ceremony, we will enter the Basilica from a rear entrance. Brother Michael will be waiting for us. Please follow him—and there is to be absolute quiet."

"Will we have time for some sightseeing today?" asked one of the priests.

"Perhaps," was all that Father Inness could mutter.

Father Crowley leaned toward Father Inness. "What kind of a ceremony is going on? I'd like to see it. Some of the others might too."

"There will be enough time for everything." Father Inness's eyes were fixed on the moving scenery. He leaned back, wishing this day were over.

The bus turned down the via del Conciliazione, crowded with cars and tour buses. At the end of the street a soldier of the Vatican's Swiss Guard, outfitted in the traditional colorful uniform, signaled the driver into the circular plaza of St. Peter's. Faces and camera lenses pressed against the windows while hands waved to the multitude of strangers.

The Police Chaplain tried to open his window for a clearer view. It would not budge. He ran his fingers along the rim of the window, feeling the rubbery texture of the glue. He turned to Father Johnson and asked him to open his window.

"Ugh. Must be stuck. Maybe the top. Nope." His hands clasped into prayer position at St. Peter's Basilica came into view. "Magnificent. I always feel at home when I come here. Simply magnificent."

The Police Chaplain joined the other admirers as the bus slowed. Father Inness pointed to the center of the facade, explaining that that was the balcony from which the Pope gave his 'benediction to the City and the World.' He then focused their attention under the portico to three doors. "The first door on the left has bronze panels and was carved by Giacomo Manzu in 1964. The bronze central door dates from the Renaissance. The door on the right is called the Holy Door, which is opened and closed by his Holiness to mark the beginning and end of a Jubilee Year."

"You're a good guide, Father," someone said.

Father Inness could not even summon a smile this time.

The bus swung around to the back of the Basilica, where more guards had blocked off anyone from entering. The brakes squeaked to a stop. A large cement-block staircase led to two more enormous bronze doors and entrance into the Basilica.

The bus door opened and a priest, wearing a brown frock with a cowl, stepped onto the bus. He had gone through the rites of tonsure; the top of his head had been shaven. Father Inness introduced him as Brother Michael, who in turn extended a gentle bow to the special gusts.

"Please follow Brother Michael, in total silence."

In single file the priests disembarked from the bus and followed Brother Michael up the stairs and into the Basilica. Father Inness was the last in line.

To everyone's disappointment a curtain of painter's dropcloths blocked their view of the interior as they traveled down a long corridor to the right.

"What are they painting?" a voice asked, bringing a fierce look from Brother Michael.

The unseen procession passed through another door, which again opened up into another hallway. On the wall was an empty glass case but the sign remained: Diagram of St. Peter's Basilica. Other than that, it was just another hallway that could have been in any old structure.

Another door came into view, and muffled groans prophesized another corridor. The door led onto a modern stairwell that had fire exit signs posted. All eyes gazed upward but Brother Michael proceeded down. A few disgruntled sighs were heard, yet still their silence remained. More dropcloths covered—covered what? Still down they went. Dropcloths appeared everywhere.

Brother Michael stopped after the third flight. From behind the line came Father Inness's voice. "Tourists are not permitted below this level. The stairs have therefore not been repaired. Please be careful. And remain silent."

The line moved downward. Stairs looked like piles of stones laid on each other. Footing demanded balance, and holding on to each other. Naked walls appeared, like old castle walls, damp and cold to the touch. Another flight lower. Loosened rock and fretful moans echoed through the ancient stairwell. The line abruptly stopped.

"Where are you taking us?" demanded a voice.

Those between the voice and Father Inness stopped against the wall until Father Inness saw the owner of the voice: the Police Chaplain.

"I ordered silence!" Father Inness harshly scolded. "Continue, Brother Michael."

The Police Chaplain remained motionless. The intimidated priest in back of him nudged the Chaplain on until finally he had no choice but to move.

Another level. Tips of noses and earlobes turned red. Brother Michael halted and, using his entire body, pushed back a thick metal door. It was brand new, hinges and all. Six rock stairs led down to a dirt floor cellar. A dozen or so hastily wired electrical lights erased most of the darkness. Broken cobwebs revealed man's recent presence here. Down the final stairs they went, until all stood on the cold ground still in single file.

Against one of the longer walls, facing the priests, were small stoned cages—individual dungeons. All eyes swiveled toward Father Inness, and then to the gun in his hand. He motioned toward the cages. "Your new home, Crossbearers." His gun hand extended.

Without protest the line moved forward, each priest

hesitating before taking the final step into his cell.

The Police Chaplain looked toward Inness as Brother Michael swiftly locked the doors behind each prisoner. "How long? At least tell us how long."

Brother Michael stood beside the Chaplain, and when there was a nod from Iness, he took hold of the Chaplain's arm and led him into the cell. The thick door boomed shut. The Police Chaplain looked through the barred window in the door again demanding, "How long?"

Father Inness handed the unloaded pistol to Brother Michael and positioned himself in the middle of the room for all to see.

"We're not going to apologize for what we did," Father Crowley stated, his hands grasping the bars on the door opening. "The Church's only hope is us. You know that, Father Inness. Release us."

"He won't let us go!" came a voice from the lone cage opposite the others.

"Cardinal Alden," a few cried in unison, their bold tones now rattled with fear.

"You consider us the plague, Inness," the Cardinal proclaimed as if he were delivering a sermon. "But we are not the plague, we are the doctors who fight against those who carry the disease. We are God's Cross-bearers, His instruments of good." His eyes were aflame.

Brother Michael brought forth a small table upon which stood the Pope's Miter. In his other hand was the Pope's seven-foot scepter, which he rested against the table. "These are the symbols of our Holy Father," Inness addressed the Cardinal. "They now belong to you—as you have always wished."

"You're a fool, Father Inness," the Cardinal shrieked. "Without us the Chruch perishes. That is why God summoned us. We are the hands of God." The others joined his outcry.

Father Inness stayed with his rehearsed speech, explaining that each cell had a bed, toilet, sink, lamp, and Bible. "Brother Michael will bring you your food. You may speak to him, but it will be of no use; he has taken a vow of silence." Father Inness turned to leave but was delayed by another outburst from the Chaplain.

"Tell us how long we must stay here, Inness! Tell us!!"

"Forever!" Inness replied. "Forever." Stepping closer to the Cardinal, but in a voice loud enough for all to hear he said, "He that is not with me is against me. The Crossbearers have been paid in full." Turning toward the others, and making the sign of the cross with his right hand, he willed "May God have mercy on your souls."

A malignant laugh spewed forth from the Cardinal as Father Inness made his way up the stairs. "You're not going to keep us here forever. Listen to me, my Crossbearers. We have done our job well and the Church is much stronger because of us. But when it weakens again, these cages will be unlocked and we'll be set free to continue our holy mission. And on that day my followers will beg me to wear the Miter and carry the Staff. Do you hear me, Inness? I am the New Order. In the name of our Lord, my Father, I order you to release me and my disciples. Do you hear me? Release us! Release us!"

Refusing to look back, Father Inness pushed his body against the cellar door and heard only silence. He only prayed that the door would never have to be opened again.

MORE BLOOD-CHILLERS
FROM LEISURE BOOKS

2329-6	**EVIL STALKS THE NIGHT**	$3.50 US, $3.95 Can
2319-9	**LATE AT NIGHT**	$3.95 US, $4.50 Can
2309-1	**EVIL DREAMS**	$3.95 US, $4.50 Can
2300-8	**THE SECRET OF AMITYVILLE**	$3.50 US, $3.95 Can
2275-3	**FANGS**	$3.95 US, $4.50 Can
2269-9	**NIGHT OF THE WOLF**	$3.25
2265-6	**KISS NOT THE CHILD**	$3.75 US, $4.50 Can
2256-7	**CREATURE**	$3.75 US, $4.50 Can
2246-x	**DEATHBRINGER**	$3.75 US, $4.50 Can
2235-4	**SHIVERS**	$3.75 US, $4.50 Can
2225-7	**UNTO THE ALTAR**	$3.75 US, $4.50 Can
2220-6	**THE RIVARD HOUSE**	$3.25
2195-1	**BRAIN WATCH**	$3.50 US, $4.25 Can
2185-4	**BLOOD OFFERINGS**	$3.75 US, $4.50 Can
2152-8	**SISTER SATAN**	$3.75 US, $4.50 Can
2121-8	**UNDERTOW**	$3.75 US, $4.50 Can
2112-9	**SPAWN OF HELL**	$3.75 US, $4.50 Can

EERIE NOVELS
OF
HORROR AND THE
OCCULT
BY J.N. WILLIAMSON,
THE MASTER OF DARK
FANTASY

ELECTRIFYING HORROR
AND OCCULT

2343-1	**THE WERELING**	$3.50 US, $3.95 Can
2341-5	**THE ONI**	$3.95 US, $4.50 Can
2334-2	**PREMONITION**	$3.50 US, $3.95 Can
2331-8	**RESURREXIT**	$3.95 US, $4.50 Can
2302-4	**WORSHIP THE NIGHT**	$3.95 US, $3.95 Can
2289-3	**THE WITCHING**	$3.50 US, $3.95 Can
2281-8	**THE FREAK**	$2.50 US, $2.95 Can
2251-6	**THE HOUSE**	$2.50
2206-0	**CHILD OF DEMONS**	$3.75 US, $4.50 Can
2142-0	**THE FELLOWSHIP**	$3.75 US, $4.50 Can